THE DIARY OF A PROFESSIONAL EXPERIENCER

An Autobiographical Journey into the Evolution of an Acting System

ALSO BY ERIC MORRIS

No Acting Please (with Joan Hotchkis)
Being & Doing
Irreverent Acting
Acting from the Ultimate Consciousness
Acting, Imaging, and the Unconscious

AUDIO TAPES

The Craft of Acting
The MegApproaches
Imaging for Acting

THE ERIC MORRIS ACTORS WORKSHOP IS LOCATED AT:
5657 Wilshire Blvd. Los Angeles, CA 90036 (323)466-9250

Internet Website
www.ericmorris.com

THE DIARY OF A PROFESSIONAL EXPERIENCER

ERIC MORRIS

ERMOR ENTERPRISES

Published by
Ermor Enterprises
8004 Fareholm Drive
Los Angeles, CA 90046

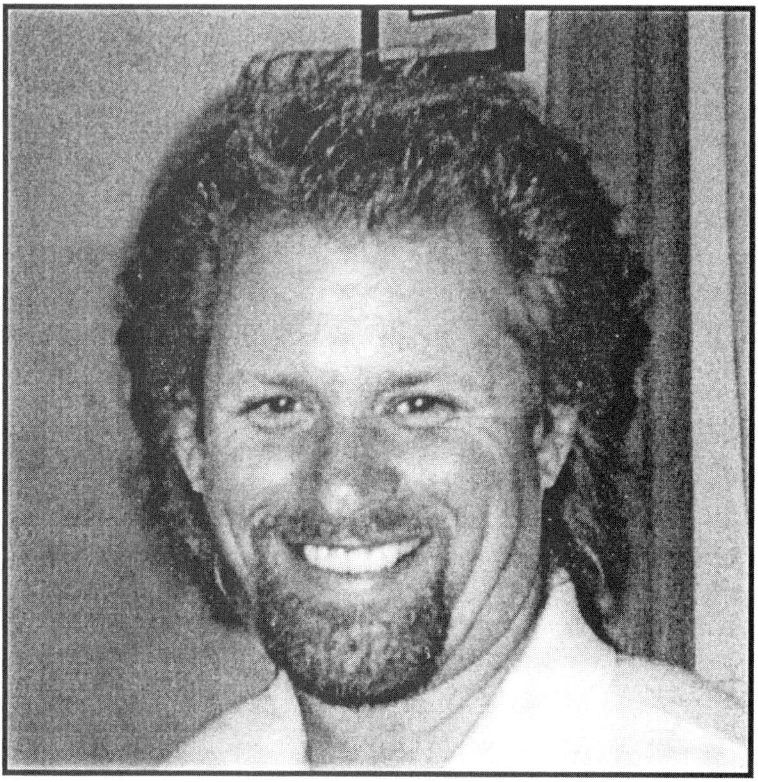

This book and my life
are dedicated to the memory of
my son Jeff, who passed away
recently at the age of 44.
He was the light of my life.
Everyone loved Jeff.
I will mourn and miss him to my
last days on this earth.

FOREWORD

I met Eric in 1974, when he coached me in one of my first films, *Stay Hungry*. Over a period of twelve weeks, we worked for several hours a day, several days a week, exploring in depth the events and experiences of my life and background that I could use as choices for my character in the film. That work was very successful, and I did quite well in the film. Eric and I established great communication and a strong creative bond. He piqued my interest in acting and was always supportive in encouraging my talent. After *Stay Hungry* I enrolled in his group acting class and studied for almost a year, during which I both witnessed and experienced remarkable emotional breakthroughs. Eric's exercises and techniques liberated actors from their fears, inhibitions and emotional obstacles, and encouraged them to act from a real, very organic place and strive to become "professional experiencers." I often heard him say that there was no separation "between living and acting," and to come from a truthful place an actor must first achieve a state of BEING. It was obvious that what he was doing was preparing each actor to address dramatic material. In his classes he could be harsh, strong and demanding of an actor on the stage, creatively manipulating him to a truthful place, but he was always nurturing and supportive, and said, "Follow your dream. Never give up. Not everyone has a dream to follow so if you do, you are special!"

Eric is truly an original and a unique contributor to the art and craft of acting. In this, his sixth book, he uses an autobiographical approach to detail his journey into the exploration and discovery of HOW to achieve reality on the stage and in film. As a result of a half century of work he has created a unique and powerful system that will affect actors for generations to come.

Even today, when as Governor I give many, many speeches, Eric's lessons still resonate. For me to communicate well, and in order to make the most of my appearances before the media, I must be believable. Good ideas and good policy would matter very little if I were unable to convey their importance to people, and the things Eric taught me help me to do that.

I am proud of him, his work, his contribution and dedication to helping people to achieve the truth in life and acting. I am happy to have him as my friend.

Arnold Schwarzenegger

TABLE OF CONTENTS

INTRODUCTION

Before starting this book, I thought long and hard about writing a book about me—an autobiography, no less! Who am I? I thought. I'm not a movie star or a famous writer or political figure, so who in the world, besides my family and friends, would be interested? Objectively I have accomplished some things and, I feel, have made a contribution to the training of actors. That, however, is not the reason or motive for embarking on this venture. *This is a book about acting!* Even though it starts at the very beginning of my life, I feel that it is well worth tracing the creation and evolution of my system, which I firmly believe will last many years after I am gone.

For centuries, since the legendary Greek actor Thespis stepped out of the chorus and uttered his first spoken line as an actor, the technique of acting had not evolved or kept pace with all the other inventions of mankind. For a long time acting was very representational. Actors learned gestures that were meant to communicate certain emotions. They would put both hands on their chest to signify strong feelings or place the back of their hand on their forehead to connote distress. Those gestures became standardized and were taught to actors as a method of acting. They even carried over into the silent-movie era.

The major transformation came from Stanislavski, a Russian actor who later became a director and teacher. He believed that if the character in a play was experiencing a certain emotion, such as grief or remorse, then the actor must find a way to experience that same emotion. That concept was revolutionary and led Stanislavski on a journey of exploration towards a new technique of acting. He started by examining the necessity for relaxation and strove with actors to establish a state of truth in their work. His contribution was enormous and changed acting—though at first very slowly and only in Russia. But as a good thing is destined to spread, sometime in the early to mid 1930s Lee Strasberg and Stella Adler went to Russia to be with Stanislavski and learn about his system. They were there at different times, though, and strangely brought back to America totally different interpretations of what Stanislavski was doing. Stella believed that an actor should not use his own life experiences in his work. In her view acting was all imagination, and that is what one should act from. Lee, on the other hand, felt quite the opposite. He believed that the life experiences of the actor were the raw material from which he created the life of the character—an interpretation, incidentally, with which I totally agree. Stanislavski's system and Strasberg's interpretation and modifications of it are, and will remain, the origins of a method of acting that has influenced thousands of actors. They both made a huge contribution to the field.

Right from the beginning my instincts were tilted towards organic reality. Before I knew anything about acting or techniques of acting, I was attracted to certain actors I saw in the movies. I felt that they all achieved a level of reality that had a great impact on me. Later I learned that they had all worked with Lee Strasberg or were members of the Actors Studio. However, over the years of my training and working as an actor, I became dissatisfied and frustrated with the huge gaps in the techniques I was learning and using. There were too many unanswered questions and blanks in an approach that was supposed to be dependable. Stanislavski himself is quoted as saying that his system was not complete, and as I learned and grew as an actor, and most particularly after I started teaching, I felt that the actor's instrument—his problems and emotional blocks—was not addressed. Nor were there any books that specifically tackled the issue. My journey into dealing with the instrument and confronting the actor's obstacles with antidotal exercises designed to eliminate them evolved with great personal aggravation and pain, since in the early years of my work I was the butt of many jokes and ridicule. The criticisms ended only when some of the people I had trained became successful actors and sang my praises.

In addition, almost all of the "master teachers" had very little specific craft, so as an actor I found myself at a loss for techniques that I needed to approach a role. As a result, I felt enormous insecurity about my ability to depend on a craft that was fractional at best.

I hope that in the following pages the events and experiences that led me to my system will become clear to the reader. I will show how I arrived at certain instrumental and craft techniques and will share and chronicle experiences and relationships I had with teachers, other actors, directors, and a vast variety of individuals in the business. I intend to be very honest about the people and events I talk about. My intention is not to denigrate or criticize anyone. In some instances my opinion might seem somewhat harsh, but I will try to separate subjective opinion from objective fact whenever possible. It is, however, extremely important that I be as honest as I can so that the reader can clearly understand the events that became crucial to my evolution.

PROLOGUE

It was a beautiful spring morning outside—not a cloud in the sky. When I arrived at my theater, I stopped at the front door and looked at the blue sky and thought how wonderful it was to be alive and living in Southern California. It was late morning, and I had a full schedule of private lessons to teach. As I sat in my swivel barber chair, the chair I have been teaching in for the last twenty years, I thought: You had better be careful what you wish for, because you might just get it! I remembered sitting at a table in Scott Hall over fifty years ago while I was at Northwestern University, eating lunch with a number of theater students in my class. We were laughing, joking and critiquing each other's scenes, the ones we had done just an hour before. It was good-natured teasing, with an underlying bit of competitiveness. The conversation suddenly became serious, and one of the people asked, "If we had one wish for our lives, what would it be?" Everyone came up with the usual fantasy wishes: being rich and famous, owning a movie studio or a house in the hills with a pool, reading scripts all day, and so on. When it came around to me, I said that I would like to spend my entire life in the theater. That was the whole sentence. I made no qualifications about what I wanted to do there or where the theater should be. I just said that I would like to be there.

I looked at the stage in my theater, the furniture we used for the scenes, and the props still on the table from the previous night's class. I turned and looked at the maroon seats, empty and waiting to be occupied. I stared into the filament of the stage lights and realized that I had gotten my wish. I have been teaching for forty-five years and always in a small theater, which I usually had built to my specifications. This was a particularly nice Equity-waiver theater with about seventy seats. What I had failed to include in my wish of long ago was that I had wanted to be in a theater on Broadway, playing the lead in an incredible play.

As I reflected on that time in school, I wondered what had brought me to this moment, in this theater. What had that journey been like? How had I gotten here? I wasn't sad about what I do. In fact I love it! However, I wondered about life and what part destiny plays in deciding its course. How did I end up being a teacher? It wasn't that I hadn't acted. I had been in over fifty Equity plays, done several seasons of summer stock, been a professional actor since 1951; I had done seventy-five feature and television films; I had had running roles in two television series; so it wasn't as if I hadn't experienced what I had started out to do. Then what were the forces that had steered me in this direction? Many actors turn to teaching in order to earn a living because their careers don't support them, but that wasn't what had brought me here. It was a series of accidents, or if you will, predestination, that had decided the course of my life.

I'm looking at the back wall of the stage now, not really seeing it because I'm on this trip, reliving parts of my life and my journey. I have regrets about not acting. I wish I had been more successful, and I believe I would have been, except for this unexplainable need to do this work from a different perspective. I can't help but feel that if I, as a young actor, had had the right teacher, the right training, maybe my life would have gone in another direction. I do feel, however, that I am in the right place doing exactly what I am supposed to be doing.

I am not sure I believe in predestination; however, as I have gone over the events of my life from childhood to the present, it seems that everything has led me to this place. I've written five other books on acting, but I feel impelled to share my experiences and journey with you. I am writing this book in the hopes that I can spare actors the frustration I felt and, even more important, help them not to waste the years looking for, and not finding, the answers and process necessary to access the largest part of their talent. The best way for me to do that is to detail the autobiographical events in my life that led me to creating a system of work that I feel is life changing. My work is based on Stanislavski and influenced by a number of other teachers, such as Martin Landau and Lee Strasberg. Over the years, however, I have gone on to innovate and discover many more techniques and approaches and have thus created what is possibly the most complete system of acting in the last hundred years. I know that sounds egotistical and maybe a little cultist, but I feel comfortable in stating it because it is true and can be proven. My hope is that I might reach some of you out there who are pursuing your dream and help you to make that dream real.

CHAPTER 1

THE EARLY YEARS

I started to smoke at two and a half and got laid at seven—a precocious, though somewhat dubious, beginning, wouldn't you say? I was born Fredric Stein, the youngest of five children, on November 19, 1931, at Mount Sinai Hospital in Chicago, Illinois. As my mother often said, I "blew in with the noon lunch whistle," or exactly at twelve noon. Since my oldest brother was almost twenty years older than I; my sister Ida, the next in line, seventeen years my senior; Phil, my other brother, fifteen years older; and my sister Helen—the closest to me in age—eleven years older than I, you might think that I was an unexpected accident of some careless amorous night between my parents. Not so! My father, a "cuddler" who loved to express love and tenderness to his children, came home from work one night and told my mother that he missed having a little one around the house, so my mother reluctantly agreed to have another child.

I was born with a full head of platinum blond hair that reached down to my shoulders. My parents must have saved their best genes for me, because I was an incredibly beautiful baby. People would stop my mother or sister on the street and stare into my buggy with awe at how attractive a child I was. Of course, all this was told to me, since I don't remember any of it! My earliest memories are of sitting around a table with my whole family eating dinner and yelling at each other. There I was in a highchair, witnessing an emotional display at almost every meal. They were not negative or angry emotions, just animated expressions, which I was lucky enough to experience at a very early age. Whatever problems I acquired while growing up, being emotionally unexpressive was not one of them.

After dinner most of the adult members of my family would light up a cigarette and sit around talking and laughing. I would lean forward in my high chair and loudly scream, "Moke, moke." At first no one paid any attention to me, although they knew that I wanted a cigarette, but finally, as a joke, my brother handed me one. I promptly put it into my mouth, took a drag, inhaled—and loved it! After that, whenever they refused to let me smoke, I would throw a God-awful tantrum until they would finally give me a cigarette. It wasn't until many years later that I found out why I was so insistent on wanting to smoke at two and a half. In therapy I realized that smoking meant being part of the family, being included in the "tribe"!

Soon I had developed a habit of six or seven cigarettes a day. Trying to wean me off smoking, my family gave me a menthol cigarette, thinking that it would turn me off. Instead, I loved it and insisted on Kools from that time on. I continued to smoke for about six months, when late one night, at three in the morning, I woke up unable to breathe. I was having an asthma attack. Our doctor, Doctor Lowenberg, came over, gave me a shot, and sternly proclaimed, "The kid has to give up smoking!"—which I did for ten years. I started again when I was thirteen and continued regularly until I was thirty-three, at which time I was smoking four packs a day. Then I quit again for eleven years, went back for a couple more years, and quit once more. All in all I have quit five times—this time, I think, for good. I haven't smoked for eighteen years. I am addicted to nicotine, not just physically but psychologically too.

I was a precocious child in many other ways. Because I was surrounded by six adults who were many years older, I started speaking at an early age and developed a vocabulary that went far beyond the norm for my chronological age. When my brothers' friends would come to visit, I would interrogate them, trying to find out what they did for a living, whether they were happy with their lives, whether they were married or had girlfriends. They would respond by asking my brothers who the midget was. I liked being around older people. That was what I was used to.

I remember being very curious about many things. At a very early age I was interested in the opposite sex and would wonder what was under the dresses of the women who came to visit. I knew it would not be acceptable for me to explore that, so I didn't, but I wanted to. I would smell the seats—the chairs and the sofa—after people would get up and walk away. As I look back, I think it was rather disgusting, but at the time I was extremely interested in odors of all kinds. Peculiarly, my olfactory sense is the strongest of my five senses. It was not until much later in my life that I realized how important my sensory curiosity was. As an actor, I have used my senses to create and respond to many stimuli. So much of what we are as people and as actors is created in our formative years.

In a sense I grew up in the theater. Both my brothers belonged to a theater group in Chicago, the JPI or Jewish People's Institute, which went beyond amateur theater. Both brothers took acting classes from a woman named Minnie Galatzer. My oldest brother was the actor in the family, while Phil was interested in the technical aspects—the lighting, the scenery, and stage-managing. I remember sitting in the front row of the theater and watching the actors do scenes and improvisations. I was three or three and a half at the time, and even though many years have passed since then, I still remember thinking that the actors were not being real. Strange as that may seem, somehow I didn't believe their acting. During the performances at the JPI, I would sit on Phil's lap and move the handles on the light board as he gave me the cues and the numbers on the board to which I had to move the lever. So I was in the light booth running lights at the age of three and a half. That is an early start! In one of the plays, they needed a small boy to walk on, holding his father's hand, and since I was available, that was my first acting job. No lines—I just walked on, stood there for a couple of minutes and walked off, stage right. In one of the performances I looked directly at the audience, studying the faces of all the people in the first row. When I got off the stage, my brother Morrey firmly told me not to do that.

"They are not supposed to be there," he said.

"But they are there. Don't they know they are not supposed to be there?" I responded.

At home Morrey's bedroom smelled of grease paint. Crepe hair was hanging from the top of the dresser, being stretched so that he could make fake beards and mustaches for the characters he was playing. Many years later, in the dressing room of the summer-stock theater I was working at, I smelled that grease paint and took an affective-memory trip back to that time when I was just a child.

I was a happy child. I loved going places with any member of my family, and they all gladly took me along anywhere they would go, because I was always "good." All of my brothers' and sisters' friends liked me and welcomed me into their homes. I would play for hours with anything I came into contact with. My imagination was boundless, and I enjoyed living in fantasy, although I knew it wasn't real. My father, a cherubic man of five feet five inches in height, with a typical Russian face and a big smile, gave me the legacy of love. He died thirty-seven years ago. I was thirty-seven at the time, and to this day I cannot think or talk about him without becoming extremely vulnerable. He loved me with such passion that I never doubted my importance in his life. He hugged me and kissed me on the mouth until a week before he died. In the Ashkenazi Jewish tradition, you name your children after relatives who have passed on, thereby giving the dead a living name and a bit of immortality; so my parents had named me after my father's uncle Frauka. Following the Russian tendency to use affectionate diminutives, however, my father used to call me Fraukushka. As a sign of love or affection Russians often add a *kushka, ishka,* or *mishka* to any name.

My parents were immigrant Russian Jews who had come to America in 1912, five years before the Russian Revolution. One day in Odessa, Russia, my father, a small man physically but a giant in character, came home and announced to my mother that he was going to America. She looked at him for a moment or two and then told him to lie down and take a nap. "When you get up, you will probably have come to your senses," she added. But he was very serious. He had indeed decided to come to the United States. Why he had made such an abrupt decision remains a mystery to me to this day. I have conjectured what might have happened on that special occasion: My father had a small business in a place called the *tolchuk*, a market place where he sold furniture and made picture frames for paintings. Perhaps he was standing in front of his store, gazing at the Black Sea, when he had a vision of America brightly shining in the clouds hanging over the water. He saw himself walking down wide streets paved with gold and teeming with people who were laughing and happy. He looked at the people around him on the *tolchuk,* who were struggling to make a living, and at that very moment he made his fateful decision. Of course, none of that may be true at all! Nevertheless, he bought a ticket, left my mother, who was several months pregnant, and sailed off to America. Being a very responsible man, however, he promised to send for my mother as soon as he had accumulated enough money to buy her a ticket.

He arrived at Ellis Island, where all of the immigrants first landed in those days, but he was almost sent back due to a slight case of conjunctivitis. They were about to deport him, but he pleaded with Immigration, and some clerk or official with a big heart finally passed him through. I have always been grateful to that nameless, faceless official for allowing my father to stay. If he hadn't, I would be speaking Russian, or maybe I wouldn't even be alive, since all of my father's family—brothers, sisters, nephews, cousins—were killed by the Nazis in World War II.

When he was interviewed by the one in charge, my father was asked what his name was, and he answered, "Vevel Shtarenshees" (I am not sure of the spelling). He was then told to spell his name, but of course he couldn't, since his English was very limited. So he was given the name of Stein, which had no relevance to our family background or history. I went through a good part of my life as Fred Stein, and my name on my birth certificate is Fredric Stein, but I never liked that name and never felt that it was who I was. Nonetheless, it was my label until I was twenty-five years old. Now *shtarenshees* literally translated from Yiddish means "shooting star," so for a brief period I thought of calling myself Fredric Shooting Star, but I soon rejected the idea, as I realized that people would expect to see an American Indian when they heard the name! In reality, though, it was my family name, and I really would have liked to have it.

My father's influence on my early life was important. He and I would lie in bed, my head resting on his naked chest, tickled by his graying chest hair, his arm around me, while he told me stories of his life in Russia and of his experiences when he arrived in America. In retrospect I understand my own fears much better because of my father's experiences. He had lived in tsarist Russia at a time when the Cossacks would raid towns and villages and indiscriminately kill Jews. I am not sure how old he was then, but I think he must have been a teenager. Those massacres, or *pogroms,* occurred without warning and could come at any time. First, there was the thunder of many horses and then the screams of the people caught in the open. The Cossacks used long, sharp swords and were experts at lopping off the heads of people who were walking in the road. When my father heard the thunder of the horses and the screams, he would quickly round up his family and they would all hide under old mattresses in the basement. The attacks lasted for about an hour, and then it was all over until the next one. I couldn't understand the reason for this. All my father could tell me was that it was that way for Jews in many parts of Europe. "Why?" I would repeat over and over. "What did the Jews do to make others want to kill them?" I remember having terrifying nightmares about the pogroms. At times I dreamt that I too was hiding under smelly old mattresses in the basement and that I couldn't breathe. I would wake up shaking and bathed in perspiration. I didn't understand why no one had done anything to stop the slaughter of innocent people. Over the years I have asked the same question about the Nazis: Who stopped *them* from bringing about the Holocaust?

While all of those stories caused nightmares and years of psychological trauma, they helped create the fabric of my character. I am stronger because of them, and while many of those fears persist to this day, I rebel against any violent injustice done to me or to anyone else. As an actor, I have also used those fears, and the anger they gave rise to, to create choices for my work.

Of course, there were other stories my father told me that were inspiring. When he came to this country, the first job he had was carrying bars of steel up ten stories for nine cents a day—imagine that, nine cents a day! I am not sure how long he kept that job, but I am quite sure that he had a number of others before he could save enough money to send for my mother and their eight-month-old baby, my oldest brother, Morrey. Some years ago I read Kirk Douglas's autobiography, *The Ragman's Son,* and I remembered that I too was a ragman's son! My father told me that he had owned a horse and wagon and that he would go riding through the alleys of Chicago in all kinds of weather, yelling, "Reks ol' ian"—by which he meant "rags and old iron"! He would dress in a heavy fur-lined leather jacket, which he called a *peltzel.* I guess that is a Russian or Yiddish word for a heavy jacket. His face would get red and chapped from the cold winter winds as he rode through those alleys, almost singing his "reks ol' ian." People would come down their back porches with bundles of rags and broken irons and other assorted junk, for which my father would pay them a few cents and which he would later sell somewhere for a small profit. He told me stories about those days on the wagon—a rickety, old wooden carriage with large wooden spoke wheels that squeaked almost as loud as he would shout. He would sit on a double wooden planked seat, much like those on the old Western buckboards, which didn't have any springs or padding to absorb the shock of the rutted alleys through which he rode; so his rear end would get blistered and sore after a time. He became very attached to his horse, which had been on its last legs when he bought it. He would talk to it as he traversed the alleys, and sometimes he even sang to it. He boarded it at some stable on the east side of Chicago and would trudge home at night maneuvering through the snowdrifts. He once told me that after staring at the hind end of his horse for ten hours every day, he knew its ass better than its face! One day, while riding through an alley at dusk, he got shot. He told me it was a BB gun, but the jacket he was wearing was much too thick for a BB to penetrate it, so I am sure it was a .22-caliber bullet, since it lodged itself about an inch into his abdomen. He was very lucky that the *peltzel* was as thick as it was, or I wouldn't be here writing this book!

Over a period of time he managed to bring to America all of the members of my mother's family—her mother, her two sisters and their respective husbands and children—but of his own family he was only able to bring over one of his seven brothers—my uncle Abie—and his uncle Frauka. I guess Uncle Frauka was older and not well, so my father probably felt that he should spend the remaining years of his life in a good place and not face the hardships of Russia. My uncle Abie later developed the reputation of a Don Juan. He was quite a ladies' man. I loved Abie! He had all of the love my father had plus a sense of fun that my father lacked. Abie was always joking and would run around the house playing with me, pretending he was going to eat me if he caught me. I knew he wouldn't really eat me, but I was scared anyway!

My father, who was the oldest in his family, had a greater sense of responsibility than Abie did, but when I say that he lacked Abie's sense of fun, I don't mean to suggest that he wasn't playful or willing to have a good time or provide one for me and everyone else. He was a champion laugher. If something tickled him, he would laugh until his stomach hurt, and since, as you know, laughter is infectious, soon all would be rolling on the floor, laughing and holding their stomachs.

My mother was more conservative in her expression. She had a hard time showing affection, and for years I thought that she didn't like me. My father made up for her lack of demonstrativeness. Years later I began to understand my mother and to see why she was emotionally conservative. As an infant in Russia, she had had a high fever and had gone into convulsions and as a result had become cross-eyed. It was never corrected, and she lived her entire life that way. I'm sure it had a great impact on her personality. I accepted it. It was just who she was, and it never seemed abnormal to me. She, however, must have suffered enormous pain because of it. I'm sure that as a little girl she was the subject of ridicule and rejection because of it. I don't recall anyone in our family ever referring to her eyes or mentioning anything about her being cross-eyed, but it did affect her vision, which was bad throughout her life.

My mother's first name was Nessie, and my father used to call her Neska. While, as I said, she was not terribly good at expressing affection, she was very vulnerable and would cry at the drop of a hat at almost anything. My father, whose one great fault was to tease, would call her *Neska Pishet Mit de Oygen,* "Nessie Peeing from Her Eyes." This, of course, infuriated her, and she would cry even harder. I'm sure that my father had no idea of the damage his teasing caused her and many other members of our family. My brother Phil, for example, suffered from insecurity his entire life as the result of being teased. My father would tell Phil that he really didn't belong to our family and that a man with a red beard had left him on our doorstep and we had taken him in. I wasn't there, of course, but I was told that my father did this to see Phil cry, which he did each time the story was repeated. I'm quite sure that if my father had realized how damaging those things were, he certainly would not have said them. The people who emigrated from Russia in those days had minimal education for the most part, and they were not psychologically sophisticated. While they were well-meaning people who loved their families, they did not have a very high level of consciousness. I'm sure that I too was teased, but I can't remember any specific incidents. Probably, by the time I came along, my father had curtailed that behavior.

I remember both my parents looking old even when I was very small. It seemed, however, that all of their friends who had come here from Russia also looked old. My father was forty-six when I was born and my mother forty. He became a citizen very quickly, while she, on the other hand, remained a resident alien until her death. My father loved this country and would make much out of the patriotic holidays. Both my parents spoke with a heavy Russian Jewish accent and used Yiddish around the house. It was one of my first languages, and I still retain a good deal of it. Even though both my parents learned English and knew how to read and write, my father, being in business, became much more proficient in the language than my mother, a housewife who stayed home, raised the children, took care of the apartment, and never worked at a regular job outside the home.

I was born in 1931, shortly after the stock market crashed bringing about the Great Depression. I remember those years and some of the events. As a little boy I wasn't aware of what was happening in the country—the bread lines and the unemployment, the people going hungry, and so on. It wasn't until much later that I learned of those things. I do remember, however, that we moved into another apartment, a few blocks from where we were living, and that we sat on apple boxes because we had no furniture. It was a time when my father was just opening a furniture store on Maxwell Street, but I wasn't worried, because there was always enough to eat. My father worked seven days a week for his entire life. He was a workaholic, and no one in the family could get him to take a single day off. He was totally committed to his family. We were his whole life.

My oldest brother, Morrey, was a rebel. He was always ranting about the inequities of our society and about how the rich grew richer and the poor workingmen suffered to make them richer. He read the *Daily Worker,* which was a left-wing newspaper, so my father called him the Communist. "Oh, ho, look, the Communist is home!" he would say. I didn't know what a Communist was at that time, so I laughed along with my father, who never took my brother seriously. I don't think Morrey was a Communist, even though he leaned a little to the left. When he became successful as a Hollywood screenwriter and was making a fortune from his work, I never heard him say anything about the poor workingman!

Morrey (he later changed his name to Edmund Morris when he began his writing career) was the source of almost all of the ridicule and abuse I experienced as I was growing up. His favorite name for me was Apple Head, and when he wasn't calling me that, I was the Moron. For a while I even thought my middle name was Moron! Why he called me Apple Head is a mystery to this day. My head was well shaped and didn't in any way resemble an apple! It wasn't until many years later that I learned that he had been abusive to all my other siblings. Because of those experiences I had growing up, I developed insecurities that plagued me for many years. After being in therapy and working through much of the damage I had sustained in an environment that was somewhat abusive, I was able to turn liabilities into assets that I could use in my creative process.

My family was very important to me as a child. Since they were all so much older, I felt as if I had three mothers and three fathers, although I knew that they were my brothers and sisters. My sister Ida took care of me, and it was really she who raised me. She died recently, and when I delivered her eulogy, I said, "She was my sister, my mother." That was really true. She would wheel my buggy through the park and sing songs to me. She dressed me and later walked hand in hand with me through the neighborhood. I'm sure that many of the neighbors thought she was my mother. When I started to go to school, I insisted that she take me there and pick me up after school. While all of the other children's mothers were young, I had an old mother, and I guess I was ashamed of that.

My brother Phil would take me everywhere. Every Saturday we would go to the Palace Theater in downtown Chicago to see a movie. Whenever a new Tarzan film was released, we would be there the day it opened. Afterwards, we would go out to lunch and walk along the lakeshore. Phil would talk about how much he loved the theater and tell me that someday he was going to go to New York to become a scenic designer. Since we spent so much time together, my father and some of the others would tease us by calling me Phil's girlfriend! Phil would laugh, but I think he was sensitive about not having a girlfriend at the time. Even though he was fifteen years older than I, I think he enjoyed being with me. He bought me gifts—a movie projector, still cameras—and always brought things home for me. I loved him. He encouraged me to be expressive, as did all the other members of my family. I was never told to be quiet or that children should be seen but not heard. I was a good child but could also be a brat prone to throwing tantrums when I didn't get what I wanted. No one ever hit me or laid a hand on me, except that my brother Morrey slapped my face once. I never forgot it! When I was really bad, my father would remove the belt from his pants, sit down in a chair, look at me threateningly, and say, *"Laygsugh,"* which meant that I was to lie down across his lap and get ready to be spanked. I would do so, but I never expected to be hurt. He would go through the motions, lifting his belt high in the air and bringing it down almost to my butt but stopping before it made any contact with my body. The first few times he did that, I was really frightened, but as time went by, it became just another way for him to express his love for me. In *Portnoy's Complaint* the main character says that every time he walked into a room, his father's face "would light up like a five-hundred-watt light bulb." That's how it was for me too. I would come into a room where my father was, and he would light up in the same way as Portnoy's father.

Dinner at home with my family was a special time. Once I got out of the highchair and sat on a regular chair with the rest of the family, I felt much more a part of it all. My mother was an excellent cook. Friday meals were especially good, a feast of homemade chicken soup with matzo balls, *kugel,* a brisket of beef cooked and seasoned to perfection, a side of *kasha* and *varnishkas,* and some salad. The desserts were always great too. We all sat around the table, talking and laughing and telling stories. My father would characterize his customers by imitating them. He would walk around the table and pretend he was a customer giving him a hard time. We always enjoyed his imitations of people. Of course, all the men would light up a cigarette. None of the women smoked, as I remember, and I just sat there wishing I could join the men; but I knew the consequences of smoking, so I didn't even ask!

After dinner, as the others all went their ways, my mother, my sister Helen, and I would listen to the radio. There was no television in those days. We had our favorite evening radio shows. We listened to "The Lux Radio Hour," which was a drama, to "Mr. Keen, Tracer of Lost Persons," and on Sundays Helen and I would listen to "The Shadow." She would open her eyes really wide, look at me, and quote the Shadow's mantra: "Who knows what evil lurks in the hearts of men? The Shadow knows!" She would laugh and pretend that the evil lurked inside of me and that *she* knew it! The radio was on a shelf in the kitchen, since that was where we always congregated. We had a living room, but no one ever used it. It was off limits and reserved for company; but when company did come over, we all sat in the kitchen anyway! My father, being in the furniture business, brought home beautiful furniture—a velvet sofa, for example. My mother immediately had plastic covers made to protect it, and then she would throw a sheet over the plastic to protect that! This was a phenomenon that I understood only many years later. My mother, who had grown up in Russia and had never had a great deal of material possessions, had developed a poverty consciousness, which lasted her entire life. Coming to America and having to struggle during the early years, as well as experiencing the Great Depression, exacerbated her insecurities. I'm sure that she felt she had better take care of every single thing she had, because she might never get others. This, of course, interfered with her ability to use and enjoy the material possessions she accumulated. Unfortunately, our parents' fears and insecurities infect us as their children. I too grew up with a protective attitude towards everything I have—mostly the automobiles that I have bought over the years. To date I have had in excess of twenty-five cars, and my relationship to every one of them has been neurotic. Not only am I meticulous in having them serviced, but I treat them as if they were living things. I am concerned with where I park them, worried over whether the doors will get dinged, wash and wax them until the paint grows thin. I have had similar feelings about my clothes and other possessions throughout the years, and that has intensely limited my use and enjoyment of them. It wasn't the same for me as for my mother. I always knew that I would eventually get another car or jacket, but it didn't seem to ease my insecurity about it. This has stayed with me throughout my life. I have gotten much better about it as a result of therapy and of elevating my consciousness, but I still retain some of the remnants of those insecurities.

Many of the complexes and fears that we accumulate over our life have been passed down to us from our parents. As an actor, I understood those things that sculpted my personality, and I used them as choices to address the demands of dramatic material. Many of my personality "liabilities" were later turned into creative assets, and I truly believe that it was the combination of many of those fears and insecurities that later led me to the exploration of techniques that became the foundation of the acting system I created—but that, of course, will come much later.

In 1936, when I was five years old, my sister Ida got married, and while I don't remember all of the particulars, I am told that I resented her abandoning me. She and her new husband, Al Satlin, moved in with us, since in those days of the Great Depression no one had much money and families lived together to save what little money there was to spend on the rent. I must have given Al a hard time, because there was a lot of conflict between us. He hated me, and I knew it. On one occasion he got so angry with me that he threw a thick glass ashtray at me. My sister Ida ran interference, put up her hand to protect me and was badly cut by the ashtray. I'm sure that if it had hit me in the head, it would have injured me quite seriously. If that had happened, my brothers would have killed Al. The funny thing about him is that his dislike for me lasted his entire life. When I was much older and would visit him and Ida, he would make snide remarks and denigrate anything I was doing with my life.

At any rate, when Al and Ida moved in with us, my sister Helen and I lost our bedroom and had to sleep on a day bed in the dining room. It was a single bed, but we quickly made it into a double by pulling out a section underneath, which was lower than the main part and much harder. I insisted on sleeping on the soft part, and I told Angoo that if she wouldn't let me, I would tell Pa, and he would make her do it. (I called my sister Angoo, I don't know why. That was just the name I gave her, and it stuck for a number of years.) So I got the soft side next to the wall, at least for a while. At night, before we fell asleep, we would listen to the radio—spooky shows such as "Lights Out" and "The Hermit's Cave," which would frighten me and sometimes give me nightmares. I will never understand the lack of consciousness of some of my family members for exposing me to things that frightened me for a lifetime. To this day I feel a certain amount of fear sleeping in a dark room alone. Helen, who was eleven years older, wasn't that impacted by the shows. Since she wanted to sleep on the soft side of the bed and avoid my complaining to my father, she told me that when I was asleep at night, a hand would come out of the wall and get me. From then on, I was on the hard side of the bed!

Other things frightened me too. I was six years old when they took me to the Lawndale Theater on Roosevelt Road to see *The Son of Frankenstein.* I was so terrified by the film that I didn't sleep for weeks afterwards. My cousin Itzie, who is only twenty months older than I, would for years frighten the life out of me by stiffening his body, putting his outstretched hands in front of him and walking towards me like the Frankenstein monster. I can watch those films now and know that it is Boris Karloff the actor playing the monster, but somewhere on a subliminal level I still feel a twinge of fear shoot through my body. For many years after I saw *The Son of Frankenstein,* I had dreams about it. I would hesitate to enter a dark room in my own house, and I couldn't be alone at home.

A number of years later, while on Christmas holiday from school, I visited the set of a show that my brother Phil was producing. It was in the early days of television, when shows were shot live and prerecorded. I believe that this one was a weekly anthology program called "The Medallion Theatre" and that the show they were recording that day was "The Thirteen Clocks," a classic by James Thurber. It had an all-star cast, including Boris Karloff and Basil Rathbone. My brother took me to Boris Karloff's dressing room and introduced me to him. I was surprised that he seemed much smaller than I had imagined. He had graying hair and must have been in his late fifties at the time. He was very gracious and friendly, very soft-spoken and extremely gentle in his manner. I later learned that he had made a series of records narrating famous children's stories. After a short conversation, I told him about my experience with *The Son of Frankenstein* and its impact on my life. He looked at me for a long time and then smiled apologetically as his shoulders seemed to elevate an inch or two. I felt embarrassed for having shared my experience with him, since it obviously disturbed him. On an impulse and without thinking, I hugged him, which embarrassed both of us, and we began to laugh with a complete understanding of what had just happened. His parting words were, "Well, Fred, you see how harmless this monster really is!" I smiled, thanked him and left.

Phil had been outside the dressing room talking to the stage manager and had heard us laughing, so he asked what was so funny. I will never forget what popped out of my mouth. I said, "Oh, nothing! Mr. Karloff and I just killed a monster!" Phil just looked at me and dismissed it. He then took me to meet Basil Rathbone, whom I knew as Sherlock Holmes and the villain in every Errol Flynn movie I had seen. I was particularly excited about meeting him since I knew his son Rodion. I entered his dressing room, and there he was in some kind of classical costume, very much like the ones he wore in *The Tower of London.* He shook my hand and looked at me with those dark eagle eyes of his and lifted his head, exposing his razor-sharp nose. "Well, well, so you are Phil's brother? Younger and more handsome, I must say!" I think he said that for Phil's benefit, since Phil was standing directly beside me. We talked for a few minutes, and I told him that I knew Rodion, as I had done two seasons of summer stock at Rodion and Caroline Fisher Rathbone's summer theater in Wisconsin. "Ah," he said in an almost Shakespearean lilt, "so you're an actor?" I guess I blushed a little, because he smiled and said that I shouldn't apologize for it, even though it was a small curse. I really didn't understand the full meaning or impact of that statement until many years later. Up to that time I had not met many movie stars or name actors, so it was an important experience to see that they were real people and that it was the celluloid image which we as an audience related to.

Not too long ago I saw Steven Spielberg on an interview television show. I think it was "Inside the Actors Studio." He was talking about all of his childhood fears and how he would imagine that the furniture in his bedroom would turn into frightening things when the lights were turned off. He imagined that the clawed legs on his dresser would transform into some kind of animated monster and come for him. He talked about some of his other fears and how they were at the core of many of his films, supplying much of the terror in them. What we are and what we do as adults are very connected to the events and experiences of our early lives.

I was uncoordinated as a youngster, not good at any sport, what you would call a klutz. The neighborhood kids teased me constantly because I was so bad. I was always the last one chosen to be on a team. In fact, it was with great reluctance that they would accept me at all. "Oh, O.K., we'll take Stein!" they would say. It made me feel that there was something wrong with me, and for years I avoided sports. In high school I didn't participate in any. I loved to go to the games and would read football magazines and fantasize about being on the team and running a hundred yards for a touchdown, but it remained a fantasy. I don't know why I wasn't any good at sports. I guess my clumsiness and lack of coordination must have been the result of overprotective parents and siblings who were always telling me to be careful. Admonitions such as "Don't climb up there! You'll fall!" can make a child fearful and destroy any physical trust that he might develop.

I must have been about eight or nine when my brother Phil brought home a Daisy air rifle, a BB gun. That rifle became one of the most important objects in my life and created a lifelong love affair with guns and shooting. I think the BB gun cost less than five dollars, but it was worth a million to me! Phil set down some very important rules: I could only shoot it when he was there, I was only to handle and load it under his supervision, and I was allowed to play with it when he wasn't there, but only as a toy—no cocking or pulling the trigger, whether it was loaded or not. It was lever action and had a very dark mahogany stock, which I polished with the furniture polish my mother used on the dining-room table. I oiled the metal parts and played Cowboys and Indians, hiding under the kitchen table and making shooting sounds. I must have killed thousands of marauding Apaches! Since I wasn't allowed to take the rifle outside unless Phil was there, all my pretend games were inside the house. On Saturdays, when Phil wasn't working, we would go to the empty lot across the street, and he would show me how to put BBs into the rifle and shoot at cans and bottles. Over a period of about six months of Saturday practice, I developed quite an eye for shooting. I may have been uncoordinated at football and other sports, but when I was shooting, my hand-eye coordination was superb, and I became quite a marksman. At last I could really do something that could be considered athletic. Naturally it wasn't running or jumping or hitting a ball over the fence, but it was something! It is hard to describe how important and meaningful that became. It bolstered my self-esteem. I felt special in a way that had been denied me, and it affected my personality in many positive ways.

After a while, we began to attract a crowd of neighborhood children to watch me shoot. Phil would set up the targets and make sure that the spectators were well out of the way. I was no longer shooting at cans and bottles; I was shooting at bottle caps at a distance of about twenty-five feet. Bottle caps are quite small and at that distance become even smaller. I would hit one every time I pulled the trigger, the cap would fly into the air, and the children would point their fingers at it and scream and shout, "Buffalo Bill! Annie Oakley!" I would stand there as if I were in the center of a ring at the circus, surrounded by admiring kids from the block, who hadn't wanted me on their team but were now looking at me with awe and respect. I think that somehow Phil knew that I needed something to make me feel part of the group. Maybe it was an unconscious knowledge that had inspired him to bring home that BB gun. I really don't know. It did, however, change my life in many ways. I wasn't aware of it at that time—I was only eight or nine years old—but over the years I realized how damaged my brother Phil was as a result of my father's teasing. I think he saw that I could also be hurt in the same way, and he identified with me on that level. He never had many friends. I think he protected himself from becoming involved with people because of the imagined rejection. When I was an adult and more psychologically aware, I realized how impacting his childhood had been. Norman Shelley, who had worked with Phil as an assistant stage manager in the road company of a musical, said to me once that Phil was "the best five-block friend" he had. When I asked him what he meant by that, he explained that he would meet Phil on a street in New York and that they would walk and talk for about five blocks, and then they would each go in separate directions and he wouldn't see or hear from Phil until he ran into him again!

Later in my life another incident made me aware of how Phil was feeling. For my fiftieth birthday, my second wife, Joy, arranged a party for me. She felt it was an important milestone in my life, and she invited exactly fifty of my closest friends, including some of my students or former students who had become important in my life. Roger, my therapist, had graciously opened his home to me, and the party was quite an affair. My brother Phil was one of the guests. For the entire evening he could not believe the number of people who were there. He asked Joy who they all were, and when she responded that they were my friends, he retorted that no one had that many friends! She assured him that not only were they my friends, but they were my closest friends. At one point he remarked that I must have sent out to Central Casting to fill the room with extras! Not believing that it was possible for anyone to acquire that many friends, he went around asking people who they were and how they knew me. Joy told me this after the party was over, and it made me very sad. It was a statement of where he was, and it hurt me deeply. But of course, as a child, I was not aware of what was going on with Phil, and I just continued to enjoy his generosity and attention.

In the early years of my life up until about the time I was eleven or twelve, we lived in the same area. I was born on Thirteenth Place, which was one block south of Roosevelt Road, and when I was about three, we moved to Grenshaw Street, which ran about two blocks north of Roosevelt Road. There was a streetcar running on Roosevelt, almost all the way to the lake, which became very important to me later in my youth. It cost two cents to ride it, and it later became the symbol of my independence. It was red and powered by electricity from wires suspended overhead. I had a favorite car, number 113, which I became superstitious about when I got old enough to ride it on my own. If 113 was the car that came along, I knew I was going to have a wonderful day, but if it was another car, I had to be careful that day.

We lived on Grenshaw Street until I was about seven years old. My memories of those years are dim. We then moved to Van Buren Street—to a second-floor apartment, since my mother would never live on the first floor of any building. She was frightened that someone would climb through a first-floor window and kill us all while we slept. This of course was a carryover from her experiences in Russia. I heard my father tell her on many occasions that there were no Cossacks or pogroms in America, but he was never able to assuage her fears.

Until that time all of my early years had been spent living in Jewish neighborhoods peopled mostly by immigrants from Poland or Russia. The area around Roosevelt Road and Keeler Avenue was like little Russia. I would go to the deli on the corner of Keeler and Roosevelt and get a chocolate phosphate for two cents and watch all the older people eating corned-beef sandwiches and speaking Russian or Yiddish. I would eavesdrop on their conversations while I sipped my phosphate, knowing that they were thinking that I was a *shagetz* (a Gentile), and would not be able to understand their comments about me. I didn't "look Jewish." I had blond hair, finely defined features and looked like a poster boy for Hitler's Aryan race! On one occasion, two middle-aged Jewish women saw me looking at them and said in Yiddish, "Look at the Gentile, long drink of water, staring at us!" I finished my chocolate phosphate, sauntered over to them and in impeccable Yiddish told them that I wasn't a *shagetz,* that I wasn't a long drink of water, and that they were very rude. Their eyes got as big as two egg yolks, and they began to stutter. I laughed and went on my way.

Growing up in a Jewish environment, I hadn't yet experienced discrimination, but that was to come very soon. Our apartment on Van Buren Street was about ten blocks north of where we had lived before. It was a mixed neighborhood ethnically, and while I had not yet felt the full impact of prejudice, at seven I knew there were different energies. There were many Jewish families in the area, but the mixture felt different from everything I had experienced up to that time. On the first floor of the apartment building we lived in, there was an Italian family who had a son named Carmine. To me he was Carmie, and while he was five or six years older than I, he took a liking to me and would sometimes ride me to school on his two-wheeler. My mother saw me on the handlebars and freaked out. She forbade me from ever doing that again. She was sure that I would be killed if I did, so I had to sneak rides with Carmie whenever I could. My best friend, Danny, lived on the corner of my block over a grocery store. He was about six months older than I. We went to the same grade school but were in different classes. After we had been meeting in the schoolyard for about six months, his parents sent him to a Catholic school; but we would still meet after school and play on the block.

One experience had an incredible impact on me and affected me for many years. It happened in front of the corner grocery store, right under Danny's apartment. Even though I knew that Danny was Italian and Catholic, I had never thought about other people's religion or ethnicity before and had not developed any prejudices on that score. Danny was Danny, Carmie was Carmie, and I liked them both very much. Each in his own way was very important to me. On that day, Danny was sitting on the sidewalk in front of a bushel of string beans, drawing on a piece of paper and concentrating so hard that he was unaware of me as I approached him. I looked down at the paper he was drawing on and saw a rendering of Christ on the cross, with many people standing around—semi-stick figures dressed in robes and obviously laughing at Christ being crucified. When he became aware that I was standing there, he proudly told me about his drawing. On the cross was Jesus, he said, and all the people around him were Jews laughing at him.

They were responsible for Christ's being crucified. I don't know if Danny knew I was Jewish. It had never come up. I remember feeling a stab of pain in my chest and other emotions that I couldn't describe. I started to cry, turned, and ran home. That experience had such an incredible impact on me that I had nightmares about it. I thought at the time that the Jews had indeed killed Jesus and that this was why they had pogroms in Russia and why Jews in Europe were attacked as my father had told me. It wasn't until many years later that I learned the true history of the Crucifixion, who Judas was, and the role of Pilate, the Romans, and so on. Fortunately, the experience did not injure my friendship with Danny, and we continued to play together.

I also had my first sexual experience on Van Buren Street. It was Danny who introduced me to Maria, my next-door neighbor. I'm not sure how Danny had met her, but he seemed to have known her for some time. Maria was an "older woman" of about nine! She was two years older than I, which is a lot at that age, and she was startlingly attractive. Her hair was short and black as night, and her eyes were so dark you could not distinguish the pupils. She had olive skin, fine features, and very straight white teeth. I really don't remember what I knew about sex at that age. No one in my family had ever talked to me about it. One day Danny and I were invited into Maria's garage, which was located directly behind the two-story apartment building where she lived. She was wearing a pink dress. She leaned against the unfinished wall of the garage, right between the two-by-four struts, and lifted her dress up above her stomach. She wasn't wearing any underwear, and her genitals were fully visible. I remember standing there knowing that this was somehow taboo but transfixed by what I saw. She opened her legs and invited us in. Danny went first, and then it was my turn. I had an erection and strangely knew what to do. I felt the heat of her on me and was very excited by the experience. Of course, we were all too young to have orgasms, but that didn't seem to matter.

After that first time, we had a number of other encounters with Maria. They all took place on the landing of my apartment building. There was a clear space between the first and second floors that seemed completely safe. There were no doors that could suddenly be opened, so we used the space for our clandestine rendezvous. I would stand lookout when Danny was on the landing with Maria, and he would do the same for me. You have to remember here that I was seven, Danny was seven and a half, and Maria was nine! How we knew what to do, and where, if any place, we had learned it, I cannot say. Once we almost got caught in the hallway by my brother Morrey as he came bounding through the entrance door of the building. We all scrambled as fast as we could, but he was very suspicious about what we were doing. He questioned me, and I remember telling him we were playing some kind of innocuous game. I don't think he believed me, but then what could he have thought? At worst, he may have figured we were playing doctor. Little did he know that his little brother was getting laid and he wasn't! So you could say that I lost my virginity at seven, but my next sexual encounter didn't take place until I was thirteen.

We lived on Van Buren Street for about two and a half or three years, and I remember that Morrey lived there with us, but I can't remember who else from my family also did. After that, we moved back into the old neighborhood, this time on Fillmore Street, one block north of Grenshaw. It's funny how we remember things that took place more than sixty years ago. I remember our address on Fillmore and our telephone number. By that time I was approaching my tenth year, so my memories are crisper. As adults, most of us know our neighbors only well enough to wave and say hello to them or maybe exchange a few niceties, but when I was a boy of ten, my block became my entire social life. I knew almost everyone who had kids close to me in age, and I constantly played with those kids. We lived on the second floor of a two-story, all-brick apartment building with an octagon front—a Chicago type of building. The owner was a man named Trombino, a thick, burly man with a heavy Italian accent and a dark tan, which was the result of his spending most of every day outside doing construction work and other heavy labor. He too was an immigrant and had somehow been able to squirrel away enough money to put a down payment on that property.

Next door was a rickety frame house that looked as if it had been there before any of the other buildings. On the bottom floor, there was a family with a son named Bobby Snell. Bobby was about my age and very short. He looked as though he had the map of Ireland on his face! He was always happy, smiling and ready to have a good time. He had something that I had wanted for a while, a yellow, twenty-four-inch bike. Of course, a twenty-four-inch was too short for my longer legs, but by God it was a *bike!*

Above him lived a family whose name I don't remember but who had a really bad kid. He was a few years older, and I always thought he would end up in the electric chair. He had a BB gun, and I remember he also had a real pistol, maybe a .32-caliber. One time, when Phil and I were shooting my BB gun out of my bedroom window on the second floor, this bad kid shot Sonny Cohen in the head, and we were blamed for it! Sonny, whose real name was Harold, lived down the block. He was a year older than I, had brown hair, and a nose that was too large for his face—a state of affairs that was probably responsible for the nasal quality of his speech. It seemed as though the words came from his nose instead of his mouth. He was also quite short and looked exactly like his mother. In fact, he looked as if he had been cloned from her!

There was also the Bylow family, who lived down the block, almost next door to Sonny, and who were a strange group. There was Albert, the oldest; Norman, the intellectual; Howard, the holy terror; and Melvin, the youngest. Howard was always hitting people and generally being a Dennis-the-Menace type of kid, only not at all lovable. My cousin Itzie, whose real name was Irving Goland and who lived about four blocks away on Roosevelt Road and Kildare, would visit almost every day and got close to Norman Bylow, who was about his age. They spent a lot of time together.

Four houses away, in another of those ramshackle frame houses that must have been built twenty-five years before the brick buildings, lived Valerian, with whom I was in love. I believe she and her twin sisters were being raised by a single father, who was away at work all day. They had a nanny, a very obese, gray-haired woman, who always sat at the dining-room table in the same spot. I don't remember ever seeing her standing. She was always knitting at that table and yelling at the girls or lecturing them. When I would visit, I tried not to get too close to her, because she had terrible body odor. I kissed Valerian once or twice, and we became girlfriend and boyfriend. She couldn't come out and play after a certain hour, so our time together was very limited and the relationship was short-lived.

Towards the end of the block there was another family by the name of Cohen, who had a son named Arnold. They had moved onto the block sometime later than we had. I met Arnie one day walking through the alley in back of our houses. He was carrying a sack that seemed to have a life of its own. I stopped him and asked him what was in it and where he was going. He said that there were four kittens inside and that some lady had given him a quarter to drown them. I was shocked, and I told him that he shouldn't do that. They were living beings, and he had no right to kill them. He said that he also felt bad about it and that he was going to let them go in the empty lot across the street. We didn't do that, however; we went door to door throughout the entire neighborhood until we had all four kittens adopted. After that, Arnie and I became fast friends.

At the end of our block, in the house next to the last one, lived a kid named Burton Altman. I didn't spend much time with him, but he was one of the kids on the block, and whenever he wanted to join in, we welcomed him. I particularly remember him because of an experience I had with him fourteen or fifteen years later when I was in the army at Fort Ord on the Monterey Peninsula. I was pulling KP at the officers' club and happened to look out from the kitchen, and there was Burton, a second lieutenant, standing eight feet away from me. "Hi, Burt!" I said. He looked at me in my enlisted-man fatigues, turned without a word, and made a hasty departure. I felt as though someone had just pissed on my head. I knew he had recognized me. I had seen that glimmer of recognition in his eyes. That hurt a lot, and I have been able to use it in my work on a number of occasions.

Directly across the street from the row of houses on the block was a huge empty lot, which ran the entire length of the block. It was filled with weeds and sticker bushes and all kinds of shrubs and sunflowers. At the back of it was an elevated cement structure about twelve to fifteen feet high, on top of which ran train tracks. Every few hours a freight train would pass by, and every time it did, we would yell, "Chalk! Chalk!" and sometimes the engineer would throw us a big round stick of chalk. I don't know why we wanted it, and furthermore, I don't know what the engineer used it for. It was, however, a treat that we celebrated every time we were lucky enough to get it. We also played games in that lot: red light, green light; statues; Red Rover, Red Rover, let Bobby come over; and so on.

Those years on Fillmore Street were very important to my development. I was almost ten, and I was becoming independent from my family; that is to say that they still fed, clothed, and housed me, of course, but that I was able to travel downtown on that red streetcar all by myself. Since the school I went to was only about a mile away, I walked to and from it every day. I remember wanting to be a crossing guard, but they thought I was too young and too small at the time. On Saturdays my mother would give me twenty-five cents; I would hop on a streetcar, go to the Central Park Theater, have a hotdog, French fries, and a Nedicks orange drink, see a double feature, a serial, and three or four cartoons, and have enough left over to buy a Milky Way candy bar. Can you imagine that? The movie cost a nickel; the hotdog, French fries and drink, fifteen cents; and the candy bar, a nickel. I would spend the whole day at the movies and get home just in time for dinner.

My father had a small furniture store on Halsted Street. At that time it was not a great neighborhood, but it was populated with similar businesses. He specialized in dinette sets, the kind that was popular at the time—the Formica-top table and matching vinyl chairs, all with chrome legs. One day, while attempting to impress potential customers by showing them that the tabletop was heat resistant, my father lit a piece of newspaper and placed it on the tabletop, which immediately burst into flames! The customers ran screaming out of the store, and my father immediately enlisted the help of the storeowner next door, who happened to have a fire extinguisher. To say the least, he never did that again. He did, however, once burn off his eyebrows, which never grew back. To heat his store in the winter he had a coal-burning stove in the rear. One day, he stepped too close, opened the door of the stove—and in a second his eyebrows were gone!

Another memorable event happened when I was three months shy of my tenth birthday: My mother and I went to visit my brother Phil in Los Angeles. He had gone there to explore the possibilities of working in the film industry or in theater. I think he felt that Hollywood would be somewhat easier than New York, although his ambition was to be a scenic designer on Broadway, and he had gone to California with my cousin Leon Brodsky, who had no theatrical ambitions but who wanted to see what the West Coast was like. It was unusual because in those days people, or shall I say people I knew, didn't venture too far from their home ground.

My mother and I took the train. Nobody flew at that time, except rich people and movie stars. We boarded the Union Pacific City of Los Angeles, which was a brightly colored, yellow train with a bold red stripe running down the middle. If I remember correctly, it was a two-day, one-night trip. We had to sit up in a seat that didn't recline far enough for us to be able to sleep, but I didn't really care, since I was so excited that I couldn't sleep much anyway. It was the first time I had been anywhere, except for summer vacations in South Haven, Michigan, which was only about 150 miles away from Chicago. Trains have a specific odor—a mixture of antiseptic, perfume, and newly laid carpet—and to this day, whenever I smell it, I have an experience of *déjà vu* from that trip to L.A. I spent most of every day on the train looking out the window at the scenery we seemed to fly by. The Midwest is very flat and there wasn't much to see there, except cornfields, farms, and grazing cows. It was quite a different story, however, when we reached the mountains. It was the first time I was seeing mountains, and I embarrassed my mother with my exuberance at the first sight of them. I must have shouted or been louder than ordinary conversation, for she quieted me with an admonishing look, and from then on I tried to keep my excitement at a lower volume. I was transfixed by the shapes and colors of those giant outcroppings and by the way the sun created shadows and spikes of light in the crevasses between the peaks. It was like visiting another planet. I'm sure I had seen movies with mountains in them, but it was quite a different experience to see them so close and so real that I felt I could almost reach out and touch the rocks.

It was the first time I had been on a train, so everything was new and different. The tunnels were long and dark, and even the sound of the train's horn sent shivers through me. During that period of my life I would spend a lot of time drifting off into fantasy, and the plethora of sensory experiences was very conducive to it. I could see myself riding through those mountains on a beautiful Palomino horse, wearing a cowboy hat and a six-shooter, always wary of marauding Indians. As the train rushed by them, I spotted places where I could camp for the night. I tasted the hardtack and beans I had cooked on a makeshift fire and slept beneath the stars with one eye open to alert me of any lurking danger.

Since my mother had packed a lot of sandwiches and fruit, we didn't spend much time in the dining car, but we did have a couple of meals there. It was exactly the way I had seen it in the movies: the tables with the clean white tablecloths and the waiters in white coats serving the passengers, who were reading the morning paper. I wondered how they could bury themselves in newspapers when there was so much to see and experience around them. I felt so excited that my appetite disappeared. We had to write our order on a slip of paper, which was picked up by the waiter and taken to the kitchen. My mother was not very secure about writing in English. Even though she did read and write it, her handwriting was difficult to decipher; so I became the hero in the dining car. She told me what she wanted to eat, and I wrote it down—which made me feel very adult and sophisticated. I quickly drank the water provided by the waiter so I could ask him for another glass. I wasn't that thirsty. I just wanted to request service from him. It made me feel like a grownup.

I would also walk down the length of the train and look at the people in the various cars and wonder where they came from and why they were there. Whenever I saw a kid close to me in age, our eyes would lock on each other, and whatever it is that passes between children of the same age would stop me for a brief moment. It seemed to be a variety of emotions and unspoken exchanges: Do you want to come out and play? Do you think you're as strong as I am? I bet I can run faster than you! I'm going to visit my brother—all those thoughts happened in a few short moments of eye contact. When I would return to my seat, my mother would be dozing and I wanted to talk, so I would nudge her gently as I took my seat, pretending that I had accidentally brushed against her. She would wake up, and I would tell her about all the people I had encountered throughout the train.

When we were almost there, I had mixed emotions about arriving. I was excited to get there and see Phil and California, but I also felt as someone does who is reading a good book or watching a movie and doesn't want it to end. As we stepped off the train and walked into the station, I felt an indescribable excitement that almost bordered on nausea. The station seemed huge. It had high beamed ceilings and was colorfully painted. Phil was there, greeting us with a big smile. He hugged my mother and lifted me off the ground, welcoming us to California. We walked out of the station into the golden sunlight of Los Angeles—and my lifelong love affair with California began! I had never experienced sunlight so rich and golden. After all, it was the same sun that we had in Chicago, wasn't it? But it was different—brighter, richer, more yellow. I looked back at Union Station and saw the big clock just as it appeared in numerous movies I had seen; only this time I was in the movie. We walked to the parking lot, to the car Phil had bought, a 1931 Model A Ford convertible, for which he and Leon had paid fifty dollars. It had a rumble seat where the trunk would usually be and was fully upholstered in light brown leather. There was room for only two people in the front, so I climbed into the rumble seat. It was the first time I had ever been in a convertible. That car became very important for the whole month we spent in L.A. As Phil drove from the train station towards Hollywood, the wind rushing through my hair and the smell of orange blossoms filling my nose made me want to shout with excitement. I did control those urges, however, and only screamed with joy internally.

I will never forget that first ride as long as I live! I was amazed at the width of the streets and the colors of the houses and other buildings. It was like being in a Technicolor Disney movie, where all the existing colors are magnified into brilliant hues. I had never seen so many open automobiles. It seemed that everyone had a convertible and was driving with the top down. It was August, and, of course, it was sunny and hot. However, it was a very different kind of heat from what we experienced in Chicago. It was not humid but very dry, and the air had a freshness to it that made me want to inhale deeply. As we rode up Sunset Boulevard, I peered into each car, expecting to see movie stars everywhere. In fact, I think I did or wished that I did.

"Oh, isn't that Lana Turner?" I shouted to my brother, who was sitting at the wheel in front of me.

"I didn't see who that was!" he responded.

As we approached Hollywood, I got a glimpse of the Hollywood sign and could not contain my excitement. "I see it! I see it!" I screamed. "We're in Hollywood!" I'm sure I startled both Phil and my mother, but they both laughed at my outburst. Looking at the back of their heads as we drove, I felt an overwhelming sense of love for both of them.

We parked in front of a brownstone apartment building that was about five stories high. It was where Phil lived. My cousin Leon had gone back to Chicago by that time, so Phil had their apartment all to himself. I remember thinking that it wasn't exactly what I had imagined. The bricks reminded me of Chicago apartment buildings, and I guess I was a little disappointed. I had expected the kind of house I had seen in the movies. We took the elevator to the second floor and entered Phil's one-bedroom apartment. He gave the bedroom to my mother and me, and he took the couch. The apartment had a small kitchen that overlooked an empty lot, which housed many discarded and unwanted appliances. Right there in the middle of the lot was an older Model T Ford, which had been abandoned there and was obviously destined to rust. It was a faded dark blue that looked as if it had been painted with a brush. My immediate fantasy was that if it had indeed been abandoned, maybe I could have it and drive back to Chicago in it. Of course, I didn't know how to drive at the time, but that was a minor difficulty that I knew I could overcome in a full month! One of the other windows in the apartment had a small view of the Hollywood mountains. I would spend my time at that window whenever I was inside. Our apartment in Chicago overlooked that large empty lot and the elevated train tracks, so this was certainly an enormous improvement.

Phil had a job at a vacuum-cleaner repair store, where he spent each of his days repairing vacuum cleaners. He had taken the job so that he could support himself while exploring whatever theatrical opportunities existed. At night he would stage-manage plays in the Hollywood area. During the day, when he was at work, my mother and I would walk up Sunset Boulevard and sometimes venture north to Hollywood Boulevard. Some afternoons my mother would stay in the apartment to nap, while I explored Hollywood. I was amazed at the orange and lemon trees that were growing in the backyards of those little bungalows interspersed between the apartment buildings. One day I stopped in front of one of those houses, and the lady who lived there approached me with a large bag of oranges and lemons. She smiled and held the bag towards me, gesturing for me to take it. I told her that I didn't have any money, which brought a big smile to her face. She was older, had gray hair that was pulled back tightly, and as she smiled, I saw her dentures shift in her mouth. "This is for you, son. Take it! There is no charge. It is my gift to you, blondie!" she said. I took the bag from her and thanked her. We stared at each other for an awkward moment, and I watched her as she walked back into her little house.

I could not get my fill of this land, which seemed like paradise to me. I walked for hours until my feet hurt. I sat on the curb watching all the cars go by and daydreamed of a life here in California. On my walks I would pass Earl Carroll's nightclub on Sunset near

Vine Street. It had thick cement plaques attached to the building wall with the autographs of famous Hollywood stars. I would stand there for a half hour at a time, looking at all the plaques and wondering whether the real stars had signed them.

My first experience at a Los Angeles supermarket was overwhelming. I had never seen one so huge! In Chicago we had markets, such as the A&P and others, but they were grocery stores, not nearly as big as these supermarkets. I wandered through the aisles with my mother, fearing I would get lost in the maze. On weekends, Phil was off, so we drove all over Hollywood, into the hills and up and down the side streets and on the boulevards. He was a wonderful tour guide. Sometimes it was just he and I exploring the city, and at those times I would stand up in the front seat and stretch my arms out to the side and yell. He took pleasure in my enjoyment and would join in with me, shouting "Yeah! Yeah!" as we drove down the streets. Until then I had never felt so free and expansive. It was as if I were experiencing a whole new way of life. I was happier in that month than I had ever been before. It wasn't because I was on vacation; it was as if I had discovered the Promised Land. Everything was more beautiful and more kaleidoscopic. The air was fresher and sweeter, and even the food tasted better!

One Sunday we took a drive to the beach. We drove west on Sunset Boulevard, and it seemed as if we were riding for hours. It was a long journey for me, who wasn't used to Los Angeles distances. In Chicago everything seemed so compressed. My first view of the ocean was an awesome experience. We parked next to the beach right in front of the water, and for a long time I just sat in the rumble seat of the car, staring at the vastness of the ocean. It was the first time I had seen an ocean. It seemed mysterious and wild to me, and the variety of its colors was breathtaking. I knew Lake Michigan, which is one of the larger Great Lakes, since I had spent time on Chicago beaches, pier fishing and boating on the lake. I had even seen other parts of it in Indiana and Michigan, but I had never glimpsed anything like the Pacific Ocean. Lake Michigan touches four states, and there is almost nowhere where you can see across to the other side, but the difference was indescribable. When I finally got out of the car and walked down to the water, I was transfixed by the enormity of the vista. Phil had had me wear my bathing suit under my pants, so when I got close to the water, I dropped my pants, took off my shirt, and ran towards the surf; but since I didn't know how to swim yet, I slowed down significantly as I approached the foam. I dipped my feet into the water and felt the biting cold all the way up to my front teeth. The odors were overwhelming. I could smell the salt, the kelp, and the fish, and the air acted as a catalyst that mixed all those odors into an olfactory experience that was second to none I had ever had before. It was like tasting wine and sucking air into my mouth at the same time, so as to experience the bouquet and flavor with greater impact. I dipped my hand into the surf and put it in my mouth. I wanted to experience this ocean in every way possible, and I had never tasted saltwater before. I thought about all the living creatures that made the ocean their home and wondered if there were any of them close to shore. I asked Phil how deep the ocean was, and he answered, "Very deep!" We spent the whole day at the beach, eating the sandwiches my mother had made us.

We also took other trips on the weekends. Once, we went to Lake Arrowhead, a mountain community about ninety miles east of Los Angeles, which has a small lake and is about fifty-five hundred feet high. As we drove up the mountain, I marveled at the differences in the geography of California. Certainly Chicago and its surrounding area were not nearly as diverse. The trees here were hundreds of feet high and maybe hundreds of years old. There were pine trees of all kinds, some of which I had never seen before, and the ground was littered with pinecones of all sizes and shapes. As soon as I got out of the car, I started to collect as many as I could carry. Then we walked along the edge of the lake. This was truly a fairyland. Even though I had never been to Switzerland, I had seen pictures of it, and that is what this place reminded me of. We ate lunch in a restaurant called the Alpine Chalet, which overlooked the lake, and I was suddenly washed over by a feeling of depression, knowing that the time of this visit was growing short and that I would have to go back to Chicago. I don't think my mother or my brother noticed my mood, for who thinks that a little boy has any reason to be depressed? My depression evaporated very quickly, however, as we explored the area further. My mother and I were standing at the edge of the lake, and I was looking at the houses that dotted the mountainside, when I told her that someday I was going to own a house up there. She smiled at me with the kind of smile one has when one's son or daughter says that someday he or she will be president of the United States. I knew that she was humoring me, but I was serious. That was in August of 1941, and in August of 1978 I did buy a beautiful house overlooking that lake, a house that I still own and where I write all my books. A ten-year-old child can make decisions that are real and in some cases are carved very deeply in his mind.

Just before our trip to California was over, Phil took me to see a rehearsal of a play he was stage-managing at a theater on Las Palmas near Hollywood Boulevard—a building that is still there, only now it's a discotheque! I sat in the front row of that small theater and watched the actors rehearse the play. Arthur Lake, famous for playing Dagwood Bumstead in the Blondie series, was the lead. I loved the Blondie movies and had seen all of them. Penny Singleton played Blondie, and Arthur Lake was her husband, Dagwood, a bumbling, uncoordinated dolt who was always falling over things and making a mess out of everything he attempted to do. Of course, it was a comedy series and therefore supposed to be funny, and much of it was slapstick. Lake had always been somewhat of a clown, predisposed to mugging as Dagwood. In this play, however, he had a very serious dramatic role and was quite different from the man I had known as Blondie's husband. I was amazed that he could be so emotional and real in an entirely different realm. That was my first real insight into what acting was and how different an actor could be when playing different characters. I guess I had thought that actors were like the characters they were hired to play and that this was why they had gotten the part to begin with.

I was very sad the day we left to go back to Chicago. Phil took us to the station, which seemed to have lost the glamour it had had upon our arrival. It appeared less colorful and much smaller on the inside. The clock too looked smaller. We boarded the train, which was the same one we had taken to get to California but which now seemed dirty and a paler yellow. The seats seemed harder, the fabric rougher, and the carpets on the floor looked frayed and worn. It's funny how feelings and moods can influence the way you see things. I was going back to drab, colorless, cold Chicago, a place that I had never liked and that I knew I would leave someday. In the evening, I was staring out the train window into the darkness, seeing only my own reflection in the glass—I guess I was off somewhere deep in thought—when my mother touched my shoulder and asked me what I was thinking about. I told her it was funny that she had asked that, because I was thinking that the first day I could, I would come back to California and never leave. She laughed a kind of warm, understanding laugh and said that I was just a little boy and that I would probably want to live in many different places. I assured her that I was very serious and that California was it for me. I really knew that at the time!

Meanwhile, there I was, back on Fillmore Street on the second floor of that apartment building looking at the empty lot across the street and listening to the freight trains rumble by every few hours. The only good thing about coming back was seeing my friends again.

I desperately wanted a bicycle. I nagged my father endlessly to get me one, but they were scarce because of the war. It was now 1942, and we were just one year into World War II. I remember the day it had started. I was at the kitchen table in our apartment working at a jigsaw puzzle, when my brother Morrey burst in through the back door. He was flushed and very excited.

The words flew out of his mouth: "The Japs just attacked Pearl Harbor!"

I turned, looked at him and asked, "Who is she?"

"It's a place, not a person, dummy," he replied.

We huddled around the radio for most of the rest of that day, listening to President Roosevelt deliver his famous "day of infamy" speech. My father was very disturbed. He was worried about what this meant for his family in Russia. When I was about seven years old and living on Van Buren Street, I had heard a short-wave broadcast from Germany. It was around 1938, and Adolf Hitler was speaking—or should I say shouting? His voice scared me. I thought it was filled with rage. After the broadcast, my father, looking disturbed and worried, had said that there was going to be great trouble in Europe. It was coming, and many people were going to die. I don't think he realized how prophetic that statement was.

Because of the war, steel was scarce, so bikes were hard to come by. My parents tried to placate me by buying me a scooter with large yellow wheels, which I would endlessly ride up and down the block. It was not a bicycle, however, and I was unhappy with it. We were just coming out of the Great Depression, but money was still an issue. Men were working for eight to twelve dollars for a forty-hour week. Finally, my uncle Abie located a used two-wheeler and told my father about it. I was playing on the sidewalk in front of our building one fine day, when my father's furniture-delivery truck pulled up. Willie, who worked for my father, jumped out from its cab, went back to the bed, lifted a bike from it, and with a giant smile wheeled it over to me. He seemed elated, almost as if it were for him. Willie, a slight black man with wavy black hair and an ingratiating smile, was always ready to take me for a ride in my father's truck. Whenever I would visit my father's store on Halsted Street, he would take me with him on a delivery. When I was smaller, he had let me sit on his lap and steer the truck. He had worked for my father for a number of years, and I regarded him as one of my extended family. I don't think he was married, but I am sure he liked children, because he really adopted me emotionally.

On that day, he placed the bike in front of me, fixed the kickstand, crossed his arms and said, "Well, my boy, what do you think of that?" I didn't know whether to laugh or cry. I had waited so long for the bike and had wanted it so desperately that I just looked at it for a very long time, running my hands over the frame and fenders, touching it as if it were made of velvet. All my life I have been very tactile. My enjoyment of any object depends on the way it feels to me. Many years later, when I had come to California, I was in an automobile showroom just as that year's new models were being introduced. There were about five cars on the showroom floor, and without awareness I was running my hands over each and every one of them. A salesman walked up to me and in an aggressive tone asked me why I was touching all the cars.

"Do they feel different from one another?" he asked me sarcastically.

I looked at him for a moment or two and replied, "Yes, they do." I meant that exactly!

He said that I was putting handprints and fingerprints all over them and that he would have to clean them. I apologized and left the showroom.

The bike was a Pacemaker, a brand I had never heard of, and it was definitely used, but I was delighted to have it, even though my dream had always been to have a Schwinn. It was brown with a cream-colored stripe on each side of the front and rear fenders, and it had a light mounted on the front fender, which was cream colored too. The light never worked, but it did add to the look of the bike. It also had big balloon tires and chrome spoke wheels that were screaming to be cleaned and polished. Before I even took it for a ride, I had made a mental list of the things I was going to do to it: wash it, wax it, get some chrome cleaner to polish it, do something with the seat, and so on. There again I felt the plastic-cover phenomenon with which my mother had infected me! Maybe I would never get another bike, so I should really take care of this one, right?

I will never forget my first ride. Even though it was about sixty-five years ago, it remains vivid in my memory and senses. I mounted the bike slowly, released the kickstand with care, and almost fell over to the left. I caught myself and reestablished my balance. Since it was a twenty-six-inch bike, I was only able to reach the ground on either side on my toes in order to balance myself. I remember pushing down on the right pedal, and the bike began to move forward. I put pressure on the left pedal, and the bike picked up speed. Right, left, faster and faster—the motion of the bike and the wind it created blew my hair in all directions. I rode down the sidewalk of that block on Fillmore Street, screaming with delight, passing everyone who was out at the time. I went by Valerian's house, down the block past the Bylows' house and towards the corner. I felt liberated, emancipated, free and elated all at once. I must have ridden that bike for two hours—or at least until I was exhausted. I remember Willie watching me take off. He was laughing and shouting something at me, but I couldn't hear him.

The Pacemaker had cost my father thirty dollars, which was about three weeks' pay for the average working man—one hundred and twenty hours of work in order to earn thirty dollars! I didn't really understand about money at the time. It was just numbers to me. I did, however, know that thirty dollars was a lot of money and that I had better really take care of that bike. It became the center of my universe. I rode it everywhere. Other kids from my block and from other blocks in the neighborhood joined me. I made many new friends and was liberated from the area. I literally rode for miles every time I took the bike out from the wooden shed we had been assigned in our basement. There was a huge bridge on Laramie Avenue, which was a couple of miles from my house. My friends and I would walk our bikes up the hill and then fly down the other side reaching speeds of forty or fifty miles per hour. Of course, it is very difficult to stop a bike going downhill at that speed, so I guess we were lucky not to have encountered cross traffic at the bottom of the bridge.

Those were happy days for me, and if I had to pick one thing out as the most meaningful in my life, I would say that the Pacemaker was my "Rosebud." I don't know what happened to that bike. We took it to our new house when we moved, and I remember riding it there, but somehow it has faded from my memory after that. My father bought me a new car in 1947, and I guess that replaced the Pacemaker. There are so many things that we own and treasure throughout our lives, as I did my bike, my BB gun, and my Tom Mix ring that glowed in the dark. What happens to those things? It is as if they go to some kind of elephant graveyard specifically designed for toys and other possessions! To this day I enjoy looking through antique and thrift shops with a secret hope that I will find my BB gun and my Pacemaker.

Around that time we also acquired a dog named Corky, a medium-sized, black-and-white mongrel. Whenever we were asked what kind of dog he was, we would say, "He is a Heinz 57," by which we meant to communicate that he was descended from a variety of breeds. He was a gentle and sweet dog for a few years. Every night, when my brother Phil came home from work, he would let Corky out. (Phil had come back to Chicago right after Pearl Harbor, because my father, afraid that the California coast would be attacked by the Japanese, had insisted upon his return.) Corky would always find his way home, except once when he ran away and was gone for about a week. I was heartbroken, but Phil felt even worse, since he thought he was responsible for Corky's disappearance. A variety of people told us that they thought they had seen him—as far away as Gary, Indiana! One morning at about nine o'clock, we heard a scratching sound at our backdoor. It was Corky. He was covered with dirt and stickers and looked as if he had returned from some distant battlefield. We were overjoyed to see him, however. The way he looked didn't matter. He was back. Phil cried, I cried, my mother cried—but that wasn't a novelty; she cried about a change in the weather! We bathed Corky immediately and put some perfume on him, which he resented because it made him sneeze.

Corky became very instrumental in our buying the first house we ever owned. One day while I was outside walking him, he was viciously attacked by a Scottie dog owned by the Ritter family, who lived in the center of the block. It was a horrible sight. I tried to break them up, but I was afraid I would be bitten in the flurry, so I started to beat the Scottie with Corky's leash and finally separated them. Corky was torn and bleeding in many places, even though I felt that he had held his own with the Ritters' dog. As it turned out, however, it wasn't a simple dogfight. For whatever reason, Corky's mind snapped. His entire personality changed, and he really went crazy. From that moment forward he would attack all the dogs he encountered, some of them twice his size. All backed down and ran away. Moreover, he would growl at us when we went to pet him and over the next couple of years succeeded in biting everyone in the family, except me, and that was because I was too fast for him. So why did we keep him? A good question! He had become part of our family, and you just don't get rid of a member of the family. He tolerated us, and we tolerated him. We would walk a wide track around each other and respect each other's space. Corky would always warn us when he wanted to be left alone, so we would just back away and avoid getting bitten. Unfortunately, Mr. Trombino, our landlord, finally issued an ultimatum: "Get rid of the dog or move!" Since my father had had other issues with Trombino before, Corky was the last straw, and it made us start looking for another place to live. My father felt that it was time to stop paying rent and to own something instead. He was a very conservative man, always insecure about making a living and supporting his family, so this was a huge step for him to take. He had come to America in 1912, it was now 1944, and he had not yet bought a house. We could have owned several houses for the amount of rent he had paid over the years, but he had been afraid to make that commitment.

We looked at several houses before deciding on one that stood about sixteen blocks west of where we lived. Now it would seem that sixteen blocks is really not a great distance, but it seemed to me that we were moving to another state! Up to that time I had spent my entire life in a one-square-mile area. In fact, until we had moved to Van Buren Street, I had lived within a three- or four-block area in either direction. Moving "way up west" was a geographical shock for me. I would be leaving all my friends and a neighborhood that I knew and felt secure in; however, I was excited about living in a real house instead of an apartment for the first time in my life.

It was a very nice one-level house on a corner lot. It had a huge basement that ran its entire length, an attic, and a very nice little backyard that Corky could enjoy. It was made of brown brick with the customary octagon front, and inside it had a huge living room that took up the whole front part. I had my own room, with twin beds, which I shared for a while with my brother Phil until he left for New York. We were still only one block north of Roosevelt Road, and that red streetcar came to the end of its line three blocks west of Monitor Avenue, which was where our new house stood.

Moving there was both a blessing and a curse for me, but at first just a curse. I missed Fillmore Street and my friends. I continued to ride my bike, but it didn't seem quite the same. It was the first time we had moved out of an area that was all, or primarily, Jewish. Ronny Meyers, who lived across the street in a yellow brick apartment building, was the only other Jewish kid in the area, which was mostly Italian with a sprinkling of Irish. I was eleven and a half and still in grade school. I transferred from Sumner, which was a fairly large school, to a four-room schoolhouse directly across the street from where we lived. Key Clark Branch, as it was called, was a branch of a larger school much further away. There were about twelve of us in the seventh grade, so we shared the room with the sixth graders, who had a separate blackboard and different lessons, but the same teacher, Mrs. Lane.

To borrow a line from Dickens, "It was the best of times, it was the worst of times..." As a family we drew closer and had a common project: the house. My father took the long streetcar ride to Halsted Street every morning and back towards evening. At least it was a single conveyance. My mother began furnishing the house, while my brother Phil, who was very good with his hands and could build things, painted the fence in the backyard, which really needed it, painted the basement floor bright red, and built me a darkroom out of one of the storage sheds. The second shed, which was larger, was converted into a rumpus room. My sister Helen, who also lived with us, had her own room in the front of the house right behind the living room. That was still off limits, by the way, though I must say that my mother did relax the rules somewhat, because when we got our first television set, which had a ten-inch screen, that is where we put it. Things were definitely looking up! My brother brought home a record-making machine. There weren't any tape recorders back then, so we recorded many after-dinner sessions on records. We had a ball! My father was a great laugher, so on one of those recording occasions all we did was laugh. We called it the laughing record. Each time we played it, it would ignite the laughter over again.

Outside the house it was a different story though. For the first time I started to experience discrimination. There were three kids in my class—Chris Rocco, Ralph Rocco his cousin, and Buddy Riggio—who made my life a living nightmare. They called me names, pushed me around and chased me home almost every day after school. I was terrified of recess, thinking I would have to deal with those boys in the schoolyard. Each day they would tell me that they were going to get me after school. Just before the school bell that ended the school day rang, I would inch towards the door, so that I could get a running start towards my house. Since I lived kitty-corner from the school, it was less than fifty yards from the exit door to my house, so as soon as the bell rang, I made a mad dash for it. I was really fast and got a lot faster as time went on. Fear is a great motivator, and I was terrified! I don't remember ever being hit or beaten up by the unholy three, but they humiliated me at every opportunity. I was a "kike," a "heb," a "sheenie," and whatever other obscenity they could think of. It seemed strange to me that they would treat me the way they did, since they all looked very ethnic, while I was very all-American looking! As I said before, I didn't look Jewish, whatever that means. I guess I didn't fit the stereotype. I hated getting up every morning and facing another day of harassment, and I loved the weekends because I didn't have to deal with those awful boys. A lot of my time alone was taken up with fantasies of getting them alone and killing them one at a time, each in a different and horrible way.

It wasn't all bad though. I made a good friend, one who lasted all the way to high school. His name was John Graef. He sat right in front of me in class and helped me get through a lot of the tests. John was very bright, while I had difficulty understanding some of the work, so he let me copy from his papers and in a way was responsible for my graduation from grade school. I found out later that it wasn't an intelligence problem that I had in grasping things, but rather an emotional one, which I will get into in the next chapter. Besides helping me with schoolwork, John became my playmate. Every day after school, we would meet in his basement and play "I must" games; for example, "I must be the general and you are my subordinate, and we are planning an offensive on the enemy." We would take those imaginary games to incredible places, often pretending incrementally for weeks at a time. Sometimes I was the hero, and at other times he was. We played those games for well over a year, and I credit those times with being the basis for my imagination in acting.

In addition, I created a fantasy life every time I went to bed. Since I hated to go to bed, I invented a reason to look forward to it. Every night I would create a story—mostly an adventure tale—in which I was a character. I was the captain of an old sailing ship crossing the ocean in the middle of violent storms, or I was on a safari in the dense jungles of Africa, fighting lions and snakes and cannibals with poisoned arrows. I always came away victorious, braving all odds and heroically defeating every foe. Sometimes those adventures were episodic, and the same story would go on for weeks. I would pick up each night where I had fallen asleep the night before. It wasn't just a mental thing. It was very sensory and emotional too. When I was trekking through the blistering hot jungles, I often woke up bathed in sweat. A lot of the time I would awaken in the middle of the night with aching muscles because I had exerted myself so much in the fantasy.

In many ways the years on Monitor Avenue were extremely important growth years. We moved there when I was about eleven and a half, and it was there I grew up all the way through high school and beyond. School was very difficult, not only because of the harassment from Chris and his cousin, but also, as I said, because I had a hard time keeping up with the class. John was my savior for that year and a half in grade school. Our teacher, Mrs. Lane, was an over-the-hill, post-menopausal bitch, who had no patience with me, and I didn't really have anyone to confide in at the time. Although my brother Phil was still living with us, he was working in a liquor store in downtown Chicago, and I saw very little of him during that period before he left for New York. My sister Helen also worked downtown and was only around in the evenings after work, so I tried to cope with the situation as best I could. What kept me going were my fantasies of revenge and my extracurricular activities. I would spend every day after school at John's house—something I looked forward to with great anticipation.

John was a typical WASP. At that time, he was a little taller than I and had light brown hair, which was always neatly combed with not one hair out of place. I often wondered if he got out of bed in the morning totally coiffed. He had very white skin, rosy cheeks, and perfectly straight white teeth that had never had a cavity. His mother looked very much like him with the very same attributes, while his father was some kind of crossover between a blue- and white-collar worker. They were a nice family and seemed to have very few, if any, prejudices. Whenever I came to the house, I was treated very well and always given some kind of refreshment. John and I usually played our pretend games in his basement, which had been set up as a room for him to use any way he wanted.

When I turned twelve, both John and I joined the local Boy Scout troop, which met in a church basement on the corner of Austin Boulevard. The three years I was in that troop were the best three years of my life. As strange as that may seem, what I learned there, the discipline and military knowledge I acquired, served me well years later when I went into the army. The Boy Scouts were a haven away from school and from the abuse I took from those guys. We met once a week on Friday evenings and worked on a variety of projects. I learned Morse code and found out how to build various kinds of fires and how to tie knots that I hadn't known existed. I also learned to respect authority and to work towards promotions and the achievement of higher ranks. We went on daylong hikes into the forest around Chicago and on weekend camping trips, where we slept in pup tents and learned to cook. We earned points for certain achievements, which was a good way to advance in rank. At first, a Boy Scout wears the "tenderfoot" badge; then as he advances, he goes to "second class" and then to "first class." After that, he can achieve higher ranks by earning different merit badges for performing various skills and accomplishing a wide variety of tasks. I became a "star Scout," which required seven or eight merit badges and which was as far as I went, because the next rank required swimming and lifesaving, and at that time I couldn't swim. I also loved the uniform, which was a cross between olive drab and light tan with red stripes on the epaulets. Each Scout in our troop, number 370, also wore a red kerchief around his neck with a Scout-emblem slide that held it in place. I was motivated to earn emblems and badges that would decorate my uniform. John and I were competitive in our zeal to achieve rank and position in the troop.

Our patrol, the Lion Patrol, consisted of about eight Scouts. Besides our Friday evenings in the church basement, we also met every other week at someone's house. Hogan, our patrol leader, was a little older than the rest of us and had been in the troop for about two years before we joined. A patrol leader wore a badge with two green stripes on his left sleeve and had to sign a Scout's card of achievements in order for the Scout to advance to the first two ranks. Hogan was a nice, easygoing guy with thick brown hair that seemed to be at war with his head. No matter what he did, he always looked unkempt. His hair seemed to grow in several directions at the same time, and he was always running his fingers through it in an attempt to make it behave. It was a lost cause, however, since nothing seemed to help. One summer he got a crew cut almost down to his scalp and was finally able to stop fighting his hair. He looked like a different person, and it took a little while to get used to him with that haircut.

Our scoutmaster, Mr. Nemec, was a short, stout man of about sixty-five with thin gray hair and the worst dentures I had ever seen. A kind man, he really enjoyed being the scoutmaster of troop 370. He loved the young boys and was always there to advise, mentor, and be helpful in any way he could. I think he was a widower, who lived alone. I went to his home once to take a test for the photography merit badge—which I got—and I remember that it had an odor, a combination of dampness and age, and that it was furnished with very old couches and stuffed chairs. There were knickknacks on every shelf, most likely selected by his wife when she was alive.

One Friday evening Mr. Nemec told us to elect an assistant patrol leader, a Scout who wore a single green stripe on his left sleeve. Nothing in the world was more important to me than achieving that rank. John and I had discussed it at length way before that evening, and we had decided that when the time came, he would cast his vote for me if I would cast mine for him. As always, John was more popular than I because he was always so much more proficient in everything he did. Besides, he was an all-American boy, one whom the Boy Scouts of America could have chosen as their poster boy. Well, the time for the election arrived at our next patrol meeting in John Graef's basement. We each cast our vote on a piece of paper, which we folded so that no one else could see what we had written. When Hogan counted the ballots, my heart was beating so hard and fast that I'm sure I set a new record. As I said, there were eight of us in all. John had gotten three votes, I had gotten three votes, and the other two votes had been cast for two other boys in the patrol. It was a tie that had to be broken somehow, with the toss of a coin or in some other way. Hogan picked a page in the Boy Scout manual, wrote down the page number, and asked John and me to each pick a number. Whoever had the number closest to Hogan's would then be the next assistant patrol leader. My choice was the closest, so I was it! I was ecstatic! I looked at John. His disappointment was obvious, but he tried to smile, shook my hand and congratulated me. I felt ambivalent about my victory because I had cheated. John and I had agreed to vote for each other, but knowing that he would probably be elected, I had voted for one of the other Scouts. To this day, sixty-two years later, I feel ashamed of what I did. John never found out about it, but I knew it and it affected my feelings about the victory.

About a year later I was promoted to patrol leader, and I suggested to John that he move to the Panther Patrol, which needed a leader. At that time we both had seniority in the troop, and since there were a lot of new and younger Scouts there, I thought that with his experience and seniority, John would definitely qualify to be the Panthers' patrol leader. At the end of every Friday troop meeting, Mr. Nemec would ask the troop for input, suggestions, or complaints. We would raise our hand and contribute whatever we had to say. It was truly a democratic group, very much to Mr. Nemec's credit. It was at one of those sessions that I raised my hand and suggested that John be appointed patrol leader of the Panthers. I could see that Mr. Nemec considered it an odd suggestion, but being as open and benevolent as he was, he asked me why I thought that it would be appropriate. I generously listed all of John's qualities and talents and added that I thought he had great leadership abilities and that he was a great advisor to me in the Lion Patrol. I also mentioned that I had become the assistant patrol leader by picking a page number that was closest to the one selected by Hogan, by then a senior patrol leader. Finally, Mr. Nemec agreed to appoint John as the new Panther patrol leader. John was elated and extremely grateful to me for making the suggestion and being so supportive of him. When he hugged me after the meeting, I felt somewhat exonerated from the shameful thing I had done.

Our troop meetings were the highlight of my week. We did a variety of things there, starting with the pledge of allegiance to the flag, the Boy Scout oath, and then the patrol reports. There were five patrols in the troop, and each leader would report what his patrol had accomplished that week. We were still at war, so there were paper drives, metal collections, and the sale of defense stamps and occasionally of a war bond to a parent. We collected tinfoil for the war effort and old appliances that could be melted down and made into weapons. We would break up into small groups and study various crafts and signaling techniques. We even had an airplane-spotters' group, who could identify enemy planes if such a terrible occasion should arise. We also sang songs and played games that brought us all closer to each other. It was a time in my life when I really needed the camaraderie, since I was going through so much in school. I couldn't talk to my father or mother. They were great to me but lacked the understanding and the language to be of any help. My father indulged my every whim and desire, gave me money, and taught me the legacy of love, which I passed on to my children, but communication was very difficult. My brother Morrey was in the army, and, as I said earlier, Phil and Helen were not around much, and I didn't feel that they could do anything about the harassment I was being subjected to. I was also a little embarrassed to tell them that I was such a coward. I was a hero in all my fantasies but terrified of getting beaten up or hurt!

It was 1944, and the war was raging in Europe and in the Pacific. Communications weren't what they are today, and sometimes we would have to wait days or even weeks to get the news about what was happening in the war. It was a time of great patriotism. We were together as Americans and very naïve as a population. We had an innocence as a country and as people which I mourn the loss of.

One day in April of 1944, when I was playing outside in front of my house, our next-door neighbor, Mrs. Castriotta, ran out and yelled that President Roosevelt had died. He was the only president I had ever known, and he had been like a father to the American people. Every week on the radio we would listen to his "Fireside Chats," which he would always start with his famous drawl: "My friends..." He spoke to us as if he knew personally everyone who was listening. His death—from a cerebral hemorrhage—was a great loss to our country, which went into a state of mourning. We felt that we had lost a close relative, and our level of insecurity was formidable. We were in the middle of a war, and the vice-president was an unknown entity. It was a dark time for everyone. There was a renewed energy to pull together, which was particularly felt in the Boy Scout troop. John and I began to wear the top part of our Scout uniform to school—just the shirt with all the decorations and awards we had earned in the two years in which we had been in the troop. I guess it was a way for us to express our patriotism and our military involvement in the war effort. Albeit we were only Boy Scouts, we could be like a home line of defense if we were needed. In the Scouts we learned first aid—how to apply bandages and stop excessive bleeding, among other things. Boy, did that create a field day for Chris and his entourage! They really let us have it. Boy Scouts? Ha! They called us Girl Scouts, pansies, and other names that I have blocked out of my memory. There were two of us, though, and I felt somewhat supported by John's presence.

One day, while we were at recess in the schoolyard surrounded by most of the members of our class, Chris came right up close to my face, so close that I could smell his foul breath, and he openly challenged me to fight him. I'm not quite sure what happened to me—it was possibly an impulse so immediate that I did not have time to think about it—but I kicked him as hard as I could with my right foot. I was wearing heavy boots, so that must have doubled the impact to his shin. He went down to the ground, screaming in pain, while I just stood there waiting for his attack, which never came. A little while later the bell rang, and recess was over. That didn't stop him from taunting me, but he at least stopped aggressing against me, and things got somewhat better.

When I was about thirteen, I talked my father into buying me a .22-caliber rifle. I had been fascinated with guns ever since Phil had bought me the BB rifle. Because I was so insecure about my abilities to protect myself against violence, it had made me feel more protected, and I was now ready to take the next step up to a real gun. My father, unaware of the inherent dangers of a .22-caliber rifle, asked me to shoot at a board that was propped up against the shed housing my darkroom. I stalled and made some kind of excuse for not firing the rifle, knowing that the bullet would go right through the board and into my darkroom and not wanting my father to know its power. I did, however, fire at old telephone books in our attic. When my oldest brother got wind of the fact that I had a .22 rifle, he came over and raised hell. He took the rifle, returned it to Sears, and told us that the "Japs" were killing American soldiers with that caliber weapon. I hated what he did. I was angry, and for a while I didn't speak to him, but later I realized that he had probably been right to do it.

Shortly after that, the war ended, first in Europe and a little later in the Pacific. The atomic age was ushered in, and nothing would ever be the same again. I was still in the Scouts, as a new phenomenon started to take place: All of a sudden our troop was deluged with returning war veterans, more than ten of them, who all wanted to come back to the Boy Scouts as assistant scoutmasters. Mr. Nemec welcomed them back. Now we had almost as many officers as troops. There were too many opinions and ideas regarding policy, and it started to become uncomfortable to attend meetings. One of the assistant scoutmasters, whose face I can still see but whose name I can't remember, started a movement among those newly returned war heroes to take over the troop and edge Mr. Nemec out. They all got together and started to pressure him to resign or to retire after so many years of good service. Considering his age, they argued, it was time for him to go and make room for younger, more vigorous men. I am sure that Mr. Nemec would have acquiesced to their demand except for the fact that John and I spearheaded a revolt among the members of the troop. At a typical Friday meeting, we all sat down on the floor and began to chant in unison that we would leave the troop if Mr. Nemec retired. The chant went on for many minutes, until finally all of the assistant scoutmasters left the room and never returned. I looked at Mr. Nemec and saw his eyes fill with tears of gratitude.

After that, I stayed in the Scouts for a little longer, but since I was already in high school, I decided that I should be working at a job after school—which would considerably limit my free time. I was fifteen years old by then, and my interests had shifted. My experiences on Monitor Avenue had had a great impact on my life and would continue to affect me in future years. I will always credit my time in the Scouts with some of the most important growing experiences that I ever had. It was an important character-building involvement. I learned what it meant to be responsible to, and for, others. I am sure that Mr. Nemec is long gone from this earth, but wherever he might be, I bless him and thank him for all that he gave us.

As I said before, I had been going to school at Key Clark Branch, but since we didn't have the necessary facilities there, every other week for physical education we had to go to the big school, which was located several miles away from our neighborhood. Those trips were a horror because of Chris and his buddies. We had to walk there and back, and in both directions I was subjected to all kinds of ridicule and harassment. One winter, on our way back, Chris hit me with a snowball in the back of the head, and it was so painful it brought tears to my eyes, which was another reason for Chris to ridicule me. I wanted to kill him. I was almost at the end of my rope with all I had taken from that group, and I was desperate to do something to make them stop, but I didn't know what. When we returned to the branch school, I walked over to Chris, who was standing next to his cousin Ralph, and looking right into his eyes, I told him in a very low voice that if he didn't stop his shit with me, I was going to kill him! I'm not sure whether it was the quality in my voice or what he saw in my eyes, but I think he really believed me. He laughed, a nervous laugh that got stuck in his throat, and then he and Ralph both walked away. Things got somewhat better after that.

Unfortunately that wasn't the only problem I had at that school. Mrs. Lane, my teacher, seemed to delight in calling attention to my mistakes. I was in the higher part of the seventh grade, 7A, when it was decided she was going to skip our class to the upper eighth grade. I'm not sure why that decision was made, but Mr. Croft, the principal, was totally behind it. One day after it was announced, Mrs. Lane asked me to stay after school and talk to her, which I did. She sat me down in the first row and told me that she was not going to skip me but that she was going to hold me back to repeat seventh grade. I was shocked and extremely upset. I told her that I was already half a year behind because of when my birthday was and asked her why she was doing this to me. She responded that I was slow and that she feared me to be "intellectually retarded." I sat looking at her for a long time, my eyes filling with tears and a lump forming in my throat. She stared at me and kept looking away, avoiding eye contact. I begged her not to do this, to please let me graduate with my class. "I'll try harder," I said, "do more extra homework!" I told her it wasn't that I was not smart, but I had a problem concentrating. I was reaching for whatever I could grasp at to change her mind about me, but nothing moved her, and I went home crestfallen.

That week I waited up late for Phil to come home from work, and I told him what had happened, what she had said and was going to do. He enlisted the help of my other brother, and they went to see Mrs. Lane without telling me. It was a week before the end of that semester when she again asked me to stay after school. This time she hardly looked at me at all. She informed me that she would skip me "on trial" if I promised to take a technical course in high school. She said that if I learned to work with my hands, I would eventually be able to support myself in the world. If I learned how to use the machines, I could get a job in a factory after high school. Of course, I agreed to her offer and six months later graduated with the other eleven students in my grade. We wore our school ribbons and pin, and we all went downtown to celebrate. Everybody was nice to everyone, even the Roccos. When we got back to the school, we all hugged and kissed. Chris shook my hand, said, "Congratulations!" and left. I think that was the last time I ever saw him. He didn't go to high school, or if he did, it wasn't to the same one I went to. I also practically lost contact with John in high school, except for occasionally passing him as we were walking across campus. I was at the beginning of my adolescence, and things were changing rapidly.

I wasn't riding my bike anymore and was working on my father to buy me a car. It was right after the war, and cars were hard to get. The shipments from Detroit were slow, and the supply couldn't keep up with the demand. All automobile production had been halted during the war years, so the last models were from 1942, and the first models after the war were the 1946's, which looked exactly like the 1942's with a different grille. It was taking the auto industry a little time to grind back into production, and cars were being delivered with wooden bumpers, because of a shortage of steel. At any rate we found a dealer who was willing to sell us a new Dodge for the sticker price plus five hundred dollars "under the table," as it was referred to. Knowing how badly I wanted a car, my father agreed to pay it, and my new life began.

It was the most beautiful car I had ever seen. It was light blue with a matching blue visor, four doors, and sparkling chrome. I learned to drive on a 1942 Plymouth at the Safeway Driving School, and my brother-in-law, Al, who had a prewar Hudson, supplemented those lessons by taking me out on weekends. It is important to know that no one in our immediate family had ever owned an automobile. We were streetcar people. Once I had my license, I drove all over Chicago—to the old neighborhood, to the lake, and everywhere. I picked up my father from work two or three times a week and started dating girls.

About six months before I got the car, I had started working at Walgreens Drugstores at the high rate of sixty-three cents an hour! I had first gone through a one-month training period, where I was shuttled from store to store so that I could learn to be a soda jerk, but after about a month of dealing with a variety of disenchanted fountain managers, I had been hired at the Walgreens on the corner of Austin Boulevard and Roosevelt Road, just a few blocks from where I lived. Austin Boulevard was the dividing line between Chicago and Oak Park, and Roosevelt Road, on the other side, separated Chicago from Cicero. I worked there all the way through high school and saved enough money to give my father several hundred dollars towards the purchase of that new Dodge.

It was quite an area we lived in! Chicago has always had a reputation for housing gangsters, and it is true several of them lived there. Many years after we had left the neighborhood, I found out that Sam Giancana, the mafia boss, had lived on our street, five or six houses north of us. As I drove my Dodge past his house, I always noticed big black limos parked in front. Cicero was the home and operating area of Al Capone, the famous gangster, who was serving his sentence at Alcatraz at the time I was working at Walgreens. He later died of syphilis in 1947 but left behind him many of his cohorts, who still lived in Cicero. A bunch of them used to come in and sit at the counter where I worked. They really had names like Lefty, Shorty, Gimpy, the Nose, and so on. At first I didn't know who they were, but as they sat around and talked about "Big Al," I got the message. If I had been casting a gangster movie, I would definitely have chosen them for those roles. Peculiarly, however, we developed a great relationship. I was just fifteen at the time and a soda jerk, and I am sure I seemed innocent to them. They liked me, and I got along very well with them. They would always give me great one-dollar tips, when the average was a nickel or a dime. They also used to tell me that if anyone gave me any trouble, they would take care of him. I don't know if they were serious or not, but where the hell had they been when Chris Rocco was giving me a hard time?

Paul was the fountain manager and a real company man. He was all spit and polish and had all of us jumping behind that counter. He was very slight, about five feet nine inches tall, and he had a skeletal face with high, protruding cheekbones and piercing blue eyes, which always looked as if they were hunting for prey. He was destined to be vice-president of the Walgreens Corporation someday. Whenever he walked into the store, everyone would snap to and pretend to be busy cleaning the fountain. I was glad not to be on his shift, the day shift, since I went to school all day and could only work at night.

People came from all over the city for my milkshakes and malteds. They were legendary. Most of my friends from Fillmore Street would hop on a streetcar and come to Walgreens just for my concoctions. One would think that a milkshake is just milk, ice cream, and flavoring—but not my milkshakes! I made them so thick that you needed a spoon to eat them. I added the flavor—chocolate, vanilla, strawberry, or whatever was requested—a raw egg, malt powder, a little cinnamon, and a lot of love. Sometimes I would mix various flavors of ice cream together, which would make for a unique taste. In my first year at Austin High School, I had made a new friend, Ronnie Magid. He was in my homeroom but didn't live in my neighborhood, and so he would take a couple of busses to come and get my milkshakes. He would sit at the counter at least once a week and help me pass the working hours. He and I were friends until his death in 2003.

Back on Monitor Avenue, Phil was preparing to go to New York to pursue his theatrical career. My sister Helen had started to date a man named Jules Green. She was twenty-five and was beginning to feel the pressure from the family to find a man and get married. In those days if a girl wasn't married by twenty, she was approaching spinsterhood! Julie was a very nice guy. He had been deferred from military duty because of a childhood handicap, a displaced hip, which made one of his legs shorter than the other and created a slight limp. He and Helen dated for a short time and then married. They lived with us on Monitor Avenue for at least a year. I don't think Helen was ever in love with Julie, which was unfortunate because he was crazy about her.

The gangsters continued to come to my counter at Walgreens and encouraged me to tell them my repertoire of jokes. I had hundreds of those. I collected them the way someone would collect stamps but never wrote any of them down. I seemed to have a computerized memory. You could name any subject, and I would have two or three jokes related to it. The gangsters would sit at the end of the counter or sometimes, when they wanted to talk privately, in a booth out of earshot. "Hey, kid," they would say, "tell us a joke! You tell jokes good!" So I would. I was careful, however, not to tell any of the many I had that might be offensive to their profession. One day, Lefty or Gimpy or Shorty—I am not sure which of them it was—approached me and asked me if I would like to come to their bar-restaurant-club on Saturday night and tell my jokes to their clientele—do a sort of standup routine. They said they would pay me for it and that I could come just on Saturdays. I agreed to try it, without telling anyone that I had just been inducted as a junior member of the Al Capone Alumni Club.

It was a little bar-restaurant with about ten tables, a bar, and a jukebox, as well as a little stage with a microphone. It was dark and smoky and reeked of stale beer and alcohol. Lefty introduced me as an up-and-coming comic and purposely neglected to say that this was my first experience telling jokes in front of an audience. I jumped on the very small raised section loosely called a stage and began telling jokes, segueing from one to another with a little improvised patter in between. Most of the audience paid no attention. They were drinking and talking or hustling women. But there was always a small group that was listening and laughing. I would spend about twenty minutes on the stage and would repeat the set about two hours later. It was an incredible high for me and the first experience I had performing, except for a small part in our school play in our room at the Key Clark Branch School. I had played a paperboy with one small scene, while some of the others had the meaty parts. I am sure Mrs. Lane, who had directed that opus, thought that I would spend my adult years working on a lathe in some factory and never would have dreamt that I would become an actor!

When the bar was closing, around two in the morning, Lefty would approach me and say, "You did good, kid." He would then shake my hand, which was suddenly filled with thirty dollars, and add, "Go home and get your beauty sleep, and I'll see you next week." Thirty dollars for a few hours' work was a fortune to me. It was the equivalent of two weeks' pay at Walgreens. I saved the money so that I could do things to my car. Unfortunately, my standup days were short-lived, since I was only fifteen and was underage to work in a place where alcohol was sold. I had been there for about six weeks, when Gimpy informed me that they could have trouble if anyone reported it. They liked me and were sorry to see me go.

Over the years I started to wonder whether those guys were really gangsters. It may all have been a big put-on! There were too many contradictions in their stories: the time frame, their various ages, and how little they knew of Al Capone's involvements. They didn't even know that the reason he had been sent to prison was that the government had finally gotten him on income-tax evasion. It's funny what people will do to heighten their visibility. I can understand pretending to be a rich and famous industrialist, a politician, an actor, or something of that nature, but a gangster? Very strange!

My interest in photography grew, and I started to take and develop pictures. People in the neighborhood asked me to develop and print their photos. Phil had bought me a pretty good thirty-five-millimeter camera before leaving for New York, and I was able to develop quite an eye for pictures. I spent a lot of time in the darkroom enlarging still lives, portraits, and other subjects. Ronnie and I would go on weekend journeys throughout Chicago to look for subjects to photograph. He was quite a talented photographer, and I have always been open to learning anything I could from anyone who knew something that I didn't or could do something that I couldn't.

I had made some friends on Monitor Avenue. There was Tony at the end of the block closest to Roosevelt Road, who was Italian and had a fairly large family. His mother was always trying to feed me. Over the years so many of my friends have been Italian—with the exception of the Roccos, who were my enemies of course. I guess my ethnic heritage has an affinity for theirs. Tony and I went hunting once. He had a shotgun, and by then I had another .22 rifle. We were looking for rabbits. He shot and killed a brown, furry rabbit, which was running for its life. I will never forget that experience. The little creature was wounded after the first shot but continued to run. Then, realizing it had been mortally wounded, it stopped and turned to face its pursuer. It stared at Tony as if to say, Why? Why are you doing this? Tony raised the shotgun for the coup de grace, but I screamed at him not to shoot again, and just as I did, the poor little thing fell dead. It was a sight I will never recover from! Tony took the rabbit home, and his mother skinned it and cooked it for a dinner meal. I never went hunting again.

There was another kid, who lived in the center of the block, whose name was Anthony and who was a couple of years younger than I. He was slight and seemed very fragile. He was always flushed as if he had just finished a long run. For some reason he adopted me. He looked up to me and was always around when I was outside. I liked him and, having been in the Scouts, felt some kind of obligation to take him under my wing. His mother, a slightly overweight woman, who seemed old to me at the time but was probably around forty, was a little overprotective of him; however, she liked and trusted me, so whenever he told her he was going to be with me, she approved of it. Anthony was about eleven when he died. A brain tumor was the diagnosis. He was the first person I had ever known to die, except for my uncle Abie, who had died from heart failure a year earlier. It had devastated my father. Abie was the only brother he had in America, and they used to meet every morning for breakfast on the corner of Kedzie Avenue and Roosevelt Road. I had never seen my father cry before, but the night my uncle died, my father came home, sat near the wall, and sobbed while he banged his head hard on the plastered wall. His sobs were heart wrenching. It is a custom in Russia that when someone you love dies—a family member or a close friend—you bang your head against the wall. I guess it is a way to inflict physical pain on yourself to match or equal the emotional pain you feel.

Anthony was laid out in a funeral parlor on Roosevelt Road. I had never seen a dead person before, and I was reluctant to approach the open coffin to look at him. I did look, however. He seemed peaceful and quiet, as if in a deep sleep. I cried and was comforted by his mother. Death is a part of life, and I know that. As I get older, I am more accepting of the inevitable. I have lost most of my family by now, and I understand that life ends, but I will always think that death is nature's joke on mankind!

CHAPTER 2

THE SCHOOL YEARS

I remember my school years as filled with trauma and loathing. The organized damage to impressionable children starts early. A single experience or statement can affect an impressionable mind and influence that person for the rest of his or her life. I started in kindergarten at Bryant School. My memories are vague and sketchy, but I do recall the teachers pretty well. They all seemed old and crotchety. Can you imagine that the restrictions began even then? Even if we had entered the school system as open, free, and expressive children, we soon learned that discipline and control of the classroom were more important than emotional freedom and expression. I was a very sensitive child, who liked playing with the other children, and my first memory is of being scolded for laughing too loud. I also remember that we had a little orchestra, which consisted of metal triangles that chimed when hit with a metal bar, sticks that would make a sound when banged together, whistles, and other noisemakers. We played under the direction of the teacher, the conductor of that orchestra. I wanted to play the triangle, because I liked the way it sounded. I felt it would be more fun than the sticks, which made a very uninspired sound, but the teacher came close to my face with her beady ratlike eyes and said, "No, you will play the sticks!" It was her meanness that affected me the most. I hated her, and I wanted to go home. Nobody at home had ever treated me that way, and I didn't like it. I said something—I don't remember what—but she disapproved, so I had to stand in the corner for an hour before being released to my seat. I was only five at the time.

Grade school was another nightmare of varying degrees for me. In first grade I had an equally unqualified teacher, who seemed miserable with her lot in life. Her name was Mrs. Meaney—and what a perfect name that was for the bitch! She looked like the kind of bird you see on the beach with a long beak digging in the sand for bugs. She was thin and hunched over like someone with the beginning of scoliosis. She would come to each student's desk and would dump on top of it little square pieces of cardboard, each with a letter of the alphabet on one side. The assignment was to put all the letters in the proper sequence, thus supposedly learning the alphabet. I had difficulty doing the task, and this frustrated Mrs. Meaney so badly that she slapped my back very hard. It hurt, but I didn't cry. I responded instead with remarkable intelligence for a child of six. I said, "Don't hit me! Show me!" but I don't remember if she did. I have always been somewhat of a slow learner, not because of intelligence but as a result of thinking differently and constantly questionings things. From an early age I was extremely curious about most things and would ask a lot of questions of my teachers, which, instead of inspiring them, frustrated them and made them impatient with me.

Second grade seemed more of the same, and I began to resist going to school at all. Every morning I would really get sick in anticipation. I even vomited on several occasions at home and a couple of times on top of my desk at school. It was an indescribable experience! It was embarrassing and humiliating to sit there with all the other kids staring at me. The school janitor would come in with red sawdust, sprinkle it on the desktop, and brush the whole mess into a dustbin. When I think about it now, I still feel the sensations of nausea in the back of my throat.

Somewhere between the second and third grades I was transferred to another school, called Sumner School, I guess because we had moved to a different school district. In the third grade some of the other children started to pick on me, which only added to my dislike of school. I don't know what grade-school teachers are like today, but in the mid-to-late 1930s they all had similar body types and features and seemed to fall into the same behavior pattern—or at least that is how I saw and remember them. My fourth-grade teacher, Miss Bloom, was the worst I had had up to that point. She was about fifty, with gray upswept hair, and she was overweight and unhappy. For an entire year she made all of our lives miserable. You couldn't do anything right. She was always critical. Even if you agreed with what she said, she would admonish you by saying, "Oh, don't be so agreeable!" It was a no-win situation. Her criticisms were extremely damaging to us. She would say such things as, "That's stupid. Are you stupid? You don't know anything!" and would actually scream at us if she felt she didn't have one hundred percent of our attention.

Miss Anderson, my fifth-grade teacher, was no better. She was a repulsive-looking woman, who delighted in catching any of us chewing gum. She would then tell us to take it out of our mouths and stick it on our noses! I sat there several times with bubble gum sticking to the top of my nose for an entire day. I had started grade school as an open and emotionally expressive child, but by the time I reached sixth grade I had learned to hold on to my feelings and to question what I was going to say before I said it. Fortunately, my home life saved me, since I was always encouraged to be expressive and say what I felt. In addition to all my other problems, all through school, and particularly in grade school, my lack of trust in my ability to understand ideas and concepts made me continue to question things on a level that would exhaust my teachers' patience. Unlike the other students, I always wanted to know why things were the way they were. The teachers would often respond that things were "just that way" and that I should not question it. "Accept it and move on," they would say to me. Although I seemed to have been born with an unending curiosity, I do believe that it was a lack of trust and my personal doubts about my intelligence that later led me to the kind of stubborn exploration and experimenting with ideas, thoughts, and techniques that created an incredible system of work.

In the sixth grade I became the target for a group of guys who fit the profile of bully. They pushed me around and goaded me to fight with them—which I never did. I was small, very thin, and not very well coordinated, and I was terrified of getting beat up. I was a good talker, so in most instances I could talk my way out of physical confrontation. The abuse lasted for a whole year and got so bad that my brother Phil had to go and speak with the teacher. That was a horrendous mistake, since she called out right in front of the class the names of all the boys who had been picking on me. I was sitting there listening while she told them to stop doing it. I wanted to melt into the seat and disappear. The impact of that experience stayed with me for a very long time. I became the subject of humor for everyone in my class. The girls treated me disrespectfully after that, so I hated getting up in the morning and facing my schoolmates in and out of the classroom. The one good thing that came out of it, however, was that the bullies did stop harassing me. I firmly believe that, even though all of those terrible experiences were traumatic because they occurred during very impressionable years, they created elements of my character that served me well later in life, not only as a person but as an actor too.

It was while I was in the sixth grade that World War II started for America. It had been going on in Europe for a couple of years, but that was another world, and it didn't concern or affect me as a ten-year-old. My father would talk about it over dinner. My brothers would chime in and voice their opinions, while I would listen without any understanding of politics. I do remember that it made me uneasy and that I would purposely change the subject as often as possible. The discussions would sometimes get loud and heated, mainly because my brother Morrey would always find a way to blame the war in Europe on the oppression of the working class by the capitalists!

On December 7, 1941, we were attacked by the Japanese at Pearl Harbor. I already talked in chapter 1 about the impact on my life of that day and the ones following it. We huddled around the radio listening to the reports of the attack and the loss of lives and felt fear, insecurity, and confusion. My parents, of course, were worried about their two draft-age sons, who would surely be involved in the war. I didn't realize it at the time, but nothing would ever be the same again. In a sense it was a very important time for the people in this country. The spirit of patriotism was at its highest, as people were concerned and involved with each other and with the war effort. They pulled together, seemed to like each other, and felt a bond that was tangible.

In school they began to sell war bonds and defense stamps. A war bond cost $18.75 and at maturity—ten years—could be cashed in for twenty-five dollars. My mother gave me a dollar a week to buy stamps that were pasted into a book, which, when filled, could be exchanged for a twenty-five-dollar war bond. There were twenty-five-cent stamps and ten-cent stamps, both with the image of the continental minuteman standing with his rifle at his side. The twenty-five-cent stamps were green, and the ten centers red. I always bought the red ones because you got ten of them for a dollar instead of four of the green ones. I don't know—I guess I thought more was better. When filled, the red-stamp books were thicker and more impressive.

Just before recess the teacher would announce the sale of stamps and bonds. We raised our money-filled fists and waited for her to come to our desks. Every so often one of the kids would buy a war bond, and everyone would ooh and aah, whispering, "Wow, they must be rich!" We also had paper drives and would go from house to house every Saturday and collect anything metal—old coffee pots, irons, old toasters, broken metal toys, and tools—for the war effort. We needed the metal to turn into bombs and bullets. I scoured the alleys for discarded cigarette packs and stripped the tin foil from the inside. I rolled it into a ball, and when the ball was as large as a softball, I turned it in at a collection center. I really felt I was doing something to help win the war. My back porch was littered with all the metal objects I had collected over the previous week. One day my father came out onto the porch and began laughing. He was staring at all the old appliances and really enjoying whatever it was that tickled him so much.

"What's so funny, Pa?" I asked.

I waited for him to stop laughing so he could respond. "I think I'll go out and buy you a horse and wagon so you can ride up and down all the alleys shouting, 'Reks ol' ian.' I guess like father like son!"

He hugged and kissed me, and his eyes welled up with tears of love and pride. It was one of those moments in life that one never forgets. I have used it as a choice in my work a number of times.

We turned in our stacks of paper in a bin in the schoolyard. The propaganda was overwhelming. The kids of today use trading cards with baseball heroes, but then we had war cards. We traded them, lagged them, mounted them, and rotted our teeth chewing gum that had war cards attached. They were brightly colored and depicted the enemy, always portrayed as a little yellow "Jap" with Coke-bottle eyeglasses and big buckteeth half the size of his face. He would always be doing something really awful to an American soldier or vice versa. The cards were very racist and importantly influenced our impressionable minds. They were the seat of bigotry, but we didn't think of it that way. The Japanese were the enemy. They had sneak attacked us and deserved everything we could do to them! The fervor ran hot and heavy for everyone. The movies characterized the enemy in the same way. Unfortunately, some people have carried that bigotry into their old age. Many years later my brother Phil married an American-born Japanese woman who had been imprisoned in one of the internment camps in Arizona for the duration of the war. Our government apologized to those people forty years later.

As I said in the previous chapter, two years into the war I joined the Boy Scouts and went into high gear. I was now actually wearing a uniform! I stood on street corners distributing written material to inform people about what they could do to help our boys "over there." We had paper, metal, and money drives almost every week. I would rush home from school, change into my uniform, go to the corner of Austin Boulevard and Roosevelt Road, and relieve whoever had already been there for a few hours. It was in many ways a wonderful time in my life, even though I was aware of people killing each other and hated the thought. We were, however, removed from the horror by thousands of miles and a shield of naïveté. Somehow it didn't seem real, until one of our neighbors returned from a Pacific-island battle, limping badly and terribly wounded. He was all of twenty-three but looked like a much older man. That brought it home to me. It made it real and anything but glamorous. I spoke to him many times about the experience, which he was very open to talking about. He had an Irish name that I can't remember. While landing on the beach of one of the islands we were invading, he had been shot by a machine gun dug into a pillbox. The bullets had hit him in the chest, followed his rib cage around to his back, and exited without penetrating a major organ. He had been very lucky. Unfortunately, his right leg had almost been severed by that same machine gun. I still have an occasional dream about that time. I see those people as they were then, only now in my dreams I am a grown man. The dreams always leave me with ambivalent feelings.

At about that time, my brother Morrey, who was in the Army Air Corps, married Estelle, whose mother and father owned vacation houses in Michigan City, Indiana, about sixty miles from Chicago. Distances in the Middle West seemed much longer than what we are accustomed to in California. I began to spend part of every summer in Michigan City, where I stayed with Estelle's family, the Davises. Their vacation houses each had seven or eight rooms, which were rented to couples and small families. It was a business and a good one. Most of the times, I stayed in the Windemere. Sometimes I had my own room, but when all the rooms were full, I slept on the couch—which was just fine by me. I loved Michigan City, which was on Lake Michigan and sported great white-sand beaches that stretched for miles. The resort area, which was only a couple of miles from the town, was divided into bus stops: Stop 1, Stop 2, Stop 3, and so on until 40 or more. The Windemere was at Stop 1, an easy walk to town. Room 7 was the smallest and coziest of all the rooms upstairs and my favorite. Whenever I slept there, I felt warm and secure. It had a fresh smell, a combination of the clean lake air with a hint of suntan lotion. That was over sixty years ago, and I still get that almost womblike feeling when I think about it. It was a special place for me. I would spend almost every day on the beach and in the evening after dinner would walk into town. There was a bridge that crossed a river just as one entered the business district. Above it, on a giant billboard, was the picture of the Smith brothers as it appeared on every box of cough drops sold in the world. The factory where the Smith brothers made their cough drops was somewhere close, so every time I crossed the bridge, the odor of licorice would hit me like a cresting wave. It was so good that my friends and I would walk back and forth over the bridge repeatedly. "Hit me again, Smitty!" we would shout and then cross again.

The town was small, with some shops, a movie theater, several restaurants, a Greyhound bus station and a couple of very old hotels. In the neon sign for the Milner Hotel, the *l* was burned out, so that all you could see was "Miner." We would pop into the lobby, which looked like a rundown movie set, replete with several old timers sitting on worn and faded velour couches and puffing on pipes and cigars. If you saw that set in a film, you would criticize the art director for being cliché. I would run up to the desk and ask the clerk if this hotel "catered only to miners." He would look at me with a look that said, What the hell are you talking about, kid? And get the hell out of here, you are bothering me! We thought it was clever, but of course we were only twelve or thirteen at the time.

When I started high school, I found out that my friend Ronnie had also been going to Michigan City since he was a kid. He loved it too, so on weekends he and I would drive there in my 1947 blue Dodge and would stay at the Sheridan Beach Hotel, which was at Stop 2. It was newer than the hotels in town and had a resort atmosphere—a little like Florida, if you know what I mean, with rattan chairs and all that wicker stuff. Ronnie and I would spend all day on the beach ogling the girls and flirting with them. We never had much luck in picking up any of them, but it was fun, and every once in a while we would manage to take a couple of them to dinner in town and maybe get a quick kiss goodnight as we dropped them off at their place.

At the end of the day there was nothing as satisfying as standing in line at Chicken in the Rough, one of the more popular restaurants in town. There was always a line to get in during the summer months, so there we stood, feeling the setting sun on our backs, our skin radiating the heat of all the sun we had absorbed, salivating at all the odors coming from the restaurant as the door swung open. We would order two baskets of chicken—four fairly large pieces—smother them with honey, and feast, moving from the chicken to the coleslaw and the giant glass of Coke. Of course, the idea of eating chicken is somewhat repulsive to me now, since I have been a vegetarian for over twenty years, but then it was an enchanted time, a time of growing up without worries or concerns. My father was supporting me and would give me money for the weekends in Michigan City, even though I did have a job all through high school.

Some nights we hung out at the arcade, which was directly across from the hotel. We played the pinball machines and the "roll-a-ball." My favorite was the machine that had a replica of a broom-handle Mauser pistol. I shot at targets that would fall if the light from the barrel hit them. I got to be quite an expert with that machine and started to attract an audience, much as I had with my BB gun when I was younger. I made it look so easy that everyone wanted to try it.

"If he can do it and never miss, so can I," they would say, but miss they did!

"So what do you do that I don't do?" was the question.

"I aim at the target."

"Very funny, Freddie boy!"

We would laugh and move on to another machine. It was simple, good-natured fun. The world was on a different wavelength. When I think about my life at that time, it makes me sad to realize that with all our technological achievements life is not nearly as simple and wonderful as it was then!

In school, however, my life was still a nightmare. When I was in the seventh grade, we moved to Monitor Avenue. As I described in the last chapter, that was like jumping out of the frying pan into the fire. I had to deal with the Roccos and Buddy Riggio. I have already talked about that time and the problems I had with Miss Lane, so I'll skip to high school. Our district school, Austin, a large four-year high school, consisted of two very big buildings—the old one, which had probably been built in the early twenties, and the new one, which was about ten years old at the time. The architecture of the old building reflected a period of European influence. The bricks were dark red and sculptured and there was a suggestion of castlelike turrets near the roof. The windows on the top floor had round arches, which gave the building an air of old-world dignity. The new building stood across a small campuslike section with grass and walkways going in all directions. It was square and made of yellow bricks, with square utilitarian windows, and it was definitely modern in every respect.

Moving into high school from grade school was a little unsettling. I came from a graduating class of eleven students into a school whose average graduating class consisted of four or five hundred students. Since I had agreed to take a college technical course, I was put into a technical division, another mismatch in my life. I was surrounded by oafish, unmotivated louts, who took great pleasure in wrestling each other before the beginning of every class. The curriculum consisted of woodshop, machine shop, and mechanics classes that taught us to dismantle and assemble automobile engines. As a departure from that, we also learned some plumbing techniques. I kept hearing Miss Lane's voice bouncing around in my head: "You have to learn a trade—how to work with your hands—so you can support yourself later in life. You know that you are slow and somewhat intellectually retarded." I don't think I really believed that, but there was a part of me that thought there was some truth to it, or I would never have agreed to take a technical course.

After a week of this regimen, I went to each of my instructors and explained that this was not for me. Surprisingly enough they were all very understanding and suggested I go to the office and change my major to General Science, which I did. I was then much happier with the kinds of classes I was assigned. They were far more intellectual and academic than woodshop. Unfortunately, I had to remain in my technical division for a short while, but I spent very little time there. Most of the tech classes were in the old building, while the other courses were in the new building. Things were looking up somewhat. I made some friends and fell in love with my first love, Joyce MacDonald. She was the most beautiful girl I had ever seen, and the fact that she responded to me was a huge surprise as well as a giant feather in my cap. We hung out, ate lunch together, and on weekends we dated—went to movies and the like. I had my own car, which was a great advantage for a high school freshman—and it was a new car at that. Joyce lived on the second floor of her building, above a grocery store. Her father was a minister. Her mother was short and matronly, and I remember thinking that Joyce was never going to let herself go like that. Her parents were both very nice. I had always thought that Joyce was an only child but recently found out that she had a younger sister, whom I never met.

I was really in love for the first time in my life. I guess none of us ever get over our first love. I would see Joyce walking across the campus and my heart would jump. I would get high just seeing her coming towards me. After returning home from a movie, we would park down the street from her house and neck in the front seat of my car. We would pet and get excited, but we never had sex. In those days girls saved that for their wedding night, and any of them who didn't was considered to be a whore! We went together almost all the way through high school and even went to the prom together. I remember that I bought her a black orchid for her prom gown. Our relationship was one of the good things about high school. Some of the teachers were also encouraging and supportive, which was quite a departure from grade school.

In my last year I tore the cartilage in my right knee while playing baseball in the empty lot adjacent to the Key Clark Branch School. I swung at a pitch, missed the ball, and spun all the way around, except for my right leg, which didn't swivel with the rest of my body! My right knee immediately swelled up like a giant balloon, and I hobbled home, which fortunately was directly across the street. As a result of the injury I was out of school for well over a month, which put me behind in my classes, so I had to go to summer school to earn my diploma—which made me miss graduating with my class.

All in all, however, my high school years were uneventful. It was as though I were putting in the time serving an academic sentence. Except for hanging out with Joyce and a few other friends, I didn't get involved in any extracurricular activities. There were a photography club and an acting group, but they held no interest for me. I was interested in photography at the time, but I felt that participation in the club would be just another school obligation. As I recall, the Masque and Gavel Club, as the Thespians were called, never mounted a production, but it wouldn't have made any difference to me anyway, because at that time I had no interest in acting or theater. I did love to go to the football games, though. I would sit in the bleachers and cheer for Austin. In a way I was a little bit like Walter Mitty. I would sit there fantasizing about being on the field with the rest of the players and scoring hundred-yard touchdowns. I guess I needed to feel that I had some athletic skills, even if only in fantasy. Some of the football players became heroes to me, and when I would see them on campus, I would follow them for a while to see what made them so good at sports. Maybe I thought that if I could find their secret, I too could be an athlete. When I think about it now, it makes me sad.

After I graduated, Joyce and I lost contact with each other. I don't know why that happened. I really can't remember the particulars. We certainly were in love. I started junior college, while she went off to college in downstate Illinois.

I started at Wright Junior College in 1949, only one month after graduating from Austin in summer school. It was too soon for me to jump back into school, and I think that had a lot to do with what happened next. I lasted about three weeks and dropped out without informing the administration; so I got "F absences" in all my classes, which later almost blocked me from returning to school. There I was, out of school and unemployed, sitting around the house on Monitor Avenue, not knowing, or even having a clue about, what I wanted to do with my life. My father was still supporting me, and I felt a little guilty about that but was at a loss about what to do or where to go. Finally, on the advice of my family, I registered with a Jewish employment agency and shortly after received a call for a job with a Mister Siegal. He was a traveling salesman, who covered five states selling women's dresses for two design houses, Marcie Allen Styles and Mitchell Frocks. He hired me to drive his car, or at least relieve him at the wheel every few hours on long interstate trips, and to carry his huge sample bags from the car into the stores he was selling to. I took the job because it was an opportunity to see five different states in the Midwest: Illinois, Wisconsin, Michigan, North Dakota, and South Dakota. I was paid fifty dollars a week and had to live on that while on the road. I stayed in cheap hotels, ate in fast-food restaurants, and was able to return to Chicago with savings of about twenty dollars a week. You have to remember here that most people in 1949 earned only about six thousand dollars a year.

For a while I liked the job. I felt very adult and independent and enjoyed listening to Mr. Siegal. He was about fifty-two or three at the time, was bald and slightly paunchy, but quite healthy and always well groomed. He wore nice suits and knew how to sell to his customers. On our long drives between locations he would talk about business, money, and his sense of what life was. He was always very formal with me and never adopted me in any other way than as a young boy-man, his employee. In later years, when I was into theater and saw *Death of a Salesman,* I was reminded of Mr. Siegal. At one point in the play, Willie Loman, talking to one of the other characters, describes a salesman he admires as a man who would "go up to his [hotel] room...put on his green velvet slippers...and pick up his phone and call the buyers." That is exactly what Mr. Siegal would do at the end of the day, right down to the velvet slippers. His entire thrust was to make money, every year a little more than the last. One time as we were driving, someone on a radio show mentioned that there were a million something—birds, trees, I don't recall—and Mr. Siegal's response was that a million of anything was a powerful lot. I am sure he was talking about dollars. I don't know whether he liked his work or not. His single goal seemed to be to acquire money—enough to someday retire. I was eighteen and didn't yet know what I wanted to do with my life or what path I was going to follow. I was just floating and wasn't very motivated at the time. I did know, however, that I didn't want to chase money as a profession in life.

During one of our calls in a dress shop in downstate Illinois, I ran into an older woman who worked in the administrative area for the school Joyce was attending, and she arranged for me to visit Joyce at her college in Jacksonville, Illinois. It was a strange and unsettling experience. It was winter, and I was dressed in a very heavy overcoat, not looking as if I were at the top of my game. I was ushered into a common room at the school and asked to wait there. I think it was a girls' school, but I am not sure about that. I was nervous and more than a little excited to see Joyce. I remember counting my heartbeats and trying to slow my heart down. About ten minutes after I arrived, Joyce walked into the room, looking more beautiful than I had even remembered. She was surprised to see me there and obviously felt a little awkward. We made small talk for a while. I asked her how she liked school, and she asked me what I was doing. I was a little embarrassed to tell her about my job, but I did. I could see almost immediately that whatever she had felt for me when we were in Austin was no longer there. I don't know how to describe the plethora of emotions that washed over me, but it was heavy! I felt hurt and abandoned, even though we hadn't seen each other in months. We talked for a few more minutes and then were interrupted by one of the administrators telling her that she had to be someplace. It was as if the interruption had been prearranged between them. I said goodbye, shook Joyce's hand, and left. I walked out into the cold, dark Illinois grayness, feeling alone and lost. I don't know what I had expected, but it wasn't that! That was the last time I saw Joyce, but as life will have it, fifty years later, I talked to her on the telephone. I had gone back to Chicago for my fiftieth high-school reunion, and a girlfriend of hers gave me Joyce's telephone number. She had just recently lost her husband and was very vulnerable. We had a great conversation recalling the old days.

I worked for Mr. Sicgal for about nine months and then decided it was too enervating to travel like that. I was unemployed again. My cousin Itzie, who was working at a factory near downtown, told me that he could get me a job there. Called United Press Products and Carron Manufacturing, it was a factory that made children's record players and some other things. In the beginning I worked on the glue machine and was responsible for putting glue on the back of the plastic material with which they covered the record players. Later, I moved over to one of the rivet machines.

So in a sense I was fulfilling what Miss Lane had said I should do. I was working with my hands in a factory, earning a weekly paycheck! I had another new car, which my father had bought for me, an incredibly beautiful 1950 Pontiac Catalina. I was going out with various women; my sex life took a large leap for the better; I was drinking a few beers and generally having a good time. Of course, I wasn't going anywhere, but at that time it didn't seem to matter, at least not to me.

It was a totally different story for my brothers, though, who became very alarmed that their kid brother was a factory worker. To this day I am not sure whether they were concerned about me or themselves. Either way, the thought of their younger brother working in a factory really affected them. Phil was in New York, and Morrey was still in Chicago at the time, but in any event they got together and decided that I needed to go into psychotherapy. Morrey knew a psychologist from school, and he arranged for me to start sessions with him. My brothers agreed to pay for it, so I thought what the hell, it might be an interesting experience, and at the same time I would be humoring them. I had never been in therapy before, and I held the same prejudice about it as the rest of middle-class America: you go to therapy if you're crazy! Nevertheless, I began my treatment with two sessions a week.

Ruby Segal, the therapist, was a short, bald, mustached man in his forties, who was slightly overweight and very serious. He would definitely have been cast in the role of a psychologist. I think he even smoked a pipe! Since he was a Freudian, he would sit behind me while I talked. It frustrated me for a little while, because I like looking at the person I am talking to, but he said seeing him would be a distraction while at the same time inhibiting me. After a while I got used to it and would comfortably ramble for an hour, after which Ruby would get up, shake my hand, and tell me that I was doing well and that he'd see me for the following session at the same time.

During the first months of my therapy Ruby arranged for me to take a battery of tests at the nearby universities. The tests took place every Saturday morning and lasted about four hours each. Some consisted of multiple-choice questions, which had to be answered with a special black pencil so they could be read and graded by machines, while others were in essay form. I also took some dexterity tests, which consisted in putting wooden blocks and triangles into the proper holes and other such things. At any rate the tests took nine Saturdays to complete, at a hefty cost of about a thousand dollars, which my brothers paid. You must realize that a thousand dollars in 1949 would be the equivalent of about ten thousand today.

Months passed and I continued my two therapy sessions each week, having totally forgotten about those tests. Ruby never mentioned them to me, so I thought that whatever information was to be gained by them was between Ruby and the people who had administered them. At that point in my treatment I really didn't know what I had accomplished or learned. In the second or third month, I had begun to look forward to the sessions, not because I felt I was growing, but because it was a place to go to talk about myself and have someone listen. Ruby said very little during the sessions. Occasionally he would ask a question or tell me to repeat what I had just said. I was still working in the factory, enjoying the mindlessness of it. There were no demands or unreasonable expectations there. All you needed to do was your job—turning in a sufficient number of units—and no one bothered you. I would look forward to the lunch breaks, when we sat up against the cement-block wall outside the factory, ate our brown-bag lunches and joked about the women inside. Itzie and Sonny Cohen were my coworkers, and we bonded, as people do when they are involved in a common activity. We hung out a little after work and then went our separate ways. I was still living at home, so I spent my paycheck on recreation.

About a year after I had taken those tests, Ruby called me into his office, which was separate from the room where we worked. He looked serious and a little preoccupied, and he invited me to sit down on the other side of his desk, which was piled high with papers and folders. I was nervous. He had never invited me into his office before, and his behavior was ominous. I don't know what I thought, but I remember being afraid that he was going to end our sessions.

There was a long moment of silence, which gave me more opportunity to become anxious; then Ruby broke it by saying, "Well, Fred, I have a problem!" He was staring at me intently, and I was working very hard to read what was in his eyes.

"Oh boy, Ruby," I responded, "don't tell me you have a problem. Where does that leave *me*?"

"Maybe you can help me!"

"You're supposed to be helping me. How can *I* help you?"

"Well, Fred, you see these papers and files on my desk? They are separated into two stacks. The pile on my right is a complete file on you from the time you started kindergarten to the day you dropped out of Wright Junior College—your grades, teachers' reports, comments, proficiency evaluations—in short, a complete 201 file of your academic life. Now, on my left are the results of those tests you took over a year ago—"

"Oh, I forgot about the tests!"

"Well, Fred, let me tell you I had a hard time getting all your school records. They were reluctant to give them to me, but I convinced them of their importance. Your school records indicate the profile of a high-grade moron, while your tests say that you have an IQ at least ten points higher than mine. Now this is where I need your help. Can you give me any explanation of that discrepancy?"

I sat there looking into his dark brown eyes for what seemed to be forever and finally broke the tension by saying, "I guess they made a mistake on those tests."

Ruby's head dropped down. His eyes focused on the desktop, the fluorescent lights reflecting off his bald head, while I sat waiting for a response, any response. I heard him sigh a deep and painful sigh as he slowly lifted his head to look at me. He shook it from side to side, as if saying no in the most frustrated and painful way, and finally replied, "No, no, Fred, there were no mistakes! Those tests—and there were more than fifty—are graded on a curve. There is less than a 2-percent margin for error. Even if you had done badly on some of them, there is a built-in compensational element that supplies an accurate result."

I didn't know what to say or how to respond. I just sat there, blankly staring at him.

"So, Fred," he continued, "what do you think is the reason for such a disparity?"

"I don't have a clue, Ruby. You're the expert. You tell me!"

"I don't know for sure, but I have some thoughts about it. I think this is the time when we have to go into high gear with your therapy. That question may be at the nucleus of all your problems and issues."

We didn't work that day. I think he wanted me to assimilate and digest what was quite a shocking revelation. In fact, I wasn't sure at the time that I really believed any of it. In the following sessions we explored the relationship I had with my family, particularly my siblings. Over the next few months many things surfaced. It seems that in addition to the constant ridicule and abuse I had suffered at the hands of my oldest brother, Morrey, I was so much younger than all my siblings that there hadn't been any way for me to compete when I was growing up, so I had unconsciously made myself unable to do so. I could not measure up to them intellectually or physically, so if I wasn't smart or intelligent, no one could expect anything from me. I was fulfilling what Morrey called me. I had made myself into that moron! The realizations were the first steps in counteracting years of conditioning. I accepted the discoveries as truth, but I still had to find ways of implementing this newfound knowledge. I couldn't read well, my study habits were poor, I was verbally articulate but could not spell, and so on. How was I going to change almost nineteen years of habit and conditioning? Ruby and I worked for several more months dealing with liberating what was unconscious into my consciousness. I became more motivated to do something with my life, but what? If I had interests, I didn't know what they were.

At about that time my brother Phil came into Chicago as the stage manager for the road company of *Finian's Rainbow*. I hadn't seen him for more than two years, so I was very happy he was there. He invited me to come and watch the play from backstage in the wings. I particularly remember the odors as I entered through the back door of the theater. It was a combination of scenery paint, freshly sawed wood, perfume, and greasepaint—a cluster of odors wafting past my nose. Phil greeted me at the stage door and introduced me as his kid brother to the doorman. As we walked into the backstage area, I saw all the reverse sides of the scenery. Some of it was canvas, while other sections were plywood, all with numbers and arrows painted on. A short, thin, balding man approached us, with a big smile and an outstretched hand. He was Norman Shelley, my brother's assistant stage manager and the understudy for the part of the leprechaun.

Phil introduced us as Norman said, "Be careful, kid, there's a bug flying around here, and if you get bit by it, it's fatal!" His statement confused me. I had no idea what kind of bug he was talking about or where to look for it.

Phil saw my confusion and explained, "He means the acting bug, dummy!"

I laughed, an uncomfortable, impulsive laugh, and said, "Don't worry, that will never happen to me."

Norman shook his head: "Oh, yeah?" smiled and walked off.

Phil ushered me to the place from which I was going to watch the show. It was right along the backstage side of the first teaser. The overture started, the lights came up with blinding colors, and in a moment the stage was filled with dancers doing the first number. My eyes opened so wide that I could almost feel the lids touching my eyebrows. My mouth dropped open, and I stood there transfixed and moved by everything I saw. I didn't budge an inch for the entire first act. I stood frozen with the impact that hits a small child who is seeing the circus for the first time.

I returned backstage every night of the four months the show played in Chicago. I made friends with some of the cast, whom I found different and delightful. Joe Yule, who played one of the leading characters in the play, invited me to his dressing room a couple of times, and I was very surprised to learn that he was Mickey Rooney's father. Once I knew that, however, I could see the resemblance. He told me that Mickey's real name was Mimius Yule III. Mimi Kelly was the female lead, and I found out that she was Paul Kelly's daughter. I knew who he was. Since I loved movies, I could identify all the character actors as well as the stars, and Paul Kelly was a well-known character actor.

Those four months changed my life. I loved the people, the atmosphere of the theater, the lifestyle, the play, the music—everything! I even loved the people who cleaned the stage! Since the first night I visited that show I have never done anything else but be in theater and pursue acting. In fact, to this day, fifty-six years later, every time I play the overture to *Finian's Rainbow,* the tears involuntarily run down my face just as though someone had turned on a faucet in my eyes.

I returned to Ruby and therapy with an energy and zeal I had never experienced before. He explained to me that the reason I had avoided any interest in acting or the theater was that pursuing a career in that area would put me in direct competition with both my brothers, and I had rejected any connection to them and their work because I had felt I couldn't measure up. He then convinced me that my interest in acting had nothing to do with them and that

I was on my own path. It made sense, and I accepted and processed it. Ruby and I had a few more sessions, and we both decided that I should return to college. Even though I wanted to learn acting and pursue an acting career, he felt that a college education was an excellent foundation for any career. Besides, I could major in acting and theater.

In those days, only about 5 percent of high-school graduates went to college. Parents expected that after high school their children should go out and find work and leave the nest. My father was the most loving and generous man I have ever known, but he was from the old country and didn't put much stock in higher education. I imagine that he had expected me to keep my job at the factory or find other such work, although he never said anything about it. For the first time in my life I wanted to go to school, even though I knew that it would be very difficult to hold down a full-time job and attend college at the same time. As fate would have it, however, the Korean War had just started, I was eligible for the draft, and everyone knew it, including my father. Since the reality was that you could get a college deferment if you maintained a B average, he not only agreed to my going to college, he insisted, telling me that he would support me all the way through.

I reenrolled in Wright Junior College and was reluctantly accepted on a trial basis, because I hadn't informed them that I was leaving the last time I had been there. It was only a year later, but it seemed like an eternity. When I think of the events of that year, I thank God, my brothers, and Ruby Segal for what they did for me. If it hadn't been for them, I might be working a lathe in some factory in Chicago. I want to say here that, like my father, I too believe that any kind of honest work a person does to make a living is just fine. I do not feel snobbish about anyone working at any kind of job, be it running a lathe or working at a glue machine. However, for me to have done so would have been a waste of my talents and contribution to the field of acting.

CHAPTER 3

THE COLLEGE YEARS

I went back to Wright in the fall of 1950. It was immediately a different experience. As much as I had hated school up to that point, I loved being in college. I was hungry to learn, and I found that my natural habit of asking a lot of questions was greeted with enthusiasm, not impatience. The first two years at any college are mostly devoted to liberal arts courses that have nothing to do with theater or acting, but I didn't care. I had a lot of catching up to do, so I absorbed all the knowledge that my brain would accept. I loved my teachers, and they responded to me very positively. It was a new and exciting world. There were no disciplinary issues, and for the first time in my schooling I was treated as an adult, not a child who had to be kept in line. At our opening orientation in the assembly hall, the college president greeted us with two or three memorable statements, which I held on to all the way through college. He told us that we were "the cream of the crop"—which meant that we were in the minority of students pursuing a college education—and that we were the future. He also said that if we left college with only one thing, being able to think, that would constitute success. I was very moved by those statements, which motivated me even further.

I enrolled in a theater class as an elective. It consisted of some theater information and some acting work. Dr. Robert Johnston, my instructor, a young man of about thirty with fine features and an abundant head of hair, looked like a movie actor himself. He was a great guy, friendly and supportive, but I truly don't remember anything I learned about acting in his class. Each semester the class would do a fully staged production, complete with costumes and lights. I had never been in a real play before, so it excited me to think that I would have the opportunity to be in front of an audience. That semester Dr. Johnston selected *The Oresteia,* the only surviving Greek trilogy, in which the major roles consist of Agamemnon, Orestes, Electra, Clytemnestra, Athena, Apollo, and a messenger. The rest of the characters are the twelve members of the Greek chorus, who appear in most of the scenes and speak in unison. I got a part as one of those twelve men. I was delighted! We were all dressed in long, bright orange robes trimmed in black. We had gray hair and long, white beards and all looked alike. I am sure that my own mother could not have picked me out of the group! We all also carried tall staffs, which we had to supply ourselves, so Mitchell Kohn—whom I had befriended in acting class—and I went out into the forest preserves around Chicago and cut down two small trees. I don't know where the other ten chorus members got their staffs. I didn't ask. The play was an incredible event for me. Being onstage, memorizing all those lines and choreographing the movements and the lines, was a wonderful first experience.

A little while later, Mitchell and I formed a comedy team that consisted of the two of us plus Marvin Kettnick. We called ourselves the Two Dots and a Dash. Mitchell and I were the dots, and Marvin the dash. We performed in all the variety shows staged at the college for the full two years I was there. I knew very little about acting at the time, but I had an innate sense of comedy, so most of our appearances were successful and well accepted by the student body.

It was in one of those variety shows, where I appeared as a native witchdoctor, that I met Jean Schubert, the woman who would later become my wife and bear my two children. I was immediately attracted to her, but she seemed to back away from me at first. Maybe it was the God-awful makeup or just that I came on too strong—I never found out. Nevertheless, we finally started dating. We went together all the way through Wright and Northwestern before getting married—but I am jumping ahead here.

I was having a ball at Wright. I was working hard to overcome my bad study habits and trying to elevate my reading skills, which even to this day are not as good as I would like them to be. I was never taught to read properly in my early years of school, and it has been a handicap ever since. I was on a first-name basis with a lot of my teachers, who often invited me to sit and have coffee with them in the faculty room. I really enjoyed them, and they also enjoyed me. I would never have believed that school could be so wonderful!

At the end of my first academic year, I did my first season of summer stock. It was the summer of 1951. I had gotten a list of all the summer theaters in the country from the Actors' Equity office in downtown Chicago, had written to a number of them while in my second semester, but had received very few responses. The outfits that did respond said that I was too inexperienced to be part of their company but that, if I were willing to pay a small fee and my own travel and living expenses, they would be open to accepting me as an apprentice. Since that did not guarantee me any stage time as an actor and the work schedule was arduous, with long hours and much physical labor, I opted to pass on those dubious opportunities. I am not sure whether my brother Morrey was still in Chicago then, but I had spoken of doing summer stock a number of times, and he knew how anxious I was to continue my theatrical education. Phil was in New York, stage-managing Broadway plays, and I guess he was between jobs, so Morrey encouraged him to take a technical-director's job in upstate New York. Since it was summer and things were slow in the city, Phil took the job, knowing that it would afford me the opportunity to go up there and work with him.

The place, called Green Mansions, was in the mountains just outside Warrensburg, New York. It was a summer resort that attracted people from the city to come up and spend a week or two enjoying everything that was provided. The environment was breathtaking, the accommodations elegant, and the food first class. I don't know how expensive it was, but I imagine that it was pricey for that time. Besides the lake and the beach with all its recreational toys, it had a great theater and a permanent company of artists, consisting of comedians, musicians, opera singers, and musical-comedy performers. Each night of the week, except Sunday, there was a different event. On Mondays they would do a standup comedy show, somewhat like "Saturday Night Live." On Tuesdays a prominent pianist might come up from the city to do a concert, while on Wednesdays they staged an opera replete with orchestra and lavish costumes. On Thursdays there was the play—a fully staged production. The management brought a company up from New York City—the Circle in the Square—whose artistic director was a very young and gaunt José Quintero. The plays were fully rehearsed in the city and ready to be performed on our stage. We were responsible for the sets, the lighting, and all of the technical support required. On Friday evenings there would be another artist performing, possibly a violinist. Saturday was the big night, with a complete musical revue including dancers, singers, and music that equaled anything you might see on Broadway. Everyone in the resident company participated in that show.

I was not part of the resident company but was one of the four members of the production team responsible for providing the sets, the lighting, and the props and for running the show from backstage. My brother Phil was in charge of us, that is, of myself plus Cameron McCardle and his wife, a shorthaired, typical techie type. Phil designed all the sets, and we built them. Six shows a week kept us in the basement under the theater stage for twelve or more hours each day. The basement had a concrete floor and no windows. We slept in a makeshift room off to the side of the construction area and only shared the stage and the dining room with the resident company. We all ate together.

I did almost everything backstage. Sometimes I would be on the light board taking cues from Phil, and at other times I was a grunt, moving scenery around and making scene changes in the dark. Once during an opera, I was taking some props off the stage between scenes, when the lights came up and there I was, in the center of the stage, with a lamp in my hand. I stood there like a deer caught in the headlights for a moment or two, then turned to one of the performers and asked, "This isn't the Martin Beck Theater, is it?" It brought the house down. The audience laughed for a full minute before the opera could resume.

Phil had an opportunity to design sets, thus getting closer to his original goal of becoming a scenic designer on Broadway. I must say that he did some incredible things. For example, some of the operas required three different sets. This would have meant a lot more construction work and, even more important, a great deal of performance time taken up to change from one set to the other. Instead, Phil had us build six three-sided flats, each six feet wide and approximately twelve feet high. We used plywood and muslin—

typical flat material—and he painted a specific set on each side of the flats, the set the opera called for in a particular scene or act. He also created a swivel instrument, which we sunk into the wooden part of each flat on the top and bottom. As the play called for each different set, the actors, in unison and as part of their behavior, would swivel each of the three-sided flats to its proper position, meanwhile continuing with the aria or dialogue they were doing. It was so imaginative and creative that it drew applause from the audience every time those flats were turned. That was only one example of a number of very inventive things Phil did that season.

The producer of the entertainment for the resort was a man named Ernie Glucksman, whose claim to fame was that he had produced a number of Jerry Lewis films and specials. He was well into middle age at the time, wore glasses, and was quite an affable man. He would pop in on us every so often to smile and cheer us on. I really don't know what he did, except be social with everyone. I never saw him offer any creative advice or input in any of the productions. He would always slap Phil on the back and tell him what a great job we were all doing. A couple of times he pinched my cheek, smiled, said, "You're O.K., kid!" and then disappeared for a couple of days.

The resident company also included a comedy team called Ross and West—Mickey Ross and Bernie West—who, for the most part, did their own material. I never thought they were very funny, but I liked them personally. Mickey was there with his wife, who seemed to be having the time of her life. He would sit at the dining table and offer me advice about acting; she would order a second dessert, while Bernie stayed very quiet. In later years Bernie West became quite a successful producer in Hollywood.

Also writing and performing his own material was Marshall Eisen, a very talented and imaginative performer. I can't say he was just a comedian, since he did skits with many voices and unique characters. Then there were the musicians, the singers, and the dancers, who always seemed to be dancing there, way across the lawn.

The Circle in the Square people were very different from the resident company. They would come up to Green Mansions the day before the performance, do a tech rehearsal with us, and then go on and do the play every Thursday evening. They would be gone by breakfast the next day. They kept pretty much to themselves, but I was very interested in them, probably because they were the "real actors." They did a number of plays that season, among them *The Voice of the Turtle, I Am a Camera,* and *The Enchanted,* which they were asked by the management not to repeat because one of the characters in it was a ghost. The management felt it was not resort fare and would possibly spook the audience, which was made up mainly of business people, corporate workers, teachers, accountants, and the like. There were a number of very talented actors in the group, and whenever I could, I watched them work. José Quintero was very soft-spoken and offered very little direction during the technical run-throughs. I only spoke to him a couple of times, mostly to inquire about things related to the play. He seemed conservative and a bit morose. This was long before he became such an expert on Eugene O'Neill.

In retrospect it was a wonderful learning time, rich with theater and people with years of varied experience. At the time, however, I was very unhappy. I was being worked to death, but that didn't bother me as much as not acting. Phil had indicated to me that I would get some stage time as an actor, and there we were in the fourth or fifth week, and I had only been building sets and running the shows from backstage with the other three. I started to voice my dissatisfaction to Phil, who seemed helpless to change anything. We were all so buried in creating the sets and doing the lighting that there didn't seem to be any time for anything else. Phil and I got into it a couple of times, which finally prompted him to ask the opera people to use me as a background actor in their operas. I appeared in a couple of them, dressed in a variety of period costumes, and was told to be involved in the action taking place on the stage. I didn't need that piece of direction. I already knew how to do that!

Midway through the season we were able to start repeating the shows of the first five weeks, which meant that we didn't need to do any more set construction, since we could use what had already been built for the first weeks. By then I was exhausted and very disappointed that I hadn't gotten a chance to act, so I decided to leave before the end of the season. Phil also gave notice, and we both left just a couple of weeks before the end. Cam McCardle and his wife took over and were easily able to manage the last two weeks, since it was all repeats. I never expressed my gratitude to my brother, who had essentially taken the job for me. I was an ungrateful brat, who really should have seen what a great learning opportunity that had turned out to be. All of us are the sum total of our experiences, and as an actor and teacher I have profited by the various exposures I have been fortunate enough to have.

When I got back to Chicago, ready to return to school for the second year, I realized how much time I had spent away from Jean. We had spoken on the phone a few times and written a letter or two, but it had been almost two months of separation, and I was very anxious to be with her again. Jean lived with her mother on Montrose and Elston in an apartment heated by a coal stove on the second floor of an old building. The first floor housed some kind of business. The first time we had dated, I had parked my car about a block away because I wasn't quite sure where the building was. As we had walked out into the street, Jean had told me that the streetcar was in the opposite direction, thinking that we were going to ride it to our destination. When I had walked up to the car and unlocked the door, I could see that she was very surprised, and it had made me feel proud. That car became a very important part of our lives. We spent a lot of time in it. At first, our dates were very formal and proper, and they stayed that way for a while. We would just kiss goodnight at the end of the evening. That was the way an average date ended in those days. After some time, however, when it became obvious that we were serious about each other, we began to make love. She was a virgin, but I had a little more experience. We would park in back of her house and make love and talk for hours. It was the first meaningful relationship either one of us had ever had.

I took another acting class in my second year, with a different instructor, Dolly Tharnstrom, a woman who must once have been very attractive but had suffered the ravages of time, as we all do. She had jet black hair, nice features, and a pleasant personality. She had been teaching for a long time and obviously loved her work, but here again I cannot remember or identify anything I learned about the craft of acting in a whole year in her class. We did improvs and some scenes but were not taught anything that specifically addressed how to approach a scene. We were encouraged to read *An Actor Prepares,* by Stanislavski, and we may have done some of the exercises in the book, but I truly don't remember anything specific. What was really important about being at Wright and in those classes was that it made me aware of how much I loved acting and theater. For the first time in my life I felt that I had found the place where I belonged. I knew what I wanted and where I wanted to go with my dreams. I was obsessed with acting, theater, the whole idea of making this my life. Every day was a twenty-four-hour day. When I wasn't in school or rehearsing, I was looking outside the school for other acting opportunities. I spent very little time at home. I was in school all day, rehearsed in the evenings, got home, studied until early in the morning, and on weekends spent time with Jean.

The first play we did that year was Thornton Wilder's classic, *Our Town.* I was cast as the drunken organist, Simon Stimson, a character much older than I. That was the way it was in college: the young actors played older people because there weren't too many older people studying theater at the time. I enjoyed playing that part. It was a preparation for doing the first leading role of my life, which would happen the following semester. Kim Novak, whose real name was Marilyn, had a walk-on in the show, as Mrs. Corcoran, an aging schoolteacher. That part had no lines. She would just cross the stage and nod at the actor playing the stage manager. Most nights after rehearsal, I drove her home, since it was late and she didn't want to ride the bus. It wasn't that far out of my way, and I enjoyed talking to her. As I remember, she spoke very little about acting and whether she wanted to pursue it. I gushed about my love for it, and we laughed at how intense I was. After the play was over, I sat with her a few times in the lunchroom, and she told me that she had started modeling and was doing a home show at the convention center. "I'm standing with my arms around a refrigerator," she said. "How do you like that? Creative, huh, Fred?" I don't know where she went after that. We lost contact. The next time I saw her, she was starring with Jack Lemmon in a Columbia picture called *Phffft!* Her name was now Kim Novak, and she was a movie star, or well on her way to becoming one.

In the second semester Miss Tharnstrom's choice of play was *Papa Is All,* by Patterson Greene, a play about an Amish family in Pennsylvania with a domineering father, who terrorizes them all with his rules and discipline. I was cast as Jake, the son, my first major role. It was a leading role with a lot of demands, including the language, the accent, and the emotional obligations. I didn't know enough to be scared, so I had a lot of fun playing it. The show was double cast to give more students the chance to appear in it.

Jimmy Matson played Jake in the other cast, and that gave me the opportunity to watch him and make adjustments in my own work. I enjoyed everything about the play: the part, the other actors, and the theatrical bonding.

Mitchell Kohn and I also went on the hunt for other theater opportunities. We both auditioned for a play at Temple Sholom on the north shore, *John Loves Mary.* He got the romantic lead, and I was cast in the part of the general, another older character. It was a community theater and had captive audiences—which insured that everybody would love the show and be very supportive. At this point in my development I didn't have a clue about how to approach a role with craft. It was all intuition and acting. This was my fourth play, and while I was delighted to be acting, I intuitively knew that there was something missing—the *how!* I could bring up the right emotions on cue, but I had no idea how I did that or whether I could do it again. I was having too much fun to be frustrated at the lack of a specific technique however. That would come later.

I am not sure about the chronology of the plays, but I know that I did five fully staged ones while attending Wright Junior. After *John Loves Mary,* I got involved with a theater company sponsored by the Chicago Park District. Surprisingly it was filled with very talented actors. Both Mitchell and I were cast in *Awake and Sing!* a Depression-era play by Clifford Odets. Again I played an older man, Myron, a man in his early fifties. I grayed my hair with white shoe polish, drew lines on my face with an eyebrow pencil, shuffled a little, and made some general technical adjustments in my voice. In the play Myron says, "I knew I was destined to failure when I began losing my hair." Since I had a thick shock of blond hair, I changed the line to, "I knew I was destined to failure when my hair started to turn gray!" It worked, I guess.

The lead, Moe Axelrod, was played by an actor named Tommy Katsoukis, who was wonderful! It was the same role John Garfield had done on Broadway. I was so impressed with Tommy's work that I followed him around during the course of the rehearsals, asking him questions about how he did what he did. Since I wasn't technically educated at that point, I couldn't be very specific with my questions, but I figured that he must have known something to produce the level of work he was doing. It was as if he had some secret knowledge that I needed to find out about. He couldn't really tell me anything about the way he worked however. It was all just intuitive. At that time I thought that if anyone in the world would make it as an actor, it would surely be Tommy. He was attending the Goodman Theatre School at the Art Institute in downtown Chicago, a theater school with a solid reputation, which in later years produced such actresses as Geraldine Page. I gave some thought, briefly, to going there after Wright but was encouraged to complete my college education instead.

After the play was over, I lost contact with almost everyone in that company. Life is funny in many ways, though: About twenty-five years later, I had been teaching for fifteen years and had an upstairs studio on La Brea Avenue in Hollywood, when in walks Tommy Katsoukis to audit my class, a much older Tommy but with the same energy he had brought to Moe Axelrod. He didn't remember me at first, but after I reminded him of incidents and events that had occurred during our work together, it slowly came back to him. He was amazed at how much I remembered and how specific the details were. I never saw him again after that night. I believe that our recollections of that time somehow had a deep impact on him. He seemed disturbed by our conversation. I had reminded him of how impressed I had been by him, and he was possibly embarrassed by his lack of commercial success. Unfortunately, that is one of the tragedies of show business: so many incredibly talented people just don't get the opportunity that would catapult them to success. Not long ago I saw Hume Cronin on a late-night talk show. The host asked him who he thought were the most talented actors in theater and film. He paused for a moment and then said, "People that you don't know or have never heard of. There are many wonderfully talented actors who have never had the opportunity to share their talents with the world." Paul Newman said essentially the same thing on another talk show I saw. He added that those actors were much too sensitive to be able to survive in this business.

Besides taking part in those five staged productions, I appeared in several variety shows at Wright Junior, sometimes as part of our comedy team, the Two Dots and a Dash, and a few other times solo. Mr. Bergschtrasser, the music teacher, asked me to be an English bobby in *The Pirates of Penzance* by Gilbert and Sullivan. The part didn't have any lines, but the costume was great! I walked around the stage supposedly keeping everyone in line by good-naturedly brandishing my billy club. At that time in my life I would have done anything to be onstage in front of an audience. The thrill was a high for me. It was exhilarating! While married to Sammy Davis Jr., May Britt was once quoted as saying that when he would open the refrigerator door and the light would go on, Sammy would do a five-minute routine in front of the refrigerator! I was just like him at the time. I couldn't get enough of it. I was too busy and too ignorant to understand that I wasn't learning a craft or process of acting. My classes were fun, the teachers were sincere and committed to teaching us about theater and acting, but they didn't know. I didn't know. We would get up onstage and do improvisations and scenes and express our emotions, always encouraging ourselves to look for the opportunity to be very theatrical and melodramatic. I guess we were told to think of times when we felt the way the character felt, to remember those feelings, and to behave as we felt we should for the scene. Of course, this only led to intellectually motivated behavior, but I didn't know enough to come up with any other way to work. At times I would truly get involved and experience some real, organic emotional life, which was exciting and felt deep and rich, but again I didn't know how or why it happened and how to access that level of reality. It was at those times that the beginnings of my frustrations would surface. As much fun and fulfillment as I was experiencing, it was now underlined by frustration and dissatisfaction. Although acting was still great, I knew that something important was missing. I began to ask, "How do you do that?" and while my teachers were very gracious and attempted to answer, they unfortunately never did it to my satisfaction.

Wright was coming to an end, and I had to decide where I was going from there. The war in Korea was still raging, so I knew my father would support my second two years in college. I didn't know where I wanted to go, but I felt I would like to go to school in a warmer climate. The thought of going away to college was very romantic. I would live in a dormitory and study on the beach. I hated Chicago. I hated the cold, windy winters, so I thought about going to the University of Florida in Coral Gables. It seemed like an exciting change from what I was used to. After all, except for my trip to California when I was ten years old, I had never been anywhere. I wrote to the university and received information, and it looked great! I thought that was *the place!* I talked to a few people I respected, however, such as Dr. Johnston, and was told that Florida U. was a "play school" and didn't garner much respect in the academic community. Dr. Johnston then suggested that I try Northwestern instead, since it had a great theater department and a good reputation for turning out fine and famous actors.

My second consideration in not leaving the Chicago area was Jean. I knew that long-distance relationships rarely, if ever, last, and that scared me because I was in love with her and didn't want to lose her. We talked about my leaving, and even though she shared some of my fears, she felt that I had to do what was right for me and my future. Of course she would miss me, she said, if I went away. After much thinking, I finally decided to apply to Northwestern.

I was interviewed by a counselor who spent almost an hour trying to discourage me from attending. When I wasn't moved by his warnings, he tried another tack and told me that I would have to take a rigid entrance exam, which was hard to pass. I informed him that I had a 3.8 average from Wright, which could not be overlooked. Finally, after passing their entrance exam, I was admitted to the School of Speech, since my major was to be theater, which is under the auspices of the speech department. I wondered for a long time why that man had been so adamant in trying to keep me out of the university. In those days there was a lot of discrimination against minorities. The blacks were segregated in Southern schools and had only recently been integrated into the armed forces. I didn't want to be paranoid, but I felt that trying to keep me out of Northwestern had been an act of discrimination against me as a Jew. At the time there were no black students at the School of Speech, as far as my memory serves me, or if there were one or two, I can't remember seeing them. I don't believe it is that way anymore, but I did grow up in an atmosphere of silently restricted schools, country clubs, and vacation resorts. In fact, just around that time, Elia Kazan made a movie about it, called *Gentleman's Agreement.*

In any case, I started Northwestern in September of 1952 as a junior and transfer student. Northwestern was very different from Wright Junior. It was a major university attended by people from all over the country. Wright, on the other hand, was a city college. Almost everyone who went there lived in the Chicago area. At Northwestern there were a lot of students from well-to-do families who had separate housing, lived in the dorms, or belonged to a sorority or fraternity. I, however, lived at home within commuting distance from the campus. Since I had my own car, I drove to school every morning and returned home at night. It wasn't the kind of college experience you see in the movies, but I was grateful for the opportunity to be there. My father paid my tuition and my books and gave me an allowance for food. Being a transfer student put me with people who had already spent two years together, so for a time I felt like an outsider.

In the third year of college you can take courses almost exclusively in your major. Since mine was theater, most of my classes were in the Annie May Swift Speech Building, an old, four-level, brownstone building with three stories and a basement. It had very traditional architecture but a great history. My classes consisted of History of the Theater, a whole-year—three quarters—course; B40, also a three-quarters course; acting classes; a class in directing; and some psychology courses, since psychology was my minor. B40 met in the auditorium and was devoted to teaching everything about the technical aspects of theater—sets, lighting, costuming, styles and period—and about how to single-handedly mount an entire production. In fact, as part of our introduction to the class, the instructor told us that at the end of the course each of us should be able to completely run a theater. There were several teachers for the course, each with his or her own expertise. Dr. Fuchs was the lighting teacher and knew more about stage lighting than anyone I had ever met. The costumes teacher was a woman, whose name I don't recall but who had all of us sewing costumes for the University Theatre plays. Actually I got quite proficient with a sewing machine! The summer at Green Mansions had given me a head start in that class, which I was grateful for.

The History of the Theater class was taught by Dr. Scott, a balding, paunchy man with a monotonous drone, who really knew his history. We started with the Greeks, finished with *Death of a Salesman,* and studied everything in between: the Romans, Restoration theater, Commedia del Arte, the Elizabethan theater—which included many writers besides Shakespeare—the Grand Guignol—the French horror theater—the Spanish theater and plays of Lope de Vega, and much much more. We had to read at least one play every night of the week and sometimes more. I read hundreds of plays that year, a legacy I will always be grateful for also.

University Theatre was the big one. All the theater students worked to be in the UT plays, as they were called. There were also staged workshop productions, which had less production value but were excellent places in which to work and learn. Alvina Krause was my acting teacher. She had a very strong reputation in the academic field and had taught such notaries as Charlton Heston, Patricia Neal, and others. She was a rather small woman, with graying upswept hair, which, it seems to me, was always severely pulled up, and a couple of crooked teeth, which affected her speech almost unnoticeably. Almost from the very beginning of our relationship, there was something negative in her attitude towards me. At first I didn't understand it but was very open to learning from her. In classes she talked about Stanislavski and his system. We did a variety of exercises, improvisations, a few scenes, and we all auditioned for the UT plays and the workshop productions. She had her favorites and made no effort to disguise it. Those were the people who usually ended up in the UT plays she directed. In my first year there, she cast me as the butler in *Ring Round the Moon.* The rehearsals were confusing. I had no idea what she wanted from me, so I asked questions about her direction, which only frustrated her. She had me crawling on the floor, wagging an invisible tail, and she finally replaced me with Robert Tack. Robert was a good friend of mine and felt terrible about replacing me, but my disappointment was with her, not him. As a consolation, she gave me a nonspeaking part as the butler's assistant, the footman, who did nothing but follow the butler around and mimic his walk and his actions—which was quite humorous and added comic relief to the play. That was one of two UT plays I did in the two years I was at NU. I also did four fully staged workshop productions. In *The Fourth Commandment,* an original play written by one of the graduate students, I played a family member and did quite well with the part.

I was in love with acting, theater, films, and comedy. I auditioned for everything and even worked outside the school. In spite of the difficulties I experienced in Alvina's classes, I was dedicated to learning anything she could teach me. Becoming an actor was the most important thing in my life, and whatever the obstacles, I was prepared to overcome them. At that time I didn't know enough about acting, process, or technique, so anything tangible that I could grab on to was a plus. I had read *An Actor Prepares,* but I had difficulty translating anything into practical technique. Krause had us do several exercises. In "transfer of emotion," each of two actors would attempt to *transfer* what he or she felt to the other. If, for example, one actor was feeling anger, the other had to be angry as a result! How that was done remained a mystery. It was a technical exercise and had very little to do with truth or reality. Those actors who were able to assume the emotion of the other received praise from Ms. Krause. Like the rest of the class, I too got up there and did it, but I instinctively knew that it wasn't real. Once, Vivian Nueberg got up onstage with another actor, the two of them sat facing each other, relating with great intensity for several minutes, and then Vivian pulled from behind her a large art board with the word EMOTION boldly written in the center of it and gave it to the other actor. Everyone laughed, and I must say I laughed the hardest. Krause just sat there stone faced, obviously angered by the joke, and after a few minutes said, "That's not funny!" I do believe that what had prompted the laughter was our instinctive feeling that this was a worthless technique.

We were also taught the "Stanislavski walk," a specific heel-and-toe movement. I had never heard of it before—and haven't since—but Krause told us that it was a specific ability that would help us walk properly and do character work. So I walked all over campus doing the Stanislavski walk. I must say I attracted some attention, since I must have looked like a peacock. Nonetheless, I thought it was important to do the work that was assigned. Krause directed us to go to the museum, pick out a statue or a figure we liked, and write a paper on how it affected us. That seemed practical, and I did it. We turned in our papers and never heard another thing about it. We were also told to go out and observe people. What we were supposed to do with our observations, or *how* we had to observe them—what to look for—was never discussed. Were we doing it to become more observant or to be able to re-create a sense of those people? I am still trying to figure it out!

We did scores of other exercises, which were supposedly from the Stanislavski system, but very few of which exist in any of the books I have read. Alvina had a host of them, which for the most part were very technical and had no relationship to accessing organic responses. She taught us how to top the other actor as he would finish a line. We were to come in immediately with our next line, "topping in on the very end of his last word." That was to insure us getting a laugh. She also taught us how to "countercross" the other actor if he were to walk in front of us, a useful technique in stagecraft, which once again had nothing to do with creating reality on the stage. When we were doing a Noel Coward play, she had us sit across from each other and throw a tennis ball back and forth on the very last word of each line, the emphasis being to respond vocally with the force of throwing the tennis ball. This, she explained, was a very good way to approach a Noel Coward play. It somehow fulfilled the characters' relationship and promoted the play's comedic style. To project our voices we stood very erect and threw them to the back of the auditorium by pumping our stomachs and forcing our diaphragms to throw the sound with great force. We would repeat the phrase "Speak with a punch and punch with your belt" over and over, until our abdomens ached with pain. It was valuable for learning how to project, and I was grateful for the technique, even though it didn't teach me how to stimulate organic emotional life.

The one Stanislavski technique she did use was "memory of emotion." This technique, also called "emotional recall," or "emotional memory," as well as a few other assorted names by a large number of acting and drama teachers, was later dubbed "affective memory" by Lee Strasberg. Alvina's instruction on how to do it was to simply recall a particular emotion and remember what had caused it. By so doing we would supposedly re-create it. Of course, this was entirely cerebral, starting in the head and remaining there, in no way restimulating the original organic experience. She went further with the instruction on how to use this technique by telling us not to dwell on the incident once we had remembered it, but to trust that it would work every time! Of course this was a fallacy. In trying to re-access a particular emotion, we were left with just conjuring it up any way we could. If she had Method or Stanislavski training, it wasn't obvious in her teaching! There wasn't any organic emphasis either in her classes or in the plays she directed. I think that was where my dissatisfaction started, with my need to have answers and to know *how* things were done. I remember the frustrations that followed me through school and well beyond. My hunger to learn was tempered by an instinctive perception of what was real and what wasn't. That isn't to say that my acting was always real, because it wasn't, and that frustrated me because I wanted to learn *how* to make it organic. I continually asked Alvina how to achieve reality, what to do to elicit true emotions. She was always vague and general in her answers and took my questions as a challenge to her teaching and her knowledge. It wasn't that at all. I really thought that she knew, but most of her answers were cerebral, general, and totally unhelpful. I truly believe that the basis of her dislike for me came from the fact that she sensed that I could see that she didn't know and that my constant need to find the *how* was a great criticism of her. In retrospect, when I think about the experience with her, I wonder how some teachers develop reputations when they really don't have a process to teach their students. Because now that I know, I realize that she didn't!

Alvina Krause had a summer theater in Pennsylvania, called the Eaglesmere Playhouse, where she would go every summer with several of her favorite students—people such as Inga Swenson, Lowell Harris, Nancy Kafesjian, and others. I desperately wanted to go up there and work. Even though I knew how she felt about me, I still thought that there was something I could get from her. After all, she was so respected at the university and by so many of her students that I thought maybe I was missing something and took the blame for not understanding what it was that she had been communicating. One day I went to her office on the second floor of the building, knocked on the door, and was invited in. There she sat behind her desk with a stern what-do-you-want look on her face.

"Miss Krause," I started. I haltingly expressed my gratitude for what I was learning, and went on: "Could I be included this upcoming summer as a company member at Eaglesmere?"

No response. She sat there without changing her expression for what seemed an eternity and finally broke the silence by simply saying, "No!"

I really hadn't expected her to say yes, but I had to try. Instead of saying, "O.K., thank you," and doing an about face out of her office, I asked, "Why?"

My question delighted her, I was surprised to see. She smiled, sat up straighter, and with delight launched into telling me why: "Fred, it isn't that you haven't any talent. You have no discipline!"

I was taken aback by her statement and really didn't know how to respond. I finally broke the silence by asking, "How do I *get* discipline?"

This delighted her even more. "You must do the things you don't want to do, and you must discipline yourself not to do the things you want to do. Make a habit of that, and you will achieve discipline!"

"Thank you," I said and left her office.

I did very well in all my classes, except Alvina's. I took a directing class from Dr. Robert Schneiderman, who looked like a seventeen-year-old boy but was a Ph.D. on the faculty of the speech department. He was small, thin, very boylike, intelligent and very dedicated to teaching. His critiques were sensitive and helpful without the critical harshness that was Alvina's style. Whenever I asked a question, he tried to answer it specifically and without defensiveness and was very able to say, "I don't know." Here again there seemed to be an absence of specificity of process, but his insights and his eye were very good. His emphasis was technical, with concern about creating a good stage picture. He had a fine sense of the dramatic, and I learned a lot from him theatrically; however, like so many of my other teachers all through my journey, he did not have any tools for directing the actor and helping him create organic reality. It seems that the emphasis has always been on achieving the result, without a specific process. I enjoyed his class, and at the end of the quarter he gave me an A and told me I was a born director.

One of the prerequisites for passing B40 was to crew one of the UT shows. It was part of the way you learned technical theater. I worked on a crew three times during that year, for *Hedda Gabler, The Glass Menagerie,* and one other show, the name of which I can't remember. On *The Glass Menagerie* I pulled a scrimlike curtain each time Amanda, Tom, or Laura walked into the dining room. You couldn't see what was behind the scrim when it was lit from the front, but when it was lit from behind, you could see all the people behind it, which produced a dreamlike quality. The director of the play wanted me to pull the scrim open every time one of the actors entered the dining room, and closed when they left. I fell in love with the play and decided that someday I would direct it—which I did about thirty years later. I will talk about that experience in another chapter.

It was in my first year at Northwestern that I made a few good friends: Bob Tack, Lee Blattner, Reed Morgan, Robert Reitz—who later changed his last name to Reed—and George Schweinfurth, who also changed his last name, to Furth. Both Robert Reed and George Furth did very well after they left Northwestern. Robert played the father on "The Brady Bunch" television series and, before that, opposite E. G. Marshall in "The Defenders," another television series. George wrote two Broadway plays, *Twiggy* and *Company,* which were quite successful. He also had a fairly successful acting career in Hollywood. Bob Tack and I would spend time before and between classes talking about bodybuilding. He had been a weightlifter for many years and had an enormous chest. His pectoral muscles were so large that he could balance a cup and saucer on top of either side of them. I was thin and had very little muscle definition at the time, so he started me on a weightlifting regimen, which I followed in my bedroom at home.

Lee Pemberton Blattner became my closest and most long-lasting friend of any of the people I had met at Northwestern. Lee was a typical WASP. He was about my height but outweighed me by twenty pounds. He had a receding hairline and looked like Leslie Howard, the actor who played Ashley Wilkes, the other leading role opposite Clark Gable in *Gone with the Wind.* Lee's hair was darker, but the resemblance was startling. The year before I had come to Northwestern, he was working on his master's degree and had played Claggart in *Billy Budd,* for which he had received the year's best-actor award. He was very bright and also talented, both as an actor and technically. He was somewhat mannered and presentational in his acting, but that was what was encouraged at NU. We became very close friends, and he helped me through some rough periods at school. Even though he and I were never in a class together, we did work on the same crew once. We also spent time together outside of school. I met his father and really liked him. His mother had died when Lee was quite young, and his father had done an excellent job of raising him. I remember that his father had bought one of those Studebaker automobiles that were made in the early fifties. You couldn't tell the front from the rear, so when it was going away from you, it looked as if it were coming at you!

Jean and I were still in a romantic relationship, even though we had spent very little time together after I had started Northwestern. My schedule was horrendous! My first class was usually at 8:00 or 9:00 A.M. and the last one did not end until 4:00 or 5:00 P.M. almost every day. If I was doing a show or crewing, I worked either in a rehearsal or backstage from about 6:00 P.M. to midnight, after which I would drive home and have to study into the early hours of the morning. I was averaging three or four hours of sleep each night, and it was the same on most weekends, for even though there weren't any classes then, there were still rehearsals and cramming for tests. Jean and I would catch a few hours together on Sundays. Sometimes we would walk up the street to Bud's hotdog place, a five-stool shack that served the best hotdogs in Chicago, and at other times we would drive over to Peter Pan, a restaurant on Western Avenue, and have an olive burger. We had both fallen in love with those thick beef burgers smothered on top with chopped up green olives. The dressing on them accentuated the taste of the burger and the olives. We used to play a little game with each other while driving around: I would simply say, "Olive burger," and we would see which one of us would salivate the most!

Jean had wanted to continue her education after Wright but hadn't had the funds to do so. Her mother, Emily, worked at a low-paying office job somewhere and couldn't afford to send Jean to college, and I am quite sure that even if she could, she wouldn't have. Emily firmly believed that as soon as you turned eighteen, you should leave the nest and never return. For many years I resented her treatment of Jean, though she mellowed somewhat in her old age. Jean had applied for a scholarship to Northwestern, had taken some tests, and been granted a tuition-free scholarship. She had come to NU in January 1953 and had taken some of the same classes as I. We were in acting class together. As a matter of fact, Alvina took a strong liking to her, which intensified her negativity towards me. It was a well-known fact that Jean and I were exclusively involved. Jean couldn't work, even part time, because her schedule was as full as mine, so I helped her buy the books for the classes she took, and we arranged our schedules so we could meet every day for lunch. I shared my lunch allowance with her; otherwise she would have starved to death. I never minded sharing everything with her. We were in love and looked forward to a life together. While at NU we served on a crew together. We spent countless hours in the basement sewing fabric that was created to look like bamboo onto a gigantic velour curtain, which was supposed to serve as the background for a play called *The Yellow Jacket.* We spent six or seven hours each day or evening sewing those strips on that curtain. It did, however, afford us the opportunity of spending all those hours together.

I was at the end of my first year at Northwestern, and I was very anxious to continue working as an actor, so I put out some letters to summer-stock companies, using my Green Mansions season as part of a resume. I got a response from a man named Robert Thompson, who came to my house to interview me. He was in his forties, had a very kind demeanor, and told me as much as he knew about the Peninsula Players, a summer theater in Fish Creek, Wisconsin. I made it quite clear to him that I was an actor, who desired to be in the company as such and not as an apprentice. He seemed happy with my qualifications and personality, and we agreed that I would come up to Wisconsin for the 1953 season. I mentioned to him that I had a friend at school who might also be interested in working up there. I was referring to Lee Blattner. He agreed to have him come up too, so Lee and I drove up to the peninsula early in June.

The theater was about 150 miles away from Chicago, in a breathtakingly beautiful area on the Wisconsin peninsula near Sturgeon Bay, about a hundred miles from Green Bay. The grounds were right on Lake Michigan. They were surrounded by trees, and everything was green and lush. The theater itself was a proscenium-type theater. It had a good-size stage, a backstage section, dressing rooms, and an ample storage area, where they kept all the folding chairs the audience would sit on to watch the play. The storage area also housed a humongous tent top, which would cover the audience area, a large empty space strewn with small gravel stones. In other words, during the winter months, when the theater was not in operation, all that was left was the stage building with a large empty lot in front of it. When the tent top was installed, however, and the burgundy director's chairs set up, the look totally changed. "The theater in a garden," as it was billed, really afforded an outside atmosphere to the productions. Besides the theater itself, there was a lodge where everyone ate all of the meals. It had a sitting area where the cast could relax, talk, and memorize lines; there were a few buildings where the members of the company slept—that is, when we had any time to sleep—with several rooms, each equipped with two bunk beds; and there was also a large, very well-equipped scenery shop on the premises.

The theater was owned and run by Caroline Fisher Rathbone, an attractive woman in her early forties, who must once have been very beautiful. Her husband, Rodion, was the son of Basil Rathbone and bore some resemblance to his famous father. Caroline's mother and father were also there. Mama Fisher was responsible for feeding the company. She was in every sense of the word a nazi! Puffy and overweight, with much too much hair, which had once been blond but was now graying, she stomped around the premises making anti-Semitic remarks, which embarrassed Caroline to no end. Papa Fisher, on the other hand, was a red-faced, cherubic man, who wobbled when he walked, was quite harmless and, I believe, always somewhat inebriated. He was most visible when we were eating but would disappear at other times, I am not sure where. Unlike Mama Fisher, he never seemed to have anything objectionable to say to anyone or about anything. Rodion was a navigator for TWA and would be gone a lot of the time. Caroline's brother, Richie, who was a Hollywood television producer attached to "The Jack Benny Show," came up for a couple of weeks during the season to direct the musical revue they did every summer. He was creative and quite gay. He called everybody "darling" and would demonstrate the dance steps in every musical number.

The resident company consisted of about nineteen actors. If there was a need to cast someone outside the company, Caroline went to the locals, but that was rare. The original theater had been founded in 1935, so it had a large local following. The 1953 season was produced by Rodion and Caroline Rathbone and directed by Robert Thompson. I don't know what the rest of the company was paid for the season, but Lee and I got room and board and a small token salary, which was paid to us because we also ran the refreshment concession.

The two seasons I spent up there were the most important and memorable times in my life up to that point. Doing summer stock is for the young and vigorous. It was an incredible experience. I am sure I could write an entire book on the two seasons I spent there. Each show ran for a full week—six nights. After each opening, we would rehearse the next week's show during the day, while performing that week's show in the evening. Everybody would help out with the scenery and lighting in his or her free time, except for the older members of the company, whose seniority precluded any extracurricular work in the production area. When I say *older* members, I mean those actors who were in their fifth, sixth, or fifteenth season with the company. Lee and I were doing our first season with the group, and since both of us had had technical training at

Northwestern, Caroline took immediate advantage of that. We were obligated to help the tech crew with the scenery and lights. We got up every morning at about seven, ate breakfast, and went to the theater to rehearse until lunchtime. After lunch, which usually lasted an hour or so, we sauntered over to the scene shop and worked for a couple of hours, depending on how large our role was in the play we were rehearsing. Then we went back to rehearsal until dinner, which was at 6:00 P.M. Mama Fisher lived up to her Gestapo rules by insisting that we be prompt or we might not eat. I must mention in passing that I once said to her in my best German accent, "Too bad, Mama, I haff no relatives in Germany!" She didn't get it, which I am glad about, since I wouldn't have wanted to hurt Caroline.

We had a little free time after dinner to get ready to do the evening show. Depending on the particular play, we usually came down at about eleven fifteen or eleven thirty, at which time the older members of the company would greet some of the audience who had been attending productions for fifteen years. The wise thing to do after that would have been to go back to our cabins and get some sleep, but that hardly ever happened. After a show we were keyed up and had to unwind, so we piled into a car and went to Egg Harbor, which was about three miles from our place. We frequented a bar, had a couple of beers, talked about the play, the audience, and so on, and then went back and fell into our beds, often too tired to undress. The typical day ended at about 2:00 A.M. or later. That gave us between four and five hours of sleep every night for the ten-week season. I loved it! It was like being in heaven—eating, sleeping acting!

Our company had quite a cast of characters, with the emphasis on *characters*. Some members of the permanent company were not actors at all but people who were there for a different experience—hobbyists and a few retired professionals who wanted to try acting in their declining years. Milton Collion was one of those retired people. Everybody called him Doctor Milt, but I don't think he was a real doctor. He was some kind of pill-pushing nutritionist, who had made a great deal of money in Florida. He was in his middle sixties and was always smiling and positive. Everybody liked him, including me. He had a round, cherubic face, which always seemed to be suntanned. He had come to the company from Florida, was the president of the Island Players and a member of the board of directors of the Sarasota Players. He played a doctor—of all things—in one of our early shows, *Boy Meets Girl.* Having appeared in *The Solid Gold Cadillac* in Florida, he had tried to purchase a gold Cadillac but couldn't find one, so he had settled on a solid gold Oldsmobile, which was really painted gold! Milt had brought his boat with him, and on rare occasions he would take a bunch of us out fishing on the lake. One time the fish were really biting, and we pulled them in one after another, which delighted Milt. He seemed very happy when he was responsible for making others happy.

The other old-timers in the company were Bill Munchow, Helen Bragdon, Judy Haviland, Sid Shertzer, Leo Lucker, Dan Scott, Bob Thompson, and Maggie Magerstadt. Bill Munchow was in his middle fifties. He was of medium height and had dark brown hair, which was slicked back—a hairstyle that seemed to be of a different era. He was a typical stock character actor, whose life was comprised of going from summer stock to winter stock somewhere in the East. He kept a small apartment in New York, which I am sure he rarely used. He was a *phumpernick* kind of actor. *Phumpernick* is a word I have either coined or heard from my Yiddish background. It simply means that he would "phumph, phumph" between lines. It was a way to stall, I later discovered, because he had trouble remembering his lines. Bill regarded those of us who were really serious about acting with humorous disdain and a knowing attitude that sooner or later we would find out that all our dreams of success in acting would end up as his had. He drank a little, maybe even too much, but was always on time to rehearsals and performances.

Helen Bragdon was a very nice older actress, who, unlike Bill, seemed very serious about her work. She was probably the oldest member of the company, having come to the Players in 1937 from the Cleveland Playhouse. She was quite versatile and equally comfortable in musical comedy. Judy Haviland, who had been returning to the company since she was fifteen years old, had a Northwestern background. Dan Scott was our resident leading man. He later changed his name to Simon Scott and had a modest career in Hollywood. He was competent in his work and seemed to be there because he wanted to continue working as an actor.

Leo Lucker had been with the Players since the beginning. He had been their leading man in fifteen of the nineteen seasons. He had come back that season from a busy schedule in New York and shared directing duties with Bob Thompson, who had also been with the company from the beginning. Leo was effete, prissy, and somewhat prone to being critical, while Bob was the very opposite, always easygoing and encouraging. He never missed an opportunity to compliment an actor on his or her work. He also acted in the plays and was a creditable actor. Sid Shertzer, also a Northwestern alumnus, had been with the company for several years. He had been working in New York before coming back for the 1953 season.

For the most part the rest of the company was made up of newcomers, like Lee and me. There was Dexter Dupont, a very young and inexperienced actor, who was in love with Johnny Ray, the singer who at the time had a hit record out, titled "The Little White Cloud That Cried." At every opportunity, Dexter would jump up on the stage and imitate Johnny. We all regarded him with warm humor. Mildred Shelton was from the Goodman Theatre School, as were a few of the others. The Northwestern actors and the Goodman people had very divergent acting styles, with a noticeable difference in delivery as well.

At that point in my development as an actor, I was still working from instinct and intuition. My curiosity and my need to know specifics gnawed at me. I had fun in the plays and was pretty good in almost everything I did; however, once again I saw no specific process or craft in anyone, including myself. I would engage the other actors in conversations about acting, questioning them about their work—what they did and how they did it. Most of the older ones regarded me with suspicion and somehow took my serious and innocent questions as a challenge of their work and talent. Around the middle of the season I lightened up and began to make jokes and imitate people in the company, as well as poking fun at myself. This change in behavior prompted a greater acceptance from the group, and I finished the season with a sense of being integrated and accepted by everyone, including Munchow.

I appeared in six plays during the first season. The first was a comedy, *Two Blind Mice,* where I played a small part as Colonel Robbins, USAF. Summer-stock audiences want to laugh and be entertained, so most of the plays we did that season were light comedies. The role was not very demanding, so I listened, was involved in the action, and said my lines convincingly. The rush came from the enthusiastic audience, who would laugh at almost everything. It is very satisfying when there is a large response after you say a line. It gives you a great feeling of acceptance. Even though I wasn't doing *Hamlet,* I was acting. Every evening after dinner, I would get to the theater an hour early, before the other actors arrived for the evening show, and I would turn on all the powerful stage lights and stand in their blinding spill. I would stare into the blackness of the empty theater and luxuriate in the feeling of being onstage, getting ready to perform. I was living my dream. I sat at the makeup table and slowly applied the Stein grease paint or the Max Factor pancake. We wore makeup for every show; otherwise, the lights would have washed us out completely. I liked doing makeup. It was something I had learned at Northwestern in B40. Putting it on gave me time for what I thought was getting into character. That process involved thinking the way I believed the character thought. I would use my costume to stimulate what I deemed were the right feelings. I didn't know it at the time, but I was using a "choice approach" that many years later would become one of the thirty-one in my system. What I did was instinctive. Since I had no specific practical craft training, I was on my own. Talent is talent is talent, and I feel it is important to say that there are many fine actors who don't have a specific craft; however, I ask, what would their talent be if they did? Craft allows the actor *to liberate his talent every time he calls on it.* He doesn't have to depend on inspiration. Craft also allows him to go deeper with more consistency.

The second play I was in was *The Dover Road,* which was billed as an absurd comedy. I played one of the four staff members. I don't actually remember the part in detail, but I do recall that it was very English. My third outing was in the summer's musical revue, called *Midsummer Madness,* a title that aptly describes what it was like. Richie Fisher directed it with great enthusiasm. Coming from "The Burns and Allen Show" and also being Jack Benny's director had given him a solid foundation in that kind of venue. Lee and I had to work hard to suppress our laughter every time Richie would demonstrate a dance routine. He would "nance" across the stage, loudly expressing, "Pu pa pa pa pa." Lee and I took to imitating him on our way to the mess hall, taking great care not to be seen by anyone. I liked Richie. He was a professional and was successful in an industry that I had not yet entered. The show was a blast. I got to sing, dance, and do outrageous comedy skits. We also did some incredible tongue-in-cheek sketches, and both the actors and the audience had a ball. I was sorry to see the show end. For years after that season, Lee and I would throw lines from it at each other and crack up. In one of the sequences, I played a Tyrolean peasant who walks into a place to ask a question, so in my finest Bavarian accent I asked, "Ish der a pool shcule in Ish-tambul?" It cracked me up every night. Thereafter, whenever I had to ask anyone a question about anything, I would quote that line. It was major silliness, but I still remember it fifty-three years later with a little tickle. That revue gave me the confidence to do things that I would never have attempted before. I took direction from Richie in choreographed numbers that would have stretched even a professional dancer. I'm not saying that I performed like one, but I did move well in those sequences. I have a fairly decent singing voice, so that wasn't as much of a challenge. We did a song-and-dance number called "The Red Rose Rag." Judy Haviland dressed as a twenties flapper and, backed by four men in the same period costumes, sang and danced in the style and rhythm of that period. We brought the house down. I still remember all the lyrics of that song. After I had spent a whole year at Northwestern dealing with Krause, my confidence and ego had been fairly damaged, but as the season wore on, I began to feel positive about myself again.

One night after a performance, Sid Shertzer came into our cabin with a gigantic watermelon, a bottle of rum, and a hypodermic needle. He was followed by the newer members of the company, whom he had rounded up on the way. I was lying down trying to get some sleep, when we were descended upon by this eager horde. Sid set the melon down in the middle of the room, with the attitude and demeanor of a surgeon preparing to conduct a very serious operation. "Watch this!" he said. "I'm going to inject this watermelon with a hypo filled with rum every night for a week, and at the end of the season we will cut it open and taste the ambrosia of the gods!" I, for one, thought he was a little nuts, but I went along with everyone else's enthusiasm. He was a man of his word: every night after the show, or when we got back from Egg Harbor, he appeared in our room with the hypodermic in his hand. "You're not going to believe what this is going to taste like," he said.

In the fourth play we did, *Boy Meets Girl,* I played a character named Green, also a small role and obviously not memorable. I do remember that Dexter Dupont was my sidekick and that we were writers at the Royal Studios in Hollywood. We were always bursting in with new ideas for a film. Dexter almost drove me crazy because he would always jump my line and cut me off in mid-sentence. I complained to him about it after each performance, and he would promise never to do it again, but he always did! Finally I decided to turn that liability into an asset: I would start to say my line, then stop and look at him in anticipation of his interruptions. This would throw him, and he would stare blankly for a moment as I continued my line. It became a funny bit in the show, and to this day I don't think he got it. I had a natural sense of comedy. My timing was excellent, and I intuitively knew when to come in with a line. Having done standup undoubtedly helped that facility. That show had a large cast, and I believe everyone in the company was in it, making the backstage area and the dressing rooms a zoo. Half-naked people kept running into each other, complaining that they were going to miss their entrance cue.

When you work with the same people day after day in that kind of environment, they start to become your family, but if there was any romance happening, I surely didn't know about it. I thought Millie was attractive, and I was aware that she liked me too, but I was involved with Jean, and we both knew that. She and I would sit around after the show sometimes and talk about what we wanted to do with our careers. I missed Jean and was only able to call her a few times that summer. Before I had left, we had decided to communicate spiritually by looking at the Big Dipper at the same time each evening. We felt that it would establish a bond between us, so I did it every night for the most part.

The next play that season was *Dear Ruth,* by Norman Krasna. I played a character named Sergeant Chuck Vincent, an endearing role and a lot of fun to play. Shortly after the Korean War had ended, a lot of plays were written that had soldiers as the main characters. The program listed this play as "a battlefield in the home, romance in uniform." We had just come out of many years of war, so it was light fare. Bill Munchow played a judge, who married my character onstage. I remember that my character was scared to death during the whole ceremony—which actually foreshadowed my real fear when in fact I did get married to Jean a couple of years later. The role allowed me to access my personality, and the audience loved me. I was able to be pretty much in the moment and allowed myself to get involved with the other actors. By that time in the season I was fairly relaxed and able to release my organic impulses. Of course, I didn't know all of that at the time. I just felt good about my work, which seemed to flow naturally. In retrospect, I realize that I was accepting the given circumstances and allowing myself to be real moment to moment, but I didn't know how that happened or how to get there in the next play.

The final play of the season was *John Loves Mary,* also by Norman Krasna, another comedy with some uniforms in it. It was a repeat of the play I had done while at Wright Junior College. I played a character named George Beachwood and had a ball doing it. The character was quite effete, maybe even gay, so I slicked my hair down, grayed it a little, wore thick horn-rimmed glasses and an awful, out-of-style tweed suit, and spoke with a slight lisp. I only had one scene, but it brought the house down every night. I guess I was using Richie Fisher as a life model, but nobody knew it, and I'm not sure that I even did until Lee mentioned to me that I spoke and moved just like Richie. One of the other characters in the play kept referring to me as Mr. Driftwood, and every time he called me that, I would correct him in an escalating indignant tone, and the audience would roar. Every night I received applause on my exit—which was totally satisfying. Most of the parts I played that first season were small but juicy, and I thoroughly enjoyed every minute of it.

At Northwestern we had been taught to eliminate the tension in our body, especially in our hands, by vigorously, almost violently, shaking them. So I would do so before every entrance. Obviously everyone observed my antics but never said anything about it. Munchow had always regarded me with humorous disdain but had never said anything to me. The night of our last performance, the actors all entered the mess hall following each other as if in a chorus line and shaking their hands vigorously. I was already seated, waiting for the first course, so I stayed there stone faced and let them have their fun. Actually, I enjoyed it. I had the last laugh though. Just before my entrance as Mr. Beachwood, I pulled up a chair in the wings, sat down in full view of everyone onstage, lifted my feet off the ground, and violently shook them in the same way as I had done my hands. Most of the actors onstage, the same ones who had earlier entered the dining room, had to bite their lips so as not to crack up. Bill Munchow laughed out loud in the middle of a line.

After the show the horde descended on my room, where the watermelon had been occupying a place under my bunk for the past nine weeks. Sid entered with a very large knife stuck out about a foot in front of him, and everyone gathered in a circle around him. He rolled the melon out from under my bunk, treating it as if it were made of thin glass. Everyone leaned in as he placed the point of the knife on top of the center of the melon. He was playing the moment for all it was worth. The suspense grew in all of us, and I must admit that I too was involved with the others' curiosity. None of us knew what we were about to discover, except Sid, who had done this before. As he sunk the knife deeper into the melon, we heard a strange gurgling sound and a whoosh. He cut the fruit in half, and as it separated in the middle of the floor, the odor filled the room—a sweet winelike scent that had retained all the freshness of a ripe watermelon. The flesh was a richly colored brownish red, oozing with liquid. Sid sliced off a small triangle and handed it to me, because, as he said, I had been the caretaker of this treasure for nine weeks. I held it in my hand, as it dripped rum and watermelon juice into my palm. I took the first bite, while everyone stared at me with great anticipation. The whole experience seemed surreal. There we were, about to eat a rum-filled watermelon, and it was being treated as if it were a momentous event. I put my lips around the edge of the triangle and took a bite. The flavor exploded in my mouth, and all my taste buds responded with glee. It was awesome! I have never been into alcohol, but this was everything Sid had said it was going to be and more. Everyone got a generous piece, and we all sat there devouring it as if we hadn't eaten in months.

The season was over and we all felt a little sad, not knowing if we would ever be together again. Lee and I stayed on for several more days to put the theater to bed. We folded the chairs and stored them, closed the scenery shop, and generally readied the theater for its winter hibernation.

I went back to school a couple of weeks later. I had been away all summer and had really missed Jean. When I got back, we made love as if they were going to pass a law against it! As usual, my car was our bedroom, and the space behind her house was where we parked to have our amorous interludes.

That year, Jean directed a workshop production of *The Country Girl,* by Clifford Odets. I desperately wanted to play Frank Elgin, the older alcoholic actor, but she didn't see me in the part or didn't want to work with me—I never knew which. It created a great strain in our relationship. We often got into large arguments about it. Whenever it was possible, I picked her up or drove her home from school. On those trips going home we fought continually about the play and her not having cast me. It almost ended our relationship, but somehow we survived it and went on. I must say though that she did a great job of directing that play. It was one of the better workshop productions I saw at NU.

It was my senior year, and I was excited about returning to my classes. The summer-stock experience had elevated my ego and self-confidence, so I felt I could deal with another year of Alvina. I decided to stop asking her *how* questions and just do what she asked us. I enjoyed all of my other classes and continued to audition for everything. I played the ghost in a workshop production of *The Enchanted,* the same play that they hadn't allowed the Circle in the Square to do at Green Mansions in my first season of summer stock. I also did a children's theater play at Evanston Township High School, called *Rama and the Tigers,* a white version of *Little Black Sambo.* I played Rama's father and had a ball doing it. The characters had been changed into Indian people from India. I guess it wasn't politically proper to do a play with a little black boy as the star. Besides, where in the world were they going to find a little black boy in Evanston, Illinois, at that time?

In February I auditioned for the workshop production of *Woyzeck,* a classic German play by Georg Buchner. He had written three major works and was still in the process of writing this one when he died. Robert Tack played Woyzeck, and I was the village idiot, a small but juicy part and a real challenge for me. As I didn't want to approach it arbitrarily or as a cliché, I tried not to be an idiot and worked on some things that slowed me down in speech, movement, and responses. I still didn't have a process, but I had wonderful instincts. The play was directed by Tom Spiva, one of the rich kids from who knows where. He drove a brand-new Cadillac convertible and dated the most attractive women on campus. He wasn't a snob, however, and seemed to approve and be sensitive to what I was doing in the rehearsals. After every workshop performance, held in the main auditorium, the students who make up the audience have a discussion about the play and the work of the actors. Even though she hadn't directed the play, Alvina moderated the discussion. Everybody in the cast came up for critique except me. One girl, whom I didn't know, raised her hand and asked, "What about the idiot?" which brought about spontaneous applause from everyone. Alvina was a little embarrassed. She said, "Small parts should not call attention to themselves," and dismissed it. It was quite telling of her attitude towards me. Everyone saw it and later commented about it to me. That, however, was our relationship: painful and difficult for me to understand.

My last year, 1954, was one of mixed emotional events. I don't know where I got the time or energy to audition outside the university, but I did. After *Woyzeck* I auditioned for *The Man Born to Be King* at the Evanston Showcase Theater. It was their second season. Hope Summers was the executive producer. The play was about Jesus and his disciples, the Last Supper, and the betrayal of Jesus by Judas. I auditioned in a rather small office in the theater for the director, Louis MacMillan, a rather small and effeminate man in his late twenties or early thirties. Hope Summers was also in the room as I read for the part of Judas. The director wanted to play against type. I was blond, had bright blue eyes, and was a picture of Nordic innocence. I don't remember the content of the reading, except that it was very emotional. Hope and Louis were both very impressed with the audition, and I got the part, which was one of the leading roles in an Equity theater. I was elated! I had gotten my Actors' Equity card a couple of years before as a result of doing that season at Green Mansions in 1951, and I was being paid to act for the first time in my life. We started rehearsals shortly after my audition. I had to do some juggling at school in order to be able to be in the play, but since I was a theater major, the faculty cut me some slack.

The play, adapted by Dorothy Sayers, dramatized the tragic events of the last few days in the life of Jesus Christ, from the night of the Last Supper through his capture at the Garden of Gethsemane, to his trial, crucifixion, and resurrection. We had an excellent cast, headed by Frederick Rolf, who played Jesus, with a lot of other Broadway actors, who were in Chicago or had come to Evanston to do the play. The director played Pontius Pilate, and Jerry Orbach played two parts: Malchus and a Roman soldier. Jerry was at Northwestern at the same time as I, but I don't remember his being in any of my classes.

I rehearsed for about two weeks, and everything seemed to be going fine. The director didn't give much direction, only an occasional blocking note. Around the beginning of the third week, this guy appeared at our rehearsals and seemed strangely interested in watching what I did onstage. I tried to talk to him a couple of times, but he was obvious in avoiding me. It turned out that he was to be my replacement—which I learned about a few days later. Hope and Louis called me into the same office where I had auditioned, which seemed even smaller and claustrophobic. They sat across from me with very serious, almost tragic looks on their faces.

We sat in silence for a very long moment, and it was I who broke it by asking, "What's up?" I knew that whatever it was, it wasn't good news.

"Well, Fred," Hope spoke first, "we feel that you are not big enough on the stage!"

Louis interrupted her to tell me that it had been his mistake in casting me. He said that my audition had been terrific but that it had taken place in a small office and that my energy was not large enough to carry to the back row of the theater. My look was just what he wanted for Judas, but I lacked the power he needed.

I was devastated! The programs had already been printed with my name in them, and I had passed a number of them out to my friends. I felt hurt and humiliated at being replaced. Besides, the actor replacing me was dark and balding and had the look of Judas! This was the second time in a year that I had been replaced or demoted in a play, and it shook my confidence badly. I wondered what was wrong with me: Was I not talented? Should I reconsider my choice of profession? I cried a lot. If it had not been that I felt I had done well in that season at the Peninsula Players that summer, I might really have quit.

Life has funny lessons and coincidences. Before sitting down to write this section, I looked at the program for *The Man Born to Be King,* which I had saved these many years, and discovered a typewritten insert with the name of the actor who had replaced me, Byrne Piven. If I am not mistaken, he is the same man who later became a very well-known acting teacher in the Chicago area. His life path paralleled mine—he in Chicago and I in Hollywood. It makes one wonder about destiny and whether there are chance happenings and coincidences.

That experience had happened early in April. I soon bounced back with some encouragement from Jean, who always thought I was really gifted. In early May, Robert Schneiderman cast me in Moliere's *The Imaginary Invalid,* which was my second University Theatre play. It is a comedy-satire, which critically assaults the medical profession and doctors in general. I had the part of Fleurant, an apothecary whose action is to administer an enema to the main character, Argan, by inserting a gigantic syringe into his behind. I got a lot of laughs, mainly because of the size of that syringe I was carrying. Later that year, I also managed to get my SAG card by doing a SAG industrial film in Chicago.

During the winter, Lee Blattner and I had driven up to Fish Creek to see Caroline, hoping to be invited for the 1954 season. It was eerie to see the place in winter. All the trees were bare, and the ground was hard and cold. The theater without the tent top looked as if the place had been bombed and only the skeleton of the stage had survived. All the buildings were locked and shuttered, and only the ghostly memories of laughter and other sounds hung in the air. There was ice on the lake and the remnants of a former snowstorm. Caroline was very happy to see us. She was warm and open and somewhat relieved to see living, breathing visitors. Over tea we spoke of the previous season and what fun it had been. I inquired about Rodion, who was away flying for TWA. Armand, the standard French poodle, who loved to chase rocks, also liked to smell crotches, so all the time we sat there talking, he had his nose in my crotch, which embarrassed Lee, Caroline, and me. I tried to make light of it by saying that I thought Armand was homosexual, and it got a laugh. I asked Caroline if we could come back for the next season. It was hard to do, since I wasn't at all sure what her reaction would be, but she was animated in her response. "Of course, you are both welcome to come back," she said. "We all loved both of you and the work you did!" We spent most of the rest of that day with her and left, filled with excitement.

I finished the year at Northwestern with pretty good grades, which were high enough to keep me from being drafted. In fact, I received mostly A's and a few Bs from all of my classes at Northwestern, with the exception of the Cs I got from Alvina Krause. That seriously brought my average down from a 3.8 to a 3.5. In the last quarter, however, I had switched to another acting teacher. He was new to the school and didn't seem to know much more than the others, but he was very committed and energetic, and he gave me an A at the end of the quarter.

Since I had deprived my mother of seeing me graduate from high school, because I had graduated after summer school, when there was no ceremony, I went all out this time. I had invitations printed, wore cap and gown, sat with all the other graduates, and looked scholarly. After receiving my diploma, I walked through the campus with my mother and could see her pride and vulnerability. It was an important moment for both of us. Jean was there too, but since she was one quarter behind me, we did not graduate together.

The 1954 season at Fish Creek was much better than the first. The plays were better, I appeared in all of them, and my parts were bigger and better. Many of the actors were repeaters, but a few new people had joined the company. Bill Munchow returned, as did Helen Bragdon, Robert Thompson, Maggie Magerstadt, Leo Lucker, Lee, and I. The new people were Mike Westfield, Gail Kolste, Robert McLeod, June Stewart, Caroline Marshall, and others.

Our first offering of the season was a play called *Lo and Behold,* by John Patrick, who wrote *The Teahouse of the August Moon.* Leo Lucker directed the opening show. The play is in the same style as Noel Coward's *Blithe Spirit* and was again a comedy, billed in the program as "giddy and inspired nonsense." It is full of zany characters, some of whom have returned from the dead to be with us. I played John McDougal, a brash criminal type, and Helen Bragdon played Minnetonka Smallflower, an Indian in full regalia. It was a fun play, and I thoroughly enjoyed doing it. On the opening night of the new season, all of the actors who have returned receive spontaneous applause from the audience, many of whom have been coming for years. The applause stops the show for a minute or two, and the actors either subtly nod appreciation or stay in character and wait for the response to subside. When I made my entrance, I got a big response, which honestly surprised me. I graciously accepted the applause and went on with my first line.

We had a couple of strange ones in the company. Mike Westfield told me that he had been in the army and held the rank of "brevet major." I had never heard of such a rank, and I told him so. He made up some strange story about it being a special rank that had been awarded to him because of some special ability he had. I always thought that he was a brevet liar! Robert McLeod was a real trip, a jokester, a player of tricks and an all-around fuck-up! I liked him a lot because he brought so much fun to everything. His antics were disturbing to a few of the older people, since they were sometimes mischievous. I remember two specific examples of his bizarre tricks: In our sixth play, *Room Service,* he played a fast-talking character named Faker Englund, who is much as his first name indicates. I played an overweight Jewish doctor named Glass, replete with a heavy Jewish accent, which wasn't hard for me to do, since I had grown up hearing my mother's and father's Russian Jewish accents. I entered the room onstage—a hotel room—and announced myself: "I am Dr. Glass. Who is sick here?" McLeod was sitting on the bed in a long overcoat. He jumped up, came close to me, and opened the right side of his overcoat away from the audience. He was stark naked and had a sign on the inside of his coat, which read, Fuck you, Freddie boy! I looked at the sign, looked at his genitals, looked into his eyes, which were intense and unwavering, the lines went out the window, but I didn't break. Instead, I made up some lines that were funnier than what the playwright had written; then I left the stage and cracked up!

The second time Bob played his tricks was on Bill Munchow. Bill had a little bit of a memory problem, and since we did one show after another and he had an enormous amount of lines to memorize, he would strategically place little pieces of paper with several lines all around the stage, hiding them behind set props in places where he knew the blocking would take him for that part of the scene. He was very adept at looking at the papers with the lines written on them without letting the audience know what he was doing. I don't recall exactly which play it was, but just before curtain Bob switched all the papers around to different places. The curtain went up, the play started, and Bill said some of the lines he knew and then proceeded to read the ones off the papers he had placed around the stage. Nothing he said seemed to make sense to him or to the other actors. Somehow he muddled through the scene and stormed offstage. He was red as a lobster and was yelling loud enough for the audience to hear. Why McLeod didn't get fired, I'll never know. The rumor was that he was having an affair with someone who was funding the theater. I am not sure that the rumor was valid, but that's what I had heard.

Lee and I often did double duty on the plays. On the first one, *Lo and Behold,* we also did the lighting. Our second outing, called *Here We Come Gathering,* was a nutty play with ridiculous antics and a lot of fun for the audience. I played a kind of street person, a peddler with a cockney accent, dressed in disgusting old clothes. One of the characters has hit a duck with her car and carries the dead carcass onto the stage in every scene, so one of the techies in the company got a duck and wrung its neck, which really bothered me a lot. Gail Kolste, who was playing Evadne Potter, was to carry the duck onto the stage. By about the fifth performance the poor dead duck began to smell really bad, and the actors had difficulty not reacting to the stench, so by the end of the run all of them had moved further and further away from poor Gail, who had no other alternative but to bite the bullet and tolerate the odor. I had a fairly small part in that play, which allowed me to run the lights that Lee and I had designed.

We followed *Gathering* with *On Borrowed Time,* in which I also played a small role. There is a dog in the cast, and guess who played that part: Armand, the standard French poodle, was Rover. He was brought onstage on a leash by one of the characters. All the rocks had been removed from the entrance to the backstage part of the theater, just in case Armand decided to pick one up and drop it onstage, where an actor could stumble on it and fall. Armand was very obedient. He didn't pee onstage, smell anyone's crotch, or carry a rock in his mouth, except on the last performance, when he entered with a boulder between his teeth! How he got his mouth open that wide is still a mystery. Fortunately, he entered and exited with the rock, so no one was worse off for Armand's obsession.

Our next production was *Mister Roberts,* by Thomas Heggen and Joshua Logan. It was probably the highlight of the season. I played one of the crew, Stefanowski; Leo Lucker directed it; and once again Lee and I were responsible for the lighting. I'm not sure why that play sticks out in my mind as so much fun, but it was. In one of the scenes, the captain calls for battle stations and every one is catapulted into action. The stage is mayhem for about three minutes. When everything settled down, I ran out onstage, looked around totally confused, and said, "Where the hell is my battle station?" The audience roared. The captain comes out on the bridge, and I'm caught with my hands on my hips. We look at each other for a moment, and I start to polish one of the gunnels of the ship. That further tickled the audience. I wanted desperately to play Ensign Pulver, but they brought in a very inexperienced young guy from outside. I was disappointed and confused as to why they didn't use actors from the company. Of course, it was politics, involving money, and I accepted it. It was a good preparation for my professional career. It foreshadowed many future casting experiences.

I had a really nice role in the next production, *The Lady's Not for Burning,* by Christopher Fry. I played Nicholas Devize, a foppish character with an affected English accent. I wore tights, a bodice resembling an Elizabethan costume, and ballet-type slippers, and I leaped around onstage being sophisticated and bored. I didn't know it at the time, but one of my "choices," without calling it that, was my costume, which made me feel very affected and prissy. My movements and demeanor were classical and very right for the character. Mike Westfield played my brother, and Helen Bragdon, my mother. In one scene I'm sitting on a bench, bored and yawning, and my mother, Helen, says, "Nicholas, why don't you go and see Alizon?" one of the female characters in the play. I respond, "Mother, I'd rather kiss the bottom of a Barbary ape!" I loved that line, and each night I eagerly awaited the opportunity to say it. Doing stock gave me the chance to explore a wide range of characters. I loved being in that play because it was almost like doing Shakespeare. The language and the style and dress opened up areas of obligations that the standard comedy fare did not provide. It was a challenge and an exciting one. The main character, Thomas Mendip, played by Robert Thompson, had some incredible lines, which I memorized and used over the years as preparations of various kinds. His character wants to be punished for a crime he believes he has committed, and his one line coming out of frustration goes as follows: "You fog-blathering, chin-chuntering, chap-flapping, liturgical, turgidical, base old man, what about my murders?" I have realized over the years, as I learned a specific craft, that a lot of what I did in my early work, which was very instinctive and intuitional, was later translated into process. The big difference is that now I know *how* to specifically access whatever the obligations of material call for, while back then I was flying by the seat of my pants.

Our sixth show of the season was *Room Service,* which I have already spoken about, and the last *My Three Angels.* For the first time at the theater, I was able to play a romantic role; that is to say, it involved a romance. My character, Paul, was the nephew of Henri Trochard, played by Lee, a stern businessman and disciplinarian, who, as I remember, was auditing the books of this establishment. I had a brief romance with one of the young female characters. I enjoyed the opportunity to be a leading man for a change! Again, as with all the other productions of the '54 season, Lee and I were responsible for the lighting as well as some of the other technical work. Northwestern had given both of us a real foundation in technical theater. Lee was brilliant with lighting, and his designs helped all of the productions.

One of the plays that season had a God-awful set. The design and construction were fine, but the color was putrid. Caroline and some of the others were very upset with it, so she called an early painting party for the next morning but then asked Lee and me if we would stay up and repaint the set after everyone had gone to bed. We agreed to do that, knowing it would probably take all night—and it did! Caroline stayed right there with us, feeding us sandwiches and coffee and cheering us on. In the morning, when the paint party arrived, they were stunned to see a beautifully repainted set in a much more pleasing color. It is funny the things you remember some fifty years later.

I loved the theater and every moment onstage, no matter what I was doing. It was a gift. After the last performance of the show, most of the old-timers bid their farewells and left. A few of us remained to close up the theater, as we had done the season before. Lee and I lingered a few days longer, I guess because we really didn't want it to be over. At the end of any play or film I'm sure every actor shares the fear that he or she might never work again. The future for most actors is very unpredictable. One might not work again for months, and in some cases years. I didn't really believe that would happen to me, but there is the feeling of finality every time you finish a job.

We hugged and kissed Caroline, said good-bye to a few of the others who stayed on, and drove out of the compound. I stopped the car, got out just before the grounds were to go out of sight, and looked back for a few minutes, while Lee stayed in the car. I knew I would never come back, and I wanted to savor the memory of those two wonderful seasons. We drove back to Chicago mostly in silence. I guess we both felt the sadness and nostalgia of endings.

I dropped Lee off at his house and made arrangements to pick him up later to head out to California. We had agreed that after the season finished we were going to go to Hollywood and pursue our careers. Most of my classmates at Northwestern chose to go to New York after graduation, but I had always been a movie buff and visualized a career in films. Lee also chose California, although I'm not sure why. Maybe it was an alternative to the terrible Chicago winters, or possibly he too had film aspirations. It seemed to me, however, that his love and orientation were the theater.

When I arrived home, my mother and father had just finished lunch and were sitting at the dining-room table. They were happy to see me. We hugged and sat at that table with its brilliantly white linen tablecloth. My father had been retired for some time. He had quit working after a heart attack. My mother fed me, and we sat around for a couple of hours chatting about the summer-stock experience. I talked about the plays I had been in and how they had gone, about the people, the audiences, and so on. Then I excused myself and went into my bedroom. I packed what was left of my clothes and some of my other belongings and then returned to the dining room, suitcase in hand. My mother seemed very surprised and asked me where I was going.

"You just came home," she said.

"I know, Ma," I replied, "but don't you remember, on the train back from California I had said that the very first day I was able to, I was going to California?"

She didn't remember it. Of course it had been thirteen years since that trip, and almost every day since then I had thought and dreamed of Los Angeles.

I hadn't saved very much money, since Lee and I had been paid only a token salary at the theater, but I had managed to put away about five hundred dollars over the previous year, and I figured that would last about a month in California. The draft was hanging over my head, and I knew that they would get me in the next few months. I tried to put that out of my mind, however, and to look forward to this new adventure. My father wanted to give me some money, but I refused to take it, since I had decided that on the very first day I was able to, I would go to California without any outside help. My mother had tears in her eyes, and so did my father. As I have already said, they were both immigrants from Russia and were very emotional and very expressive. They both kissed me on my lips, we cried for a few minutes, and I left. Lee was still packing when I arrived at his house, and he was a little harried and confused about what to take along with him. We piled into my Pontiac Catalina, secured all the baggage in the trunk, and were off to California, singing, "Hi, diddle dee dee, an actor's life for me!"

CHAPTER 4

CALIFORNIA HERE I COME

I felt excited as we passed out of the Chicago city limits. It was a city I had never liked, and I was happy to see its outskirts in my rearview mirror. We figured that the drive would take at least three full days, but we hadn't counted on staying in hotels, since money had to last. The plan was for Lee to sleep while I drove and vice versa. It felt like the beginning of a new life, and I experienced waves of excitement all the way there. We talked and sang and made plans and felt very high.

The trip had a few memorable highlights: We were in the mountains somewhere in New Mexico; it was nighttime and very dark, and as we crested the peak where the road started to descend, laid out in panorama were the lights of a fairly large city in the distance. I pulled the car onto the shoulder and got out to drink in a view such as I had never seen before. I started to cry, not out of sadness but of joy. It came to me at that moment that I had been "Midwesternized" and hadn't really seen much of our country nor any of the outside world. I was almost twenty-three years old, and I was leaving the nest for the first time. I don't know how long I stood there, but it was a significant moment in my life.

When we reached Arizona, just outside Winslow we came to a meteor crater. I think at the time it was called the Berringer Crater, but when I passed it again many years later it was just the Meteor Crater. Lee wanted to stop and see it, so we paid the small entrance fee and were allowed to go through the gates. The crater was awesome! I had never seen anything like it before, except in science-fiction movies. It was enormous—several miles in circumference, at least two miles across, and it must have been a thousand feet deep. We stood on the rim for a very long time, feeling insignificant in the realm of the universe. A loudspeaker was telling the tourists about the meteor: It had hit many thousands of years earlier and must have been felt for thousands of miles, but of course no one knew that for sure. It was buried very deeply below the red clay bottom, and the narrator estimated that it possibly contained enough metal to build a whole fleet of battleships. I'm not sure why—maybe he was curious or it represented a challenge of some kind—but Lee decided to climb down to the bottom of the crater. It took at least two hours for him to make the roundtrip, and when he reached the rim on his return, he was totally exhausted. About fifteen years ago I went back to that crater and saw that it is now fenced and that no one is allowed to climb down into it anymore. Lee slept for hours after his excursion. I woke him so that he could see the Painted Desert and part of the Grand Canyon. Only the very tip of it was visible. We didn't stop, since we were anxious to get to California.

We arrived in Los Angeles on the fourth day in the early afternoon. My sister Ida, who had come here about seven months earlier, invited us to stay with her. She and her husband, Al, lived at 830 South Fairfax, in a typical California apartment building with a stucco exterior and a quadrangle surrounded by numbered doors. Their apartment had two small bedrooms, one of which was occupied by Ida and Al, and the other by my niece Bobbie and my nephew Gene. Bobbie was fifteen and a half, and Gene fourteen. We were invited to dinner and told that we were welcome to stay.

I have already explained how Ida had actually raised me for the most part and how I had always regarded her more as a mother than a sister. Al, on the other hand, had never been too fond of me but seemed pleased to see me in California. After dinner Lee said that he was disappointed that we had missed seeing the La Brea Tar Pits on the way out here, so Al offered to drive us over there after we had had our dessert, since it was just about a mile away. Lee was shocked. He had obviously thought that the tar pits were in some other state, and not in the middle of the Miracle Mile on Wilshire Boulevard. We went to see them that evening, and I must say that by then I felt more like a sightseeing tourist than an actor looking to start his career!

Lee and I were set up to sleep in the living room. Since it was a small apartment, we were all very crowded, but what could we do? I didn't have much money, and for that matter neither did Ida or Al; and Lee, who was on some kind of milk-drinking protein diet, consumed a half-gallon of milk daily all by himself!

We went out every day attempting to meet people and find out what the regimen was in Hollywood. I had one contact from my brother Phil, a guy he knew from the JPI in Chicago, who had gotten the nickname Fluffy from the enormous amount of wavy hair that stood up about six inches from his scalp. Evidently, he and Phil had been close friends until Fluffy had moved to California. I remembered him slightly, having met him at the JPI theater. Phil had told me that I could probably find Fluffy at a small theater in Hollywood, the Players' Ring on Santa Monica Boulevard, so we drove there and parked across the street. The building was recessed from the street, and there were about six cement circular steps leading to the box office. I felt anxious since I didn't know what, if anything, I could expect Fluffy to do for us. There was a small woman in the box office, who looked half Indian, from India. I asked her if Fluffy was there, and I could see that she didn't have a clue who Fluffy was; then I remembered that Fluffy's real name was Joe Mell, so I asked if Joe was there. "Oh, Joe," she responded, "yeah, he's in the theater. I'll go and get him." We were invited into the lobby, where the walls were all covered with the pictures of the actors in their current production, and I remember feeling envious that my picture wasn't there. From inside the theater, on the other side of a double door, I heard, "Fluffy? Fluffy?" The double door burst open, and out walked a short, pudgy, round-faced, bald man. He stopped and looked at Lee and me, wondering who the hell we were and where in hell anyone had come up with a name he hadn't heard in over twenty years.

I broke the uncomfortable silence: "I'm Phil Stein's brother Freddie."

"Oh, my god, Freddie, the last time I saw you, you were this big," he exclaimed, sticking out his arm about three feet above the floor.

Joe had moved to California about eight years earlier, just about the time World War II had ended. He worked in the office of

Meyer Mishkin, an agent whose most famous client was Jeff Chandler. Joe was Meyer's secretary and gofer and did whatever else needed to be done. I'm sure he received a salary, but it was also a good place to be to get submitted for work, and Mishkin made sure that Joe got a small part here and there. Joe had also been acting in some of the shows at the Players' Ring, which at that time was the best showcase in town, where actors could be seen by agents and casting directors. In fact, many actors got their start in the business as a result of appearing in a play there.

I introduced Lee and briefly filled Joe in on what we had been doing—Northwestern, summer stock, and all the plays I had done in Chicago. I also told him that I was a member of Actors' Equity and the Screen Actors Guild. He seemed impressed. He had been totally unaware that I had followed in my brother's footsteps, and he was also impressed that Lee had a master's degree in theater from Northwestern. He ushered us into the theater and gave us a tour, including the backstage areas, the dressing rooms, and the light booth. It was a theater in the round—or actually in the square. The stage was in the middle of the room, surrounded on four sides by a total of over a hundred seats. The light grid was packed with expensive instruments, which Lee took notice of immediately. All in all, it was a very well-equipped plant.

After we had seen the whole place, Joe took us into an office in the back and introduced us to Paul Levitt, the owner and producer of the theater. Paul was in his middle-to-late thirties and had dark hair that seemed to come to a point in front and receded at his temples, which made it evident that he had been losing his hair. He had a very subtle, almost unnoticeable lisp, which I think was caused by the way his lips moved as he spoke. Joe did a great sales pitch, telling Paul that he had known me when I was four years old and listing our credits like an experienced agent selling his clients. As a result, Paul offered us very low-paying jobs as stage managers for their productions. When I say low paying, that is exactly what I mean: thirty-five dollars a week for both of us! We accepted, thinking that it would at least pay for our food and that we would be working in a theater. What could be better than that? Paul also said that he taught a small class for the apprentices and the techies who worked around the theater. It would come with the package and supplement what he was paying us, and it would culminate in an evening of showcase scenes with an invited audience.

Paul always talked "poor mouth," while being the most despicable exploiter of actors in the world, a fact I did not know at the time. He had a partner, Ted Thorpe, a little guy who resembled what we picture as a siding salesman, replete with the blue suede shoes.

Lee and I were invited to see the current production, a play called *Pick-up Girl.* It was the first play I would see in California. I was stunned at how good it was. I thought some of the performances were terrific. If this was the kind of work they were doing there, I was really lucky to have had the connection with Joe Mell. Corey Allen was one of the leads, and I was incredibly impressed with his work. He was Brando-esque in his behavior, but that had a lot to do with the nature of the part he was playing. He later did quite well as a film actor. He was the guy who menaced James Dean in *Rebel without a Cause,* the character who went over the hill when they were playing chicken. In later years he turned to directing and had a somewhat successful career in television. It was much later that I got to know him personally.

The actress playing the pick-up girl was Beverly Long. I fell madly in love with her at first sight. She had long blond hair, blue eyes, skin that looked like a baby's, and a face that angels would have envied. She was quite good in the play and also later appeared in *Rebel,* as one of the high-school kids.

I was curious about the way some of the actors were working but afraid to approach them with any questions of process. I saw some of them around the theater, since I was involved in the play that followed *Pick-up Girl.* I ran into Beverly a couple of times and may have said no more than ten words to her. I was intimidated by her beauty. Writing this in retrospect more than half a century later, I find it incredible that I now know the outcome of those people's lives. Beverly had a modest acting career and in later years became a very successful casting director and commercial teacher.

We were going on a month, and Lee and I were still at my sister's house. I wanted to get out of there, but I think Lee was concerned about having enough money to get an apartment. It wasn't only the cramped quarters that concerned me, but also the extra expense for the food that we were consuming. My sister Ida seemed to be between a rock and a hard place, caught between helping her brother and the pressure she was getting from Al. I felt the tension and didn't know what to do about it. Finally, Ida suggested that she would help us find an inexpensive single apartment. She jumped into my car, and we rode around the cheaper areas of Hollywood.

We found a one-room apartment on Normandy Avenue in a five-story, red brick building, which dated back to about the early 1930s, had an elevator, and seemed clean. The apartment had a small kitchen and a Murphy bed, which folded up and was stored in a double-door closet. If memory serves me, I think the rent was seventy-five dollars a month. Those of you reading this must remember that this was November of 1954. You could buy a new car for about two thousand dollars! Lee and I rented the apartment, figuring that with what monies we had left, plus our salary from the Players' Ring, we could each come up with $37.50 a month. I felt that I was on borrowed time anyway. The draft hung heavy over my head. In fact, I had received a notice, which my mother had sent me, informing me that I was to report to an induction place in Chicago. I had immediately sent off a registered letter to my draft board there, informing them that I was now residing in California, and a couple of days later had received a very gracious response from them informing me that they were transferring my file over to Los Angeles. I was very relieved for a number of reasons: first, I felt that this would give me more time, maybe even months; secondly, I thought that the California draft board might have different quotas and there was the possibility that they might never call me up; and finally, if I was to be inducted, I would rather be in California at some military facility that had better weather than Kansas or Missouri. It was early November, and I had only been in L.A. for a month or so. I was soon turning twenty-three. My birthday was the nineteenth of the month, and I did not want to celebrate it in the army.

Since we had some time, one sunny afternoon Lee and I decided to go visit this contact of his, an older woman, whom I think his father knew somehow. She was a friend of Grant Withers, an old character actor, who had been in the movies for the last fifty years, had had an important role in *The Grapes of Wrath,* and had done at least fifty other big movies. He lived in the same building as she did, somewhere on Hollywood Boulevard near Highland. It was an old residence hotel from the silent-movie years, with a large front porch populated by old retired people, who sat in rocking chairs and talked about the good old days. The woman was also there, in an old rattan chair, which had been painted over many times in a number of different colors that were peeling in various places. It had what we now know as a tie-dyed appearance. She was about eighty years old and was wearing a flowered dress with bows on it and a large hat like those you might have seen in 1920 on the boardwalk in Atlantic City. She looked as though she had just stepped out of a Tennessee Williams one-act play. Lee spoke to her about their mutual connection and asked if she could help us by introducing us to someone who could open a few doors at the studios. She said that when she knew we were coming she had invited Grant down to meet us. While waiting for him to come down, we had some tea, and then the woman launched into some anti-Semitic rhetoric. Knowing that I was Jewish, Lee turned red, but I winked at him as if to say it was O.K., considering the source. Not only was this dinosaur of a woman a bigot herself, but she came from generations of prejudiced daughters of the D.A.R.

About an hour after we got there, Grant Withers limped out onto the porch. I recognized him from having seen him in dozens of movies, even though he looked like the skeleton of the man he used to be. His speech was slow and halting, and there was other evidence that he had had a stroke at some time. He was lucid and still had most of his mental faculties but spoke very slowly, and since he was also somewhat hard of hearing, we had to repeat everything we said. Lee asked him for advice—what we should do to get started in the business. Did he know anyone who could help us? All he came up with was that we should go to the studios and apply for employment. Maybe that was how it used to be done, but even as new to Hollywood as I was, I knew that it was not the way to break into acting in films. He told us he had been away from it for so long that all the people he knew were probably dead or no longer in the business. He seemed honestly willing to help us but had long since hung up his mantle. We thanked him and politely left, saying good-bye to "Baby Jane"! Lee was infinitely more disappointed than I was. I guess he had expected more from the contact.

We went back to the Players' Ring for our first assignment as stage managers, which was for *The Rose Tattoo,* by Tennessee Williams. We divided the duties: Lee spent most of the time in the light booth, handling the light cues, while I took charge of the props and dealt with getting the actors in the right place at the right time. A large number of people were attached to the theater, and each of them seemed to do something around there. Lee and I had come in right at the beginning of rehearsals. The play had already been cast: Penny Santon, an Italian actress living and working in America, was to play the main character, an Italian woman who had lost her husband some years back; Jerry Riggio had been cast as Mangia-cavallo, which translated into English means "eat a horse"; Susan Kohner was to play Penny's daughter; and Jody McCrea, the daughter's boyfriend. Jody was a tall, good-looking young man about my age. He had two famous parents, Joel McCrea and Frances Dee, both very successful actors in the forties, fifties, and well into the sixties. Jody was a sweet guy, always polite and sensitive to other people's feelings, and I liked him a lot. Susan was the daughter of Paul Kohner, a very large and famous agent. I think the play was being directed by "Boomie," whose real name was Alan DeWitt and who was a real character.

Briefly this is what the play was about: Penny's character was still mourning the loss of her late husband and kept his ashes in an urn on the mantel. In the play she talks about having spent each night in his arms for twelve years. Jerry's character comes into the house for some reason I can't recall. Penny and he are adversarial in the beginning, he being defensive about his name—which she jokes about—and she still attached to the memory of her husband. Their relationship changes when they find out they both have a rose tattoo. Susan loves her boyfriend, but Penny doesn't like him, which provides additional conflict. The actors were pretty good. They all seemed to have a sense of truth and were quite natural, except at times of emotional outbursts, when they were a little over the top.

As part of our stage-managing responsibilities, Lee and I were obligated to find, purchase, or requisition the props. Being the cheap bastard he was, Paul instructed us to get as many things as we could for free: beg, borrow—he stopped short of telling us to steal, although he wouldn't have minded even theft to avoid spending any money. Lee and I went out on the town with an elaborate list of things we needed for the play, most of which were easy to find in thrift stores. If they needed to be new, we purchased them at discount stores.

The only prop we couldn't find was the urn that was supposed to contain the ashes of Penny's dead husband. We brought back a few jars and vases that could have been used to house the ashes, but Penny insisted on a real funeral urn. "Let's go to a mortuary or a crematorium and see if we can buy an urn," I said. Lee didn't think Paul would approve, but off we went. I don't recall exactly where the crematorium was located, somewhere on the south and west side of L.A. The owner, or manager, greeted us with open enthusiasm. The one thing we had learned fast is that if you say you are working on a movie or a play, people are very accommodating. It is as if they get some kind of pleasure from being involved, even from a distance. We explained our need, and the man said he could help us but asked if we would first like to take a tour of the facility. At first I hesitated to give him a response, but my conviction as an actor has always been to be interested and curious about everything, because you never know when you might need that information or experience; so I acquiesced. He took us directly to the furnace room—which was actually called the crematorium—and opened the heavy metal door, exposing the burned skeletal remains of some unfortunate dead person. It was a shock to see them totally intact.

"I thought that there would be nothing left except ashes," I said.

"Oh, no, the bones have been burned through, but now they must be ground by this machine." He led us over to what looked like a large-scale meat grinder and continued to describe his profession with a sense of pride: "We take the bones, which are now very hollow and brittle, and we put them into the top of the machine, grinding them into smaller particles, which are the ashes. Of course, we only give the survivors a small portion of the total amount produced by a normal-size cadaver."

I was getting a little light-headed but was too embarrassed to mention it. We completed the tour and purchased the least expensive urn there. We thanked the man for his kindness and left. On the ride back we sat in silence for a long time, both of us recovering from the macabre experience. I broke the silence by saying, "When I die, Lee, I want to be stuffed by a taxidermist and sat on my living-room couch with my hand in the air and a smile of greeting to anyone entering my house." We both laughed at that and went on to other subjects. That experience has never left me, however. To this day I am affected by what I saw there.

Penny was very pleased with the urn and thanked us for getting it. Even though it was never opened in the play, we filled it with ashes from a wood-burning fireplace—a touch of reality, I guess!

We opened to large audiences. The theater always seemed to be sold out. I found out why: Dorothy Roth, who was in charge of that part of the business, was constantly on the phone in the back office talking to organizations and selling large blocks of tickets. The audiences were therefore comprised largely of theater parties, mostly from Jewish organizations, who were very zealous in their support of theater.

One of the perks of being at the Ring was the people. There was a great bunch of people who populated the theater. I made many friends who would stay in my life for years to come. We had a lot of get-togethers outside the theater. We would often go down the street to Barney's Beanery, a greasy-spoon bar-restaurant, where a lot of the theater people hung out. We would also visit some of the people's houses, drink beer and listen to music. It is always hard to go directly to bed after a show. Everyone is keyed up and still in performance mode, even if not appearing in the play. Ellie Kay, a theater groupie who hung around outside and backstage, was always willing to take the party to her house. A group of us would go over after the show and hang out for a few hours. She was delighted to play hostess and supply the food and beverages as well as the music. Ellie was grossly overweight, wore Coke-bottle glasses, and had short, frizzy brown hair and a questionable complexion. She was very sweet and obviously very lonely, and what she didn't offer in looks, she attempted to make up for in generosity. She asked me what kind of music I liked, and when I told her I preferred Broadway musicals, and in particular *Kismet,* she went out and bought the album. What did we like to drink? It was in her refrigerator. I don't know where she got her money, but it was obvious that she had a source of support. She wasn't employed and lived in a nice little house in what is now West Hollywood. Her brother, Hershy Kay, was a fairly famous American composer in the style of Ferde Grofé. Ellie was very attracted to me but never expressed it openly. She asked me about my relationship to Jean: Was it serious? Were we going to get married? Was I exclusively involved? I knew where she was coming from, and I answered her questions honestly but with sensitivity.

On Mondays, since that was the dark night for the play, the acting class Paul conducted was held at the theater. It had between ten and fifteen students. We did improvisations and scenes, but Paul wasn't much of a teacher, and I think he knew it. Besides running the theater, he acted in films, usually in very small parts. His thrust was making money. That's what his greatest drive was, to acquire a lot of it. I am sure he had that class so that the students would work for nothing in the theater. I knew that I had a much better theater education and also knew more about acting than he did, but I was still hungry to find a teacher who could fill me in on how to create reality on the stage. Paul's critiques were general and directorial, but I was there to get whatever I could out of it. I was eager to do the showcase scenes, thinking that I might land an agent out of the evening.

The scene I chose was from *Home of the Brave,* a war play focused on relationships. I was to play the part of Coney, a young Jewish soldier in World War II, who shares with the other character, his friend Finch, all of the discrimination and anti-Semitism he has experienced while growing up. In the scene we were going to do, Finch and Coney have just been in some kind of firefight with the enemy. Coney does something stupid, accidentally putting them both in jeopardy, and Finch impulsively responds angrily, "You dirty, rotten Je…erk!" Coney knows that Finch meant to say "Jew," and Finch recognizes the pain on Coney's face. There is a very poignant moment between the two. Finch is crestfallen with shame and hurt that he said what he did, and Coney has this wonderful monologue about what it has meant for him to be Jewish and the abuse he has suffered from people who weren't his friends. The monologue concludes with, "If you're a Jew, you stink," which contains all the pain of a lifetime.

We rehearsed the scene for about three weeks, in and out of class. I can't remember the other actor's name, but he was good and he gave me a lot to work off of. Of course, I had many living experiences and parallels in my life that totally fit Coney. For one thing I had the Roccos and Buddy Riggio as impetus. At that time I didn't have a specific craft to be able to turn my experiences into choices that I could use, but instinctively, and because they had become part of the fabric of who I was, those experiences totally affected the work I did in the scene. On the night we did the showcase, the theater was packed with friends, relatives, and, I hoped, also some industry people. Our scene was towards the end of the program. When we finally did it, I was totally connected. I was on fire, and when I said the last line, "If you're a Jew, you stink," there was an audible shocked response from the audience. After that line we left the stage as if we were changing our battle positions. On my exit this bald man grabbed my arm, squeezed it hard, and said passionately, "Brilliant! Brilliant!" I nodded subtly and exited. I got three feet off the stage and realized that the man was Joseph Schildkraut, a character actor I had grown up watching in a hundred films. I figured that the reason I hadn't immediately recognized him was that he wore a hairpiece in all his films. After the show was over, I went out into what was left of the audience to speak with him, to thank him and tell him how much I admired his work, but he was gone. To this day, fifty-two years later, that experience stands out as one of the most impacting and important moments in my life.

If there were any agents or casting directors in the audience, I didn't know about it. None of the other people had been approached after the show either. This was already the middle of November. I had been in California for only a month and a half, so I guess I caught myself being a little impatient.

The Players' Ring attracted a lot of very well-established character actors. I was in Hollywood and was not accustomed to coming face to face with people I had seen in the movies or on television. I don't believe I have ever been star stuck, but it was very different seeing actors in the flesh. Paul Kohner would stop by quite frequently to visit Susan, and occasionally he would bring his beautiful wife with him. She was either a Mexican or a Spanish actress well into her middle years and probably retired from acting at the time. The years had not taken a toll on her beauty. Paul, on the other hand, was overweight, had a protruding belly and thinning hair, and paraded around the theater making sure everyone knew how important he was.

Ralph Riskin was someone I struck up a friendship with. His father was either a successful writer or a producer. Ralph had an interest in the theater, but I don't believe he was an actor. A close friend of his was Roger Moore, who came by a couple of times. Besides being young and handsome, at that time he was at the beginning of his career, way before "The Saint" or James Bond. If I had had a crystal ball or been clairvoyant, I would have known that much later, after teaching for many years, I would have as students both his son and his daughter, who were not even born yet when I met Roger. Life is very strange indeed!

I really missed Jean. I spoke to her on the telephone almost daily, and I wanted her to come to California. I was soon to have my wish. In late November, or it might have been early December,

I received a notice from the Selective Service System to report for a physical exam on a certain date. In the interim I had auditioned for a play to be staged at a theater in Palm Springs. The play was *My Three Angels,* and the producer was Herb Rogers, who for years had run the Tenthouse Theatre in Highland Park, a suburb outside Chicago. I hadn't known him then, but obviously he was in California now. I told him I had done the play recently in stock and would love to do it again. He liked my audition and gave me the part. We were to start rehearsals in late December. It was the same role I had done in stock, and it was an Equity company, so I would be getting paid Equity wages.

The play at the Ring was going well and everything seemed to be falling into place. I was working in theater, I had been cast in an Equity play, my money issues were under control, and I felt that the future looked very good, except for the damned draft. It isn't that I am not a good American. I'm very patriotic. I just didn't see any value to me or the army for me to give up two years of my life when I was just at the beginning of my journey in my chosen profession, which I had prepared for. The Korean "police action" was over, and the world was at peace—except for the cold war and for some of our senior senators who were looking for Communists in the bushes and under rocks. How could I be of value in the cold war? I didn't speak Russian, and I hadn't any known talents that might be valuable to the army, so why waste two years of my life being somewhere and doing something that took me away from my passions? I started thinking, How could I get rejected when I took my physical exam? Play nuts? Hobble in and tell them about my trick knee? Pretend I had a hearing problem? I was stressed out over the whole thing. Several people told me that as an actor I could go in there and convince them of anything. But I rejected the being-nuts idea; I didn't think my trick knee would get me out, since I had passed the physical in Chicago a couple of years earlier; and there were other ways they could tell if I had a hearing problem. So what could I do? Aha, I thought, I'll be gay! I was sure they didn't want homosexuals in the service. I had long, blond, wavy hair and blue eyes and was very sensitive. I qualified physically, so all I had to do was pretend to be gay. After all, what was fair about the draft anyway? In the old days in England, so-called "press gangs" would go into pubs, hit men over the head, and drag them into servitude on ships that would sometimes not see land for two years. Well, wasn't that what they were doing to me? I felt indignant and justified in trying to beat the draft. I decided that on the day of my physical I would just do Mr. Beachwood but would tone it down a little, make it subtler. I discussed my plan with Lee and a couple of other people, and they were all supportive of it. Bernie, one of the students in my class at the Ring, even said he would come down there and kiss me on the lips right in front of the building, where everyone could see! I thanked him and refused his suggestion, telling him that I thought it might be overkill and that, besides, we might get the shit kicked out of us by some of the rednecks down there!

The day arrived. I got up early and began to "nance" around the apartment, making adjustments to my behavior, since I didn't want to be too obvious. I went down to the building and stood in line with the rest of the potential draftees, staying in character the whole time. I got a few raised eyebrows, but no one said anything. Before removing our clothes, we were given a questionnaire to fill out, which had several questions about our health and our mental state. Wherever there was a question about moods or depression, I checked that I had suffered from those. There was also a question about ever having been in psychotherapy, and since I actually had been, I checked that too. My answers were guaranteed to get me a trip to the psychologist, and they did. I was ushered into a small office. Sitting behind the desk was a man they must have gotten from Central Casting. He was about fifty, I would guess, had dark, curly hair, and was staring at some papers on his desk. I stood in front of the desk, adopting a gay attitude. I did nothing obvious, just took on the manner and facial expressions of a gay person. Before I left the apartment, I had made sure to coif my hair so that it would be piled high on my head, and I had accentuated its waviness. I stood there for a few minutes, waiting for the psychologist to acknowledge my presence, and when he finally looked up at me, he regarded me from head to toe for at least a full minute. There was no denying it: I was in that character, a younger Mr. Beachwood. I am sure he got the message. I started to say something, when he abruptly rose from his chair and very aggressively, almost shouting, ordered me to sit down and not say anything until asked. I complied obediently. I sat down as he stood over me asking me why I had been in therapy. I told him that I had depression problems and that I had been unhappy, meanwhile making sure I retained the feminine stance the whole time I spoke. He continued to be aggressive and authoritative, but he never spoke about sexual orientation, and, of course, neither did I. I am sure he got it, but he never mentioned it. He asked me what I did for a living, and I told him that I was an actor and a dancer. I threw in dancer because I knew that people think a lot of dancers are gay. He asked me a couple of questions about the army and about how I felt about being a soldier. I was very careful not to expose my real feelings about being inducted and was somewhat vague in answering those questions, but not at all negative. When my answers went on for too long, he would cut me off abruptly. What I thought at the time was that this guy had some real issues and hated his job. It was later, after I had been in the army for a while, that I understood his behavior. He was treating me that way purposely to see if I would respond to authority and behave—take orders, as it were. If I had responded to him aggressively or defensively, I would have been rejected. If, for example, I had said, "Hey, fuck you! Don't talk to me like that! I'm still a civilian, and you can take the shit you are laying on me and shove it up your ass!" I would have been out of there. You see, it's O.K. to be an obedient homosexual in the army, but it's not all right to be belligerent or hostile. You must respond positively to authority. Of course, I didn't know that until I had been in the service for several months. Most of the guys who got discharged for insubordination and pattern inadaptability got so because of their antisocial behavior. They received undesirable discharges or what are commonly called *yellow* discharges. So in order to avoid that kind of problems, the army screens inductees before they get in.

After all those questions, the psychologist sat down in his chair, and his attitude changed. His voice became softer, and the hardness disappeared from his eyes. He looked at me and smiled, added that I would make a fine soldier, stamped my papers, and dismissed me. I left the building with a sheaf of papers in my hand and tears in my eyes. I got into my car and drove back to Hollywood. I had been told that I would be notified when to report for induction but that it would most probably be after the Christmas holidays. I was thinking as I drove that I had a few more weeks of freedom before serving a two-year sentence. At that moment I realized what it must be like for people waiting to start a prison term. I felt insecure, and I really missed Jean. The telephone wasn't really helping my loneliness any more, and now, more than ever, I wanted to be with her. I called her as soon as I was back in the apartment and told her to come to L.A. right away. She agreed. At least we would have a few weeks together.

I had to give up the part I had gotten in Palm Springs, but I went back to the Players' Ring, committed to do my job for as long as I could. The play was going well, and a lot of people depended on me to be there and do what I did. I informed everyone that I would be leaving for the army after the New Year. They were all very sad but encouraging.

One evening during intermission, while I was standing at one of the urinals relieving myself, I looked over my shoulder to the left, and standing right beside me was Tennessee Williams, also relieving himself. I was stunned for a moment, not knowing what to say or if indeed I should say anything.

Finally, I interrupted the uncomfortable moment by saying, "Mr. Williams, I love your work."

He turned to me, smiled, and said, "We are just going to have to stop meeting like this!"

I laughed, he laughed, and I asked him what he thought of our production. We were on the way out of the toilet when he said that it was one of the better productions of *The Rose Tattoo* he had ever seen and that he was enjoying it immensely. I thanked him and returned backstage to alert the cast of the second act.

Jean arrived in L.A. and moved into the Normandy apartment, while Lee moved out. I can't remember where he went, but we had the place all to ourselves. It was a bittersweet time. I took Jean to the theater and introduced her to everyone. She saw the play and liked it. When the time came, the cast threw me a huge going away party. Everyone was there: the entire cast, all the production people, Paul, Ted—everyone who was attached to the theater and even some people I didn't know. Paul was very sweet to me. He told me that I was part of the Ring family and that I was welcome to come back when I got out of the army. Everyone came with a gag gift, some of them related to what I might need in the army: an enema, a joke book on how to escape from Alcatraz, and so on. They had also all chipped in to give me a beautiful stopwatch. I was very moved by the outpouring of so much affection, and Jean too was very impressed by the whole thing. One of the people who were there, whom I didn't know—possibly a friend of someone I did know—said something to me that I will never forget. He told me that he had been in the army a couple of years earlier and that he would not take a million dollars to go back in but that he would not take two million to give up the experience. I didn't know what he meant at the time. I thought that he was just doing his best to encourage me to look forward to the experience instead of anticipating it with dread.

During the time I had been in L.A. my father, mother, and older brother, Morrey, had moved out to California. My brother had been given a contract to write films for Columbia Pictures. Knowing that I was going into the army, my father persuaded me to sell my Pontiac to Morrey, and since I figured that I wouldn't have any use for it in the army, I did so. It was as hard to say good-bye to that car as to the people I was leaving behind. After all, it had played such an important role in my life and my relationship with Jean. It was our private place to talk and make love in, and our attachment to it was great.

The day arrived, as all days do, January 4, 1955. I got up that morning with a terrible hollow feeling in my stomach. Jean and I had breakfast, and she tried to talk about good things in the future, but I knew what she was trying to do, and it wasn't working! I was to be at Union Station downtown early in the afternoon. There were a bunch of us there. Everyone was saying good-byes, and there was a general sense of sadness. I kissed Jean and boarded the train to Fort Ord.

CHAPTER 5

THE ARMY YEARS

The train left Union Station at about five thirty in the afternoon. I was anxious about the unknown and didn't sleep for most of the night. A bunch of us sat around in the club car talking. I felt the tension from almost everyone and during the silences heard the rattling of the train along the irregularities on the tracks. The movement of the train and the plethora of odors brought back my trip to California when I was ten years old; only this time the excitement of a new adventure had turned into fear and loathing of what was to come.

The sound of the train finally lulled me to sleep, but I was awakened by loud voices and a general tumult signaling our arrival in Monterey. Military buses were waiting to take us to the fort. We climbed down from the buses into a dark, cold, and unfamiliar place. I was dressed for the Los Angeles climate and not prepared for the sharp and cutting wind. I stood there shivering in the dark with all the other inductees, not knowing whom or what we were waiting for. I was trembling uncontrollably, and my teeth were chattering, but I felt the need to hide my fear. No one spoke. We all stood there, silent and cold. I later found out that Fort Ord had been nicknamed Fort Pneumonia by the Sea!

After what seemed like half an hour, a surly noncom appeared, ordered us to form up, and then marched us to the mess hall for breakfast. I really felt like a "new fish" starting to serve a two-year sentence in prison. The servers who were dishing out the food were wearing white jackets and all looked like the convicts in a prison movie instead of a bunch of hapless privates pulling KP. The eggs were powdered, the French toast hard and cold, and the oatmeal lumpy. Each portion was divided into separate sections on a very scratched metal tray—which added to how unappetizing everything was—but I was hungry, so I ate what was in front of me. Even before I had swallowed the last of the oatmeal, however, I heard the same noncom screaming orders from the other side of the mess hall: "O.K., take your trays, scrape whatever is left on them, and pile them up on those stands by the door! Your mommy isn't going to clean up after you here. Get your asses out in front of the mess hall and form a line three deep. Do it now!" I complied, of course, all the time wondering why he had to scream at us. We could hear him just fine without the dramatics.

It was the first day of processing in. We were in the section of the fort that must have been the oldest, since all the barracks were wooden and painted in the same yellowish tan institutional color. There were quite a few administration buildings and what appeared to be small storage facilities. First, we were marched to get our haircuts. While standing in line, we witnessed the awful shearing of good-looking young men with mounds of healthy hair, who were being shaved to within a quarter of an inch of their scalps. I waited my turn, mourning the loss of my beautiful, wavy blond hair and thinking that it might never grow back as rich and full as it was. I had fantasies of grabbing a razor and cutting the barber's throat, and I visualized him falling in slow motion into the sea of hair lying on the ground. I could see him disappearing under the mixture of colors and textures on the floor.

When my turn came, I slumped into his chair and jokingly said, "Just take a little off the top, please!"

Very funny, Fanny," he replied, as I immediately realized I shouldn't have said that.

He turned out to be a butcher, not a barber. He shaved my head so close to the scalp I might as well have been totally bald. I felt the tears running down my face as my hair drifted slowly down the front, some of it even landing in my mouth.

"O.K., Fanny," he said, "throw your comb away and get a washcloth."

"Thank you, *Sweeney,*" I replied.

I am sure he didn't know whom I was referring to—the demon barber of Fleet Street, who used to cut his clients' throats. I exited the building, terrified I might see my reflection in some windowpane. I reached up to my head, where my hair used to be, slowly brought my hand down to my scalp, and was horrified to feel nothing but short, sharp stubble.

Our next stop was the infirmary, where we stripped to the waist and stood in line to get our shots: typhoid, tetanus, and whatever else they deemed necessary for us to avoid contracting rare tropical diseases. What immediately struck me was how impersonal all the doctors or medics were. They hit us in both arms at the same time, repeating their "Move along!" command. I asked one of them if I should expect some kind of reaction to the inoculations, but he didn't even look up at me.

Uniforms were next on the agenda. We filed into a warehouse piled high with stacks of shirts, fatigues, boots, and field jackets and were given a duffle bag to store all the things we were to be issued. "What size waist? shirt? collar? inseam? boots?" The sergeant threw those questions at me as if they had been prerecorded. I stood there silent for a moment, long enough for him to look up at me. He was a full foot shorter than I and looked like a character actor in the movies—a craggy face with an unlit cigar stub stuck in the right corner of his mouth. "Hey, dummy, I asked for your sizes!" he shouted. I bit my bottom lip, trying hard not to express my immediate response to his calling me a dummy, then spit out all my clothing sizes as if the words were going to penetrate his body and draw blood. There was an uncomfortable moment between us, as he stared hostilely into my eyes. I diffused the situation with a phony smile and a "Thank you, sergeant." I don't know why he had asked for sizes, since nothing fit me anyway. It is truly like what you see in the movies. They give you clothes miles too big for you.

The first full day in the army was over, and after we had "chow," I collapsed onto my bunk. I was fully clothed and must have slept for a couple of hours before removing my clothes and getting under the covers. I slept hard—a dreamless sleep of the dead.

"Get your lazy asses out of the sack, you freaks!" My eyes sprung open as if powered by internal springs. For a long moment I didn't know where I was. I stared at the decaying wooden beams of the barracks and felt sick from the shots I had received the day before. Everything looked like a Salvador Dalí painting, surreal and distorted. I felt a wave of depression wash over me like a thick blanket. I'm never going to make it through this, I thought. As melodramatic as it may seem, I felt that my life was over. I had only been in the army one day, but it already seemed like an eternity, and I had 729 more days to serve! The corporal was still belting out commands: "I said, get your asses out of the sack and hit the floor!" It was 5:00 A.M. and still dark outside. I had an awful taste in my mouth, metallic and bitter, and couldn't move a muscle in my body. I was frozen on my back in the top bunk. As hard as I tried, I couldn't move. Out of the corner of my right eye, I saw the corporal approaching our bunk area. He looked like the direct descendant of prehistoric man, a throwback to Neanderthal; or else he had had an overactive pituitary in his adolescence, which made his head larger than his body, jutting his chin forward and recessing his eyes deep into his skull. He was wearing a blue helmet liner, which is what all the cadres wore. *Cadre* is a term used in the army to designate the counterpart of a Marine drill instructor. He approached my bunk, looked directly into my eyes with his own beady, black, recessed eyes, and said, "What are you waiting for, freak, an invitation? Get your fucking ass out of that bunk, or I'll pull you out!" I just looked at him for a second, thinking, This is not happening to me! It's a nightmare and I'm going to wake up any minute. It took everything in my power to swing my legs over the side of the bunk. Since I was in the top bunk, it was a little bit of a drop to the floor, but I held on to the blankets as I eased myself down. The floor was hard and cold, as was the entire barracks. I looked at this guy, and if ever I had wanted to kill someone, this was the moment! I branded it into my memory, knowing that someday I could use it in my acting. If only I could kill him, I thought, I would be doing the world a favor. It was as if time had stopped. His mouth was moving, but I only heard every third word: "You got ten minutes to shit, shower, and shave and form up in front of the barracks. If you're one second late, I'll have your ass." He was close enough for me to smell his foul breath, and that, mixed with the rotten taste in my mouth, made me almost barf in his face.

I walked over to the latrine and almost gasped in horror: It had two rows of commodes sitting right next to each other, with a scant two feet between them—which meant that if you had to defecate, you would be doing it right next to another guy. I could not imagine that lack of privacy, not to mention the mixture of disgusting odors wafting up my nose. It's one thing to smell your own shit and quite another to digest the smells of thirty defecating recruits! At any rate, I had a thing about moving my bowels if there was anyone within a hundred feet of me, a throwback to my painful toilet training as a child. What the hell was I going to do, not shit for two or three days? I took my shower, shaved quickly, ran back to my bunk and locker, and put on my fatigues, which were the uniform of the day. I got into formation just as the corporal was blowing his whistle. We marched to the next orientation.

There was still a lot of processing in to do. We took a whole battery of written tests to determine our intellectual state and IQ, which I guess would decide our future assignments, and we had lecture orientations on what was expected of us as soldiers in the United States Army. We were reminded of the Uniform Code of Military Justice, which is quite different from civilian justice. At our induction in L.A. we had been sworn in, and that code had been read to us. In the military you are guilty until proven innocent, which is the opposite of civilian law. We were also told that we would be issued a rifle upon our assignment to a basic-training company and that that rifle was the most important part of our uniform. Even if one became a cook or a clerk-typist, everyone was a rifleman in the army, and if an emergency arose, even cooks were expected on the line, ready to kill the enemy.

By then we were close to the end of our second day of processing, and I really had to go to the toilet. It had been thirty-six or more hours since I had moved my bowels, and I was approaching the danger point of not being able to hold it any longer. Fortunately, we were marched to the mess hall, and I was able to sneak away to find some place where I could have privacy. I passed a building that had a sign saying Officers' Lounge. Aha, I thought, there must be a toilet in there, and I'm sure they would not make the officers shit together. I walked in with an air of purpose, grabbed a cloth napkin on a nearby table, and started to dust whatever furniture existed on my path to the toilet. I found it, quickly jumped into one of the private stalls, and relieved myself. I had never known before the pure pleasure of defecating! It was a completely new experience, akin to having a gourmet meal. I rejoined my group in the mess hall and ate hardily, even though the meal was "shit on a shingle," an army description of thick sliced beef on bread covered with gravy.

Again it had been a long day of orientation, and I fell asleep quickly; however, this time I had dreams and nightmares all night: I was being chased by sergeants and running through thick underbrush, being shot at and narrowly escaping death. One nightmare followed another, and they got worse as they progressed. In the morning, I awoke exhausted, feeling as though I hadn't slept at all. This was our third day, and the major processing was over; however, we had to wait for our assignments. In the army a new recruit must do something, so some of the men were chosen to police the area, which meant that they were to go all over picking up papers and other debris, while I, unfortunately, was assigned KP (Kitchen Police) duty. I reported to the officers' mess, was provided with a white apron, and told to wash the pots. It was a sweaty, dirty job, and I hated it. When I was finished, the cook sergeant told me to stack plates out in the dining room. This is when the episode I referred to in the first chapter took place: Near the table I was working at, I saw my old childhood friend Burton Altman, now a second lieutenant. "Hey, Burt," I called. He looked over at me, and I could see he recognized me. "It's me, Fred!" I insisted. Without saying a word, he turned and quickly walked away, as if he had just come too close to a leper. I stood there with a stack of dishes in my hand, just watching his hasty getaway. I had never been so hurt or humiliated in my life, but I got it! He was an officer, and I was a lowly private on kitchen duty. It's funny how things stay with you, though. Even after fifty-one years I would love to meet him and confront him. Silly, huh?

Towards the end of the day, we were moved up to the new barracks to start our first eight weeks of basic training. Those barracks were quite a departure from where we had been: brick buildings three stories high, with block walls cleanly painted in a light green color accented with darker green borders. They even had toilets with separate stalls and doors that closed. Still, they were Spartan and institutional. I was assigned to Fox Company of the Sixty-third Infantry Regiment. A company is made up of about three hundred men, a number of companies make up a battalion, and several battalions make up a regiment. Each company is divided into platoons, and each of those platoons is assigned to a platoon room. There are six platoon rooms per building, each housing fifty men. I was on the top floor to the left of the stairway and was assigned to the last bunk next to the far wall of the platoon room. This time I had the bottom bunk and an open space between me and the wall, which was to my liking. I wasn't hemmed in by bunks on both sides. There were offices and administrative areas on the first floor, as well as a complete supply room in the basement. The first sergeant, as well as the cadre, had private quarters. Each platoon was assigned a leader, usually selected from the older retreads in the platoon. A retread is someone who was in the service before, has re-enlisted, but has to go through basic again. Our platoon leader, a thirtyish, balding man, was gay—a fact I was perhaps the only perceptive one to pick up on. He often jumped on top of guys in their bunks, pretending to wrestle them like some guy thing. He stayed away from me, though. I guess he saw my awareness of him.

On the first day, we were issued our rifles and warned never to forget their serial number. We had a standing locker and a footlocker, where we kept our toiletries and uniforms. Leaning against the wall by my bunk, I looked around the room, taking in all of my platoon mates, with whom I would be spending the next eight weeks. It was very depressing! Most of those guys had enlisted in the army, possibly as a career. Only about a third were draftees. Most of them were young, anywhere from nineteen to twenty-three, and none too swift in the head department. At the beginning I thought the English language had deserted us. It was "fuckin' " this and "motherfucking" that, "cocksucking motherfuckers," "fuckwads," and so on. I heard profanities I had never heard before—and I thought I had heard it all. It was as if those guys couldn't speak any language that didn't contain "fuck" or "fucking" in every single sentence. This kind of exchange went on in the platoon room for a couple of weeks before I began to pick up on the variations of meaning. For example, "motherfucker" could be an expression of delight rather than an attack, and "fuckin' " this or that could mean a variety of things, based on the vocal inflections; so after a while I started listening to those inflections to determine whether they denoted a good thing or an angry response. Fortunately, John Vose, the guy in the bunk above me, and Karl Takazawa, who slept in the bottom bunk to my right, were great guys, both college graduates and very bright. The three of us shared the same opinions about our neighbors.

Each day was ten hours long, and the training was rigorous. We awoke at 5:00 A.M., showered, shaved, dressed, and bolted down three flights of stairs, screaming at the top of our voices, as if attacking the enemy. We were instructed to do this every time we ran anywhere. The logic was that the sound would frighten the enemy and make them turn and run. It was an interesting concept, but I don't think it ever worked in a war! We marched, hiked, ran, almost always with a full fifty-pound backpack on our backs. We attended classes on how to disassemble our rifles, aim them, use the sling in proper ways, and shoot in various positions. Fort Ord has tens of thousands of acres. It is a vast expanse of land that contains shooting ranges, obstacle courses, athletic fields, a small airstrip, and hundreds of buildings. A small hike could be ten miles long. At the end of each day, we fell into our bunks, totally exhausted. It seemed to me that this would never end. I kept remembering what that guy at my going away party had said to me, that he wouldn't take a million dollars to go back into the army but that he wouldn't take two million for the experience. It kept bouncing around in my head. For my part if I had had a million, I would gladly have given it to them to let me go home.

Our drill sergeant was Sergeant Carey, a tall black man who seemed very physically fit and truly enjoyed his job. When we went on marches, he would lead us in cadence songs, to which his marching gate would respond, and he would inject a little of his own marching style as he walked. One of the songs went something like this: "You had a girl home when you left." On the word "left" we were supposed to be in sync with our left foot. "You're right." At that point we had to lead with our right foot. "You had a girl home when you left. Jody was there when you left. You're right. Jody was there when you left. You're right." Then he would call out cadence count: "One, two, three, four, one-two…three-four." I really tried to keep up with everyone but got so exhausted carrying that fifty-pound pack that I would drop back and stagger into the barracks ten or fifteen minutes behind everyone else. Sergeant Carey was on my case and would berate me in front of the platoon. I didn't like being in the army, I was there against my will, and I made no attempt to hide the way I felt. Because of my attitude and my inability to keep up with the rest of the men, particularly on long marches, I got a lot of shit from some of them. I even received company punishment a couple of times. I had to sweep the stairs, clean the latrine, and do some other menial jobs. I didn't care much if they gave me extra work; and if it made them feel better, it was O.K. with me.

Whenever my depression overtook me, I would call Jean in L.A. She was sweet and very supportive and would encourage me. It was clear, though, that she didn't have a clue how tough it really was. I felt very alone. We were given weekend passes about every second week. Everyone took off for Monterey, the closest city, a place rich in history, at one time the capital of California. It was filled with restaurants, bars, movie theaters, a Fisherman's Wharf, and a lot of things that a young soldier can find to do. Jean came up on one of my passes, and we checked into the San Carlos Hotel. I hadn't seen her in over a month, and when I did, I trembled with love and romantic anxiety. She was beautiful! I stood there drinking in every part of her. She had hazel eyes, long chestnut brown hair, which hit her shoulders and draped slightly down her back, and white skin with naturally rosy cheeks. Her mouth was perfect, and when she smiled, it wrinkled at the corners. She had a wonderful figure with all the curves exactly in the right places. At that time she could have been Janet Leigh's sister. The resemblance was incredible! I remember cutting out the pictures of Janet Leigh that looked the most like Jean. Making love to her was overwhelming. I couldn't seem to get enough of her. It was some of the best connections we had ever had. Being with her that weekend was like returning to the real world. I had really missed her, and the warmth of her body next to mine was reassurance that there was a future for us after the army. We went to dinner at a restaurant that was very romantic, with candlelight and red wine, then went back to the hotel and made love for most of the night. After breakfast the next morning, we walked along the ocean and then went back to bed. After lunch we also went back to bed. It was like a fantasy weekend. Going back to the unit was very hard, and the next day even harder. It seemed as though the weekend had been a beautiful dream that had never happened.

On one of our scheduled weekends off, our platoon lost their weekend passes because of me. In an inspection the inspecting sergeant found that one of the buttons on one of my shirts in the locker was not buttoned. He lifted our pass privilege and made sure everyone in the platoon knew it was because of me. That certainly didn't endear me to the guys, who already regarded me as an "intellectual fuckup." Our gay platoon leader took every opportunity to put me down after that. At one point during the eight weeks, someone planted Zade Green's wallet at the bottom of my duffle bag and made sure that Zade would look for it there. That could have been a serious problem for me. The army hates thieves and usually prosecutes them and sends them to the stockade. I hadn't taken Zade's wallet, and I told him so. Zade was in his middle to late thirties, a retread and a genuinely nice man. I think he believed me and didn't pursue it. Later we were partners on the rifle range.

Fortunately for me, bivouac was a different story. I had learned a lot about camping in the Boy Scouts, which paid off in the wild. I knew how to pitch a pup tent, make fires, and create comfortable sleeping arrangements, and I enjoyed the departure from other military activities. It didn't affect my reputation in the platoon though. I was still regarded as a fuckup and a lousy soldier; however, there were several guys who liked me and regarded my war with the army with humor. I am sure that they felt the same way about being drafted, but somehow they did what they had to do to survive the experience. It wasn't that I was a rebel or even wanted to be. I really tried to do everything I was asked, but never having been very athletic or coordinated, I just couldn't do the physical things. I couldn't hike ten miles with a fifty-pound pack on my back, and when I approached exhaustion, I couldn't keep up with the group. I did, however, make a game out of certain things. On the bayonet course, where we were bayoneting straw dummies, I had a little fun burlesquing it. I would run up on a dummy, stop, stick my bayonet into the straw, and in a very fey way say, "Take that, you dummy!" John and Karl, who were right behind me, broke up, almost dropping their rifles.

There were things that bordered on the dangerous and were uncomfortable. We had to crawl under barbed wire while a .30-caliber machine gun fired live rounds ten or eleven inches over our heads. At the same time, there were demolition pits all over the course, which would be set off at intervals. If you happened to be near one, it deafened you for a couple of hours. Then there was the gashouse. We were supposedly being trained to use gas masks, so they took a group of us into this corrugated building and instructed us on how to put a gas mask on, clear it, and walk in a circle while they exploded canisters of teargas, filling the room so full that we could not see the man in front of us. At a certain point during the exercise, we were instructed by the corporal to remove our masks, and we did. The pain was unbelievable! Tears ran down my face, as if a faucet had been turned on in my eyes. My skin, nose, lips, and lungs were on fire. We walked around in that circle for about a minute before they released us from the building. There were guys lying on the ground coughing, vomiting, and gasping for air. I was pissed! I started yelling, "What the fuck was that for? What were we supposed to learn from teargas?" My lungs felt as though someone had put them in an oven at high temperature. I was really angry. One of the noncoms in charge of the exercise approached me and aggressively asked me if I had a problem. We stood looking at each other for a couple of minutes, and in my moment of rational judgment I responded, "No, corporal, I don't have a problem. I just think that exercise was cruel and inhuman—and what were we supposed to get from it?" He didn't reply. He just turned and walked away.

Of all the things that a soldier is supposed to learn in basic training, firing and caring for his rifle are the most important. Marksmanship is at the highest level of priority. Before we were taken to the range, we had a whole week of classes and demonstrations about the rifle, a Garand .30-caliber semiautomatic rifle, with a clip of eight rounds, which weighed nine and a half pounds but on a ten-mile march, slung over the shoulder, felt like *ninety* and a half pounds! General Patton had been quoted as saying, "The Garand rifle is the greatest battle implement ever devised." We were taught to fire it in a number of different positions—prone, sitting, standing, and kneeling—and instructed on how to use the sling as a way of steadying the rifle. I found it extremely interesting because of my fascination with guns and shooting. In fact, it was the best part of basic. We hadn't fired the rifle at that point. That was reserved for the range, which we were about to spend five days on.

The morning before the first day, we assembled in front of the barracks, ready to take the march to the range, which on the other side of the highway faced the ocean in an area restricted to any kind of boat traffic. Sergeant Carey paced up and back in front of the platoon, giving us a lecture on how important it was to be a marksman. "In battle you want to be in a foxhole with a man who can shoot," he said, "because that man might just save your ass. No one in this platoon is not going to qualify on that range. Is that clear?"

Qualification means that you have hit a certain number of targets somewhere inside the target circle to get enough points. There is no marksmanship medal that comes with qualification, but there are three marksmanship medals a soldier can earn: the Marksman Medal, a two-inch black cross with the name of the weapon hanging from its bottom; the Sharpshooter Medal, the same black cross with a rendering of a target in the middle; and the Expert Medal, a smaller cross with a target in the middle surrounded by palm leaves. Each medal has its category imprinted on it. To get each one you must attain progressively higher scores by hitting the bull's-eye more and more times.

We stood in the hot sun, sweating and anxious to go, but the sergeant continued his lecture: "I mean no one—repeat no one—will not qualify!" He looked directly at me as he walked over to within a foot of my face. "Not even you, private Stein!" He spit those words into my face with an obvious threat behind each one of them. I didn't say anything. I just stood there with absolutely no expression. The smile I felt rising up inside of me filled my body. If there was anything in the world I could do, it was shooting. I had been shooting a rifle since I was seven years old, albeit it was a BB gun, but the principles are the same.

On each of those five days, we spent about eight hours on the range, shooting at targets that ranged in distance from two hundred to a thousand yards. That is a lot of shooting! Many of the men ended up with black eyes and M1 thumbs. When inserting a clip into the rifle, you must quickly release the slide, which springs closed and cycles a round into the barrel. If your thumb gets in the way, or if you are not fast enough to get clear, the slide mashes your thumb between the barrel and the rear of the slide, causing a painful injury and a big swollen thumb, called an M1 thumb. A black eye is caused when you extend your thumb upward instead of around the stock of the rifle. The kick from firing off a round is quite substantial and propels your thumb right into your eye. After a couple of days of shooting, our barracks was filled with M1 thumbs and quite an assortment of black eyes, but I had avoided any injuries.

We fired at the targets from all shooting positions in slow and rapid fire. When you miss the target altogether, a red flag, referred to as "Maggie's drawers," is hoisted by the target tenders. They wave it back and forth, and everyone in your immediate area is aware that you missed. Sometimes, if the man next to you isn't busy shooting at that moment, he will make an oohing sound, calling further attention to your not hitting the target. I never got a Maggie's drawers. Zade Green, my shooting partner, was grateful to me for giving him some pointers that raised his score. When we were finished on the range, we went on to other shooting exercises. We practiced on a course where men targets pop up, which you have to shoot within a certain time frame; otherwise, they are supposed to have killed you. I did well on that exercise too, even though I had trouble with a jamming rifle. We also threw live hand grenades and fired 3.8 rocket launchers at old junk cars that were supposed to represent enemy tanks. I fired two rockets and had a direct hit both times.

As memory serves, I think we were just beginning our sixth week of training, and I was sitting on my bunk polishing my boots, when one of the platoon guys ran in and shouted, "Stein, Sergeant Carey wants to see you in his quarters right now." My first response was, I didn't do anything. I must admit I was scared. One of the byproducts of the training was to instill fear and respect in all of the trainees. They had succeeded in scaring me, but I didn't respect any of the noncoms, with the exception of Sergeant Carey, whom I liked and respected for his commitment to soldiering. I bolted down all three flights to the first floor. Never having been to Sergeant Carey's quarters, I had to locate them first. Halfway down the corridor I saw his name on a door. I stood there for about five minutes before knocking gently. When I heard, "Come in," I opened the door meekly and stepped inside. It was the first time I had seen the sergeant without the blue helmet liner on his head. He looked different. He had pitch black, wavy hair, which was longer than I had expected, and he seemed taller, thinner, and better looking than outside in the field. "Sit down, Stein!" he said. I tried to read the expression in his eyes but couldn't. I took a seat and was very still. Nothing was said for what seemed an eternity. He paced back and forth and at times circled my chair. It was a small room, so he was never too far away from me.

Finally, he bent down directly in front of me, put his face right next to mine, no further than five inches, and said, "Where does a fuckup like you learn to shoot like that?"

His question surprised me. For a moment I was speechless. When I recovered, I blurted without thinking, “Well, Sergeant, you see, I love to shoot. I just hate the army!”

He stood upright, looked at me, and with a mixture of anger and respect said, “Get the fuck out of here!”—which I did.

As it turned out, my score on the range was among the highest in the whole company of three hundred men. I guess I had earned the name Buffalo Bill those kids on Fillmore Street had called me many years back. I think I had also earned Sergeant Carey’s respect, because he never singled me out again or made any negative remarks about me.

I had three weeks left of basic when I came down with a terrible strep-throat infection. I had a high fever and a really bad sore throat. I could have gone to sickbay, but I was afraid the doctor would put me in the hospital, which meant that I would have been recycled to another company to repeat the week or weeks that I had lost. The prospect of being in basic training for ten or eleven weeks and of being transferred to another company where I didn’t know a single person was totally unacceptable to me. I thought that I would rather die of a strep infection than face that alternative, but what was I to do? I certainly couldn’t go out with the company on some field exercise, and I wasn’t going to report to sickbay. I approached our platoon leader, fully expecting no help, and I was pleasantly surprised at his response. He was understanding and told me he would talk to Sergeant Carey. Everything in the service operates on the chain of command. In order to speak with the company commander, for instance, you have to first go to your platoon leader; he in turn goes to the platoon sergeant, who goes to the first sergeant of the company, who in turn goes to the company commander with your request. My platoon leader came back to me within the hour and said that Sergeant Carey would allow me to stay in the barracks for the next day. I was more than a little surprised by his response but also extremely grateful. After twenty-four hours in the barracks I was almost fully recovered and ready to report for duty.

The next day, while in formation in front of our barracks, as Sergeant Carey was passing me in line, I muttered, “Thank you, Sergeant.”

He looked at me and smiled, "It's O.K. Even expert marksmen get sick once in a while." I guess he never knew how much that comment meant to me.

We were finally at the end of the first eight weeks of basic training. It was the last day, and we were instructed that the uniform of the day was to be our class-A dress uniform, which I don't think I had ever worn yet, since on weekend passes I wore civilian clothes. We were to fall in at a certain hour to receive our shooting and good-conduct medals and some special ribbon awarded to all U.S. soldiers from the president of Korea. In addition, we would be receiving our assignments for the second eight weeks of training. I was terrified that I would have to do a second eight weeks of infantry basic at Camp Hunter Liggett, which had the reputation of being a hellhole. I knew that I had a B profile because of the knee I had injured while in high school, and I thought that it would surely disqualify me from being an infantry rifleman. I also had a college degree. Why wouldn't the army take advantage of that? I shuddered at the thought of being a grunt. The moment arrived, as it always does, and we were handed a manila envelope containing our new assignment, report date, and transportation information. We were told to fall out, and we went to the day room in the barracks. John and Karl descended on me from two sides.

"So, what did you get?" They spoke in unison.

"I haven't opened it yet. I'm too afraid to see what's inside."

John grabbed the envelope from me and said, "I'll open it, damn it!"

He did it ritualistically, making sure that he elevated the suspense. He removed the papers and read them slowly. His jaw dropped; his face became grave; he looked at me and back at the paper, milking every moment: "I am sorry, Fred, I guess you'll have to go get your rifle." My stomach dropped to the floor. I was numb, without the ability to feel anything, when he started to laugh. He handed me the papers, and as I read the assignment sheet, I too began to laugh. My heart leaped up into my throat, and I began to cry. I had been assigned to Fort Lee, Virginia, to study to become a clerk and to undergo quartermaster training. I thought, Eight weeks of being civilized, properly dressed—and no more learning how to kill people! John, Karl, and I promised to stay in touch, but of course we never did. It is really sad how many people come in and out of our lives over the years.

Before I had to report to Fort Lee, I had two weeks furlough, almost two weeks in Los Angeles with Jean, my family and friends. Coming back to L.A. was like getting a massive B12 shot. Even though I had lived here for only three months, I felt it was home. I didn't know what to do first. I was like a kid in a candy store wanting to taste all of it right away. Jean and I decided to get married. We found a little jewelry store, bought his-and-hers wedding bands, went downtown, took our blood tests, and applied for a marriage license. We were married by a judge in a little chapel in Hollywood—actually called the Hollywood Wedding Chapel—with Lee and his girlfriend, Pat, as our witnesses. Pat took pictures of Jean and me but lost the camera on top of a mountain she and Lee climbed later that day. After the ceremony, we visited my folks—my father, my mother, and my sister Ida—but got a very cold reception from them. Jean was not Jewish, and that was a big thing for them. I felt embarrassed and hurt by their response and left very quickly. I apologized to Jean for the way they had acted, and she was very gracious about the whole thing. Dressed in my summer khakis and wearing my medals of course, I visited the gang at the Players' Ring Theatre and got a great reception from everyone. They were truly happy to see me and made a big fuss over me, so big that one of the actors in the new play they were doing came backstage, looked around, stared at me, and said, "Who's this, Audie Murphy?" and then walked away grumbling to himself.

After the furlough, the army flew us to Virginia. There was a whole group of us going to Fort Lee. A couple of days later, Jean joined me, so I applied for separate rations and an allotment for her. We rented an upstairs room in an old Southern house in Petersburg, Virginia, which was about fifteen miles from Fort Lee and reachable by bus. I don't remember how we found the place, but it was fine for our eight-week stay. Mrs. Yancy, the owner of the house, was a very sweet overweight lady with a thick Southern accent, who had probably been living there her whole life. Jean got an office job in Richmond, which is about fifteen miles from Petersburg, and secured a ride from a woman who worked in the same office and also lived in Petersburg. I hopped a bus to the fort every morning at about 7:30 and was ready for my classes at 8:00 A.M.

This was a different army. No one was yelling, barking orders, or insulting me. We were treated with courtesy and respect. It was very much like being back in school. I had typing classes and inventory classes, learned about army issue, memorized codes and numbers, was taught how to check out equipment, and so on. We went from one class to another, had time off for lunch, took breaks during the day, and at 5:00 P.M. went home. It seemed more like a real job. Jean and I had an evening life. We made some friends and went out to dinner and the movies. We had weekends off, so we took in some of the sights. I had never been in the South before, so I had some prejudices and prejudgments that were quickly dispelled. The environment was green and lush, and the people couldn't have been nicer.

My time at Fort Lee was so uneventful that I really don't remember much about it. As we drew closer to the end of the training, I had a new worry to deal with: Would they send me overseas? While that would have been appealing to some, it wasn't to me. I wanted to stay in the States and serve out my time as close to L.A. as possible. Happily, I got my wish. I was being sent back to Fort Ord, incredibly to the Sixty-third Infantry Regiment, as a supply clerk in King Company, a basic-training company. I could live off post with Jean and come home from work every evening. Jean and I were both delighted at the assignment. I went back to Fort Ord, while Jean returned to L.A. to give me time to settle in and find a place for us to live in.

I was working in the basement of the new barracks, two buildings down from where I had taken basic. My immediate superior was Sergeant Noble, a nice and very officious black man, from the Caribbean Islands, I think. He didn't know about my war with the army yet, but he was due to find out. Our company commander, First Lieutenant Kite, had a real rod up his ass and was a tall but slouching asshole with an acne complexion. He was all army as far as I could tell. The company first sergeant was Ramos, a Puerto Rican with quite a dark complexion and oily, slicked-down black hair, who was doing his twenty or thirty years. The company clerk was a full-blooded Navaho Indian, whose name I can't recall. I wore pressed fatigues and a silky blue neck scarf signifying infantry. At this point I was an E2, which is the automatic rank after you finish your sixteen weeks of training. Recruits are E1s.

I did my job, which was to hand out rifles to the new recruits, log the serial numbers, and give them blankets and other supplies as needed for their training. On weekends I hunted for a place for Jean and me. I found a nice one-bedroom in Pacific Grove, between

Monterey and Carmel, in the Summerhill Apartments, a long, green, one-story building with about five apartments in a row next to each other. We had the front one facing the street. The following weekend I picked up Jean in San Francisco, and we drove back to Pacific Grove. I didn't have a car yet, so one of the recruits had offered to let me borrow his older MG. I regretted having sold my Catalina to Morrey, since I really needed a car now. Jean liked the apartment, and we settled in. She got a job in the finance office at the fort, and we were able to meet for lunch a couple of times a week.

The days passed slowly. I wasn't excited about spending the next twenty months in that airless basement. While the experience was quite different from basic training, I was still in a place where I didn't want to be, doing work that was boring and unchallenging. I went home to Jean every evening, had dinner, watched a little television, and went to bed. I made up a little three-by-five card with small squares indicating all the days until my discharge, and each night upon returning home, even before I washed up for dinner, I would draw a line through another day. The card hung next to the kitchen, so I could see it from almost any point in the apartment, except the bedroom. Jean regarded my obsession with a mixture of humor and sadness. Even at those times when we were both tired after a long day, we made love. It seemed like an interlude away from thinking about the army. For however long our lovemaking lasted, it seemed like a transformational state away from reality. I escaped into her body and her eyes and often held on to her tightly all night. I loved the way she smelled, and often while I was buried in that supply room, I would get a sense of her odors and would smile. I wonder what Sergeant Noble thought at those moments, because I would sometimes catch him staring at me.

It was difficult getting to the fort by bus. The busses seldom ran on time, so I was late repeatedly, which frustrated Sergeant Noble. I needed a car. On a used-car lot, I spotted a lovely 1950 Chevy convertible, which I really liked. I had never owned a convertible and had always wanted one. All the Hollywood movies I had grown up watching were filled with actors riding along the California coast with the top down and their hair blowing in the wind. That image had branded itself in my mind, and I knew that someday I would be in California and have a convertible. Jean and I looked at the Chevy, but it cost a thousand dollars, which was more than we could afford. In order to get financing one had to be an E5, a sergeant. E2 privates did not qualify, so we had to pass on the Chevy; however, at a dealer in Monterey, we found a 1951 yellow Studebaker convertible that cost seven hundred dollars and seemed in pretty good condition, so we bought it. It was our second choice, but at least we were able to scrape up the seven hundred.

I drove to the fort every morning with the top down, no matter what the weather was like. Sergeant Noble was pleased that I arrived on time. My hair had grown back as blond and wavy as ever, and he was always on my back to get a haircut. "You look like a girl!" he repeated. Of course that wasn't true, but it was army consciousness. I had always been pretty independent, but now everybody with a stripe on his sleeve was telling me what to do—something I had never liked. I was a private in the army and could easily be punished for insubordination, so I developed a passive-aggressive behavior that couldn't be interpreted as insubordination. I was a hell of a lot smarter than the people who surrounded me, so I used my intelligence and perception to manipulate my superiors—and I use that word with great qualification. Suppose Sergeant Noble told me to stack a bunch of blankets in a certain way. I might say, "Of course, you know what is the best way, Sergeant, but don't you think that if I put them here in this way, it would avoid doing it twice?" There was a silent "asshole" at the end of each sentence, but because I had complimented him on his vast experience, Noble would almost always accept my suggestions. One day, however, I really pissed him off. I don't remember exactly what I had done, but he was very angry with me.

"I'm going upstairs to tell Sergeant Ramos to block your promotion," he said.

I was sitting at the typewriter filling out some bullshit form. I stopped typing, looked up at him, and said, "Oh, please, Sergeant, would you do that? I don't need the responsibility."

He became bright red, his nostrils flared, and his eyes opened wide enough for me to see the whites above and below his pupils. He turned and stormed out of the supply room. I was in line to become a private first class, an E3, but I didn't give a shit about the stripe. The only PFC I wanted to be was a poor foolish civilian, and they were not about to give me that one. Noble did block the promotion. It was several more months before I got that lonely stripe.

On one occasion, while on a trip to the first sergeant's office, I passed Lieutenant Kite screaming at a frightened recruit, "I'm your commanding officer. You don't ask me where the mailroom is!" His voice was so loud and angry it could be heard all through the first floor. As I passed him, I thought, What a complete asshole! Wouldn't it have been simpler to tell that poor recruit where the mailroom was? I never found out whether Lieutenant Kite was regular army, a reserve officer, or what. I did know, however, that he had found his calling.

On September 30, 1955, a beautiful afternoon on the peninsula, I was on my way home from the fort. The top was down on my yellow Studebaker, and the wind was blowing my hair across my forehead, which felt wonderful, since my hair had been short for so long that there had been nothing there to dance in the wind! I was listening to "The American Airlines Classical Hour," when they interrupted the program to announce that James Dean had been killed in his Porsche race car on the way to the Laguna Seca Raceway. I wasn't sure at first that I had heard exactly what they had said, or I couldn't believe it, so I started hunting for a news station, but it was, in fact, all over the news that he had been killed on Highway 46. At that moment I was about a hundred miles from where it had happened. I was shocked! Although I had never met him, I really liked his work, and I felt very sad hearing about his death.

When I got home, I broke the news to Jean, who was also shocked and saddened by it. We talked about it for the rest of the evening, feeling very fortunate that we were alive and healthy. It is unusual for a twenty-four-year-old to think about mortality, but Dean's untimely death was a very impacting and sobering experience. After all, he and I had been born in the same year.

All that time I had really missed acting. I hadn't even thought about it through the ordeal of basic training, but I was now hungry to be in a play somewhere—anywhere. After checking the local newspapers, I spotted an ad for a play that was being done at the Wharf Theatre in Monterey, so I went down to check it out. The theater was on Fisherman's Wharf, jutting out over the water, so that when you went out the door backstage, you were on a small deck right above the ocean. It held about a hundred seats and was a very well-appointed plant. Tom and Bob, who were lovers and had somehow got the job of running it, kept it spotless and were very conscientious about keeping it up. I think it was owned by someone else, possibly a couple of people. I introduced myself to Tom and Bob, told them about my background, and asked if I could audition for their next production. They seemed impressed with me and invited me down to see the current play. I don't remember what it was, but I thought the work was on a professional level, especially for a community theater. Ruth Warshawsky had the lead, and I thought that she was very good. I introduced myself to her, and we became great friends. Our friendship lasted for years after that.

Ruth was married to an artist many years her senior, Abel G. Warshawsky, nicknamed "Buck"—which is what everybody called him. They lived in Monterey, in a large house with a huge skylight that illuminated the area where Buck did his paintings. He was in his middle fifties and had a shock of black hair sprinkled with gray, which seemed to have a mind of its own. He would often run his hands through it with an admonishing attitude, as if saying, Lie down and behave! He suffered from crippling arthritis, which affected the lower part of his body, causing a pronounced limp. He was a great artist and had been awarded the French Legion of Honor for his paintings, which hung in almost every major museum in Europe and the United States. Ruth was in her early thirties, very much an actress in personality and behavior. Their relationship seemed one of convenience and not romantic in nature. They both took a strong liking to me and often invited me to their home.

After making contact with the people at the Wharf, I felt more hopeful about the future. I shared my feelings about the theater with Jean, who was also interested in doing something there. My attitude became different in the supply room. It wasn't that I liked being there any more than I had, but now I had something to look forward to. I auditioned for *The Caine Mutiny Court-Martial* and got the part of Doctor Bird, a navy psychiatrist with the rank of lieutenant, a pompous and articulate character, who was called to testify against Captain Queeg at his court-martial. It was a nice little part with a very good scene. A second lieutenant in the army played Queeg's defense attorney, while Mike Monahan was the young ensign. Mike had called Carmel his home for all of his growing-up years. He had recently been discharged from the navy and had returned to the peninsula. While in the navy, he had continued to pursue his love for acting, doing some theater at the Globe in San

Diego. We became friends and continued our relationship long after both of us went to Los Angeles.

Curtain time was 8:00 P.M., but my character appeared at about 8:45, which I thought would give me plenty of time to leave the supply room and either get home or go directly to the theater. The play was due to run for five or six weeks. For the first few weeks I had no trouble getting there, but around the fourth week of the run, Sergeant Ramos summoned me to his office to say that the entire company had gone on bivouac and that he wanted me to find six three-foot chains and six padlocks to lock the platoon rooms. It was about 7:45, and I had been rushing to get out of the supply room. I had an hour before I had to make my entrance, and the theater was about twenty minutes away. I felt panicked. I couldn't tell Ramos I was in a play in Monterey, and I had no other excuse I could come up with, so I left his office and went to a couple of the other companies' supply rooms but had no luck. Realizing that it was already 8:15 by then, I jumped into my car and headed for the Wharf. I ran down Fisherman's Wharf in my fatigues to get to the theater and burst in backstage as they were contemplating how to get around not doing my scene. I quickly changed into my navy uniform and, just as I finished tying my tie, heard my entrance cue. Filled with the attitude and arrogance of the character, I sauntered out onto the stage, sat in the witness chair, and gave the best performance I had given so far in that play! I didn't stay for the curtain call, since I was very anxious to get back to Sergeant Ramos. It was a little after ten when I got to the barracks. I took a moment to prepare for my next performance and then entered the office. Sergeant Ramos was still behind his desk working. Breathing hard and having created real perspiration, I blurted, "Sergeant Ramos, I've been all over the fort, and nobody has chains or locks." I continued to act exhausted, hoping to play on his sympathy. It worked! He looked up at me, smiled, and in his best Puerto Rican accent said it was "O.K."

"Go home. I see you in the morning," he added.

"You know, Sergeant Ramos, I could go to a hardware store in Monterey tomorrow and get the locks and chains." He smiled and assured me that I had done the best I could and that we would deal with the problem later.

The theater became my haven away from the army. I felt that I was part of a company. I made a lot of new friends and looked forward to the weekends. When the play ended, I felt a little empty, as most actors do at the end of a play or film. I had now been in the service for 184 days, and I was still crossing off squares on my three-by-five card every night. One day, Sergeant Noble was transferred somewhere else and replaced by a corporal who was serving time just like me. Things got mellower in the supply room. We smoked and sat around telling jokes and making fun of the "gung-ho assholes." I was bored and hoped that something would come along and get me out of that damned basement.

I think God was listening to my prayers, because the very next day I was sent to regimental headquarters, to the motor pool in the basement of the building. There, at a desk surrounded by acres of unoccupied cement floors, sat Master Sergeant Calvano, a short, very Italian-looking man, with a large nose and coarse features. His shirt was unbuttoned at the collar, and he was reading a mystery novel.

He looked up at me and said, "So what can I do for you, Ace?"

"Well, Sergeant, King Company needs a half-ton to transport some stuff to one of the ranges."

"I don't have a half-ton. How about a two-ton?"

"O.K. It's a truck, isn't it?"

"Yeah, it's a truck. Sit down, Ace, take a load off. What do you do at King Company?"

"I work in supply."

"Yeah? I did that shit once a long time ago. Boring, huh?"

"You can say that again!"

"O.K. Boring, huh?"

I laughed, and he laughed, and I immediately knew that he was a different kind of army sergeant. He continued to speak. I knew that he was hungry for someone to talk to.

"I spend twelve hours a day in this dungeon, running the motor pool for the whole regiment. I work from six in the morning to six at night. I brownbag it because I can't even go to the mess hall for chow, and I have no help here, just me and my desk and my mystery stories."

It wasn't as if he were whining or complaining. It was a statement of fact, and that's how he expressed it.

He went on: "Say, how would you like to get out of that supply room?"

"Are you kidding?"

"No, I could get you assigned to me TDY (temporary duty)."

"You could really do that?"

"Yeah, if you want to. I'll go upstairs talk to Major Boren, and I'll have you here tomorrow."

I was really taken aback. I didn't know how to feel. "O.K., Sergeant," I said, "if you can do it, go ahead. I would give anything to get out of that place."

"You know you'd only be working six hours a day, from six in the morning to twelve noon or twelve noon to six in the evening. We'd split the shifts."

Wow, I thought, this is too good to be true. I left and went back to the supply room with a smile in my stomach. I still didn't believe it, but it was a possibility, and that opened a door to hope. At about three in the afternoon "Chief Sitting Bull" came down to the supply room and told me that Lieutenant Kite wanted to see me in his office. I don't know what I thought. I walked a large circle around "General Custer" and stayed away from him as much as I could. The fact that he wanted to see me in his office could mean anything. I straightened my uniform, put some water on my hair to mat it down a little, and went up to his office. I knocked and heard "Come in." He was sitting behind his desk, arms folded, with a scowl on his face.

"Sit down!" he barked.

"Yes, sir."

"I don't know how you did it, Private, and you can bet I'm going to find out, but Major Boren at regiment assigned you to the regimental motor pool. God damn it, where am I going to get a replacement for you?"

"I don't know, sir, but orders are orders."

He looked at me with disgust oozing out of every pore on his pockmarked face. He didn't say anything, but I knew that he knew I had fucked him. The thrill for me was that the son of a bitch couldn't do anything about it.

The next morning I was sitting at the desk with Sergeant Calvano, who was teaching me how to run the motor pool. I was still in a basement, but the environment, the job, and the hours were a thousand percent better. If I worked the noon-to-six shift, I still had plenty of time to audition or do a play. The motor pool always shut down at 6:00 P.M. on the button—no late hours or last-minute assignments. Sergeant Calvano was a prince. He was easygoing, had a great sense of humor, and never pulled rank. It was as if we were equals in rank. He called me Fred, and I referred to him as Sarge. This new job endowed me with incredible power. I was still an E2, and I was running the whole show. Nothing moved in or out of the regiment except through Sergeant Calvano or me. Every first sergeant or company commander had to come to me if it was my shift. They only got what I would give them, and if they gave me any shit, I would call up to Major Boren and with a humble act tell him how the company commander of Easy Company, for example, was abusing me. In less than fifteen minutes I would get a call from the commander of Easy Company with a full apology for his behavior. No one bothered me, and no one ever came down into that basement to talk to me. I could have been watching pornos, and no one would have ever known! Of course, the drivers of the trucks would occasionally come to me for certain instructions. Every morning our whole allotment of trucks would arrive from the central motor pool of the fort, the assigned drivers would park them in allotted spaces in the regimental parking lot, and as the orders for vehicles came in, I would dispatch them to the companies that had ordered them. When a driver finished his work for a specific company, he would report back to me. I kept tables on what was in the parking lot and spent a lot of time reading. I was infinitely happier now than in the supply room. I was able to have a better and fuller social life. Jean and I spent time with Ruth and Buck, had dinner with Sergeant Calvano and his blond, attractive wife, or hung out at the Wharf Theatre. It was recessed from the main street of the wharf, so if you didn't know it was there, you couldn't see it. Right next to it was the bar owned and run by Sonny and called "Sonny's Bar," of all things! Sonny was one of the characters who appeared in Steinbeck's *Sweet Thursday,* the companion piece to *Cannery Row.*

On my way home from the fort, I drove by all those abandoned, large, windowless boilers where the people in Cannery Row used to live. Cannery Row was still as it had been when Steinbeck had written about it, but Doc Fern and all the other people were gone. I didn't know it then, but I was in a place that was part of California history and legend. Unfortunately, it has now become a tourist site filled with T-shirt shops, malls, ice-cream parlors, and so on. The old sardine factory is now an aquarium.

Once again I auditioned at the theater, and I got the part of Danny in *Night Must Fall,* by Emlyn Williams. It was the lead in the play and the largest role I had had to date. Danny was a serial killer who preyed on older widows, well-to-do women who hired him to work in and around their house. He was young and good-looking and was able to charm his way into the favor of his victims. A cockney from a lower-class English family, deprived of a normal life and education, he had probably grown up on the streets. After establishing a trusted relationship with the various women he worked for, he would kill them, take their heads as souvenirs, and carry them around in hatboxes. I suppose that he also took their valuables before disappearing.

Fortunately, my job at the motor pool allowed me to have the time to rehearse and do the play. At that point, my knowledge of a process of acting was as limited as it had ever been; however, there were a lot of available realities in my life that I could use and translate as choices for the character: I hated the army, I felt trapped and helpless to do anything about it, I had a lot of resentments against the people I dealt with on a daily basis and fantasies about taking revenge on them, and I envied people who were free and doing what they wanted to do with their lives. Similar feelings were part of what formed Danny's personality. His envy and bitterness were at the core of what drove him to kill the kinds of people he blamed for his lot in life. There were distinct parallels between his feelings and mine, the big difference being that I wasn't psychotic. I used those similarities to power my behavior as Danny. Because of the existing *available realities,* my level of truth was very high, and it was my best work up to that time. In many ways this play was a crossover experience for me. I was more honest and real in my work than I had ever been, but I wasn't quite sure I understood the reasons for the difference.

Jean had a smaller part as a housemaid. It was great to be at rehearsals together and in the same production. We had spent a lot of time at Northwestern in some of the same classes and had worked on some of the same production crews, but we had never appeared in a play together before.

Because I was doing what I loved, my job in the army was more tolerable. I was a PFC, and all the first sergeants and company commanders were kissing my ass to get what they needed. Every once in a while an officer would drop by the motor pool, sit down, and chat with me. I knew what he was doing and why, but I played along with him. I probably had more power than any private in the history of the United States Army, and I enjoyed the position.

Around the third week of the run, I invited Sergeant Calvano to see the play. He was blown away by my performance. After the show, while we were walking to our cars, he impulsively embraced me, which was embarrassing for all of us. I had never before been embraced by a master sergeant! He looked at me with great confusion and said, "What are you doing in the army? You should be in Hollywood, acting in movies."

For a moment I was speechless. Didn't he know I had been drafted? "Sarge," I reminded him, "I'm here against my will. I was drafted right out of a play I had been hired to do."

"Oh, yeah," he responded, "I knew that, but I have to tell you that I was so impressed with your acting that I really forgot for a moment."

I was on a real high all the way home. I guess that he knew me in the context of being a soldier, and even though I had told him I was an actor, he had probably never processed it until he saw me on stage.

One night after the show a very interesting looking man came backstage. He was fairly tall, bald, and had very piercing eyes. He looked at us and with outstretched arms said, "A fond embrace to all of you. What a wonderful evening in the theater!" He looked directly at me with his intense eyes, walked over to where I was standing, extended the index finger of his right hand so that it made contact with my chest, and said, "Young man, you have a great future ahead of you!" I thanked him, he shook my hand, and he left.

"Who was that guy?" I asked.

Nick Lefevre walked over to me and told me it was Henry Miller.

"The writer?"

"Yes, he lives in Big Sur."

I couldn't believe it. I had read his book *Tropic of Cancer* in college and was totally impressed with him. The next day, a messenger delivered one of his paintings on a giant postcard, which reiterated his enjoyment of the previous evening. I wish I had that original painting now.

The play ran for six weeks and was very well received by the community. Most theater companies attract a following of people who attach themselves to the theater. In this case some of those people were retired from the army and had decided to remain on the peninsula. Ruth was very popular with everyone and often had us over to her home for drinks and conversation. We sat around talking about theater, politics, and the weather in Monterey. Among the guests were Colonel Mason Wright, a retired army colonel who had taken up acting in his twilight years, and a retired general, who didn't seem interested in acting but was attracted to the people who hung around Ruth and Buck. So there I was, a private in the army, defending my position on acting with colonels and generals and feeling secure in their company. I had gained respect because of my work at the theater and because I was so damned articulate! Mason Wright was in one of the next plays. He played Caesar in *Caesar and Cleopatra.* I hoped he had been a better army colonel than he was an actor. He did, however, look the part. He was of medium height, slightly paunchy, and bald, with a gray band of hair that ran just above his ears. In his toga and with the wreath around his head, one might have believed he was Caesar.

About once a week I would drop by and visit with Buck. I was fascinated with his work. I would sit behind him and peer over his left shoulder at the canvas he was working on, while he talked about his work—how he used color and shape. He had invented a process of underpainting the skin of his subjects to create a translucent quality and add a dimensional element to the person's face. He had spent many years in France and had received many awards for his works. He took a fancy to Jean and asked to paint a portrait of her—which he did. It was a fine painting, as were all of his works, but he missed Jean's youthfulness and somehow didn't capture her attractive sexual qualities. The woman on the canvas appeared dowdy. I think that he too was somewhat disappointed in the painting. He gave it to us as a gift when I was discharged from the army.

I loved my visits with him and enjoyed listening to all of his experiences. He had been a prizefighter in his younger years, which was hard to believe when one looked at his arthritic body. His house had a great amount of wall space, but only a few of his paintings adorned it, and those that did were out of his view. To the right of where he sat to paint, there was a very large cabinet, which ran the entire length of the room and where he stored all of his finished works. I had been curious about it for some time but was reluctant to mention it to him. I finally mustered up the courage to ask him why he didn't hang some of those stored paintings on the walls. His answer has stayed with me for all these years: "I don't hang them, Fred, because I would continually see the flaws in them. I would have to take them down and work on them, which would prevent me from painting other pictures." I was very affected by that. I thought that if an artist of Buck's caliber was still reaching for perfection, not satisfied with his creations but wanting to grow, that was to me a significant statement about art and creativity. I think that my attraction to Buck was related to that creativity, which was so absent in the army. He was a haven away from uniforms, rules, and orders.

I was accustomed to just drop in on Buck without telephoning first, and he seemed O.K. with that. He was always happy to see me. On one occasion I walked into his living-room/studio smack into Bing Crosby, who was sitting in his finest golfing garb, posing for a portrait that Buck had been commissioned to do for the Pebble Beach Organization. I was embarrassed and just about to excuse myself, when Buck introduced me to Crosby and invited me to stay. I was delighted! There I was, in the presence of a living legend, an actor and singer whom I had grown up watching and listening to. In fact, he was so famous that Adolf Hitler had known who he was and dubbed him "Der Bingle"! As usual, Buck chatted away while painting. Crosby seemed quite relaxed. They both included me in their conversation. I was very nervous at first, but after a while I relaxed and enjoyed the experience. A number of years later, I was in a film at Twentieth Century Fox with Gary Crosby, one of Bing's sons. We liked each other and talked a lot in the ten days I was on the film. Gary often spoke about his father and how abusive he was to all of his sons. It was clear that Gary was carrying a lot of pain in relation to his father.

Meanwhile, back at the fort, I was still in that basement, shuttling trucks to the various companies, working my six-hour shift, and looking forward to my other life, which involved all of my friends at the theater and on the peninsula. One sunny morning I was summoned upstairs to speak with Major Boren. I liked the major. He was a good guy, laid back and cordial, middle-aged and serving his twenty, I think. I sat at his desk waiting to see what he wanted.

"Why aren't you an officer, Fred?" he began. "You're bright, a university graduate—why don't you apply to Officer Candidates School?"

I was at a loss for words for a few moments and didn't know how to respond to his question. I knew that he liked me and was sincerely trying to suggest something that he thought would be to my benefit.

Finally, I said, "Well, sir, you see, the army is not my career. I'm going to pursue a career in films. I'm an actor, and with all due respect to you, Major Boren, going to OCS would mean extending my enlistment for at least another year, and sir, I wouldn't extend my time in the army for one more day, even if they made me a general!"

I could not believe what had just come out of my mouth. I am sure all the color drained out of my face. Major Boren started to laugh, I mean laugh so hard that the other personnel came out of their offices to see what was so funny. He laughed for a long time, and I was relieved that I hadn't alienated him.

"You are something else, Fred!" he said. "The reason I called you up here was to tell you that Sergeant Calvano is being sent overseas, which means that you will have to take full responsibility for the regimental motor pool. Do you think you can handle it?"

"Yes, sir, I can!"

"Good! It will mean working longer hours, you know."

"Yes, sir."

"O.K. then, I'm depending on you. It is a big responsibility."

"Thank you, sir," and I left.

I didn't like the idea of working from 6:00 A.M. to 6:00 P.M., but I was my own man, and no one was going to give me any shit!

I was very sad to lose Sergeant Calvano. He had become a good friend. He gave Jean and me a small, tan-colored young dog with fairly long fur, who was really cute and very mischievous. He chewed our shoes, books, and everything he could get his teeth into. We called him Devil, which was a proper name for him. He was sweet, and we got very attached to him. One day he ran away, and we never saw him again. I scoured the neighborhood for days to no avail.

At about that time, the Wharf was casting *Tea and Sympathy,* a play I had seen on Broadway on one of my Christmas vacations from school, with Deborah Kerr and John Kerr as the leads. I loved the play and wanted desperately to play the leading role. I auditioned and thought that I had done quite well, but I was beat out by Bill Christopher, who later played the clergyman on "M*A*S*H." Bill was in the army at the same time and had heard that the Wharf was casting, so he had auditioned and gotten the part. I was very disappointed but later realized that he was physically better for the role. Ruth played the female lead. They were both excellent in the play.

A month after I took charge of the motor pool, the Second Infantry Regiment returned from Germany and absorbed our motor pool into theirs. I was now working in a different location and was surrounded by a number of sergeants and other noncoms. They were a lousy lot, a bunch of rednecks whose only interest in life was putting in their time, drinking, and hunting for pussy. Once again I was the low man on the totem pole. Everyone with a couple of stripes was giving me orders. On one occasion I responded to a sergeant first class by saying, "Get off my back!" It was the wrong thing to say at the wrong time. He jumped all over me, threatened to have me punished and to do whatever else he could to make my life miserable. I apologized, and he dropped it.

That motor pool was much larger than the Sixty-third Infantry Regiment's. I think it was because it was servicing both regiments, but I don't recall if that was actually the case. I do know that there were about ten people running it. The officer in charge was a first lieutenant named Johnson, a very nice guy, who never had much to say but was always in his private office doing whatever it was he did. The second officer was a young second lieutenant who obviously was not regular army but probably ROTC from college. He and I hit it off very soon after I was transferred to that motor pool. He never seemed to have anything to do, so he sat around and watched the rest of us work. He and I would sit together at a desk and talk for long periods of time about books, movies, plays, and the meaning of life. The regulars didn't like him, which was very obvious in the way they related to him and the things they said behind his back. To them he was just a college ROTC punk serving his draft time in the service. It is amazing that most people resented college graduates at the time, even outside the military.

However, he was, after all, a commissioned officer, so they had to treat him accordingly. Besides being only a PFC, the lowest rank at the motor pool, I was so chummy with the lieutenant that the others resented me all the more. My relationship to him had a double edge though. The noncoms didn't like my fraternizing with an officer, particularly that one, but they walked a wide track around me because of it. I was not happy there at all. The hours were long and the work uninspiring, and I had to deal with those assholes!

Since Jean worked on the base, I met her for lunch several times each week. It was a little bit of a walk to her office, but I didn't have a fifty-pound pack on my back! I was on separate rations, so I had to pay for my lunch at the mess hall, and so did Jean. It was all of about fifty cents a meal. Sometimes, we ate at the PX (post exchange), where they had a little sandwich bar. I complained about the motor pool and bitched about the people there, so Jean told me to do something about it.

"After all," she said, "you got out of the supply room, didn't you?"

"Yeah, I did," I replied, "but that was a kindda accident."

I decided to use my lunch breaks to sniff around the base. I found out where the Special Services Office was and went down there. I was greeted by Darryl Hickman, whom I had seen numerous times as a child actor in the movies and who was now an enlisted man working there. I told him who I was, what I was doing, and that I was an actor looking to do something in that field. He was very nice, and he related to me as one actor to another. Acting is like a huge fraternity. Knowing what the field is like, most actors have an intuitive understanding of each other. I told Darryl that I was married and lived off post.

"So, Fred, do you go home in the evenings?" he asked.

"For sure," I said. "I blast out of here the moment I can."

"Well, even if I could get you into special service, you would have to do a regular job in the daytime, such as clerk typist or whatever, and at night you would be working in the entertainment area."

"Hey, I don't want to do a double shift, even if it would mean entertaining the troops!"

He laughed and totally understood. "Special services are for single guys," he concluded.

I thanked him and went on my way. Around four years later we were in the same play together, an experience I'll talk about in the next chapter.

I picked up a copy of the Fort Ord directory, which listed all the activities and services on the base, and noticed that the base hospital had a radio station, so on one of my lunch breaks I went over there. It was a small closed-circuit station, which broadcast only to the hospital patients and personnel. I was greeted by a master sergeant, whose name was Makamoto, I think, and I told him that I had been a professional radio announcer in Chicago at station WNUR—which was only partially true. Actually, WNUR was the Northwestern University radio station, and though I had done some work on it, I lied about being a professional announcer. I told Makamoto what I was doing in the army and how frustrated I was at not being able to do what I did in civilian life. He understood and asked me if I could get permission from my commanding officer to be assigned to the station on a temporary-duty basis, since all four people who worked there needed to go on leave, one at a time, and there was no replacement. It would definitely mean about three months of work at the station. I told him that I would talk to Lieutenant Johnson to see if he would let me go. The next morning, I knocked on Lieutenant Johnson's office door and was invited in. He signaled me to sit down and asked me what was up. In the next ten minutes I probably did the best acting job of my entire life.

"Well, sir," I began, "I have this great opportunity to do work that I went to school for. I was working in radio in Chicago before I was drafted. I am a member of that union, and it is what I intend to return to after I complete my service. At any rate, I have an opportunity to work at the hospital radio station on TDY, if you, sir, will approve it."

I was shocked at how quickly and positively he responded to my request: "Of course you can go. I wouldn't hold anyone back from doing what he wants to do."

"When should I plan on leaving, sir?"

"How about now? Good luck, and come back when you are finished there."

I thanked him and skipped down the street, singing, "Hi, diddle dee dee, an announcer's life for me." I got a few strange looks from other soldiers passing by, but at that point I didn't care. Things were actually looking up. I took the rest of the day off, figuring that I could report to the radio station the next morning. I then went home and waited for Jean. I could hardly contain my excitement. As soon as she walked through the door, I jumped her and blurted out the good news. We went to a very expensive restaurant in Carmel to celebrate. We really couldn't afford it, but we felt that the news warranted it. We had wine with dinner and then went home and made love.

The next morning, I reported to the station, release form in hand, and was escorted through the procedures. Our job was to play music all day, interrupted by five-minute news reports five or six times a day. I was shown how to cue up records so that when I released my hand the music would play immediately. Being a disc jockey involved more than playing music though. I had to do intros and patter between selections; so knowing a little, or even a lot, about the various selections and the artists was mandatory. Well, I knew very little about popular music and even less about the people who sang or played it, so I really had to fake it, and quickly. There were four other people manning the station: the master sergeant, Jay Henderson; an overweight country guy; another enlisted man, whose name I have forgotten; and Makamoto. Makamoto was very formal in his presentation, without much humor or inventive patter. Jay was hip and cool and sounded like a CBS professional. The fat guy from Kentucky only played country music, but he had the proper accent to make his patter authentic, while the younger guy, who had enlisted with the promise that his MOS (military occupation specialty) would be radio broadcast specialist, had no personality at all. He was monotone and dry. If he had ambitions to be a disc jockey, he might have to wait until the next life to attain those goals. I glommed on to Jay, watched, listened, and learned. I read record jackets and promo information to acquaint myself with the various recording artists. At first I quoted verbatim what I had read, but later I added my own twist to the patter. The great thing about the job was that I worked in civilian clothes and only one week a month. The station broadcast from 8:00 A.M. to 10:00 P.M. seven days a week, but since there were four of us, we took turns each doing a full week once a month. No one checked on us, and as long as the station was broadcasting regularly every day, no one cared who was doing the talking. It was incredible! I was now in the army only one week a month, and the rest of the time I was a civilian.

Every day I slept until I felt like getting up and then spent part of the day on the Pacific Grove beach, sunning myself and reading books. On some afternoons I visited Buck or hung around the theater.

At that point I had been in the service for thirteen months. I had eleven left and planned to work it out somehow so that I could finish out my service at the radio station. The army worked on a rotation system. They moved personnel around the country and around the world. I don't know the reasons for that, except to assume that the powers that were sat around and figured the best way to make the troops miserable! Don't let them get too comfortable! After all, the military is not a country club. That was their thinking. Well, almost everyone at the station was rotated overseas, except me, and the reason for it was that if you had less than a year left to serve, you could not be sent out of the country. I was therefore the sole survivor at the station. My TDY assignment turned into a permanent position. I had experience there, which all of the replacements lacked, and even though some of them outranked me, I was the senior guy, and everyone allowed me to call the shots. I did all of the scheduling and handled some of the paper work. When I was on the mike, I had a specific signoff at the end of every evening: "Goodnight to all of you, RAs, and remember, for you it's just another day, and for you US's another day less. Goodnight! Get well soon!" RA in front of a soldier's serial number meant that he was regular army and had enlisted for four years. US in front meant that he had been drafted and his tour of duty was only two years. I did that signoff for months, and no one said anything about it until one day, when I was collecting my pay, a lieutenant colonel came into the office where they were distributing the money and asked me if I was the guy on the radio station with that unique signoff. I knew what he meant, but I didn't know what to expect, so I said, "Yes, sir, that's me."

"Well, cut it out!"

"Yes, sir." He left, and I stopped signing off that way.

I was winding down, becoming a "short timer," and my three-by-five card was getting filled with cross outs. I looked at it every night and counted the remaining days until I would be free again.

They were doing *Pal Joey* at the Wharf. Mike was cast as Joey, the lead, and Jean opposite him, as one of the female leading characters. She could always dance and sing, and when she had auditioned for the play, she had surprised everyone there. Bob and Tom had only seen her do a small part in *Night Must Fall* and knew her as my wife. Since she was going to be away every evening for rehearsal and then performance, I took a small part in the play in order to spend those evenings with her. I had very few lines as Papa Tellier. Johnnie Nerris and I just sat at a table in the background, drank what was supposed to be wine, and commented on the action that was taking place in front of us. The play had a limited run. Mike, who thought he had been miscast and had at first refused the part, had only taken it because Tom and Bob offered to pay him two hundred dollars, which, coincidentally, was the exact amount he would have to pay the hospital to deliver his firstborn daughter. He received scathing reviews and was quite upset by the entire experience. Jean, on the other hand, was delighted to have gotten the role and did quite well with it. It was probably the last opportunity I would have to work at the Wharf, since my time was growing short.

By then I had spent thirteen months at the radio station all in all. That qualified me for a new MOS—which I got—radio broadcast specialist. Any job you do in the army for a year or more becomes your MOS. Not that it really mattered what my MOS was when I was discharged, since I had no intentions of doing anything further in the military. I was very lucky: I had gone into the army twenty-seven days before they cancelled the Korean Bill of Rights, and I was eligible for all its benefits, none of which I ever used afterwards, except for the most important one, which was that I didn't have to be in the reserves for two more years. That would have meant attending meetings a couple of times a month and spending two weeks in the summer at some army base doing maneuvers. Just twenty-seven days had saved me from two more years of attachment to the military.

With only a week or so left before my separation, I sent Jean back to Los Angeles, where my parents had rented us an apartment in the building where they lived. I stayed in our apartment in Pacific Grove until the last minute, when I had to move back into the old barracks in order to process out. There I was again in those rotting buildings, but this time the experience was quite different. Instead of fear and loathing, there were joy and excitement. Processing out involved turning in various parts of our uniform. We were not allowed to keep our overcoats or field jackets, but the rest of what they had issued us was ours. We went from one administrative office to another, receiving all kinds of documents, particularly the magic one, the discharge diploma, which stated that we were honorably discharged from the United States Army. The processing center had a mixture of soldiers, those coming in and those of us going out. During that period I wore my fatigue uniform, on which I had never sewn my PFC single stripe. The only uniform that had my rank on it was the class-A dress uniform, and the only reason I had put the stripe there was that I had to wear that uniform to receive my monthly pay. The last day at the processing center, a corporal approached a group of inductees near where I happened to be standing and told us to line up and follow him to the mess hall to do KP. Under my breath I said, "Fuck this!" turned and went in the opposite direction. I imagine that if he had seen a stripe on my sleeve, he would not have included me. I certainly was not going to pull KP on my last day in the army!

Because of the Christmas holidays, we were getting an early release, so I would be out on December 13 instead of January 3. Two weeks may not mean a lot in the space of a lifetime, but it was a lifetime to me. We marched in a column of twos in a long line to the last office to receive our final papers, and I was singing at the top of my voice, "This is my once-a-year day," a song from the musical *Pajama Game.* I drew a lot of attention from other soldiers marching past us in the opposite direction, but I could have cared less about anybody or about what anybody thought at that moment. After two years of underlying fear, I no longer worried about anything having to do with orders, rules, discipline, or any of the other crap I had lived with.

After receiving all of our separation papers, we were dismissed. I was a civilian again. I looked at my wristwatch and computed the time I had spent being a soldier. It was one year, eleven months, seventeen days, four hours, and twelve minutes! I threw my duffle bag into the back seat of my Studebaker and headed out of the fort.

Before leaving for Los Angeles, I wanted to say good-bye to all the people I had worked with at the Wharf Theatre and to my other friends. I dropped by to see Buck and Ruth, had lunch with them, and promised to keep in touch. I visited a few other people connected to the theater—much to their surprise. They wanted to know why I was leaving the peninsula. When I told them that it was because I had been discharged from the army, they were very surprised that I had been a soldier in the first place. They didn't know that I wasn't just living in the area. Most of the people outside the army had never seen me in uniform. I had just assumed that they knew.

I didn't return to the peninsula for many years. I guess it was tainted with the army experience. About five years later, Buck had a heart attack and died. Ruth moved to L.A. shortly after that to pursue her acting career, while Tom and Bob absconded with fifty thousand dollars of the theater money. It was rumored that they had fled to Mexico.

It was many years before I came to understand what that guy had said to me at my going away party—that he wouldn't take a million dollars to go back into the army but wouldn't take two million for the experience. Even though I hated being kept from my profession and felt that I was putting in time that didn't serve any purpose, except to make me two years older, I learned a lot. I matured in the service, became more self-sufficient, and understood the military consciousness and how it affects our country. I learned self-defense tactics, how to survive in the wilderness, and how to take orders. On top of that, I have played numerous parts in films as a soldier, sailor, or marine and been able to call on my military experience many times in my acting.

CHAPTER 6

THE TRAINING AND WORKING YEARS

I was OUT, and back in Los Angeles. My parents had rented us a one-bedroom apartment on the first floor of the building where they lived. They were across the courtyard from us but on the second floor, since—as you may remember—my mother had always been terrified that a first-floor apartment was an invitation to burglars. Small and dark, our apartment was located south of Pico Boulevard, the wrong side of town for my taste. From the time I had been in grade school I had dreamed of living in Hollywood. I enjoyed looking through movie magazines and reading about movies, movie stars and their lifestyles, and I wanted to live where they did. Still, this was my first civilian abode, and I was so grateful to be out of the army that I overlooked all of the drawbacks of the apartment, including the fact that my father seemed to pop in unannounced any time of the day or evening. I adored my father and still get very vulnerable when I think about him, in spite of the fact that he has been gone for over thirty years, but after all, I was still almost a newlywed, and it was stressful to be in such close proximity to my parents.

As soon as I arrived, I threw my duffle bag containing all of my uniforms, discharge papers, good-conduct and shooting medals into the storage facility provided by the building, and I never saw it again. In the following years I regretted having discarded all those things, since some of them would have meant a lot to me later on.

Since I had been discharged during the Christmas holidays, I had to wait almost two weeks to get started on my career. I was chomping at the bit to get out there and beat the bushes. The first thing I wanted to do was to get into a good acting class to continue my training, but I had no idea where to begin looking for one. The only class—if one could call it that—that I had had since leaving Northwestern was the one I had attended at the Players' Ring before going into the army. Paul Levitt was no acting teacher, and I had come away from the experience without having learned anything. Even though I had continued to act while in the army, I was no further ahead in my knowledge of craft. I knew I was talented, but talent without specific process is not only undependable but also extremely frustrating.

My brother Morrey, who had changed his name to Edmund Morris many years earlier, had recently come to L.A. from New York after the opening on Broadway of his play, *The Wooden Dish,* which had had a moderately successful run there but had been received with much more enthusiasm in London. He had been given a contract at Columbia Pictures to write a number of features. The acting coach there, a man named Benno Schneider, had a wife, Batami, who was teaching a class in Hollywood. Ed arranged for me to take that class. Batami was up in years, possibly in her early sixties, had long, gray hair flowing down past her shoulders and very deep wrinkles, which seemed to form a maplike pattern on her face. When she spoke, the lines around her mouth and eyes seemed to be keeping time with her words. She moved as if she had been a dancer in her early years, and I think she had a slight accent, but my memory isn't clear about that. I really wanted her to have some of the answers I was hungry for, but that was not to be the case. She was pleasant, articulate, and somewhat perceptive about the work she saw, but she was general in her approach to acting, and her critiques were directorial. She would sit with her chin resting on her open hand, take a few dramatic moments before saying anything to the actors, and then make comments such as, "You need more energy. You don't want to put your audience to sleep, do you?" She would continue commenting about the blocking of the scene, which was not what I wanted to hear. I would be thinking that she might discuss *how* the actors had stimulated their behavior, but that never happened in any of the classes I attended. She also made me think of Alvina Krause, which carried with it unpleasant memories. I stayed in her class for a short time and never did anything onstage. I discussed my feelings with Ed, and to my surprise he was very understanding. He told me that he would continue to look around and would ask people at the studio for referrals.

In the meantime I returned to the Players' Ring and renewed some of my contacts and friendships. Lee Blattner was no longer there. He had married his girlfriend, Pat, and had gone to work for Jimmy Doolittle at the Greek Theatre. Barbara and Sy, however, were still around. I had gotten to know Barbara before going into the army. She was not an actress per se, but she loved to hang around the theater and the people there. She was very helpful and always willing to do things for the actors who were preparing to present a scene. She was dating a guy named Sy Cedar, with whom I had hit it off well. He had a good sense of humor and enjoyed going out after class and talking about acting and what his ambitions were at the time. While I was away, he and Barbara had gotten married and had a little girl. Sy had changed his first name to Jon. The four of us became really close and spent a lot of time together. Jon was also an actor, so we had a lot in common.

Paul and Ted were still up to their old trick of paying the actors union wages and then making them return the checks—a practice called "kickbacks." We complied because it was the only way we could work at the Ring. Paul and Ted were raking in a fortune from the theater, not only from regular theater-going audiences, but also from the theater parties that filled every seat in the house on most weekends. The Equity Union salary for a theater the size of the Ring was very nominal, at most possibly fifty dollars a week, which wouldn't have made any of us rich; but a salary would have meant that we as actors were being paid for our efforts, and that, at least, would have lifted our morale.

Nevertheless, I auditioned at the Ring and got a small but nice part in *Girls of Summer.* It was my first job since I had left the army, and I was thrilled to be onstage, instead of backstage stage-managing. The leading roles were being played by Mike ("Touch") Connors—whose nickname came from his having been a football star at UCLA—Carole Mathews, and Bobby Driscoll. Mike was at the beginning of his acting career. Later on he became fairly successful on television as the lead actor in two different series, "Tightrope" and "Mannix." Carole Mathews was a busy working actress in B films, while Bobby Driscoll, as a child actor, had done such films as *Song of the South* and several other big ones. A great guy, always smiling and seemingly happy, he was then in his early twenties and was attempting to carve out a career as an adult. I really liked him, and we established a close relationship during the run of the play. Almost every night during the intermission, Robert Blake and Dean Stockwell would visit Bobby, and the four of us hung out in the dressing room backstage. I listened to them talk about the old days—the people, the other actors, the directors, and some of the gossip that wasn't written about in the newspapers. I was fascinated by their conversations. They had grown up in the studio classes, taught by teachers the studio brought in. That was my first meeting with Robert Blake. In later years our paths crossed several times, and we became friends. A few years after the play, Bobby Driscoll died. He had been addicted to drugs earlier in his teens, and even though he had freed himself of the addiction by then, it had already wreaked havoc on his body, so that he was never able to recover.

Around the fourth week of the run I was approached by Ivan Green, an agent who had come to see the play and been impressed with my work. He was a short, balding man with a very birdlike appearance, whose direct and opinionated demeanor was totally incongruous to the way he looked. He said what he felt and pulled no punches when he was expressing his views or his criticisms. He invited me to visit him the next day at his office, which I did with great excitement and anticipation, since I had never had an agent before. We sat looking at each other for a long, uncomfortable time. He said nothing, and I said nothing. I could see that he was appraising me in the light of day, away from the ambience of the theater and the applause of the audience. I was sure that I could read his thoughts as he looked me over. I imagined that he had changed his mind about representing me and that he was having difficulty telling me so. The longer I waited for him to say something, the deeper I sank into my depression.

Finally, to my surprise he said, "O.K., Fred, I like you. I think you're talented and even somewhat good-looking, but you have to change your name—it's too ethnic—and do something with that shock of blond, wavy hair!" My hair was long and light blond, and it had a pronounced wave in the front. I guess I had let it grow a little longer as a rebellion to the crew cut they had given me when I was inducted.

"O.K.," I said, "I'll change my name and cut my hair. What else do you want me to do?"

"Nothing at the moment," he replied, "except get pictures—headshots—and let's start building a résumé. It's not going to be easy for me. You don't have any film credits, and casting directors for the most part don't have a lot of respect for theater credits. I'm going to have to work very hard to get you going, but I believe in you, so I'll do it!"

His words really affected me, and I had to do everything in my power not to cry. I think he saw how moved I was.

So what was I going to change my name to? My brother Ed had already suggested that I use the same last name as his so that when he introduced me to people in the business, it would be less confusing. I decided on Fredric Morris and informed the Screen Actors Guild of my decision. They in turn rejected the name, because there was already a Fred L. Morris in St. Louis who belonged to the union, and you cannot use the same name—or even one close to it—as any other member. They suggested that I choose two other first names to submit. Thinking that Eric was half of Frederic, I chose Eric first and Gregg as an alternative. They accepted Eric, and so in 1957 I became Eric Morris. A funny addendum to this whole name thing is that if they had rejected Eric and chosen Gregg, I would have become Gregg Morris, and the black actor who later played on "Mission Impossible" would not have been able to use his real name, since I predated him in the business by eight years.

I cut my hair and started to audition. My brother, who knew several people from his years in New York, arranged for me to meet Ted Post, a movie director who was doing a film at that moment. Post was very nice. He asked me if I could handle a leading role, and of course I said yes. Thank God I wasn't given the opportunity to do that, however, since I certainly was not technically ready to carry a film at the time. Nevertheless, Post did give me a part in the film he was directing, the story of Barney Ross, titled *Monkey on My Back.* Barney Ross was a prizefighter, a contemporary of Max Baer, who had developed somewhat of a reputation as a fairly good boxer in the late forties and early fifties. I was cast as a soldier, of all things, in the segment of the film where Barney Ross served in the Second World War. I didn't have any lines, but I was one of the soldiers walking through the swamps and crawling through the Pacific jungles. There were a lot of scenes and a bunch of close-ups—which delighted me. It was my first Hollywood movie, and I was very excited to have the opportunity to work in films so soon in my career. Cameron Mitchell was playing Ross. He had somewhat of a name and had done a lot of work in smaller films, but I found his behavior and attitude really objectionable. He yelled at all the actors and kept telling everyone what to do. He had assumed the role of director, and I thought he was an arrogant shit; but of course, being the new kid on the block, I didn't say anything.

Unfortunately, my silent performance never reached the screen, since they replaced Ted Post the next day with another director, who scrapped all of the footage Ted had shot; but I got paid and had my first film experience and a credit to use in building a résumé. I was very excited about being in the movies. I had watched movies all my life, and being in them was something I had dreamed about.

Ed spoke to another director he had worked with in New York, and I got a part on a television show. It was a one-hour live show, called "Matinee Theater," which was in color, aired at noon five days a week, and was a very ambitious undertaking for that time. They did classics and contemporary material. Alan Cooke, the director for that episode, was a displaced Englishman with a very heavy British accent. I did *Arms and the Man,* by Shaw, where I played a Prussian soldier in classical costume, who came in and out of scenes, inserting a line here and there. It was an "under five," which meant that I could have no more than four lines and that I qualified for a lower pay scale. I didn't care. Alan gave me a lot of silent things to do, so it looked as though I had a featured role. Albert McCleery, the executive producer, obviously liked my work and attitude, since I was brought back for two more shows.

I had a bunch of lines in my second outing. Almost all my scenes were with Marilyn Erskine, the lead, whom I remembered having seen in a film called *Westward the Women.* I thought she was a really good actress and felt very honored to be working with such a seasoned professional. She really related to me in our scenes together. The involvement was wonderful. It was the first time I completely lost myself while acting in front of the camera. I played a mentally challenged, disturbed young man, who had been hospitalized for being unable to function in society. Marilyn's character, also a patient in the hospital, was mentally in a much better place than I, so she took me under her wing and brought me out. While this did not constitute the major plot of the story, it became an exceptional part of the show. Not being able to articulate in craft terms exactly why the work was so organic and real, I just accepted that it was because of the way we related to each other as actors.

Larry Shwab, the director, was a real character. He made each of the actors write a five- or six-page biography of his or her character. My part was relatively small, but I created a background that took up ten pages! He read it and told me that it was so interesting and psychologically accurate that we should do a show just on my character. Larry was also a psychologist and an inventor and later taught acting. He was a very sweet guy but for whatever reason was never very successful at any of his careers. Once, when I was working on the show, I walked into his office to ask a question, and there on his desk was a box painted red with a big button in the middle. On top, printed in large white letters, it said, "Panic Button."

I asked him what the button did, and he replied, "Nothing! It does nothing. When you feel stressed or panicked, you push the button and release your tension."

"Oh," I said, "is that one of your inventions?"

"Yes," he replied," and I think it's going to do well."

He and I became friends and remained close until his death about fifteen years ago. He had some very creative ideas. He would have the actors improvise before starting the lines of a scene they were about to do. It was a great lead into the words, and it established a relationship, which connected to the first written line. I am not sure what the producer or the other people involved in the show thought of some of his unorthodox directing techniques, but I for one loved it! I think it was Larry's audaciousness that attracted me to him. He could probably have been an important director if he had continued to explore and grow in his knowledge of craft. His idea of creating a character background, while not new, was part of his intention to get the actors to supply dimension to the characters they were playing, but putting ideas and descriptions on paper really does very little to carry them into behavior. I didn't know it then, but in order to profit from creating a character background, one must have the tools to implement it into pragmatic, organic behavioral results. At that time I didn't have those tools.

The third "Matinee Theater" show I did starred Robert Culp and Shepperd Strudwick, both seasoned, well-established actors. Robert had not yet played "I Spy," but he had done some shows in New York and was thought of as a very good actor. Shepperd had been around for a long time and had established himself as a very competent character actor. The show was a period piece in a rural setting, and I played one of the village youths, who was involved with a pretty young girl from the same village. While the show was definitely not about my character, his was an interesting side story to the main plot. It was a difficult show, not because of the acting responsibilities, but because of the many costume changes, which—this being a live performance—had to be done on the run between sets. There wasn't any room for mistakes. When the camera opened on the set where you were supposed to be, you had better be there! I loved every minute of it.

Ivan was thrilled that I had gotten those shows on my own, but he also did send me out regularly. I did a number of "court" shows, also done live: "Divorce Court," "Police Court," and a show called "Court Martial," which, as its name indicates, had to do with the military. I had some knowledge on the subject, which helped my performance. Marvin Page, who cast most of those shows, liked my work well enough to use me over and over again. There was a section in the *Hollywood Reporter,* the business trade paper, that had little news quips about what various actors were doing. In one of the columns, someone had planted a blurb about me, which read, "Eric Morris has done so many court shows that he fired his agent and hired a bailiff." Of course it was meant to be funny, but to this day I haven't a clue who had put it in.

In those early years, '57, '58, '59, I was averaging a few days' work every month. It seemed likely that it would continue and structure a successful career. I still didn't have a class to go to, however, and pursuing my training was a priority. I was happy about working but very frustrated with my work. Quite often I would connect with something, and my behavior would be real and organic, while at other times I struggled to feel the emotional life I was obligated to. Something quite wonderful had happened when I was doing the mental patient on "Matinee Theater." I had connected with his realities. They had become mine, and I had really experienced the torment he felt. It reminded me of when I had played the village idiot in *Woyzeck* at Northwestern. Unfortunately, I couldn't tell why or how it had happened. It was an intuitive response sprinkled with some inspiration, but how could I repeat it if I didn't know how I had gotten there? That was what plagued me. Not a single one of the teachers with whom I had studied had given me any concrete answers or specific tools I could use and depend on.

As it happens, my brother had worked on some television show in New York with Jeff Hayden, who at that time was a floor manager for one of the networks. Jeff had since moved to L.A., where he was directing and also teaching an acting class on Beverly Boulevard. Ed spoke with him and arranged for me to attend his class.

Jeff was a very good-looking guy with a charming personality, so it was easy to like him. He was married to Eva Marie Saint, a movie star who was wonderful in *On the Waterfront.* She would occasionally visit, sit in the back and watch the work. She was very friendly with the people she knew and also very supportive. The class was filled with working professionals, some of whom I had seen in movies and on the tube, and as I was the youngest member of the class, in the beginning I was very excited to be surrounded by such experienced actors. Jeff would talk a lot about acting, using much of what I later learned was Method terminology, mostly from Strasberg. I don't know if he had ever worked with Lee, but he seemed familiar with the language. The actors did scenes, and many of them were working on projects. Charles Aidman spent months on *Spoon River Anthology.* He was a pretty successful actor, who did a lot of television and voiceovers, but he reminded me of Bill Munchow in that he was also prone to *phumpernick* when he acted. Also in the class was Majel Barrett, who later had a running role in "Star Trek" and then married its producer and director, Gene Roddenberry. Walter Barnes—an older character actor—Christine White, Steve Marlo, Jack Ging, and other established actors rounded out the group.

At first, I was quite intrigued by what I saw. Some actors would get up onstage and say they were working for their eyelashes being the wings of monarch butterflies. Another actress said that her body was filling up with hot volcanic lava, and still there were those who came up with even more bizarre images. Jeff would compliment and encourage them. I thought it was imaginative but failed to see the translation or application of their exercises. In the beginning I thought that I was either being impatient or missing something. I was too new to feel comfortable asking questions, so I kept quiet. The word *how* continually echoed in my brain: How do you use any of those involvements to access emotions that fit the scene? I thought that there were some very talented actors there, but I never heard any of them, including Jeff, talk specifically about what they did or how they did their work. I was afraid to get up and do anything in front of the group, so I remained an observer.

The group was doing a project that consisted of scenes and sketches, some with music and dance. About ten or twelve actors were involved, and I was asked to do the technical stuff—light cues, tape-recorder sound cues, and so on. It was fairly complicated, since there were many cues and changes, but because of my Northwestern and summer-stock background, it was a piece of cake for me. Nevertheless, Jeff and the others were impressed with my abilities. Mo—originally Morris—Miller, who had changed his name to Steve Marlo, took me under his wing, and we became friends. He was in a number of the scenes and was quite dependent on my being able to come in with the sound cues at exactly the right moment. Being the youngest and least experienced actor in the class made me feel insecure. I thought that Jeff had accepted me because of his friendship with my brother Ed—which may have been true.

Around that time we heard that there was going to be a big theater conference at the UCLA Conference Center up at Lake Arrowhead, the purpose of which was to promote live theater in Los Angeles. Abbott Kaplan, who was responsible for organizing the event, was part of the hierarchy at UCLA. Because of the stature of the organizers, many luminaries and show-business celebrities were invited, including Jeff, who was asked to bring anyone who might add to the energy of the conference. He decided to take the members of his class who were doing the project we had been working on, and he asked me to come with the group to do the technical management. I told him that I couldn't afford to pay for the food and lodging and that I was really embarrassed about it, so he graciously offered to pay for me, saying that I was indispensable to the project, that they would not be able to get a replacement on such short notice, and that he would be delighted to sponsor me. I accepted reluctantly, knowing that he was right about not being able to replace me.

On a beautiful summer night Mo and I drove up the mountain in his 1955 yellow Thunderbird convertible, with the top down. He had recently purchased that beautiful sports car with his earnings from a film he had done. I sat in the passenger seat, my head tilted back on the headrest, looking at the thousands of stars that studded the night sky. The mountain air filled me with a sense of well-being. I was excited by the prospect of this adventure. I was about to be surrounded by some of the biggest names in the film industry and was experiencing California the way I had fantasized about it. I felt like the valued mascot of the number one team in the country. Mo did most of the talking. He had come to L.A. to do the lead in a film, *Stakeout on Dope Street.* He spoke about his career in New York, the plays he had done on Broadway, and what he had worked on in Hollywood since finishing that film. If his goal was to impress me, he succeeded. He was five or six years older than I and had been in the business all those years before me. We talked about Jeff's class and how long he had been there. I wanted to ask some questions about process, but I didn't. When we arrived at the conference center and were assigned cabins, I was relieved to find out that he and I would be sharing one, since I felt comfortable with him. The accommodations were lovely and the food great! I felt very special to be there among all these famous people: Robert Ryan, James Whitmore, Lee Strasberg, and many others, including producers and directors.

We convened in a large room, where Abbott Kaplan spoke about the goal of the conference. Referring to the wealth of talent that existed in L.A., he said that Hollywood should have important live theater in addition to a film industry. "The audiences are there," he went on, "just waiting for us to bring them theater equal to what's on Broadway." Emphasizing the fact that we had an even larger talent pool than what existed in New York, he spoke for about fifteen minutes before introducing the major guest speaker, Lee Strasberg. He gave Strasberg an introduction befitting the king of a large country. I was sitting pretty far back in the room, and when Strasberg walked to the podium, I stood up to be able to see what in my mind was a legend. I would have thought him to be well above six feet in height, but instead this little gray-haired man stepped up to the podium and had to adjust the microphone so it wouldn't block his face. In less than two minutes he changed the entire atmosphere of the meeting. He was very negative about the whole idea of creating a theater in L.A. While being very articulate, he cited numerous reasons why theater would never flourish here and put the kibosh on the whole idea. He said that New York was a theater town, Los Angeles a film town, and that we should accept it and promote what we did best. He spoke for over half an hour, and I felt the excitement dissipate in the room. It was actually a tangible pall that fell over the crowd. It was my first encounter with the legendary Lee Strasberg, and while I felt that he was totally discouraging to the people who were so hopeful, I couldn't help but feel privileged to be in the same room with him.

We did our show, but while everyone was very attentive, I don't think it went over very well. It seemed out of place in that venue and smacked of the classroom rather than ascending to the level of the conference. After the event was over, everyone gathered in the lobby of the conference center. Lee Strasberg was standing alone near the registration desk, so I walked over to tell him how much I had enjoyed his speech. When I was within range and our eyes met, I started to speak: "Mr. Strasberg, I really—" at which point he abruptly turned away from me, leaving me standing there to finish my statement to an empty space. I was shocked and humiliated, but because I have a sense of humor, I continued talking as if finishing what I had to say to the air in front of me! I must have looked bereft, because Christine White approached me, wondering what had just happened. She knew Strasberg from the Actors Studio. She had dated James Dean and been his scene partner when they had auditioned for the Studio. I think she was still having a tough time over his death. She tried to explain Strasberg's rude behavior to me: "He's very shy, Eric," she said, "and he avoids face-to-face contact whenever possible, so don't take it personally." I was feeling as though someone had just pissed on my head and didn't know how not to take it personally. Christine obviously saw how hurt I was, and she was very sweet. That was my first encounter with Strasberg. I didn't know it then, but there were to be many more experiences with him in the future. I have often thought that if he had been more encouraging and supportive at that conference, we might have generated more vital live theater in Los Angeles.

After that, I continued in Jeff's class, attempting to make sense out of some of the work. Talent is talent is talent, and I saw some good work, but I continued to be frustrated by the lack of clarity and specificity. After a few months in class, I mustered up the courage to comment. It was after a scene done by the same woman who had been working for her body being slowly filled with hot lava that I raised my hand and was acknowledged by Jeff.

"What would you like to say, Eric?" he asked.

"Well," I responded, "it's more in the framework of a question than a comment. I would like to know the purpose of working for the lava choice. What was it supposed to do for her, and how did she go about creating that reality inside her body?"

There was a silence in the room for a long enough time to make me feel as if I had just committed a crime. Jeff started to comment and was interrupted by the woman who had just done the scene. "I don't understand the question," she said, "and I don't even know where you're coming from."

Every eye in the class was on me, and I felt like sinking into the floor and disappearing. After a short pause I spoke: "Well, I don't mean my question as a challenge to you or anyone else in this class, but in order for me to learn something here, I would like some specific answers as to how and why you did what you did. What was the purpose of the choice, and what was it meant to stimulate?"

Wow, I thought, that was awesome! I had really said what I felt, and now I thought the ball was in her court. She stumbled around for a few minutes trying to answer my question but was totally unable to be specific about the how. She did say that it was to make her feel a climbing rage filling her being. When Jeff saw the spot I had put her on, he interrupted to say that the choice she had made was imaginative and that acting was very dependent on the imagination. I could see that some of the other people respected my question and weren't satisfied with her answer or Jeff's.

One evening when Jeff was directing a television show, Steve brought Anthony Quinn in to conduct the class. Everybody was excited to do something for Quinn, and there were a lot of scenes that evening. His comments were also general, directorial, and vague. At one point I overheard him whisper into Steve's ear some very disparaging comment about an actor who was onstage doing a scene. I was within earshot of them, and I heard everything Quinn said. It was awful and insensitive, and coming from one actor in relation to another, shocking to me. I had always thought, and still do, that Anthony Quinn was a fine actor, but he was also a crude and vulgar human being. That incident has stuck with me for forty-eight years!

Soon after, Jeff cast me in a play he was doing, as one of the town boys who hung out in *Weinsberg, Ohio.* I had some lines and a lot of stage time hanging out. We were going to do the play at the Geller Theater, a beautiful theater on Wilshire Boulevard, and I was happy to be doing the part. The leading roles were played by Darryl Hickman and Pamela Lincoln, a descendant of Abraham Lincoln. Darryl remembered me from the army, and we spent some minutes reminiscing about our time there. He later married Pamela, and they had a couple of kids.

We were in our second week of rehearsals when Jeff approached me and told me, "It isn't working out, Eric. You're just not right for the part. It isn't anything you're doing or not doing; it's just not a good fit for the look of the play." I was shocked. I had thought it was going well and had established a relationship to the other two actors I had my scenes with. I was hurt and confused, and Jeff saw it. He went on to tell me that it was his mistake in casting me. Why is it that when a director replaces you as an actor, he thinks that saying it was his mistake will make you feel better? It doesn't! In my short career, that was the third time I had been either demoted or replaced. I went home, drew a hot bath, and cried until the water got cold. I don't remember whether I went back to class or not. It seems a little vague now. I'm sure I was embarrassed to have been replaced, but I truly don't remember if I continued in the class. I didn't have any bad feelings towards Jeff. He was a hard guy not to like, and to this day when I think about him, it brings a smile to my lips.

By that time Jean had gotten a job as a secretary-receptionist in an advertising agency on Wilshire Boulevard. Our lease was up on the Robertson apartment, so we moved to Hollywood into a one-bedroom with a pool and underground parking, on Detroit Street between Santa Monica Boulevard and Fountain Avenue. I was a Chicago boy and had never lived anywhere with a swimming pool. I was really going Hollywood, and I loved the idea. We were too far away from my parents for my father to pop in on us, and that was a relief. I loved the place and spent a lot of time in the pool area. Our next-door neighbor was an older woman, named Hennie Mohr. Her son, Gerald, a character actor who had done a successful television series in Europe, called "Crosscurrent," in the trenchcoat style of Humphrey Bogart, came by every day to sit by the pool and take the sun. He smoked strong, exotic Egyptian cigarettes and was the epitome of what he thought was a Hollywood movie star. He and I got very friendly and spent almost every afternoon sitting in the poolside loungers, talking about acting and films. He knew that I was just at the beginning of my journey as an actor in this town, and he took full advantage of being the older, more successful actor giving advice to a novice. He talked about his career and his many roles in television and motion pictures, and I listened and was impressed. I didn't know it at the time, but he needed me more than I needed him. The afternoons were nonetheless pleasant, and I began to look forward to them.

I was still driving my yellow Studebaker, which had such front-end problems that when I was on the freeway it looked as if it was doing the rumba! It attracted a lot of attention from the other motorists, who pointed at it and laughed as they passed by. Jean and I decided to buy a new car, a bright red 1957 Corvette, with a red leather interior, a white canvas top, and wide whitewall tires—my very first sports car. I was ecstatic! We put a small down payment on it and financed the rest. Our apartment rent was $110 a month, and the full price of the Corvette out the door was $3457. Jean was working full time, and I was collecting unemployment compensation and pay on an occasional acting job, so we were making it financially. We were happy and looking forward to a successful life together. We could make our rent and car payments and still have enough left over to go to dinner and a movie once a week. Sy and Barbara, who were renting a two-bedroom house in Hollywood, came by a couple of evenings a week, and sometimes we would visit them. Mike Monahan, whom I had met at the Wharf, and his wife, Sherry, moved into a small house on Detroit down the street from us. Mike had come to L.A. from the peninsula just a few months before me. The six of us hung out together. They all had children, and since money was tight for all of us, we spent a lot of time at each other's houses, playing charades and goofing around. It is amazing how much fun one can have without spending much money. When I think back to those times, I feel that they were really the good old days.

Ivan had arranged for me to audition for Owen McLean, the head casting director at Twentieth Century Fox. I did a scene in his office, and he was so impressed with my audition that he cast me in four big Twentieth films over the next two years. The parts were small, just below featured roles, but I did have a few weeks on each of them. This was a big break for me. They were all A films, and I worked with four of Hollywood's legendary directors.

In the first of those films, *Rally 'Round the Flag, Boys!* Leo McCarey was the director. The film starred Paul Newman, Joanne Woodward, Tuesday Weld, Joan Collins, Jack Carson, and Dwayne Hickman, Darryl Hickman's brother, who later starred in "Dobie Gillis," a successful television series. I was a soldier again. By that time I was wondering whether I had really gotten out of the army or just been reassigned to Hollywood! I met Tommy Gilson on this picture, the first of two we worked on together. Leo McCarey was a quiet director, who gave little verbal direction. He would spend most of his time talking to the director of photography, and if they agreed that the take looked O.K., he would call, "Print." It was fun being at a major studio, driving through the gate every morning and being a working actor. I didn't have too much to do. I had a line here and there and hung around with all the other soldiers on the train and in the restaurant, watching Tuesday Weld move that incredible body of hers past our tables. We didn't have to be told how to respond. It was very natural!

The second film I did was for Henry Levin, a well-known director, famous for doing romantic comedies. He was a very sweet, very soft-spoken man, sensitive to the actors. Here again, I was in the armed forces, as an air-force military policeman. The film, *Holiday for Lovers,* starred Gary Crosby and a whole bunch of other Twentieth actors. I don't remember who the other stars were, but I had a nice little scene with Carol Lynley, who was the female lead. Gardner McKay, who was under contract to Twentieth at the time and most likely knew that he was going to be the lead in an upcoming series, "Adventures in Paradise," spent all of his time hiding behind the other actors so that he would not be seen playing a glorified extra. He was very tall, so he had to bend his knees to get low enough to hide from the camera. In one scene, as I turned around, I smashed right into his face, which was at the level of my bellybutton. Gary Crosby and I hit it off and spent a lot of time talking to each other between scenes. He was a great guy, and I really liked his honesty and simplicity. I told him that I had met his father when Buck was painting his portrait for the Pebble Beach

Organization, but I immediately saw that he had a lot of issues about Bing.

The third film for Twentieth was *A Private's Affair,* the director for which was the famous Raoul Walsh, also somewhat notorious for having directed most of Errol Flynn's swashbucklers. He hung around with Flynn and the Wild Bunch. I guess he did everything Flynn did, which was no small feat. There is an interesting story that was circulating around Hollywood, which I think is worth retelling here. The Wild Bunch of Hollywood included Walsh, Errol Flynn, John Barrymore, and some other drinkers and partygoers. When Barrymore died, some of the rest of the group stole his body from the mortuary, brought him back to one of their homes, sat him in a high director's chair with a drink in his hand, and then invited the rest of the group over to celebrate. Those who didn't know that John's body would be there got quite a shocking surprise when they came through the door!

At any rate, Raoul Walsh was a very colorful character. He came to the set every day, wearing a long tweed riding jacket, riding pants, and knee-high boots without spurs. He had a black patch over one eye and moved with purpose. In the film, I was again in the army but this time dressed in whites as a hospital orderly. Each morning when I arrived on the set, Raoul would greet me with, "Good morning, Eric, are we going to have a good day today?" and I would respond very respectfully, "Good morning, Mr. Walsh. Yes, sir, we are going to have a very good day." He would smile and move into the area of the first scene of the day. He was very easygoing and nice to work for. He said very little after a scene was shot. Sometimes he would ask to do another take. If an actor blew a shot, he took that as part of making movies, never attaching any blame to his responses.

The fourth picture I was in was *Wake Me When It's Over.* It was directed by Mervyn LeRoy, another legendary Hollywood director. Dick Shawn was one of the stars, and again I was playing a soldier. I had a nice little scene with Dick: We were sitting next to each other at a radarscope, it was a tight two-shot, and he was doing one-liners and otherwise being silly, while I was supposed to be totally serious about my work. It was a funny scene. Shawn was a well-known comedian, who had started out as a standup. I had several scenes in that film, but I think the one with Shawn at the radarscope was cut out of it.

I was still without a class and growing more frustrated by the day. My career was going well, my home life was good, I enjoyed the friends I had, but I felt very incomplete as an actor. I was working in television and on an occasional movie but was still frustrated with my work. I was on the hunt for a good class. I checked the trade papers every day, sat in on a couple of classes, but didn't find anything that I thought had the answers I was looking for. Since the Horseshoe Theater on Melrose was auditioning actors for a play, I went down there and met Robert Beecher, who was in charge of the theater and who informed us that they had an acting class taught by one of his associates, Fred Gallo. I didn't like the play they were reading for, but I was interested in checking out the class, which was being held in a basement theater on Gardner.

Fred Gallo was a somber individual, a day player in films and television, who professed to directing ambitions. The first night I was there, we all did improvisations. Fred would create the structure of each situation, and we had to act it. I was to be a doctor aiding an accident victim. At one point I mimed giving him a shot, probably morphine. When the improvisation was over, Fred went on and on about how authentic I had been in administering the syringe. He asked me if I had been to medical school, or if not, where I had learned to give shots. I was flabbergasted at how much time he was devoting to an activity and nothing to the behavior in the improv. That surely wasn't the class for me!

I therefore kept on looking and one day heard that Lucille Ball was going to do a workshop at Ben Ari's studio. I had heard about Ben Ari, but I didn't really know much about what he taught. It was the name of Lucille Ball that had gotten my attention. I loved her work and thought that I could learn something from her and that this would be a great showcase for me. I therefore enrolled in Ben Ari's class, which met upstairs of the Coronet Theater on La Cienega.

Raiken Ben Ari was a short man with dark black hair, which was sprinkled with wisps of gray and stood high above his scalp. He had a largish nose, which curved towards his mouth, and a crooked finger on his left hand, which he extended upwards for emphasis when he spoke. He had a pronounced Russian accent, not foreign to my ear. I liked him immediately, and he took to me also. When I had lunch with Robert Easton recently, he told me a couple of very interesting stories about Ben Ari and his involvement with

Vachtangov, an associate of Stanislavski before and during the Moscow Art Theater years. He said that Ben Ari spoke very often about Vachtangov and credited him with a lot of the knowledge he had gotten while in Russia. As the first vice-president of the Screen Actors Guild, Robert Easton represented the United States in the International Federation of Actors. They had a number of meetings in Moscow and in Leningrad, where he asked whether he could visit the old actors' home. There he spoke to all the retired actors who had populated the Russian theater and had worked with Stanislavski and Vachtangov, and all of them said that it was Vachtangov who had the greatest talent and insight and was the more creative and talented of the two. Ben Ari told an amusing story about Vachtangov: While the latter was directing a play, one of the actors approached him and asked him whether it was possible to do a particular movement in the middle of a scene, and, said Ben Ari in a very heavy Russian accent which imitated Vachtangov's, he answered, "Yes, it ees possible, but ees it necessary?" Later, Ben Ari left Russia for Israel, where he was very instrumental in the creation of the Habima Theater.

I worked with Ben Ari for several weeks before Lucy was scheduled to show up. The class included a fairly large group of actors, but if one really wanted stage time, one could get it. I spotted very quickly the most active people in the group and worked with them. Rudy Solari and I did a number of scenes together for Ben Ari and later for Lucy. Ben Ari was kind in his critiques and attempted to be helpful, but again there was not much process involved in his teaching. He did have some good tips, however, on how to get involved with the other actor and stay that way. I learned how to listen better and concentrate on what was happening in the moment. That was a lot more than I had ever gotten from Jeff. Ben Ari was a very kind man, who genuinely cared for his students, especially me. I might be sitting on the bench, deep in thought, waiting for class to start, and as he was passing, he would stop, look at me, and say, "Eric, why are you so depressed? You are a beautiful boy with talent!" It would make me smile, and he would smile in return, "Dat's better. You see how easy it is to be happy?" I guess I was prone to brooding in those days, mostly about my work and the need to find security in a process.

Rudy and I did scenes from *The Crucible, Home of the Brave, The Glass Menagerie,* and several others. I was anxious to meet and work for Lucy, and when she finally came, I was one of the first onstage. That time with her, which lasted about ten weeks, was the most memorable in my life. I learned some life-changing lessons from that woman, one of the most generous people I have ever known.

Lucy, the famous redhead, had aged some since I had last watched "I Love Lucy." There were more lines in her face, and she seemed a little sad just under the surface, but her hair was still that famous flaming red. During that same lunch with Robert Easton that I mentioned above, I learned a lot that I hadn't known at the time I had been in her class. Robert, who had worked with her in the Desilu workshop and had played parts on "The Lucy Show" told me that he thought the reason she had started teaching was that her marriage to Desi was falling apart and that she needed to fill her life with activity and creativity. As I look back at that time, it seems to make sense to me. I was excited to be working in front of her. She was an icon, and I felt privileged to be getting her attention. She was amazing. She sat in the back of the theater, and from the moment she arrived, the class atmosphere became positive and encouraging. She was able to be inspirational to all of us. She worshipped talent. In that ten-week period I never heard her utter a negative criticism to anyone. The students would sign up to do scenes on a particular evening, and she would watch them and comment on them afterwards. She did, of course, have a critique and suggestions about how to make a scene more effective. She used the word *truth* often, and while she never made an actor feel bad about his or her work, she was very direct and right on target with her critiques.

There were some very interesting people in the group: Vic Tayback, who later played the cook in the movie *Alice Doesn't Live Here Anymore* and subsequent television series "Alice"; Robert Easton, an actor who later became the best dialect teacher and coach in the world; Mark Herron, who was later married to Judy Garland for a short time (I never understood that relationship, since Mark, a very pleasant guy, was obviously homosexual); Rudy Solari, who in later years created a fairly successful theater in Beverly Hills; and the wife of Oscar Levant, who never seemed to do anything in the group except complain about people smoking. Some years later Vic Tayback saw me play Jocko De Paris in *End As a Man* at the Store Theater in Hollywood and was so impressed that he sponsored me to become a member of the Angels Company—but more about that later.

In the beginning I had thought that Lucy was going to talk about the craft of comedy, but to my surprise she seemed more interested in serious dramatic scenes. Many more people volunteered to do work on the stage after she arrived than before, which was not surprising to me, since I knew that most of them wanted to get work in the industry. I was onstage almost every week with a scene. All in all I did about seven scenes in that ten-week period. I played a priest in a scene from *The Crucible,* which I did with four other actors. Rudy Solari and I worked almost exclusively with each other. We did a scene from *Death of a Salesman* and one from *The Glass Menagerie,* and I repeated the scene from *Home of the Brave* with which I had had so much success before going into the army. Lucy never said anything to Rudy or me other than that our work was wonderful or terrific or that she was impressed with our talent. She always responded to my work with great enthusiasm and support. She was obviously impressed with me and told me so every time I worked. I was very pleased, and so was Ben Ari.

I learned two important lessons from Lucy, one of which was life changing. Quite often we would ask her questions about how she worked or about her life, her career, or her experiences as a major star. She was always very accommodating with her responses. She didn't seem to have a privacy issue and would gladly share her feelings on almost any subject. One evening someone asked her if she ever got to the set of "I Love Lucy" hung over or exhausted from the evening before. She was quite open about the fact that quite often she would get there tired and uninspired because of a party or other activity that had gone on too late. "So I would sit at the makeup table," she explained, "and would wake up and begin to encourage what I called *an enchanted sense of play.* I would then walk into the set and get deeply in touch with that childlike energy, which I called sense of play, and make some barely audible childlike 'wee' sounds internally. Very soon I would feel that exciting energy climb up in my body, and I was ready to be Lucy."

Robert Easton related a story that he had heard her share with the group at Desilu: Sometimes, when she was doing a scene with Vivian Vance, it seemed stilted and unreal and not very much fun, so they would decide to approach it as if they were two little girls playing in some backyard. It always worked for them. They were able to get into that magical state of play. Listening to Lucy reminded me of my summer-stock experience when I would get to the theater a full hour ahead of everyone else, turn on the blinding stage lights, and stand in their filaments looking into the darkness of the theater. I would raise my arms high above my head, make a sound something like that a gleeful child would make, and feel that exciting energy climb up my body as if it had come from the center of the earth through the stage floor and up my body like hot liquid filling me up to the top of my head. I didn't know then that I was stimulating my own version of an enchanted sense of play, but when Lucy told that story, I immediately identified the experience.

One evening someone asked her how she was able to do all the varied things she did—do "I Love Lucy," run a studio, have some kind of home life, raise children, and so on. She replied, "I do 100 percent of what I'm doing when I'm doing whatever I'm doing, and when I'm finished with that, I go to the next thing and do that with 100-percent involvement." When I heard that, it was like experiencing some kind of religious revelation that in itself meant a great deal more than the actual words. I raised my hand and asked her if she would give us an example. I think she saw the effect of her statement on my face. She paused for a moment and then said, "All right, Eric, suppose I was sweeping this stage with a broom. I would give 100 percent of my attention and energy to doing the best job of sweeping that I was capable of, without giving one thought to what I had just been doing before or what I was going to do next. When I finished sweeping the stage, I would move on to the next activity without giving the stage another thought. I would then commit myself to the next activity with the same 100-percent involvement." It may not seem like such a profound statement to the reader of this book, but it changed my life forever. Until that very moment I had always been in a state of worry about the variety of things I had on my plate. All through college I had suffered over how to apportion my time, what subject needed the most attention, and when I was going to be able to move on to the next activity; and when I had forced myself to do so, I had been miserably preoccupied with my last involvement—which had made me unable to fully concentrate on what I was doing at the time. I had consistently been fragmented and unable to relax and enjoy moments of zoning out. It had also affected my acting. I would be distracted with a thought about an obligation and forget the next line sometimes. My angst and worries made life less enjoyable and fulfilling. After that evening, I began to practice the 100-percent phenomenon. At first it was difficult. I had established quite a powerful conditioned response, and like most habits this one was hard to break. That is when I learned another important lesson for life, which was not to attempt to break a habit but rather to create a better new one. That's how I was eventually able to succeed in my focused commitment to activities.

Robert asked Lucy to recommend some reading material, expecting that she would suggest something on comedy. Much to his surprise she mentioned *The Art of Selfishness,* by David Seabury. The book was psychological in content and extolled the virtue of becoming selfish in positive ways and the need to do so. At first, Robert thought that it was a strange recommendation, but on pursuing Lucy's reasoning we all understood. She said and felt that so many of us, and actors in general, were so giving and into other people's needs that we didn't take the time to create a foundation of self-esteem, and that giving to oneself was necessary in building a strong ego state. It seemed almost like a contradiction, since Lucy was one of the most unselfish and giving people I had ever met up to that point in my life. She never seemed to be self-impressed, and God knows she had every reason to be! As my life has evolved, I can trace much of what and who I am directly to Lucille Ball and those wonderful ten weeks with her. I live by two important credos: always to stay "hungry," forever reaching for more knowledge and growth, and never to be self-impressed. I really think that both those beliefs started with Lucy.

While she was always encouraging in her critiques, Lucy would spot the areas where the work in a scene wasn't truthful or real, and she would suggest ways to approach those places or the relationship between the actors. It wasn't that she had a defined or specific technique or language, but she really possessed uncanny instincts about performing and was somehow able to communicate those ideas to us. I, of course, wanted more specifics in craft terms, but I was very impressed with her insights. We spent a little time discussing the business and how tough it was, how insensitive some producers and studio heads could be, which led her into one of her early experiences as an actress under contract to RKO. They had thrown her into all kinds of little parts—secretaries, elevator operators, and an occasional other-woman part—mostly straight or serious roles. One day they called her into the head office and invited her to sit down. Flanked by a number of paunchy, balding studio executives, she was then informed without much ceremony that they were dropping her. They were not going to renew her contract. It was a blow, which had come without warning, but she maintained her composure, stood up, looked directly into the eyes of everyone in the room, and said, "Gentlemen, someday I'll come back and buy this studio." She walked out with her head held high and a number of years later bought not only RKO, but also RKO Pathé, the other RKO studio in Culver City. Now to me that is the pinnacle of payback!

Shortly after she ended with us at Ben Ari's, Lucy did another workshop, on the lot at Desilu, which included most of the people under contract at the studio. Desilu was doing "I Love Lucy," "The Untouchables," "Star Trek," and a few other shows. Nick Georgiade of "The Untouchables," Roger Perry and Majel Barrett from "Star Trek," as well as Robert Easton, were involved in that workshop. Robert told me that he and Bobbette Bentley had done a scene from *Bus Stop* and that Lucy had told them that they were better than what she had seen on Broadway. Lucy was not given to exaggeration, so Robert was quite pleased with her critique.

On the last evening of our session, Lucy called me over to a quiet corner of the studio and told me that she was very impressed with me, that I was incredibly talented, and that she wanted to do something to help me in the business. Needless to say, I was overwhelmed and had to fight to hold back the tears. I hugged her, thanked her, and told her that I would never forget the experience of the previous ten weeks. I haven't. Unfortunately I never followed up on her generous offer. She went to New York to appear in the Broadway production of *Wild Cat.* She had told me to call her when she got back to Los Angeles, but for whatever reason I never did.

After Lucy left, I stayed in Ben Ari's class and continued the journey and search for tools. Ben Ari was helpful but lacked the components of a process. Most of the people who were there for Lucy had left, and the class was much smaller, which was good for the students but not for Ben Ari. I am sure his income suffered as a result of the exodus. He cast me in a play that he was planning to tour all over the Los Angeles area, S. Ansky's *The Dybbuk,* a play with a classical Jewish theme. There were three characters in it: a rabbi, a young man named Channon, and a young girl, Leah. I was to play Channon, and Robert Middleton, a well-known character actor, who had appeared in scores of movies and television shows, was cast as the rabbi. Robert was quite overweight and had a jovial round face, thinning hair, very expressive eyes, and an infectious laugh, which he shared often. The actress who was to play Leah was from Pasadena and was very plain and not especially attractive. She had frizzy, light brown hair, which always seemed unkempt, so I silently committed myself to present her with a large comb on the final evening of performance! She was quite talented and almost always acted from a place of truth and reality. Robert was wonderful, and I was insecure.

As I remember, the dybbuk was an evil spirit, which inhabited Leah. Channon, who was in love with her, wanted to free her from that possession, so he enlisted the help of the rabbi to do the exorcism. Here again I felt very privileged to be working with such a seasoned professional as Robert, and my relationship reality to him worked for the relationship between the rabbi and Channon. Ben Ari directed with insight and sensitivity. We did the play podium style at a number of synagogues and some other venues all over Los Angeles and in some of the suburbs. When I say "podium style," I don't mean that we stood behind a podium and didn't move. Quite the contrary, we moved. Leah danced, I embraced her, and the rabbi made physical contact with us. It was just not done in a conventional theater stage set—which allowed us to move around without huge trucks and stagehands. I think that we did the play over a two- or three-month period. It was a great experience, one that I treasured for many years after. I felt like a working actor. I received much praise from people in the audiences and was encouraged by their comments to take more acting risks. After a number of performances, I was able to quell my insecurities and look forward to the next show. As Channon, I was able to access very strong emotions that came from very deep places. It was the first full-length play that presented such dramatic obligations, and I felt that I had learned something from the experience. I had done some very heavy scenes before, but never a full-length play that demanded sustaining heavy emotional life for such a long period of time.

Shortly after the play ended, I left Ben Ari's class. I felt the need to move on and hopefully find a teacher who had some of the answers I had so long been searching for. I auditioned and got a part in *The Cold Wind and the Warm* at the Players' Ring Theatre. It was a fairly small role of a love-struck young man, who followed Barbara Bain's character around, mooning over her. Barbara was Martin Landau's wife. The two had come to Los Angeles with a Paddy Chayefsky play, *Middle of the Night*, and had decided to stay in California. "Marty" was at the theater visiting every night, and I got to talk to him before the play started and during the intermissions. We had a good cast, and I enjoyed going to the theater every evening. Besides Barbara, there was also Frank Wolff, a curly-headed, gregarious, full-bodied guy with a prominent nose and a large mustache. When he smiled, his entire face became involved. He had a deep voice and a great laugh, was a friend of Marty's and Barbara's, and attended Marty's class. He was one of those people who could have been the subject of the *Reader's Digest* section on "The Most Unforgettable Character I Have Ever Known." I think I had a scene or two with him, and I believe my character was his younger brother. Frank had one of the most unusual abilities as an actor: he could fart on cue. I mean that all you had to do was ask him to pass gas, and without fail he would!

I would prepare outside in back of the theater, shaking my hands violently—as they had taught us to do at Northwestern to eliminate tension—and pacing vigorously back and forth, which I thought at the time would elevate my emotional state and physical energy. Actually, unbeknownst to me, all I was doing was increasing my tension. I had many long conversations with Marty about his work, about the Actors Studio, of which he was a member, and about his career in New York. He made some subtle suggestions that I might be better off saving my preparation routine to use that life on the stage. I don't think at the time I got the full impact of what he meant, but I certainly understood it later.

Frank had a 1954 green MG, and since I was into sports cars, I expressed interest in it. He invited me to take a ride one sunny day. We rode up Sunset Boulevard with the top down and shared our passions about acting and cars. He pulled over to the curb abruptly, parked, turned to me, and very seriously said, "Eric, I like you! I am going to give you a great gift, one that will affect the rest of your life." I was taken aback by the unpredictable abruptness of his actions and the serious tone in his voice.

I smiled uncomfortably and asked, "So, what is this gift?"

He replied, "I am going to invite you to Marty's class. I really think that it will change your entire approach to acting. I know how much acting means to you, and I've seen you struggle to get where you want to be. Marty has some of those answers you have been looking for."

I was a little reluctant to say, "O.K., I'm coming," for a couple of reasons: (1) I was in the play with Barbara, and (2) I didn't know much about Marty. He was tall and gaunt and had a tendency to stoop a little. He had strange offbeat features and seemed a little reserved with me or at least withheld some of the things that I think he would have liked to say to me about my work. I did, however, agree to visit the class, which was on Monday night, a dark night at the theater.

Marty had a little studio on Gardner, just a few doors north of Melrose. It was a cute little place with a slightly raised stage area and folding chairs for seats. It had an acting-class atmosphere and was decorated with warm colors. Marty greeted me warmly and invited me to take a seat. I sat in the last row of chairs. The class began with several students' getting up onstage one at a time and doing the singing-and-moving exercise that Marty had gotten from Lee Strasberg. As I watched them going through it, I was taken with the amount and variety of emotions that evolved with each actor. After that, there were various individual exercises and a couple of scenes. Again I witnessed some bizarre behavior, followed by abstract and somewhat confusing explanations of process. It seemed a little like Jeff Hayden's class in that the choices people spoke of were strange. Marty's critiques seemed direct and benevolent, but I was uncomfortable with the work I had seen. My instincts told me that this was not the place where I wanted to study. Frank asked me what I thought, and I said that I was impressed, but confused, by the nature of the choices people were using. He told me that they actually worked to produce the life in the scenes. Here again I didn't hear a specific *how,* and I was desperate for that how. I had one week to decide whether to take the class or pass on it. That was a tough week, because I was still around all those people in the play. We had another month of run, so I decided to avoid the discomfort of not going to the class and having to make excuses. I figured I would enroll for one month, at which time the play would have ended, and then I could drop out without all the explanations. Besides, I really liked Frank and didn't want to disappoint him, since he really felt that he was giving me this life-changing gift. That phrase *life changing* has become such a cliché! I use it in my life presently to describe the work I teach, but it is only a cliché if it isn't true. I was soon to find out whether Frank was right.

The following week, I arrived early and waited outside the building. When I got to the studio, I saw a young, good-looking man leaning against the bricks near the entrance. I said, "Hi," stood there for some moments, then added, "You look familiar." He responded by telling me that I too looked familiar to him.

"Maybe we have run into each other at auditions," I said.

"Yeah, probably," he responded. "What's your name?"

"Eric Morris. What's yours?"

"Jack Nicholson."

I shook his hand and proceeded to tell him what little I knew of the class. That was my first meeting with Jack and the beginning of a long friendship. Marty arrived, and I took a seat in the second row. I paid my twenty-five-dollar tuition for that month and officially became a student in the class.

In this, my second viewing, I began to see and hear things that piqued my interest. I heard some of the *hows* related to the work I was seeing. Unlike in Jeff's class, there seemed to be an explanation of how people were creating the choices they said they were using. For example, if one of the actresses had been working for her eyelashes being the wings of monarch butterflies, she might have said that she used fake eyelashes to get a sense of their weight and extension and that from that point she used her senses to create the butterfly wings; or in the case of that woman filling up with hot lava, she might have explained that she had started by feeling her own body heat and also using her senses to elevate it, while creating a rising energy climbing up her body; or someone might have said that he was using an impacting person in his life to stimulate the desired emotional life. For the first time in all of the training I had been exposed to, I heard things that began to connect with a system, a process, the *how* I had been looking for. Marty explained the purpose of the singing exercise, what it was meant to accomplish. He emphasized the need for an actor to free himself from blocks and obstacles and some of the ways that was accomplished through the use of certain exercises.

At one point Marty asked me if I knew how to do sense memory, and I proudly responded with a yes.

"We learned sense memory at Northwestern, and I use it in my work," I said.

"O.K.," he replied, "bring in a sense-memory exercise that you work on with something to eat or drink for next week's class."

The following week, when he called my name, I jumped up onstage, arranged myself in a chair in front of a small table, and proceeded with what I thought was sense memory: I took a dramatic moment, then lifted the imaginary glass to my lips, mimed drinking the imaginary milk, and put the imaginary glass back on the table. The whole exercise had taken about one minute. There was a spontaneous outburst of laughter from the whole class. I flushed red, looked out into the audience with a mixture of confusion and embarrassment, and turned to Marty, who sat in front of the people, on the right. He was kind enough to suppress his own impulse to laugh at what I had just done. He took a beat and very kindly said, "Eric, that is not sense memory. That isn't even good pantomime!" I must have looked as though I had just experienced humongous humiliation, because he came up on the stage, put his hand on my shoulder, and said, "Listen, how can you expect yourself to understand a technique when you have never been taught it properly?" That made me feel a little better, and at the same time I was angry with Krause, who had told us what sense memory was and how it worked.

This was the beginning of the journey—one that was truly life changing for me in every area of my life. I took to the class with a fervor and passion that went way beyond what most of the other people in that class were experiencing. I felt that I had finally found what I had been looking for during all the years I had been an actor. We did a variety of exercises, each of which had a different purpose or was supposed to address a different issue or block. The singing exercise was designed to access whatever emotional life was underneath the vocal expression. Singing one word of a song and holding each note for a period of time were supposed to allow whatever the actor was feeling to surface. It was amazing to watch. An actor would, for example, sing "Happy Birthday," and halfway through would come apart and start to sob uncontrollably. The movement part of the exercise pointed out any vocal-emotional or physical-vocal "splits." What that word simply means is that the actor's instrument is not functioning from a together place. Splits indicate that some problem, block, tension, or commentary is getting in the way of the instrument's behaving naturally, as it does when nothing interferes. Some of the other exercises, also from Lee Strasberg, were "private moments," the basic sense-memory exercise with a cup of coffee, and the original "being," which was very helpful in not taking anything for granted. Years later, in the early period after I had begun to teach, I used a couple of the same exercises. Marty would also do group improvisations, sometimes structuring a circumstance and at other times saying that we were all in a bus station in the middle of the night and letting us do whatever we wanted from that place.

The second half of his class was devoted to scene work. Usually there were two or three scenes per class. There were some very talented people there, but it's hard to remember who was in the class when I started and who came in after I did. As was my habit, I looked for, and found, the people I felt would commit themselves to hard work and be there to rehearse the scenes I wanted to do. There were several people whom I didn't get to know very well, either because they didn't stay in the class or because they were there as observers and never worked onstage. One exception was Monte Hellman, who was there a lot of the time and was, and still is, a film director. He directed Jack Nicholson in a few pictures in the Philippines and received critical acclaim for one of his films, *Two-Lane Blacktop.* I don't know the chronology of those films or at what point they were done—probably not at that time in 1959–1960. Some of the other people, such as Stella Stevens or Bruce Geller, didn't do anything in the class that was memorable or stimulates my memory of their being there at the time. I do remember Gretta Tyson, however, who was married to Ron Starr, another student there and someone I still see occasionally. Gretta came into class one night wearing a full-length mink coat with nothing underneath. She didn't expose her naked body, but by something she said or did, everyone knew that there was nothing there but mink and skin!

The people I worked and bonded with were Sondra Kerr, Jack Nicholson, Harry Dean Stanton, Dale Wilburn, Sandra Knight, Marsha Park/Perron/Pessis—I never knew what last name she chose to have at any given point—Rupert Cross, Connie Buck Marlowe, Beverly Anderson, and Don Spruance. I did scenes with most of those people, or at least with most of the women. All in all, I must have done fifty scenes in the three years I was there. In the very beginning I rehearsed a scene from *The Glass Menagerie* with Shirley Knight, who was a beautiful girl and quite talented, but a little egocentric. She left the class before we could do the scene, because she couldn't tolerate the cigarette smoke. I thought that Sondra Kerr was enormously talented, so I tried to work with her whenever she was available. We did several scenes together, from *The Rainmaker, Desire under the Elms, Dark of the Moon,* and something else that eludes my memory.

What was different about this class from any of the others I had attended was that the Method was less cerebral and more applicably practical, instead of consisting of vague intellectual directions, such as, "Think of where you are coming from before you enter the stage!" In itself that is a good thing to address, but thinking about it does nothing to create the reality of having just been there. In the same way writing elaborate backgrounds for a character is an exercise in writing rather than acting, unless one has the tools to implement those realities into one's own behavior. The entire Stanislavski concept of "actions and activities," which I had been taught in a variety of Method-acting classes, was debunked in Marty's. Lee had proven that attempting to address an action or activity would only lead to concept and premeditation for the actor. An action is divided into three parts:

What am I doing?

Why am I doing it?

How am I doing it?

Understanding the first two parts is O.K., but the moment you plan on how you are going to do something, it becomes premeditated behavior. Unless the actor supplies an impetus ("choice") that impels him to behave, his behavior ceases to be organic or real. Activities are also planned behaviors. I once heard an actor on a television interview say that when he was playing Happy in *Death of a Salesman,* he decided at one point to get up from the kitchen table, walk over to a mirror on the wall, and comb his hair. He said it was an activity he thought would fit the character of Happy; but it was his *decision* to do that, not a real impulse or need. Lee had thrown all that out and substituted it with obligations and choices, and Marty, taught and influenced by Lee, did the same. After identifying the obligation in a scene—what it is that is impelling the behavior of the character—the actor can address it by working for a choice from his own life experience that will create the need and impetus to behave in the same way from a real place. Instead of making *decisions* about how to behave, the actor has the responsibility to create an impetus that makes him *need* to do so. Those were entirely new concepts for me. They made real sense and were backed up by specific applicable approaches, which had been missing from the beginning of my training. When I asked, "O.K., how do you do that?" I now got an answer that I could immediately apply to creating an emotional state.

The understanding came rather quickly, but the ability to do the work wasn't so swift. When I came into Marty's class, I had already been acting for nine years. I had done forty plays and a number of films, and my habits were well worn in, so a lot of my work remained impositional and conceptual. I was onstage every week, often twice in the same evening, once for an individual exercise and sometimes also for a scene. I always had at least one scene prepared and quite often was working on two or three at the same time. I was obsessed with the class, the work, the craft, and the organic nature of acting after all those disappointing years. You might say that I had become a newborn actor. I was still living at 1211 North Detroit Street, and my home life was good, but I now had to juggle time spent with Jean in order to do my daily routine. She was working at a nine-to-five job at the advertising agency, so my days were free to work on my craft. When she came home, I felt as though I too had put in a full workday. The big difference was that she was getting paid for it and I was growing as a person and an actor. I also had to rehearse with people from the class and found myself spending more time with them than with Sy and Barbara, Mike and Sherry, or Lee and Pat. It seemed as though there weren't enough hours in the day, and I had to reserve the weekends for my wife.

Ivan was sending me out fairly regularly, and I was booking jobs at least one out of three auditions. During the two years I was with that agent I did about fifteen film jobs. Often I would be rehired several times on the same show. For instance, I did six episodes of "The Silent Service," a series about the submarine service. We actually filmed the show on a real World War II sub, the USS *Sawfish,* which was moored in Long Beach. Here again I was playing a sailor. I couldn't get out of the service! As a departure from all the soldiers and sailors, I was cast as a dope addict on "Police Court."

So I was working but was still not satisfied with my acting. I did a lot of the shows and films in the early months of being in the class, when I wasn't as yet secure in making the transition from the kind of work I used to do to what I was now being taught to do. Marty was pretty hard on me. Some of his critiques were brutal. One time, after I finished a scene, he looked at me for a very long time—I think he was searching for the right thing to say—then blurted, "Eric, that wasn't even good bad English acting!" Well, you can imagine how I felt after that comment, but I didn't get angry, because I knew he was right. I was frustrated and cried a lot on the way home. There was a period in that first year that was very depressing. I thought of going home and sticking my head in the oven but fortunately never acted on it! I remember calling Jack Nicholson up on a particularly bad Tuesday morning after a very disappointing class the previous evening. I was in tears and wanted to share my depression and frustration with someone who was open and sensitive to me, and Jack always was. After my blubbering tirade, he simply and benevolently said, "You know, Eric, you are a good actor, whether or not you can do this work." I really needed to hear that, especially from someone I respected.

As I said before, I picked people in class who I knew were as passionate as I was about the work, and I did a lot of scenes. I worked with an actress named Rosalyn, whose last name I can't remember, on a scene from *Golden Boy,* and even though it was one of the earlier scenes I did for Marty, I did have a moment or two of connection with reality. He pointed them out to me and told me why I was connected and real in those moments. In *View from the Bridge,* another of my early works, however, I got trapped doing an Italian accent. Nonetheless, my relationship realities were growing. I found it easier to become involved with the other actor and to respond to her as I was affected in the moment. That was a big breakthrough for me. I have already talked about all the scenes I did with Sondra Kerr. She was as committed to the work as I was, maybe even more so if that was possible. I also did a couple of scenes with Sandra Knight, and I worked with her on *Talk to Me like the Rain and Let Me Listen,* by Tennessee Williams. Barbara Bain and I worked on *Elizabeth the Queen.* I truly enjoyed that experience, because I would drive out to Paradise Cove in

Malibu to rehearse with her. She and Marty had rented a house there, which belonged to Will Rogers' son and was near the ocean and full of atmosphere. Going there to rehearse had the added advantage of being able to see and talk to Marty outside the class environment.

I did Marchbanks from *Candida* also with Barbara, I think, and, as a departure explored a scene from *The Moon Is Blue.* I was good with comedy, so I ventured into some comedic scenes but found that they were filled with traps for me. I could easily lapse into shtick, so I stuck to the more serious stuff. The scene I repeated about twenty times was from *Desire under the Elms.* I had to work with five different actresses on it, because each of them in turn got tired of the repetition and quit doing it with me, maybe because I was so obsessed with it. I was very intense in those days and sometimes a little hard to take. I played Eben, a farm boy preoccupied with the place—the farm—and the ownership of it. Abbie, the other character in the scene, had married Eben's father and laid claim to the property when he passed away. In order to win Eben over, she has decided to seduce him. I included Eben's rural accent in my work and found ways to dislike the other character, but I had problems with the characterization. Every time I did the scene, Marty's comments were the same: "Eric, you are a nice Jewish boy from the big city of Chicago, and you don't have dirt under your fingernails, and you don't have cow shit on your shoes, and you don't even know what cow shit looks or smells like! I don't believe you as Eben!" I can't even begin to describe the frustration I experienced doing that scene. I tried many things to be less sophisticated or intelligent, but nothing seemed to work or to change Marty's comments.

One evening in class—I think I was on my third actress—Marty asked if anyone had a scene. I, of course, raised my hand, and he asked me what scene I was doing. *"Desire under the Elms,"* I replied, at which point Harry Dean Stanton stood up and in a loud, tortured voice exclaimed, "No, no, I can't take it another time. I can't!" and he walked out of the class. His response didn't deter me, however. I hopped up on the stage and did the scene again. Harry Dean, for whatever reason, either didn't like me very much at the time or just delighted in teasing me mercilessly. Whenever he saw me leaving class or at Schwab's Drugstore, he would ask me in a loud voice if I was going home to practice sense memory. I didn't like it, but I accepted it as a personality quirk of his. In spite of the way he treated me, I always liked him. When I left Ivan Green, Harry Dean helped by introducing me to his agent, Betty Wookey, whom I went with after Ivan. I'm sure that the rest of the class was also getting tired of seeing me struggle with Eben, but Marty never told me to drop the scene. To me it was more than a scene. It was a challenge to my talent and craft, and I was not about to throw in the towel.

Marty had told the class to go to the zoo and study animals for use in characterization. He had instructed us to watch each animal for its rhythm and limitations. At Northwestern Alvina had told us just to observe animals and people, and nothing more—no process, no technique, nothing about what to look for. Marty at least gave us two elements to use in getting a sense of the animal.

I decided to go to the zoo and find an animal that might create the spine of Eben, one that would address my sophistication and my urban background, affect the manifestation of my intellect, and so on. After looking for a couple of days, I settled on the gorilla. I watched a particular one and studied him in relation to his rhythm and looked for his limitations. It wasn't much to go on, but it was a good start. I went to the zoo for a couple of hours every day and stood in front of the gorilla's cage. I tried to get a sense of him as subtly as possible so as not to call attention to myself, but I got to know the keeper and, after a few visits, established a nice relationship with him. I told him why I was there every day, and instead of lifting an eyebrow, he was very helpful in telling me things about the gorilla's habits.

When I felt secure with a translated sense of the gorilla, I got up onstage with Connie Buck, the fifth actress in this saga, and did Eben. When the scene ended, I looked over at Marty, expecting him to say that I looked like a Jewish boy from Chicago imitating a gorilla! Instead, he stood up from his chair and said, "O.K., Eric, you did it! I believed you. I believed that you were raised on a farm and had cow shit on your shoes. You even approached Connie with a sexual animalism." I was ecstatic! I sat down and got very vulnerable. Being vulnerable and very emotional was never difficult for me, but this was different. It was a kind of triumphant vulnerability. The class comments were equally full of praise. It was the beginning of my journey into the exploration of what in my work I now call "externals."

Having satisfied myself at last with being able to address that scene and accomplish a sense of the reality of the character, I went on to other material. I worked with Beverly Anderson, who later changed her name to Beverly Ballard and moved to New York. She was a very attractive, blond Swedish girl from Minnesota, and I enjoyed working with her. She did quite well later in commercials. Another actress in Marty's class with whom I did some scene work was Jackie Raskin. She was a little difficult, because she would always say a line in the scene, listen to the way it sounded, and then repeat it over and over until she was satisfied with it. This was very distracting if I had something going for me, but I liked her anyway. She later married Monte Hellman. They were together for some years. Jackie died about twenty years ago, and this brings to mind a funny anecdote about her. She was a vegetarian and into health and nutrition, and at a dinner party she said, "I wouldn't put anything into my stomach that I wouldn't put in my eye," at which point B. J. Merholtz responded, "Well, you wouldn't stick a stalk of celery in your eye, would you?" B. J. was, and still is, a close friend of Jack Nicholson. All of us hung out together, and quite often B. J. and some of the other people in the class would come over and hang out at the pool at my apartment building. B. J. also came to Marty's class as an observer. Since he was a writer, I am sure his interest in the class was profitable. Not too long ago at a dinner party at John Shaner's house, B. J. said to me that as a result of watching my work in Marty's class, he had thought I was the best actor in Hollywood and that he was sad I hadn't stayed with it. Be that as it may, in class I felt the need to reach a level of craftsmanship that would give me the confidence and security that would allow me to do the kind of acting which I knew inside I was capable of.

Towards the end of the first year in class, I called my agent, Betty Wookey, and told her not to send me out for a while, until I was ready. She was shocked at my request, since, as she told me, I was working regularly and she was getting good feedback on my auditions. I tried to explain to her that I knew that with a little more training time my work would be incredibly better. I fully expected her to drop me, but she didn't. She agreed to hold back as I had asked.

Those three years were a very special time for all of us, for the relationships that were formed, the bonding, and the camaraderie.

In the beginning, we all went to Norm's coffee shop on La Cienega after class. We would sit around and talk about class and the work we had seen that evening, and we shared our ambitions as actors. I really felt as though I had found a home and those people were part of an extended family. Later, we all started to hang out at Jack's place after class. He was renting a little house on Fountain Avenue, just west of Gardner. We would buy a half-gallon of Gallo wine and listen to Harry Dean Stanton play his guitar. My favorite was "Cucurucucu Paloma," which I would request all the time. We sat around talking about everything, but mostly about acting, other actors, and the business. Sometimes we stayed all night, and I would walk home just as the sun was coming up. Jack's bedroom was just off the dining room, where we hung out, and when he got tired he just went to sleep. The after-class activities became almost as important as class. I looked forward to those nights.

Many years later, I went up to Samuel Goldwyn Studios to see Jack to ask him if he would write the foreword to *No Acting Please.* He was there, prepping to do a film, and was on the phone talking to a lawyer to try to find out if he could collect a million-dollar bet he had won on a basketball game. When he got off the phone, he called me into his office. I was laughing, so he asked me what I was laughing at, and I replied, "Jack, you're talking to a lawyer about a million-dollar sports bet that you won. Do you remember when we didn't have sixty-nine cents between us to buy a half-gallon of wine after a Monday class?" He laughed, and we reminisced about those days. "We tore your house apart looking for pennies, nickels, and dimes, and we finally found enough in the cushions of your sofa," I reminded him. We continued speaking about the class and the people who were there at the time, and he said that he had thought we all felt like a very representative group of actors in Hollywood, but, he continued, "We really weren't. We were unique and special, and we didn't know it then, but as it turned out, almost everyone in that group has made a mark in the business." We went on for some time, and Jack agreed to write the foreword—which of course he did.

Quite a number of personal relationships evolved directly from Marty's class. At one point, I was rehearsing a scene with Sandra Knight, who was living with Robert Blake at the time. Quite often he was there at her apartment, where we were rehearsing, and we would spend some time talking about when we had first met and about Bobby Driscoll and the Players' Ring Theatre. Robert and I hit it off well and on many occasions talked about his early years in the business. Sandra and I also became very close friends and did a couple of scenes together. It was about that time that *The 2000 Year Old Man* came out on record, and as she and I loved Mel Brooks and Carl Reiner's comedy, on many occasions in class we would throw one-liners from the record back and forth across the room. It made us, as well as some of the other members of the class who were familiar with the record, laugh.

One weekend Jean, Sandra, Robert, and I went up to Lake Arrowhead, checked into a hotel, and spent Saturday and Sunday in that winter wonderland. Bobby and Sandra took the upstairs bedroom, while Jean and I had the lower one. It was as cold as the North Pole. We had a lovely little fireplace on the first level, but the management had only provided us with a small bundle of wood to burn, so when we exhausted our supply, Bobby and I went looking for more. There weren't any markets in the area, so we decided to requisition wood from the stacks outside the houses along the road. Because it was like stealing, we were very careful about how we approached the stacks. I was the lookout, while Bobby grabbed the logs. When we had enough, we made our way back to the hotel. To the girls, who wondered where we had gotten so much firewood, Bobby said that some guy who was driving along had asked us if we would like to buy some. We spent the rest of that evening in front of the fireplace, drinking Burgundy and eating cheese and apples. We talked about acting, our relationships, and what we wanted out of life. It was very mellow, and when we were ready to leave to go back to Los Angeles, we all hugged and promised to remember what a great weekend it had been. That was forty-six years ago, and I still remember it fondly. It was a very special time in all of our lives.

I'm not sure that every acting class breeds such closeness and relationships on the outside. One could write an interesting novel about the nature and changes of all the relationships that evolved in that three-year period. Almost everyone in Marty's class was affected by the work, some more than others and almost no one as profoundly as I. I had come to that class with creative malnutrition, hungry for answers and willing to work feverishly to learn the how. I was aware of many of the relationships that evolved and changed in the three years I attended the class, but only recently did I find out there were others I had not known about. After not seeing Sondra Kerr Blake for about twenty or more years, I had lunch with her and found out that her memory was precise about many of the events of that period. She told me that she had been seriously involved with Frank Wolff, who had asked her to marry him and go to Europe with him. She didn't want to do that, so I guess that's what had caused the split. Sondra was very open about the various relationships she had had during and after that time. She had had a short affair with Jack Nicholson, but she was so terrified of him that the relationship had turned from a romantic involvement into a friendship. Her intimidation had been so great that in a rehearsal for a William Styron scene they were doing for class, she had made them relate through a closed bathroom door in her apartment. They had said the lines while he stood on one side of the door and she inside the bathroom. When they did the scene in class, it was so outrageous that Marty stood up and said, "What the hell was that?" Jack threw his hands up in the air and in a most frustrated way replied, "She made me rehearse with a closed door between us!"

Jack had also been involved with Georgianna Carter for some time, but later, when he got involved with Sandra Knight, Dale Wilburn married Georgianna in what was a short-lived relationship. Sondra told me that one night during class, Jack came and sat down next to her and in a whisper asked her if she thought Sandra Knight was wearing anything under her dress. I imagine he had been interested in Sandra for a while, and that was his way of expressing it to Sondra. Sandra Knight was still living with Robert Blake at the time, but everything changed very quickly, as Sondra told me, on the evening she herself was appearing in an Equity Library Theater production of *The Grass Harp*. After the show Robert went up to her and said, "I'm going to marry you!" He left Sandra Knight standing alone, so Jack sauntered over to her, and I guess shortly after that Robert was with Sondra Kerr and Jack got involved with Sandra Knight. Both couples later married. Jean and I attended Jack's wedding, an intimate affair with about a dozen people in attendance, in a small house around the corner from where he lived on Fountain and within walking distance from where Jean and I lived on Detroit Street. Jack was young and had all the good looks of a leading man, and Sandra was, and I might say still is, beautiful. They stood there looking into each other's eyes with love and intense sexual energy. I remember thinking how much I envied what they felt for each other. I was in love with Jean, and we had a good relationship, but the envy came from a romantic place that makes people cry at weddings.

Much of my time out of class was spent with people from the class, such as Dale Wilburn, Don Spruance, and later Jon Cedar, whom I brought into the class. Dale used to come over every day. We would sit around and talk about class, the work and the people. It was a very special time in my life. One afternoon Dale, Jack, Don, Jon, and I were sitting in my living room and as usual talking about acting and class and what each of us was doing outside of class, when I suggested we play around with my eight-millimeter movie camera. I said that in addition to working on scenes and exercises in class we should also deal with the technical demands of film. I had a long hallway between the living room and the toilet, so I suggested that we set up the camera on a tripod just outside the bathroom and that each of us come out of the bathroom on "Action" and walk past the camera without being self-conscious or aware of its being there. It seemed like a very simple thing to do. I volunteered to be first, so I waited in the bathroom for action to be called and then proceeded past the camera into the living room. I was greeted by spontaneous laughter from all of them. Obviously they had all seen a self-conscious awareness of the camera, which I had tried to compensate for in my behavior. They all did the exercise one by one, and every last one of them fell into the same trap. Dale sauntered past the camera with an impositional relaxed attitude, with his head cocked to one side, very obviously compensating and attempting to be natural. Jack was very direct and moved very quickly past the camera looking straight ahead as if focusing on a particular destination. It was obvious that if there hadn't been a camera there, we would all have just walked out of the bathroom naturally without any obligation to be anything other than ourselves. We roared with laughter because all of us found different ways to compensate and attempted not to be affected by the presence of the camera.

We did a lot of things in that period of time. Don was into Western quick draw. He had a single-action colt revolver, like that which the cowboys wore, and he had become very good at drawing and cocking it in one very fast movement, so quick that he challenged me to beat him by holding and flicking the wheel on a Zippo lighter to ignite the flame faster than he could draw, cock, and fire the pistol. I thought that it was a sucker's bet, since I already had the lighter in my hand and my thumb on the wheel, but he beat me every time! I thought that I would be doing a lot of Westerns on TV at that time, so I was eager to learn how to do what he had done. I knew I would never be nearly as good as Don, but I believed I could learn, so he proceeded to teach me. Of course the gun was never loaded, so we were confident that we would never have an accident; however, Don did tell me of an experience he had had in the desert a few years earlier: He had been practicing his quick draw with a loaded .22-caliber single-action pistol, when it went off as he was pulling it out of the holster, and he had shot himself in the leg just above the kneecap. He was able to crawl out, reach his car, and drive to the hospital. That was the last time he practiced his quick draw with a loaded gun! Don was a very amiable guy, and we spent a lot of time together. He and his wife, Dolly, would come over to our apartment, or, quite often, we would go to their place or out to dinner. One day, Dolly returned home from work to find Don in his underwear, standing in front of the mirror with his gun and holster strapped to his waist, practicing quick draw.

At that time Westerns were very popular in the movies and on TV. There were no less than eight regular Western series on television. I, of course, wanted to work, so the quick draw was not only fun but, as I thought, a preparation for doing parts on Westerns. I got pretty fast with it and was anxious to have the opportunity to use it in a part. My brother Ed, who was writing for a variety of TV shows, wrote a small part for me on the series "Lawman," starring John Russell. I was interviewed by the director, Christian Nyby, who didn't see me in the part at all! The producer, Jules Schermer, was a little embarrassed, since my brother had described me to a T in his script. I was called in a week later for one of three leads in another segment of the show and was asked if I could ride a horse, because there would be several fast rides through town. I had been told to always say, "Yes, I can do that," no matter what the activity was, so I said that of course I could ride, even though I knew that the last time I had been on a horse was when I was five at a Kiddieland Park with my father leading me around in a circle.

I got the part. I had one week before I had to report to the studio, and I was terrified of riding a galloping horse. I called around and got the name of a guy, Johnny Carpenter, who was an expert horseman, wrangler, rider, and teacher. We agreed to meet at his ranch in the north valley, and for three days he had me on that horse's back jumping on and off, doing running stirrup mounts, galloping, jumping off the horse before it was completely stopped, and so on. I was scared but committed to the training. He told me to hold the reins in such a way as to conceal that I was holding on to the saddle horn for dear life. After those three seven-hour days I was pretty good—still frightened, but at least I looked good sitting a horse.

The day of shooting arrived, and there were the horses! I got up on one and took special care to look as though I had been riding since the cradle, and I think that part was the best acting I did on the show. I sat bolt upright and related to the horse as if I had helped deliver him from his mother's womb. The show was called "The Young Toughs." It was about three wild, young cowboys who come into a town to cause mischief and mayhem. Tommy Gilson was the leader of our group. I had worked with him on *Rally 'Round the Flag, Boys!* at Twentieth, and we were pretty good friends. The other rowdy was an actor named Van Williams, who was being groomed by Warner's to be an up-and-coming actor as part of their contract stable. The director was Les Martinson, a really nice guy and quite a character. Les would always shout to any group being photographed, "If you can see the lens, it can see you!" The irony of that experience was that the only riding required was to walk slowly into the town, stop, look around, and slowly walk out of camera range. I could have done that without Johnny Carpenter! I was grateful for the training experience, but I wished I had spent the time on the script. A while after we did that show, Tommy was tragically killed by an estranged girlfriend when attempting to break down the door into her apartment. She shot him with a shotgun, and he was killed immediately.

During that time I continued working very hard in class. I had created a daily workout ritual. While Jean left for work every morning around 8:00 A.M., I slept in until about 10:00, then got up and had my coffee, which was not only my morning breakfast beverage but also the beginning of my sense-memory exercise workout. I drank the first cup to the bottom, refilled it, and started the process. I would ask sensory questions about the cup of coffee, directing each question to the part of the sense I wanted a response from. I worked with the object and without it, moving it out of sight and attempting to re-create it when it wasn't really there in front of me. I worked at least two hours, had some cereal, got dressed and went out for the next part of my ritual. The first stop was at Jack's house on Fountain. Sometimes Jack was there, and at other times he wasn't, but the visit was not only to see him but also to check out who might be there. Almost anyone who was part of our group might drop by and visit with whoever was there. David, one of Jack's roommates, was a metal sculptor and was almost always in the backyard welding a piece of metal to another piece of metal to create an objet d'art, so the house usually smelled like burned metal wafting in from outside. I began to associate a visit to Jack with that odor. In fact, I would begin to smell it just as I was leaving my apartment, which was about six blocks away. Of course, since I was so obsessed with sense memory at the time, I congratulated myself at the sensorial response. Jack's house was a meeting place for a lot of us, and on any visit it wasn't unusual for me to run into Dale, Harry Dean, or Bill Duffy. We usually sat around for a while talking about the class, the business, or a scene we were working on. Sometimes Jack would walk through the front door, see us in a huddle, and throw a wise quip at our little group. He had a great sense of humor and quite a sharp tongue.

On one of those daily stopovers, halfway into the room I was knocked off my feet and thrown to the floor by something that jumped on my back from behind. I landed on my back staring up into the huge eyes of what looked like a leopard! I was too scared to scream, so I just lay there motionless until Bill came and lifted his pet ocelot off my chest. It was considerably smaller than a leopard but its markings were very much the same. It was three times the size of an ordinary house cat. Bill thought it was very funny, but I didn't share the laugh with him.

"For God's sake, Eric," he exclaimed, "it's just a cat and it's very friendly. All it wanted to do was play!"

It took me a second or two to respond, "Oh yeah, Bill? If I wanted to play with jungle animals, I would have gone to Africa!"

I can't remember what Bill told me about where he had gotten the animal, but the next time I visited Jack's house, I entered with great caution.

My next stop was Schwab's Drugstore, which was anything but just a drugstore. It had a long counter and a dining room filled with booths. Four brothers ran it, all of them pharmacists, who took turns being there. Usually you would find one or more of them behind the drug-and-sundries counter on the left side in the back. There was a Hollywood legend connected to Schwab's: It was supposedly at its fountain that Lana Turner had been discovered, sipping an ice-cream soda. Sidney Skolsky, a fairly famous Hollywood columnist, had an office right above the pharmacy and would often sit with a bunch of us in the dining room, sharing stories of what the old Hollywood was like. I found those times very interesting and informative. Schwab's was very important to a very large group of actors, who needed a place where they could go to see other actors and share their lives with them. The dining room was always filled with a wide variety of types, most of them actors. We usually occupied a large corner booth to the right as one entered the room. I had done some shows with a few of the others, which was always a good subject of conversation.

One of the regulars was Clegg Hoyt, who was a real character, one you might see in a funny movie. He was very overweight, had a short crew cut and was always red faced and sweating, even on cold days. I think he had some physical disabilities and conditions, not the least of which was a glass eye. Without warning he would turn, put his face close to yours, and the glass eye would be a large American flag rather than an eye. It was somewhat unnerving and a little shocking, to say the least, but it was his kind of humor, and everyone accommodated it. One evening I dropped by for a quick cup of coffee and saw Clegg sitting alone in that large booth, so I joined him. He was seriously engrossed in devouring his soup. He greeted me and continued to eat, when all of a sudden his glass eye dropped into the soup. He paused, looked at the glass eye floating in the plate, and said, "Now that's a hungry eye!" He fished it out of the soup, wiped it off with a napkin, placed it back into his eye socket, and continued to eat. I just sat there speechless and changed the subject.

Sometimes, if there was no one I wanted to join in the dining room, I sat at the counter. An actor's life is a lonely one. If he isn't working, then he is waiting for a call from his agent. Schwab's became a haven away from the boredom or depression. It seemed that all of us there bonded and shared what we felt, even if we didn't talk about it. I read the trade papers and made note of what was casting, so I could mention it to my agent. It was, at any rate, a good excuse to call her to see what was happening.

I spent about an hour or so at Schwab's and went back home. If I hadn't scheduled a rehearsal with someone from class, I would then do another couple of hours of sense memory. My daily workouts became very important to me. I was obsessed with making the process work, but for several months it was very frustrating. I think that is why most actors desert sense memory as an acting tool. Most of the time I was working on at least two scenes, so I rehearsed almost every day. Jean would come home around five thirty, and I wanted to be there waiting for her. We would have dinner and watch a little TV. She would retire fairly early, while I stayed up and worked with various objects, using sense memory to re-create them. I averaged between four and five hours every day on the process. I worked with a wide variety of objects: the coffee cup; fruits of all kinds; more meaningful objects, such as pictures of my family; odiferous objects to isolate the olfactory sense; and so on. I filled my pockets with "feelies"—smooth rocks, fabrics, small bottles of perfume, prickly things, an assortment of small pocket knives, marbles, and so on. I would sit at an outdoor restaurant, the Plush Pup, put all of the objects on the table in front of me, close my eyes, and explore them one by one tactilely. I would put the perfume bottles under my nose, then take them away and attempt to sensorially re-create the odors when they were out of range. The first couple of years were very frustrating for me. I achieved limited success with the process, but only some of my senses responded to imaginary stimuli. I could actually feel an object, smell it, and sometimes hear it when it wasn't there, but the visual sense was the hardest to convince. I would stay with a single object for months if I wasn't having the kind of responses I wanted to have. I would get obsessed with certain elements of the exploration. For example, I worked with matches for at least two months, not because I wasn't able to create the matchbook, but because I couldn't isolate that microsecond when the match would ignite after I had dragged it across the part of the matchbook that ignited it. It happened so fast that I was unable to re-create that moment. I guess that was somewhat obsessive, but it was important to me, and I pursued it, almost getting asphyxiated from the sulfur fumes! I was finally able to do it, and that was an important victory on my sensory journey. Another stumbling block occurred when I was working with a pencil. I could re-create it when it wasn't there, but if I tipped my hand forward, I couldn't quite get that very moment when the pencil started to move forward in my palm. I worked on that one for a month or so. There were, however, great breakthroughs sensorially. I was able to masturbate without touching myself, just by supplying the sensory stimuli that brought me to an orgasm, and that also took a great amount of time and effort. It had occurred to me that if it was possible to have a wet dream without actually physically masturbating, it should be possible to achieve the same goal using sense memory. I tried a number of techniques, employing sexual fantasies and supporting them with sensory responses. When it did happen, I was so elated that I shared the experience with a table full of actors at Schwab's. Clegg Hoyt was there, as well as Harry Dean, and when I finished sharing this momentous experience, Harry Dean leaned over and in a whisper said, "Eric, I don't think you should have told us that!" Boy, was he right! The very next time I visited Schwab's, I walked through the front door, and from the other side of the room Clegg came running towards me waving a paper napkin in the air and shouting, "Here, Eric, use this!" To say the least I was very embarrassed and at that moment decided to be very careful about sharing my sensory breakthroughs.

The visual sense continued to be elusive. I could get somewhat of a response, but it wasn't like really seeing the object when it wasn't there. It was more like a negative picture, instead of a positive one. My first real breakthrough with the visual area came quite by surprise: I was talking on the telephone with Sondra, attempting to set up a rehearsal time for a scene we were doing, while at the same time working with a half-gallon carton of Arden's milk. I worked with the carton in front of me, asking mostly visual sensory questions and responding with the visual sense. Sondra and I were having some difficulty nailing down a specific time to rehearse. I continued to work with and without the carton, moving it to the side out of sight when trying to re-create it. I was distracted doing two things at one time but continued throughout our conversation to work with the milk. I was staring directly at the carton in front of me, when I happened to glance to the right and saw it sitting on the table there. I freaked! I had been seeing the milk carton in the flesh, so to speak, totally as if it were there in front of me. It wasn't my imagination. I had really seen the object when it wasn't there but had been moved to the side. I had obviously forgotten that I had moved it and was tricked into believing that it was still in front of me. Because I had been involved in that conversation with Sondra, I had believed that the milk carton was still in front of me; so, as it happens with what is called "the expectancy illusion," I had seen what I had expected to see. I became so emotional that I couldn't continue the conversation with Sondra. I excused myself awkwardly just before I started to cry. I sat there for many minutes looking at the empty space where the milk carton wasn't and felt overwhelmed by the experience. This was a major breakthrough for me. I realized that not only did I have to ask and respond to sensory questions, but I also had to work on getting my brain out of the equation. If I could convince myself that the object really was there when it wasn't, then it might be possible to see objects as though they really were there. That experience helped me to have greater success with the visual sense. While I wasn't always as successful with seeing the object as I had been with the milk carton, I did have continued visual success when working with and without objects.

A second important experience occurred about a year later. I was sitting at my dining-room table, where I had been doing most of my sense-memory workouts for the past year and a half, working with a Sunkist orange. I explored the object going from one sense to another, experiencing, however, *no* sensory responses. It was as though my entire sensorial system had just shut down. I was so frustrated that I slammed the orange down on the table and walked into the living room. I figured that I would take a break and return to the object a little later. It wasn't a relaxing break, however, because I could not stop worrying about why I wasn't getting any sensory responses. I waited about half an hour before returning to the orange, and when I did, the same thing happened again. I just sat there with the orange in the palm of my hand, asking no questions, just staring at it as if it was somehow in a conspiracy against me. I had some vengeful thoughts about the object and threatened to eat it if it continued to defy me! I decided against devouring it and put it down. I stuck my empty hand out in front of me, and all of a sudden I felt the orange as fully as if it were really in my hand. I smelled the acrid citrus odor and even had visual flashes of it. I saw the color, the texture of the skin, and so on. It was an incredible realization. MY SENSES HAD BEGUN TO ASK AND RESPOND TO THE OBJECT AUTOMATICALLY! When I had asked the questions, it had short-circuited the process that had started by itself. My senses were way ahead of my questions, so they had shut down. It wasn't that I never again had to ask sensory questions, but I had to allow the senses to do a great deal of the work without the questions. A note to the reader here: this happened about two and a half years into the process, and I was working as many as five hours a day!

As I remember, most of the choices used in scenes in Marty's class were approached sensorially—which made sense memory a very important tool for creating choices that addressed the obligations of a scene. We also used affective memory, which is totally dependent on sense memory. Affective memory is a complicated process, which demands that the actor be very facile with sense memory. I used affective memory quite successfully in the scene from *Dark of the Moon,* which I did with Sondra Kerr. In fact, that scene was a crossover experience for both of us. It was my very first "ultimate consciousness" experience onstage. Of course, that concept and phrase were not used in the class. I introduced them later, after I had started teaching, and the actual name of the phenomenon was coined by one of my students, Anna Ivara. I describe the entire experience in great detail in my book *Irreverent Acting.* In the scene, I played the Witch Boy, and Sondra was Barbara Allen. It was the scene where Barbara dies in the Witch Boy's arms, because she has been unfaithful, and he has to return to being a witch instead of a person. My "rise-ability" to supernatural phenomena is very high because of my experiences in childhood. Sondra was an incredibly talented actress, but since she had never died before, she wasn't sure how to approach that obligation. She remembered that for a time in her life she had experienced fainting spells, and she decided to work for the stimuli that she felt would induce fainting. I, on the other hand, chose an experience I had had at the age of fifteen, when my aunt was dying of stomach cancer in the hospital. I had been left alone in her room while her daughter went to answer some questions for the doctor in the other room. It was a bright, sunny day outside, and the windows were open, but all of a sudden the room grew dark, almost as if there had been an eclipse of the sun. It was the middle of summer, but the room was suddenly very cold. Abruptly, my aunt sat upright in bed, her eyes wide open and huge, looking at a part of the room as if there were someone there, and as loud as she could, she screamed, "I'm not going with you!" She promptly fell back on her pillow, and in a moment the room was filled with doctors, nurses, and emergency personnel. She had obviously flat lined on their monitor, but they were able to bring her back, at least for a short time. I will always insist that I did not see, but felt, the Angel of Death in that room. The feeling was tangible! It frightened me so much that even to this day when I think about it, I experience a strong emotional response. I used that experience as a choice for the scene, and the next thing I knew, Marty was onstage shaking me, and someone was rubbing Sondra's wrists and forehead to bring her to consciousness. Many of the people in the class were on their feet looking at us. Sondra had indeed fainted, and I'm not sure exactly what had happened to me, but I know that I hadn't been onstage; I hadn't been in that theater. The Witch Boy's line at the climax of the scene goes something like this: "I hear the flapping of eagles' wings, and they are coming for me!" That was the last thing I remembered before the stage was filled with people. After we came around and back to normal, Marty said something I thought was hilarious. After acknowledging that the work was wonderful and that both of us had had an inspiring experience, he asked what we would have done if there had been a third act after that scene! I am certain that I would not have been able to create that experience had it not been a result of all the fears in my early life.

During the time I was in Marty's class I had a couple dozen acting jobs in television and feature films. I had told my agent to take me off the market but eight months later had reinstated myself as an actor ready to work. As I grew with the craft, so did my acting in films. I was cast as Freddy Barker, a criminal and a lead in *Ma Barker's Killer Brood.* At that point in my development I was able to get my tension under control, be present in the scene, and work for choices that produced the desired emotional results. This was an enormously important thing for me, since I had spent so many years acting without a dependable process. I played a shady character on "The Jim Backus Show" and did a number of episodic series that were popular at that time on television. I was cast as a slick character on "The Case of the Dangerous Robin," starring Rick Jason, where I spent most of my time kissing Dawn Wells in the front seat of a car. She later went on to success in "Gilligan's Island." Lurene Tuttle, who had played my mother in *Ma Barker,* was again my mother in "Dangerous Robin." She and I would often run into each other at the bank on Hollywood Boulevard. On one occasion, while we were in the teller line with each other, I turned around and said to her, "Hey, Ma, why don't we knock over this bank?" I guess my voice was loud enough to be heard by several customers behind us, who seemed to show some panic. Lurene turned to them, explained the situation and defused it. I thought it was funny anyway. There was an assortment of other TV shows and films on which I had a day or two. In those early years I worked an average of once or twice a month.

I also did a couple of plays. I auditioned and got the role of Captain Connors in *Time Limit* at the Morgan Theater, a juicy role, which allowed me to be killed by the other soldiers onstage. I loved dying onstage or in front of the camera and did so frequently. I thought that it was quite melodramatic to have a death scene in open view of the audience and that I died well! In my acting career I did it no less than six times in full view of the audience or camera. In *Ma Barker's Killer Brood,* I was shot to death in a Florida farmhouse along with Ma. After I had started teaching, I died in George Peppard's arms in *Battle beyond the Stars,* again in *Wavelength,* on the men's room floor no less, and in "Strategy of Terror," a two-part Kraft Suspense Theater that was later distributed as a film in Europe. I was shot to death on the lawn of a sprawling estate while attempting to assassinate a dignitary from the United Nations. As I became more of a craftsman, my choices for creating death were more organic. I worked for things that made it really look as if I had died. I once saw in a movie a death scene where, when the character died, it was as if the light in his eyes suddenly went out. I remembered that and attempted to work sensorially for that phenomenon by creating darkness creeping into my vision until it was totally black. It really worked on camera. I was also able to create a limp numbness all over my body at the same time.

There was a film casting that I really wanted to be in: *Pork Chop Hill,* which starred Gregory Peck. It was about a famous battle over a hill in Korea, and it seemed as though everybody in Hollywood was in it: Bobby Blake, Marty Landau, Harry Dean Stanton, and so on. I called Betty Wookey every day, asking her to get me an audition. She obviously couldn't get me up for it, and the film finished without me. I'm not sure why it was so important for me to be in it, but it was! About a month and a half later, I received a call from Betty, who told me she had some really good news for me. They were adding some scenes to the film, and she had gotten me two days on it. I was delighted! She told me that the part had no lines but a lot of action and coverage and that I was sure to be on camera a lot. I asked her why they didn't just hire extras, but she said that they had particularly specified that they wanted actors. Finally I was going to be in *Pork Chop Hill!* I reported to the Samuel Goldwyn Studios on Santa Monica Boulevard, got into makeup and costume, and went on to the set, which was filled with a bunker and trenches and a whole lot of dirt. It looked as though it might be on top of a hill somewhere in Korea. There were only two of us who had been hired as actors, Stan Young and I. Stan was a young, good-looking actor, who was fairly new in town and as eager as I was. The director, Lewis Milestone, had won an Academy Award for *All Quiet on the Western Front,* a World War I movie starring Lew Ayres and filmed in the late thirties. I believe that was the last notable thing he had ever done. He was a stubby little man with a shock of salt-and-pepper hair and a thick German accent. He looked at Stan and me as we entered the set and said, pointing at me, "You, get a rifle and stand over there!" Regarding both of us with obvious suspicion, he told Stan to kneel down in front of the bunker. Mr. Peck entered the set, picked up an M1 carbine and approached the bunker. He stopped and introduced himself to me and asked my name. I was very excited to meet him and thought it was strange that he would tell me who he was as if I didn't already know. I told him my name and added how pleased I was to be working with him. He smiled and moved into the bunker. There were about forty people on the set, mostly extras dressed in combat gear. The first day was mainly fill-in shots of soldiers jumping in and out of trenches, firing their rifles at imagined enemies. The special-effects team was setting off explosions all around us. I had a couple of close-ups firing my rifle at advancing Korean troops. I ran, jumped in and out of trenches, and was followed and surrounded by scores of extras screaming in my ears. It was an exhausting day, but I was delighted to be working on the film.

On the second day, I arrived at the studio and saw Gregory Peck walking towards me. He smiled and said, "Good morning, Eric."

I was surprised that he recognized me and that he remembered my name from the previous day's introduction. I replied, "Good morning, Mr. Peck," and we both continued going in our separate directions.

The second day was almost entirely devoted to action inside the bunker. Just before lunch the director called Stan and me over and asked us in his heavy German accent, "Which one of you can handle a line?"

I was so taken aback by the question that I looked directly into his eyes, began to stutter, "Gi...ve ve it...ttto hhimm!" and walked away. I had been so insulted by the insensitivity of that schmuck that I had purposely stuttered! I had played *Hamlet* in college and had been pretty good. Certainly I handled Shakespeare quite well, so I felt humiliated by the question.

Stan asked me, "What was that all about?"

"That son of a bitch purposely asked for actors. What did he think we were? It is an insult to be treated that way. That's why I did the stuttering."

Stan laughed and I guess was pleased to have a line to say, although I don't remember what the line was or whether he even said it. We spent most of the second day of shooting in the bunker. Mr. Peck was in every scene, and I liked being there with him. At one point in the action, the special-effects team was spraying fire through the eaves of the bunker, and I guess I was a little too close to the flames. Mr. Peck put his arm around me and gently moved me towards the middle of the bunker. He smiled and said that he didn't want me to be a casualty and that besides, if I stood next to him, the way he positioned me, I would be on camera. I thanked him and moved close to him. Gregory Peck was a wonderful human being. He was unassuming and down to earth and was always supportive of good causes and humanity. He never seemed to be self-impressed and would reach out to people in need. I was very sad when he died.

To this point in my acting career I had been a soldier in the Civil War, World War II, and the Korean War. Not many people can say that they have had such longevity or have spent so many years in the service!

At the same time, in Marty's class I tried to do a variety of scenes in order to explore the craft. I learned to go with what was there, use it, and allow myself to include my impulses in the lines. If I needed to be attracted to the actress I was working with, I looked for the things that I found attractive about her. I also learned to include impulses that weren't necessarily related to the concept or behavior in the scene. This allowed me to be more in the moment and much more unpredictable. Those things seem like common sense now, but I hadn't acted from those places before coming to Marty's class. I had been very loyal to the concept I had established, and I had stuck to that behavior, without including my own moment-to-moment realities. Just that realization and adjustment elevated my acting to a new level of authenticity. I was able to use sense memory to create environments, sounds, music, or odors that would affect me. I also learned how to endow the other actors with physical properties that they didn't possess.

In *Golden Boy* I worked to create a physical disability. The character was slightly cross-eyed, which affected his confidence, as well as making him defensive. As I mentioned in the first chapter, my mother had been cross-eyed for her entire life. It could have been corrected but never was. She had been born and raised in Russia before the turn of the twentieth century, and I guess her family didn't have the knowledge or sophistication to seek medical advice about the condition. As a result, she would compensate in every way she could to hide her affliction. In order to see clearly she had to turn her head in such a way that the bad eye could see as much as the eye that was straight. I worked sensorially to affect my right eye. I explored a number of possibilities—blurring my vision, creating dark spots in my right eye, partially closing my eye—which did have some effect on me. I played around with cocking my head in a variety of positions so as to block the vision in my right eye. I don't remember what I settled on, but the exploration did bear fruit. Every time the actress playing Lorna looked at me, I felt like turning my head in such a way that it would hide my bad eye. That really happened on an organic level. I had other choices for the attraction to Lorna, and I used Chris Rocco, my old grade-school nemesis, to stimulate my anger and hostility. All I had to do to create Chris was to sensorially create that particular look of hate and prejudice he had every time he looked at me. For the character's love for music I used my relationship to acting, which was very available to me. Since the scene we were working on takes place on a park bench, I thought we might as well use a similar environment, so we rehearsed on a bench in Griffith Park. When we did the scene in class, I worked sensorially to re-create the same environment. It was near a road, so there were cars going by, and since Joe talks about wanting a car like Gary Cooper had, I used the cars that I related to. When I did the scene in class, I responded to the cars that passed by the workshop and included my response to them in the moment, which delighted Marty. He made a special point about how I had grown in my ability to include my moment-to-moment impulses.

When I did *A View from the Bridge,* I used my attraction to the actress I was doing the scene with. For the conflict between my character and Eddie, her uncle, I worked for my older brother Morrey. I sensorially created his voice and his criticism of me, which was quite frequent. Every time I referred to Eddie in the scene, I was actually relating internally to my brother. The character wants desperately to become a citizen of the United States, and for that intense need I related to my own need as an actor to be working. To deal with the character's frustration I used whatever my own frustrations with my work and the scene were at any given moment in the rehearsal and when doing it in class.

I really enjoyed doing *The Rainmaker* with Sondra Kerr. I had a lot of fun with that character, Starbuck. He has a huge ego and is very flamboyant, and of course he is a con man, who has learned how to convince people to buy his services. At the time I was doing the scene, I was also lifting weights—bodybuilding. As a matter of fact, Connie Buck, an actress in class, a full-blooded Native American and a fine painter, said that she wanted to capture my arrogance on canvas, and so she did a portrait of me in oil. When the painting was finished, I looked like the average bodybuilder at Gold's Gym, maybe just slightly smaller than Arnold Schwarzenegger! As a choice for the scene I worked sensorially to create the wonderful feeling in my body after I finished a workout. All my muscles were filled with blood and I felt invincible. I also worked to create a piece of music that helped me to feel inspired, the music from the film *The Big Country.* In addition to those choices, I used Sondra, who by that time had done several scenes with me. To address Starbuck's relationship to Lizzie I used what I knew about Sondra and what I really felt. We did the tack-room scene, where Starbuck seduces Lizzie. I thought that Sondra was attractive, and I used all of the physical stimuli, as well as the emotional ones, to impel myself to want to seduce her. Starbuck is definitely in control of the situation in the scene, but I never felt in control with Sondra. She was always a little difficult and somewhat harsh with me, and I felt intimidated by her most of the time. All of this, of course, was contrary to the demands of the relationship in the scene, so I had to address that obstacle, which I did by emphasizing all of the things that made me feel superior to her, such as my size and physical strength. I also concentrated on everything that was attractive and desirable about me. It worked! The scene went quite well. I was using the work with some success, and even though that success was spotty, I felt that I had some handles and I looked forward to using them. Marty's comments about my work were taking on a kinder and more encouraging tone.

The next scene I attempted to do was *Cat on a Hot Tin Roof.* I think I did it with Connie Buck, who certainly filled the bill sexually. She was beautiful and sensual and could easily pass for Maggie the Cat. That scene had a multitude of responsibilities, which I relished as a challenge of my craft. Brick has a broken leg, which is in a cast, he hobbles around on crutches, he drinks constantly, and while he is not falling down drunk, he is certainly affected by the alcohol. He is repulsed by Maggie's advances and has a great deal of ambivalence towards her. He is fighting his own sexual-identity demons and drinks to numb himself. I started my process with sensorially working for the broken leg and created the effect of a cast on my right leg. I couldn't identify with the sexual-identity demons, since I had known at the age of three that I was definitely heterosexual! I therefore substituted my enormous sexual attraction for other women, which was really a demon at that time in my life. I had married very young, lived in a society in which most women remained virgins until they were married, and since I had been involved with Jean for five years before marrying her, I hadn't had the opportunity to sow any wild oats. I was curious and frustrated. I had the conflict of being married and not wanting to cheat on the one hand, and being subjected to overwhelming temptations on the other. I used this reality as a parallel for Brick's conflict with his sexual identity. At that point in my craft development I didn't have an approach technique for how to pragmatically use that as a choice, so I just thought about the conflict. Since then, of course, I have created a huge number of techniques for making those realities practical. For Brick's ambivalence towards Maggie I was able to use Connie in terms of some of the conflicts that we had in our rehearsals. Connie was a very nice person but very opinionated in her interpretation of the scene, and we had gotten quite heated at times in our rehearsals. I reminded myself throughout the scene that she was difficult and that I wanted to avoid getting into any conflict with her.

I had quite a bit of trouble, though, with Brick's drinking. I had never been drunk, and while I used to drink some beer and ale while at college, I was not a drinker and didn't enjoy even the slight buzz that I had gotten from drinking. I did work sensorially for the effects of alcohol—the lightheadedness, the inability to focus, the thickening of my tongue, the slight loss of equilibrium, and so on. What was difficult for me was creating a need to take that next drink. There is a line in the scene where Maggie asks Brick when he is going to stop drinking and he says it will be when he hears "the click." That wasn't real for me, and I didn't want to fake it! I discussed the problem with Marty, who came up with a brilliant suggestion: He told me to think about the most terrible things I could conjure up about my life—horrible memories and fears of future tragedies, the kinds of things that haunt you in the middle of the night or in your nightmares—and suggested that to stop myself from those awful thoughts, I could take a drink from the glass of water I had in my hand and, for the time I was drinking and several minutes after that, I could stop thinking those torturing thoughts. It worked! I used it effectively and was able to achieve a great deal of organic success in that scene.

I have already spoken about *Desire under the Elms,* so I won't repeat myself. Working on that scene was a real turning point for me as an actor. I learned not only how to use certain choices, but also how to address characterization on a completely new level.

One of the next things I did was a short one-act play by Tennessee Williams, *Talk to Me like the Rain, and Let Me Listen.* Sandra Knight and I did the entire play. Since both characters are on the stage together, you might think that they have a relationship, and I guess they do, but they never directly relate to each other, since both of them are out of it. My character is lying on the floor, and Sandra's is sitting in a chair upstage right of me. Both are very depressed, and my character is also extremely hung over. His first line is, "I woke up in a bathtub filled with ice cubes and Miller High Life beer. They passed me around like a dirty postcard!" Reading that first line, I got an immediate hit on the character. I worked to create a squalid environment with an overwhelming stench of urine, water-stained walls and ceiling, garbage and rotting food all around me, and an omnipresence of doom. Sensorially

I created a huge hangover, replete with a pounding headache and a rotten taste in my mouth. I blurred my vision and worked for a swollen tongue, which affected my speech and created slurred words. The scene is essentially divided into separate monologues, hers being the longer one, as I remember. For what my character is feeling in the scene, I "selectively emphasized" all of the depressing things in my own life. A side note here: some of the techniques I am specifically describing, such as selective emphasis and some of the other specifics, did not exist at that time or in that class. I developed an incredible number of them later in my teaching years, which I will get to in the next chapter. Besides what I had learned in Marty's class, a lot of what I did was instinctive. Concentrating on my own depressions seemed to fit what the character was experiencing. In the piece, my relationship to Sandra was one of not relating but feeling her presence throughout. I loved working with her, so it was difficult not to relate to her directly. I felt that the scene went well, and Marty seemed impressed with our work. I was getting more specific with the craft, and that was satisfying to both my teacher and me.

I also worked on *The Hasty Heart,* a play that takes place in a veterans' hospital. The character is a dying Scotsman named Lachie. I spent too much time on acquiring the Scottish accent and not enough on creating the other realities. My accent was superb, but I had some difficulty with the sense of dying. I was all of about twenty-nine years old, filled with a sense of immortality and convinced that I was going to live forever. Of course, I don't feel that way anymore, but I'm too old to play that part now! I nevertheless attempted to create illnesses in various parts of my body, which became increasingly hard to believe. I did, however, connect with the character's charm and humanity. In spite of the fact that he is dying, he has an incredible spirit and is childlike in his demeanor. I don't recall the process I used to access that part of me, but I did it as a character element, which made the scene nice to watch.

When I did the scenes with Barbara, Marty's wife, from *Elizabeth the Queen* and *Candida*, a lot of what my characters were supposed to feel about hers was already available realities, so I had very little difficulty. I looked up to both Marty and Barbara and also found her attractive and wanted her to care about me, so I was able to access those realities.

Somewhere in the malaise of those many scenes I took a shot at *Orpheus Descending.* I approached the role of Snakeskin, or Val, or whatever his name was in that rendition of the play, which had had four different titles. One of the original titles had been *Duel of Angels,* then it had become *Battle of Angels,* then *Orpheus Descending,* and when they made the film with Brando, it became *The Fugitive Kind;* so I'm sure they changed the name of that character several times too. I liked "Snakeskin" because the character wore a snakeskin jacket throughout the play. I had recently bought a black leather blazer at a men's shop on Sunset Boulevard, before leather sports coats were popular. I had paid what I thought was a fortune at the time and was very proud of it. Every time I wore it anywhere, people stared at me, and I felt that it affected my personality in specific ways; so when I did the scene I wore it and used it as a choice for the character. Later, many years after I had started teaching, when I began to create what I called CHOICE APPROACHES, this would have fallen into the category of "objects that come into contact with the body," one of the thirty-one choice approaches that are part of my system. The choice of the jacket elicited a subtle sexuality that really worked for the character. That was not the only choice I used for the scene, but the others are vague after forty-six years.

We also did an occasional improvisation in class, when there was time to squeeze it in between individuals and scenes. I remember doing one with Jack Nicholson. We were in each other's faces, our noses were about one inch from touching each other, and we were yelling at the top of our voices. It was very emotional and filled with anger. At one point in the exchange Jack said, "You know you have bad breath!" My first response was embarrassment, which gave way to humiliation, and finally I got angry and said, "You don't smell so good either," which made him laugh. When the improv was over, I sat down in the back and cupped my hand close to my nose and mouth attempting to see if I really had bad breath. All my life I have always been very sensitive to odors of all kinds and have taken great care with my hygiene, so his comment really affected me. I couldn't detect anything foul about my breath, but when we took a coffee break in the middle of class, instead of going to Winchell's with the rest of the people, I jumped into my car, went to the drugstore, bought some mouthwash and used it on the way back to class. To this day I don't really know whether I did have bad breath that evening or whether Jack in his Jack way had just used it in the improv.

I was growing rapidly in class and for the first time in my acting life felt that I had some tools I could count on. I had been in Marty's class for a little over two and a half years, and I was chomping at the bit to work outside in a stage production. I didn't want to start auditioning for the theaters around town. I wanted to have more control over what I did and whom I worked with. I had seen a play in New York on one of my Christmas vacations, *End As a Man,* by Calder Willingham. The leading character, Jocko De Paris, had been played by Ben Gazzara, and I had been very impressed with him and the production, so I decided to do that play and began to put the project together. Jack Nicholson was perfect for Jocko, and I was going to play Marquales, also an important character in the play. I spoke with Jack, who agreed to do Jocko. As fortune would have it, though, he got a lead in a motorcycle movie for Roger Corman and couldn't do the play. I was disappointed but undeterred. I decided to play Jocko and cast Don Spruance as Marquales. I needed a good director, so I approached Bruce Dern, whom I had met a couple of years back when he had arrived from New York. Bruce and I had never worked together. We just had long conversations at the counter at Schwab's Drugstore. I liked him and what he had to say. He was also a member of the Actors Studio, which promoted similar approaches to acting. Jack Garfein, who had directed the play on Broadway, was also connected with the Actors Studio. Bruce was familiar with the play and agreed to direct it. Since it was my baby, I used as many actors from class as I could and cast others from outside, mostly people I knew or who were my friends. I can't remember where we got the money for the production, but I believe everyone involved chipped in, and we had enough to secure the rights and pay for the theater. I rented a small theater off Western Avenue, the Store Theater, a perfect name for a theater that had once been a store! John Shaner owned it, and since he was a good friend of Jack's, I approached him—which was as dramatic an undertaking as doing the play. John was officious, businesslike, and a complete pain in the ass. Doing business with him was like dealing with David Merrick's attorneys for a Broadway theater rental. We did not get along at all. Over the years he and I have become very good friends, with a tremendous amount of affection for each other. I guess we both became much more successful and mellow after forty or so years.

The theater had about fifty or sixty seats and was better than a black-box theater. I was disappointed that Jack couldn't do the role, since I thought he was perfect for it. It was a little bit of a stretch for me, but surprisingly I was very good as Jocko De Paris. I worked very hard, explored a large variety of choices, and settled on the ones that really worked. I used an eagle as the spine of the character, which brought an ominous quality to Jocko.

During the rehearsals some of the actors got together and revolted against Bruce Dern. They thought he was too hard and critical in his direction. They approached me and demanded that he be replaced, but I was adamantly against it. Yes, Bruce was a little tough, but I liked it. I, for one, felt that he never let me get away with anything less than reality, and even when his criticism hurt a little I knew he was right. I had a line where I ordered one of the actors out of the room, and when I said it one time while rehearsing in my living room on Detroit Street, I pointed to the wall. Bruce stopped me and said, "Eric, do you expect him to walk through the wall? Why not point to the door?" I know that seems like a little thing, but it isn't. It relates to maintaining authentic reality, and I loved it! As harsh as Bruce could be at times, his direction was right on target. Unfortunately, all of the other actors ganged up on me and threatened to quit the play unless he left. I went to him and explained the situation, and he said that he understood and opted to step down. Everyone else was pleased except me. A couple of actors also dropped out, because different things came up, but they were replaced by other guys I knew from the business. One of those replacements, Erik Holland, was terrific in the play. In fact, he recently told me that he had gotten his first film job from doing it. I replaced Bruce with Lincoln Demyan, an older actor with a slight Southern drawl. He and I did not get along from the very beginning. He wasn't even on the same planet with Bruce as far as talent and insight were concerned, but it was getting late in the day and we had to proceed with rehearsals and open the play, so I felt stuck with him. I was exploring choices so that I could stimulate the life of the character and his relationships in every scene, while Lincoln was giving result directions and getting in the way of my exploration as well as of everyone else's.

The play takes place in a military academy. All the characters are young men. Jocko is a sociopath, spoiled and devious, who controls the action in almost every scene. He delights in hazing underclassmen and getting exactly what he wants at any cost. Like many sociopaths, he is also extremely intelligent and cunning. In one scene he gets a slow-witted football player drunk and then whips him with a fencing foil. The title of the play reflects the goal of the academy: that everyone who graduates from there will "end as a man." I enjoyed doing the play and was able to access the ugly part of my personality to address that evil in Jocko. I was so successful at achieving it that after one of our performances, while I was leaving the theater, I passed a man who had been in the audience, and he screamed and quickly backed away from me, which made me laugh. Wow, I thought, I must have really scared that poor guy!

Vic Tayback also came to see the play and was blown away by my performance. I had known Vic from around town but had never been very close to him. He was a pudgy, dark-haired man with thinning black hair and a Middle Eastern face. He had the unique distinction of never having read a book cover to cover, and he seemed proud of it. After seeing the play, he approached me and asked if I would like to be a member of the Angels Company, a theater group of professional actors, which had a very good reputation around town. I replied that I would be interested, so he brought my name up to the board with such an incredible recommendation that they accepted me immediately. When the play closed, I started to attend their sessions. There were a lot of very good actors there, and I saw a couple of the plays, the first of which was one I had done at the Wharf Theatre when in the army, *The Caine Mutiny Court-Martial.* It was a good production, with one actor, Tony Carbone, standing out from the rest. I intended to work with the company in their next few productions, but I never auditioned for anything, I'm not sure why. After a while I drifted away from them. My relationship with Vic was renewed when we were both at the Actors Studio about ten years later.

I was still going to class but was unable to continue my scene work, since all of my energy was directed at the play. Shortly after we closed, Marty got the part of the general in *Cleopatra* with Elizabeth Taylor and Richard Burton. It was a big part, which meant that he would be gone for a year. I felt as though the bottom had fallen out of my life. There I was, doing some of the best work in all my acting life, and I was being abandoned in midstream! Of course, I was happy for Marty but very insecure about my training future. I spoke to him about how I felt, and as always he was supportive and encouraging. On the day he left for Rome I drove him and Barbara to the airport. It was a happy and a sad day, all rolled up in insecurity and confusion. I loaned Marty my eight-millimeter movie camera to use while in Rome, and when he came back he told me that he had photographed Liz and Richard's budding romance. They were both still married to other people, Elizabeth Taylor to Eddie Fisher, and Burton to I don't know whom.

There I was, without a teacher and at a point where I felt I still needed to be coached. After Marty left, one of the newer members of class suggested that we stay together and continue working on our craft. I thought it was a good idea but was insecure about not having a teacher to guide us through the instrumental work as well as the craft process. We met in the same place where we had been and collected dues from everyone to pay the rent. Unfortunately, it only lasted for the month we had rented the space. Without a teacher the democratic nature of the class, where everyone contributed insights and comments, soon turned the meetings into confusion and resentments. I spoke to Jack about my feelings, and he invited me to sit in on a class that he was checking out.

The class was being taught by a woman named Donna Roman Dru—I'm not sure about the spelling of her last name. It met in her apartment, which was on the corner of Fountain and La Cienega, in the same building, as rumor has it, in which Marilyn Monroe had lived before she became a big star. It was one of those thirties buildings with high ceilings and rococo wainscoting in floral designs. Donna was in her early forties at the time. She was semi-attractive, while the lines in her face signaled her waning youth. She was married to an actor named Rick Roman, whom I had never seen, so he remained a shadow character in my mind. Three rows of wooden folding chairs had been set up facing an open area that had been occupied by a couch, which had been moved against the opposite wall. Jack and I sat together in the second row, waiting for the seats to fill and the class to begin. The slats on the wooden chairs relentlessly attacked my butt, and soon my bones ached. The odors in the room were like stale incense and that smell you experience when visiting an old antique shop in a small town off the beaten path. There were about twelve students besides Jack and me, and when all the seats were filled, Donna began to speak. Her voice was authoritative and a little harsh. She instructed two people in the front row to get up and do their scene. Even before reaching the center of what was supposed to be the stage, the boy, a young scarecrow of a lad, began speaking the first line of the scene. I could hear the tension in his voice. The muscles in his face were tight and restricted. The girl he was working with had a shrill, high-pitched voice and started to speak even before he had finished his first line. When the scene ended, Donna gave them a directorial critique. There was nothing of craft in her comments and less than nothing that either of those two young hopefuls could learn from what she said: "Good! Do it again next week and take more time with it!"

Two more young actors walked onto the stage, took a few minutes to prepare before starting the scene, and were interrupted by Donna: "You cannot take that kind of time before starting the scene. They won't allow it on a movie set!" She stopped them several times to give them blocking direction, and when it was over she admonished them for being indulgent. "You have to be professional at all times, and you should know enough not to step on each other's lines!" she said. There wasn't any craft or process in her teaching, and she was damaging the confidence of those impressionable young people. I suffered through another scene, looked over at Jack, gently nudging him with my right elbow, and whispered that I would like to leave. He whispered back that I should give her a little more time and that it was rude just to get up and walk out. I considered what he had said and agreed that it would not only be rude, but disruptive. As for giving her a little more time, even if I had given her up to the second coming, nothing would have changed! She had little insight and even less knowledge of process. Having been with Marty for two and a half years had really spoiled me. When the class took a break, Jack thanked her, and we quietly left. Neither of us took the class.

We spoke about where to go from there to find a place to study. Jack, who didn't seem as desperate as I, said that he would look around, that I should do the same, and that we would share our findings with each other. Since it was my habit to drop by his house every day on my way to Schwab's, I knew that we would eventually come up with something. In the meantime I felt abandoned and depressed, even though Jack had said to me on more than one occasion that I was a good actor whether or not I could do all the work we learned in class. I continued a daily workout program, working with sense memory and with a variety of choices and monologues.

By then my personal life had become quite involved and demanding. Jean and I had waited seven years to start a family, and she was getting discouraged about it. We had a number of conversations on the subject, some of them quite heated. It was true we had agreed to wait until my career would take off and I could support a family, but, well, we all know what the business is like, and although I was working pretty regularly, I still wasn't quite earning enough to carry the entire load. Jean drove to Chicago to see her father and took her sister and mother with her. During the time she was gone—about two weeks—I decided that we should start trying to have a child. I was moving up on thirty and figured that I didn't want to be a grandfather to my child, so it was certainly time to commit. Besides, there is an old Jewish saying that a baby comes and brings along his own loaf of bread. The day Jean returned, she informed me that she wanted a divorce. She was disenchanted with our relationship and wanted to move on; but when I told her that I had made the decision to start a family, she lit up like a Roman candle. She told me that she had always loved me and that it was all she had wanted. In very short order she got pregnant, and we were expecting our first child.

All of a sudden my life really changed. Up until then I had been collecting unemployment and getting acting jobs frequently enough to almost match Jean's salary. On occasion I would even out earn her, which really made me feel terrific. Nevertheless, even though she was still working, she would eventually have to quit to give birth to our child, so I knew that I needed to get a steady job; but what kind of work could I do that would allow me to go on auditions? My cousin Leon ("Lee") Brodsky and a guy he was in business with had an auto-mechanics shop, called Four Star Carburetors, up on Western Avenue. I had never understood why they had named it that, since they did all kinds of automobile repairs there, not only carburetors. Lee, who was my mother's sister's son, was about fifteen years older than I. We had had little contact during all the years I was growing up. He had gone to California with my brother Phil before World War II and was in the navy during the war, so I hadn't seen him for many of those years. He was closer to my two older brothers than to me. Even though I was sure that I didn't know enough to qualify as a mechanic, I asked him for a job, telling him that I thought I could be a helper—clean up the place, go for coffee, and chase parts around the city. After he checked with his partner, they agreed to hire me part time as an apprentice mechanic, who would learn to do simple repairs. I was delighted, sincc I loved cars and wanted to know how to work on them. Lee and his partner could only afford to give me four or five hours in the mornings, which was not enough to pay my bills, so I looked for an afternoon and/or evening job to bridge the financial gap.

I asked my sister Ida if her husband, Al, needed any help at the liquor store he managed. She told me she would check with him but added that she would be very frightened for me to work there, particularly in the evenings. The store was located in South Central Los Angeles, a predominantly black area and quite a rough part of town. There were a lot of homicides there, and I was a blond, blue-eyed, fair-skinned white boy! I told her that I really needed the job and that I liked black people and had always been able to communicate well with them, so Al hired me as an evening clerk. I started at 5:00 P.M. and worked until midnight, when the store closed. There was another clerk working with me, a very nice black guy named Marvin, who took to me immediately. Al showed me the ropes and left the additional training to Marvin. So now I had two jobs: mornings at the auto shop and evenings at the liquor store. It was a lot of hours, especially considering that the morning job was very hard physical work. I bored out cylinders, changed oil, gapped and replaced spark plugs, did minor tune-ups, got very dirty, and had to work for hours to get the grease from under my nails and out from the crevices on my hands.

Jean was still working, but after she started to show, she had to leave her job at Stevens, Biondi and Di Cicco and instead got a job as a secretary for a curmudgeon of a man, named Victor Bloom. Victor could have won a contest as being one of the most unattractive men in the country. He was just slightly over five feet tall, with a bulbous nosc, which bore evidence of the ravages of youthful acne. His voice sounded as though it came from the lower depths or much like a tractor grinding over a gravel road. His shirt and jacket let you know what he had been eating in the previous few days. He was gruff and aggressive and said exactly what he felt at every moment. At first meeting he was intimidating, but after you got to know him, you found that he had the biggest heart any chest could hold. He was really a sweet man. He sold ads to a number of small papers—the *B'nai Brith Messenger,* a small Hollywood neighborhood paper, and a few others—and had a number of other men working in boiler rooms selling ads over the phone.

I felt as though I was no longer an actor, but a grease monkey and a liquor clerk—a total loser. Jean saw the change in me and tried to encourage me. She had always been able to lift my spirits, but it wasn't working this time. I wasn't training, and my auditions seemed to be few and far between. My career seemed to be slipping away. I fell into a major depression. I did my work, I was on time and dependable, but I hated every minute of it. Nevertheless, there were things in each of my jobs that I liked: I felt great about learning how to repair cars, and I enjoyed the clientele at the liquor store. We had a wild and crazy group of winos, who waited for me to come to work every day. They stood outside, shaking from withdrawal and waiting for their daily ration of Thunderbird wine. Since they never had any money, I bought them a fifty-nine-cent bottle, which they promptly drained before I could drop the change into the cash register. The fix usually worked within minutes, and I received a grateful nod as they disappeared down the street. Crazy Max came in every evening at about nine o'clock, singing popular songs at the top of his voice, but with made-up lyrics that didn't quite fit the melody. He was quite large, very overweight, with long kinky hair, which usually obscured one of his eyes. He always had the exact amount of money to pay for a small half-pint of bourbon. I don't know what he did for a living or where he got the cash to buy the bottle, but, like clockwork, there he was every night exactly at nine. After a while I began to look for him, expecting a new tune with crazy words each night. One evening he walked into a store filled with people, singing as loud as his vocal cords permitted and extolling how he loved this white boy who saved him from suicide every night. I recognized the melody but the lyrics needed a lot of work!

Jean and I were still living on Detroit Street but knew we had to find a place more suitable to raise a child. For a number of years while I was going to grade school and later to high school, I had lived in a single-family house. Those years had been important. I had felt different living in a house, instead of in the apartments where we had resided for most of my early life. I therefore decided that we should look for a house to rent, since we didn't have the money to even consider buying one. After looking at a few places, we found a cute Hansel-and-Gretel house in Burbank. Some builder back in the forties had built a number of those gingerbread houses, most of which were sprinkled along Hollywood Way. Ours was on a corner and was very quaint. It rented for $110 a month, but we had to pay the first and last months in advance. When I look back at that time, it's hard to believe that I didn't have the last month's rent to put up. We borrowed it from Jean's mother, Emily, who by that time had migrated to California.

I continued looking for an acting class to get into, but I wasn't happy with any of the ones I audited. Because of the preceding three years with Marty, I was very demanding about how to work. Everywhere I went I found generalities and nonspecific techniques.

One day, I was lying on jacks under an old Buick, trying desperately to free the lug nut on the crankcase so I could drain the oil. It was really frozen, so I pounded on it with a rubber-headed hammer, used a large wrench, and sprayed oil on it to no avail. Finally, in total frustration I hit it with a metal hammer as hard as I could. The bolt cracked in half, and the entire reservoir of oil poured onto my face. Fortunately, the oil wasn't hot, or I would have been burned and most likely disfigured. I crawled out from under the car, and just as I was wiping the oil from my face, Jack and Sandra drove onto the lot where I was standing in coveralls drenched in black oil. At the time, Jack was driving a convertible Volkswagen Carmen Ghia, and he had come into the shop to check a problem he was having with the generator. I don't remember ever being as embarrassed as I was at that moment. Jack looked at me, flashed his incredible smile, and said, "Hey, Eric, are you doing research for a racing-car movie?" In spite of my discomfort I laughed, full well knowing that he had seen my embarrassment and had wanted to take the curse off the moment. Sandra was equally supportive.

A number of months had passed since Marty had gone to Rome, and I was still without a class. I also felt that Lee really didn't need me to work for them. He was being kind and helping me out, but it was a drain on them financially. He never said anything or indicated that he wanted me to leave, but I really felt that I wasn't doing enough around the shop to justify my being there. He would look for things for me to do, and when it was obvious that there wasn't anything, he would send me to lunch. I told him that I was very grateful for what he had done for me at a very difficult time in my life, and I quit. I was still at the liquor store, but I needed another part-time job to be able to take over when Jean delivered our son. I sensed it was going to be a boy, and I was delighted by that.

During that period I booked three or four television shows, mostly for a day or two each. At that time the SAG minimum was ninety dollars a day, so after taxes I would come home with a couple hundred dollars, which was a great supplement, since we could live on a hundred dollars a week. However, I didn't work as an actor every week. I auditioned and got the part of a gas-station attendant-mechanic on a show called "Manhunt," starring Victor Jory and Patrick McVey. It was definitely ironic that one of the roles I had landed was exactly what I had been doing for the past several months. Maybe Jack was right about my researching that job for a part in a TV show! I was very impressed to be working with Mr. Jory, having grown up watching him on screen. I remembered how much he had scared me playing the evil Indian in the movie *Tom Sawyer*. I had a one-scene part in the show. It was a cop show about the San Diego police. My scene was simple: The police drive into the gas station, and I come out of the lift stall and say, "Can I help you?" Jory flashes his badge and asks me if I have seen a man drive into the station in a big white Imperial. I say, "Yes, I did—yesterday," and go on excitedly talking about the car and what a humongous engine it has. Could I describe the man? they ask. I respond by saying that I was more involved with the car and that the man never got out. Jory asks me for anything about the man that I can remember, and I tell him that I think he was a big man with black hair and that he was smoking a cigar. He thanks me, and then they drive off.

We started the scene. They drove into the station, which was really a set on one of the little studios in Hollywood—I think Ziv Television—Mr. Jory got out of the car, walked up to me, and said a line I had never heard before! I stared at him blankly for a moment, and he asked me what was wrong. Did I forget my first line? "No, sir, that is not my cue!" I responded. He proceeded to say another line, which was equally unfamiliar to me. Fred Jackman, the director, walked into the set and asked me what the trouble was. I told him that I hadn't recognized any of the lines Mr. Jory had said.

"Let me see your script, Eric!" he replied.

I quickly ran over to my trailer, retrieved the script, and handed it to Mr. Jackman.

He just looked at the title page and freaked out. He started yelling at the assistant director, the continuity person, and anyone within earshot: "This is next week's show!"

Both scripts had a gas-station scene but with different content. For a few moments everything seemed to go into tilt. No one said anything. What to do?

I broke the silence: "If you give me five minutes," I said, "I can memorize this week's script, and we can do it."

Jackman looked at me with a you're-kidding-me-kid look, but I repeated that I was sure I could do it, since it was only about eight or nine lines. He agreed and said we could shoot it in incremental takes. I went over to one of the parked cars, laid the script on the hood, and began to memorize it. I have eidetic imagery, which allows me to quickly retain anything that is on a page in front of me. It's like a photographic memory, but one step down. I took about seven or eight minutes and told them I was ready to do the scene. We took our places, Mr. Jory said the first line, and I responded. He continued, and I did the entire scene in one take. Mr. Jory looked at me, put his hand on my shoulder, and said, "Eric, you're a real trooper!" I felt proud to be complimented by an actor I respected so much. During that period of time I worked on a couple of other shows, but I can't remember what they were.

Like my sister, Jean was worried about my working late at night in the liquor store, even though I told her that I felt safer on those streets than on Hollywood Boulevard. I had gotten to know the people in the area, and they had taken me into their lives. When I walked down the street, I was greeted by my first name by almost everyone, usually with a big smile. Nonetheless, Jean wanted me out of there and suggested that I speak to Victor Bloom about a telephone sales job. I told her that it was strictly a commission job and that there were no guarantees. She reminded me that I had done very well at telephone sales all the way through my first two years of college, so I spoke to Victor, who said he would give me a shot and see how it worked out. Since I could keep my liquor-store job in the meantime, there was nothing to lose.

I sat and watched several older men in a room filled with telephones. They all looked like siding salesmen—you know the kind, the ones who wear blue suede shoes. The atmosphere was a downer. The room was filled with stale smoke and a cacophony of voices reading words off a pitch sheet. All of the men sitting at those miniature desks looked as though they were past middle age and life had left them with an endless line of cul-de-sac jobs. I listened to a couple of them and felt that I was much more qualified to sell than they were. It was a depressing experience. I sat looking at those guys and had the morbid thought that maybe I would be sitting at a small desk with a telephone in my hand thirty years from then, doing the same thing.

I took the job and went to another boiler room with a group of younger men. That in itself made me feel better. I immediately did very well. I was outselling everybody in my room and the other rooms as well. Perhaps it was my past experience with telephone sales, or maybe it was because I was an actor and could relate to people much more personally. Victor called me into his office and offered me a management position with his company. I quit the liquor-store job and started working almost full time for Victor. He wanted me to set up a number of rooms in the valley and hire telephone salespeople, and he said I would get a commission on everything they sold. I jumped at it. I rented an apartment in a medium-size building in Van Nuys and had the telephone company install seven phones in various parts of the place. Since we had no furniture, most of the telephones sat on the floor. I hired many of my actor friends and a few of their friends, but none of them could sell a single ad! The turnover was overwhelming, and I had to make my living by being on the phone. I closed the apartment and found a place in Pacoima directly across from the Whiteman Airport. It was a bare industrial room with faded white walls and a cement floor pockmarked with patches of varying colors. I moved a couple of tables that I had used in the Van Nuys apartment and placed them against the walls. I figured I would work there and get one other person to work with me. Finding someone who could sell was not going to be an easy job, however, but I ended up hiring my friend Mike Monahan, who already had a wife and a couple of kids to support. He did O.K. We both worked there for a few months.

Going to work every morning was really difficult and quite depressing. I wasn't on my way to an acting job, and I hated the area and the place where I was going to spend the next six or seven hours of my life. On my way to work every day I made up a song that I sang. The melody was ever changing but the lyrics remained the same: "This is what I do so I can do what I want to do!" I sang it over and over like some kind of mantra, and it did make me feel better.

Every day, I would open the front door and stand there for a minimum of five minutes looking at that God-awful room before I would actually enter. The telephone on my desk looked ten times bigger than it actually was, and I felt as though I would not be able to lift it off the cradle. Finally, when I made the first sale, I relaxed and felt more like working. It was, however, a daily routine, and I wondered how long I would be able to maintain it. Jean was closer to delivery and had stopped working, so the entire responsibility was now mine.

I decided to take a day off from work. While I was sitting at the table in the breakfast nook of my house, drinking my morning coffee, my thoughts flew all over the place: What was I going to do? Where was I going? What about my acting career? Would I ever be able to support us just from acting? Was there a teacher out there anywhere? I had talked with Jean about going to New York and studying with Strasberg, but that was financially impossible. Making a move like that would cost a fortune, not to mention that I didn't have an income, even if I could get there. I had been very optimistic and upbeat all of my life, except for that particular time. I was despondent and filled with a feeling of hopelessness. I'm not religious, although I do believe in a higher power, and at that exact moment felt completely powerless. I looked up at the beamed ceiling that the former tenant had painted in pastel icky colors and said, "O.K., I'm giving the whole thing to you. If you want to help me, please do!" I felt a little silly, since I wasn't in the habit of praying; and besides, why would that higher power take any interest in my problems when there were so many more important things to attend to? I refilled my coffee cup and resumed my brooding. At the pinnacle of my self-pity the telephone rang. I answered. On the other end a very raspy, deep voice asked if I was Eric Morris. At first I thought it was a telemarketer trying to sell me something I couldn't afford; then I heard the voice say, "This is

Curt Conway. I spoke with Marty, and he suggested that I call you, since you were the leader in his class." The word *leader* wasn't mine. I had never felt like a leader, even though I had done more work in the class than almost anyone else. "I've moved here from New York," Curt continued, "I want to start a class, and I thought that maybe you could speak with a few of Marty's students and see if they would be interested."

I looked up at the ceiling and under my breath said, "Thank you, God, for sending me Curt Conway!"

"Are you there, Eric?" he resumed.

"Oh, yes, I'm sorry," I replied. "I was distracted for a moment." I knew that Curt had been Marty's teacher and assumed that they worked in a similar way. "Yes, of course," I continued. "I will talk to all of the people, and, incidentally, I want to work with you."

"That's great, Eric! Here's my phone number. Feel free to give it to any of your people, and thanks."

I was elated. My prayers had been answered so fast that I thought I should make a list and continue communicating with the higher power. I was able to get several people to go to Curt's class. He rented a little space in an upstairs studio, and I was excited about being there. During the first class we didn't do much that was related to craft or process. I had totally expected that Curt would be teaching the stuff that Marty used to, but he didn't even use the same terminology. I figured that I would give him some time to acclimate himself to Los Angeles, get his feet grounded, and then we would get the real stuff.

Curt was a real piece of work. At that time I believe he was in his late forties or early fifties, was of medium size and built, with a shock of gray hair that was thick and full. His voice was his most distinguishing feature. It was really deep, guttural, and gravelly. I wondered at the time how it had developed in that way and later found out that he was an alcoholic. I imagine that all those years of drinking had injured his larynx and that the sound came from that injured place. He had been fairly successful as an actor on Broadway, and I'm sure that he had also worked in television. He had, however, been blacklisted during the McCarthy era. Called in front of the House Un-American Activities Committee, he had refused to name names and incriminate others, so he had been classified as an unfriendly witness and blacklisted. He couldn't get any work as an actor, so he had started teaching—which had brought him to this place in his life.

I went to two other classes and decided that there wasn't anything there for me. Curt was knowledgeable and articulate but didn't have a method of creating reality on the stage. He would give good critique, but when it was time to tell his students how to fulfill what he had pointed out, there wasn't any process. I had spent too many of my training years in similar environments, and I wasn't going to spend any more time or money doing it. Now I had the job of telling Curt that I was going to drop the class. I created half a dozen scenarios to justify my leaving, but none of them sounded too convincing. I finally settled on what was very close to the truth: Jean was due soon. I had to work evenings to support my family and was extremely tight financially. Curt offered to give me a scholarship, which I thought was either very generous or due to the fact that he might be afraid that if I left, others would follow. At any rate, I thanked him and told him that when I had adjusted the hours of my working schedule, I would be back but would pay for the classes. It has been my experience that students who don't pay for their classes create all kinds of issues with the teacher. If the critique is harsh, they think it is because the teacher resents them, or they may feel guilty about not paying their way, and their work suffers for it.

There I was once again, flapping in the wind without a teacher. I figured out that what Marty taught he had gotten from Strasberg, not Curt, but I hadn't known it until I experienced Curt's approach.

Since nothing had changed in my career life and Jean couldn't work, I figured I would look around for some other opportunities in the film world. I remembered a discovery I had made while still living on Detroit Street: One afternoon, while sitting on the couch and looking at the telephone on the divider between the kitchen and dining room, I had made the decision that I was not going to spend my life waiting for my agent to call me for an audition. I had seen too many actors destroy their lives because of this business, some of them actually drinking themselves to death. I had decided that I would ultimately find a way to diversify my talents and become a "hyphenate" in my field. I would get involved in various aspects of filmmaking, at first just in production and then maybe also as a director. I hadn't yet thought about writing or teaching. I have never lost interest in acting, not even to this day. I just felt that because of the nature of the career I had chosen, I would have to continue my journey with a few intelligent adjustments.

What I Learned in Marty's Class

1. I learned that there was a *how.*
2. I was introduced to what an obligation is in relation to dramatic material.
3. I learned how to read a play or film and identify the character responsibilities.
4. I found out what choices are and how to access them from my life.
5. For the first time in all my training I was taught what sense memory is, how to create an object—a choice—using the technique, and how to practice and train my senses to memorize objects using a specific method.
6. I understood how important relaxation is to the creative process and how it is impossible to create when one is tense.
7. I discovered a number of relaxation techniques that one uses to eliminate tension.
8. I found out about instrumental exercises that put one in touch with one's emotions—such as the singing-and-movement exercise that Marty had gotten from Strasberg—and other instrumental exercises to purge tension and elevate one's emotional state.
9. I came to realize how important a healthy ego is to the creative process.
10. I was able to understand conceptual traps and avoid hooking into the logic of a scene or playing the emotional results.
11. I learned how to go with the moment, allowing myself to express what I was affected by in each moment and also to include my impulses in the lines of a scene.
12. I found out how to identify and use available stimulus, to allow the other actor and the environment to affect me and to express my responses organically.

I am sure there were many other things I learned in that class that I have either forgotten or haven't listed. The reality is that it was the first and only class up to that time in my life where I learned HOW to do the things that lead to the organic fulfillment of material and how to use my instrument from a real place. I had what I felt at that time was a process. The class put me on the road and the journey I have been on for the last forty-five years. I always say to people that as a result of being in Marty's class and with the indirect influence of Lee Strasberg, I went from A to E with a process and that in all my years of teaching I have gone from E to T on my own. I feel that I have gone light years beyond the original Stanislavski System and really innovated a process that stands by itself in training actors to become PROFESSIONAL EXPERIENCERS.

In the next chapter I will describe in detail how my process evolved and how what I started with became much more dimensional and specific.

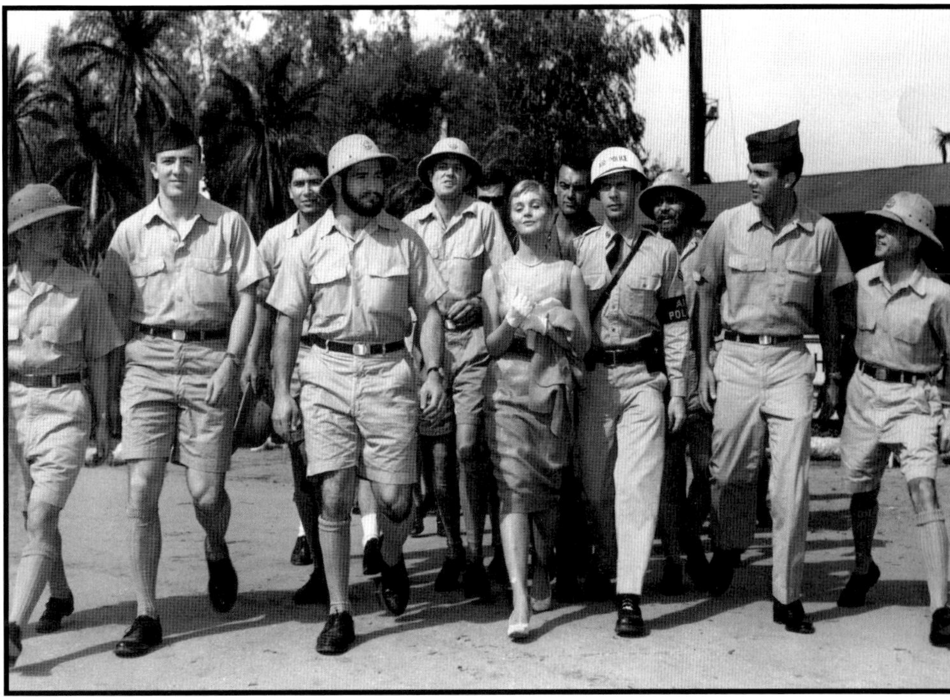

In *Holiday for Lovers* at 20th Century Fox,
I had a nice scene with Carol Lynley.

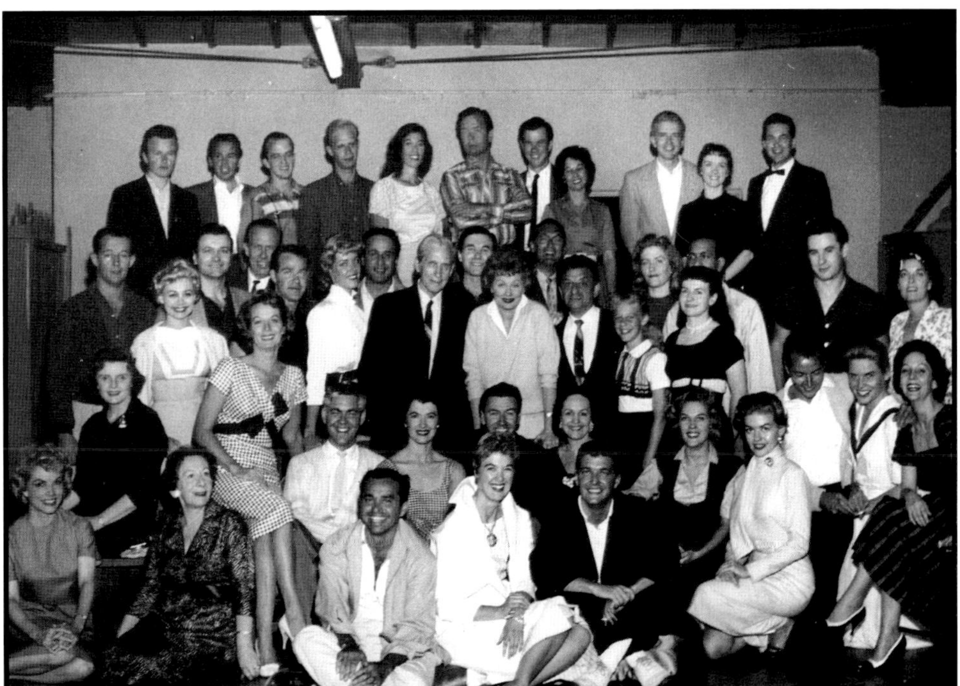

The whole gang at Lucille Ball's workshop:
Ben Ari is on her left, and I'm in the top row.

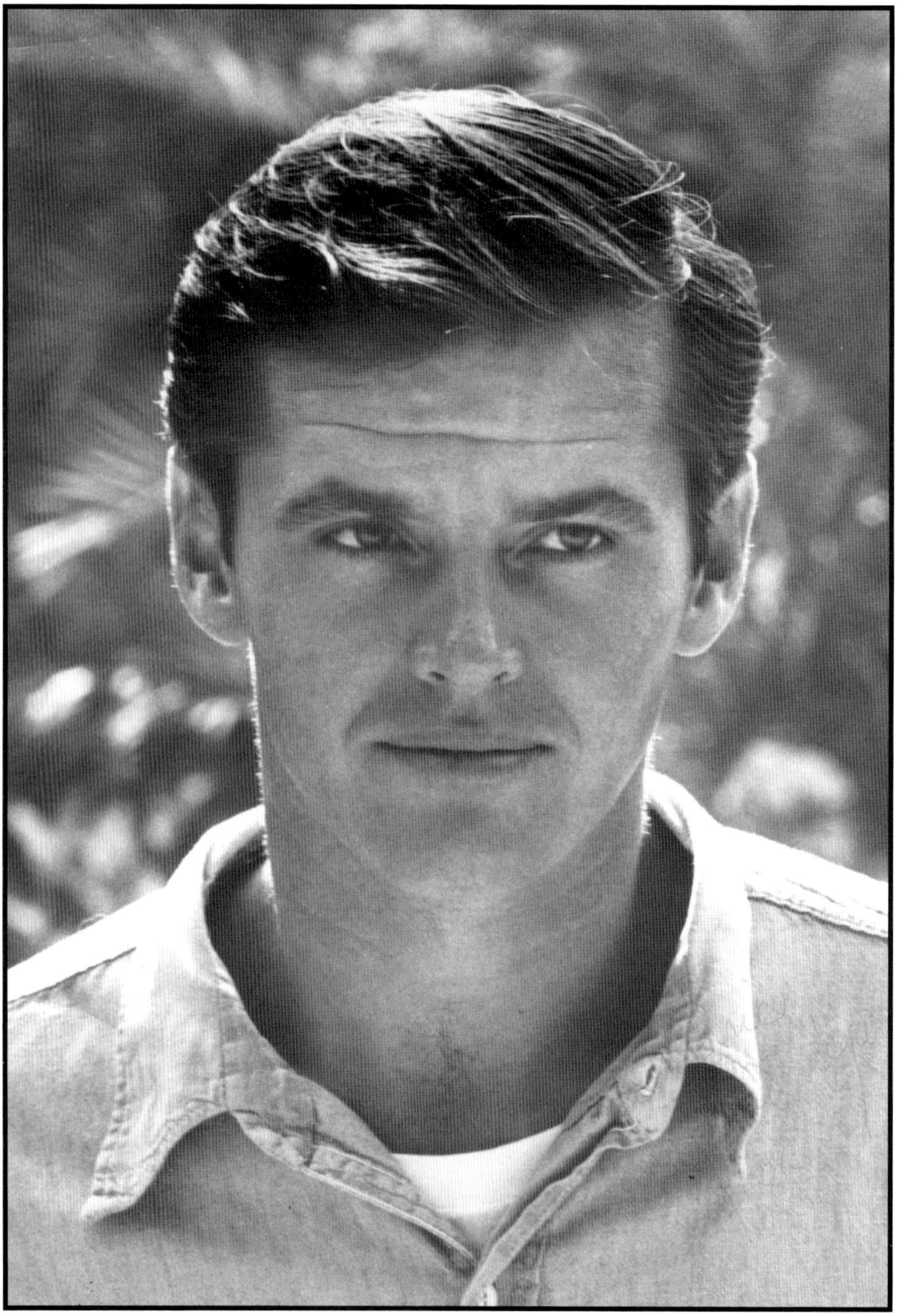

As a young actor, I supplemented my income
by taking headshots of other actors.
This is one of the pictures I took of Jack in a sitting.

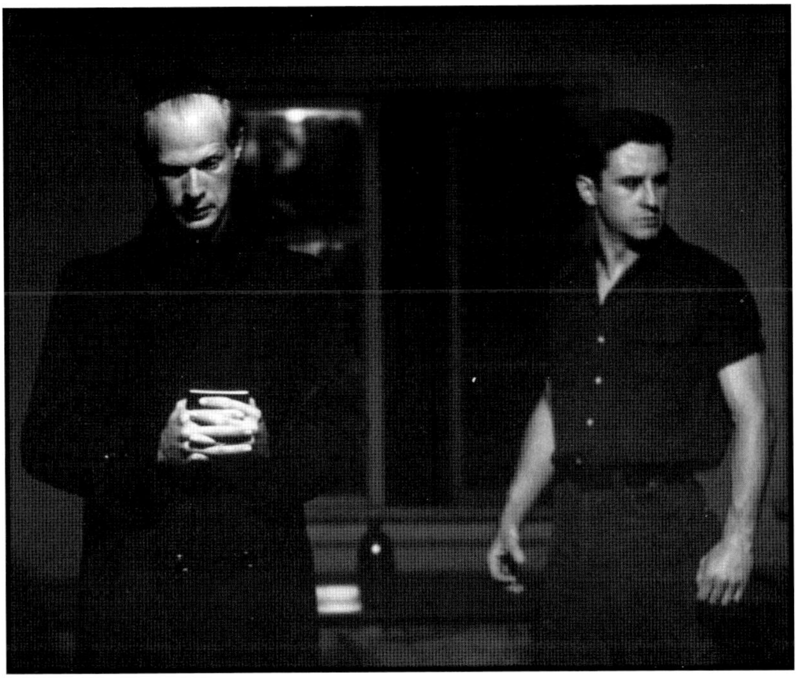

I played a priest in *The Crucible* with Rudy Solari for Lucille Ball.

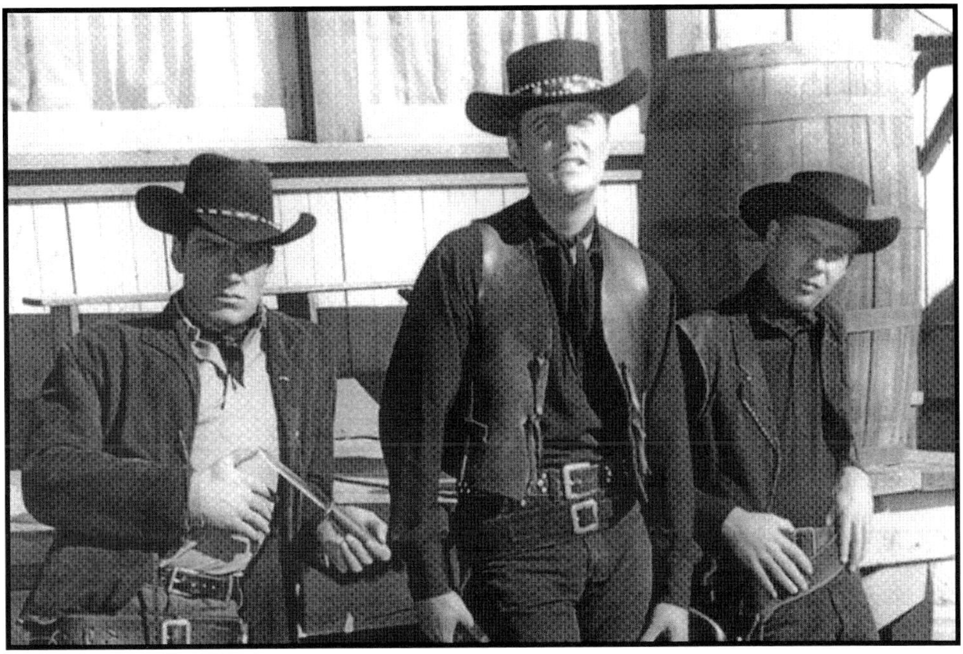

Van Williams, Tommy Gilson and I
as "The Young Toughs" in "The Lawman" TV series

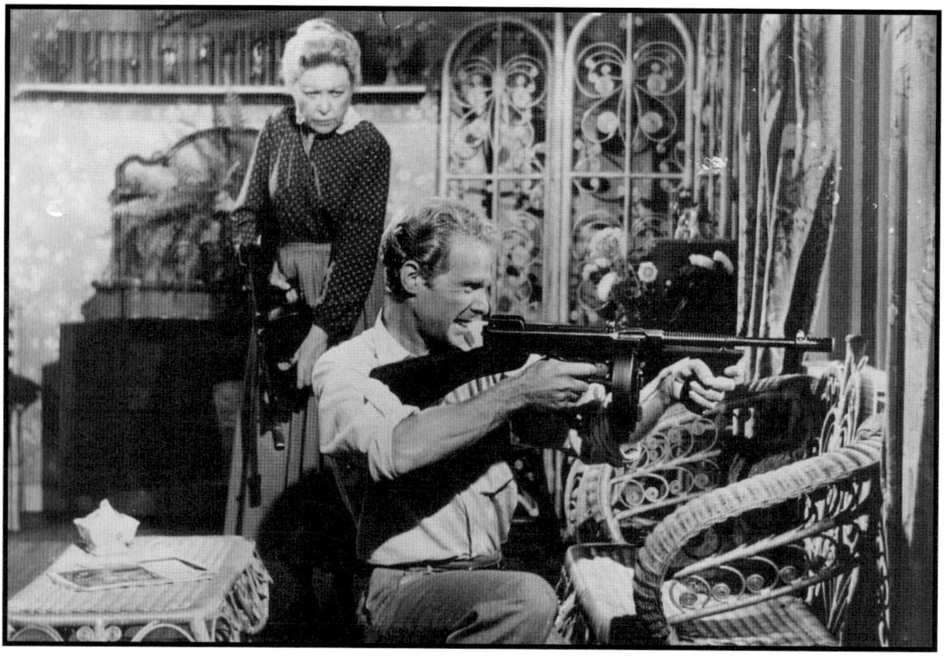

In *Ma Barker's Killer Brood* I was cast as Freddy Barker, one of the leads, with Lurene Tuttle as my "Ma."

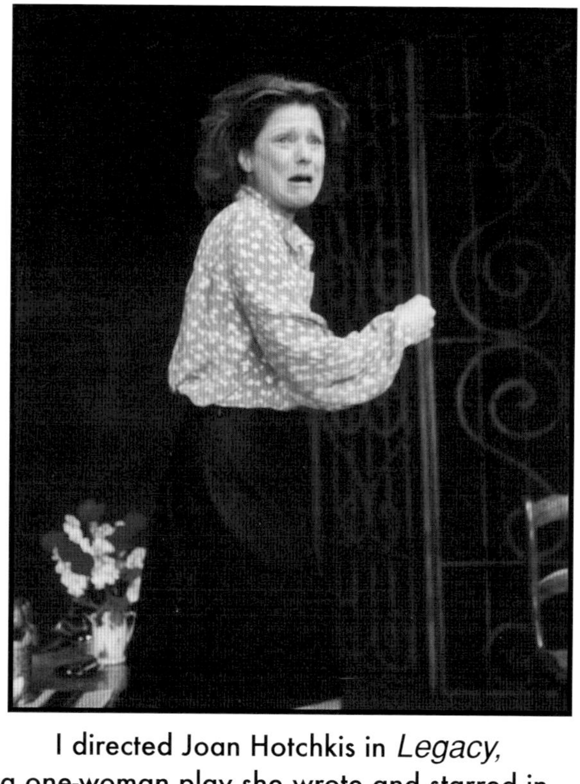

I directed Joan Hotchkis in *Legacy*, a one-woman play she wrote and starred in.

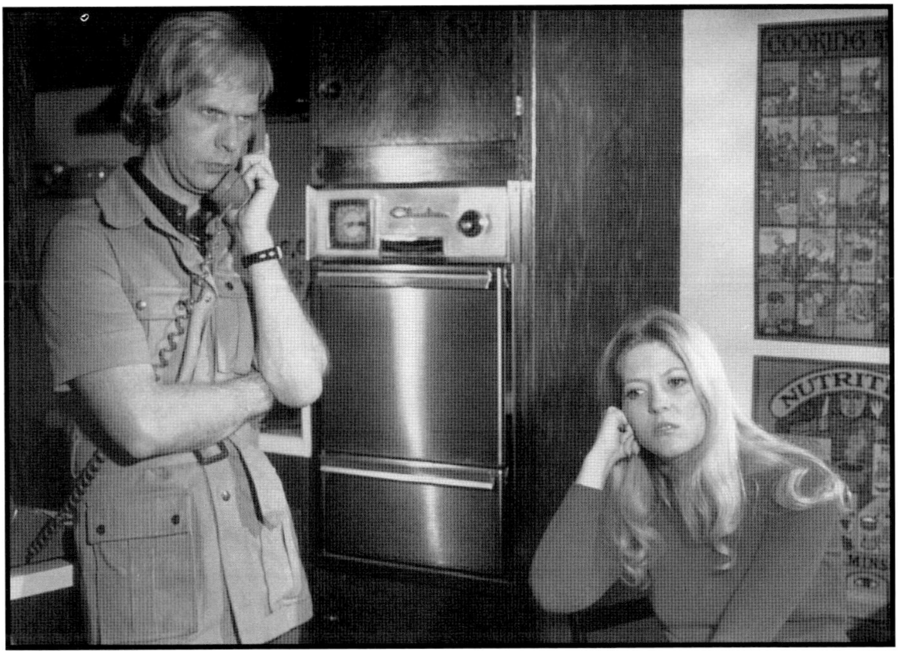

In *Echo of a Massacre* I was a psychiatrist opposite Meredith MacRae.

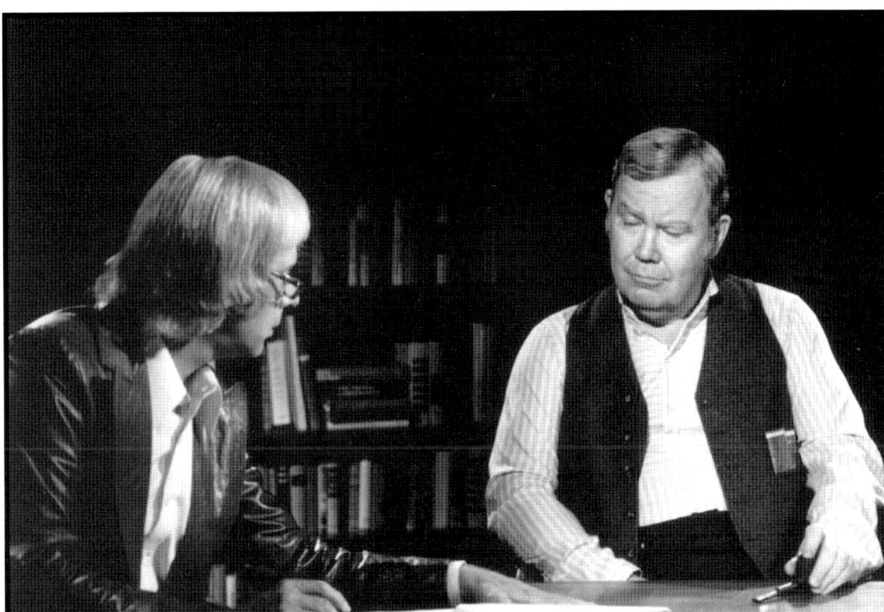

Interviewing Father Banahan as one of the characters in "Eyewitness to the Past"

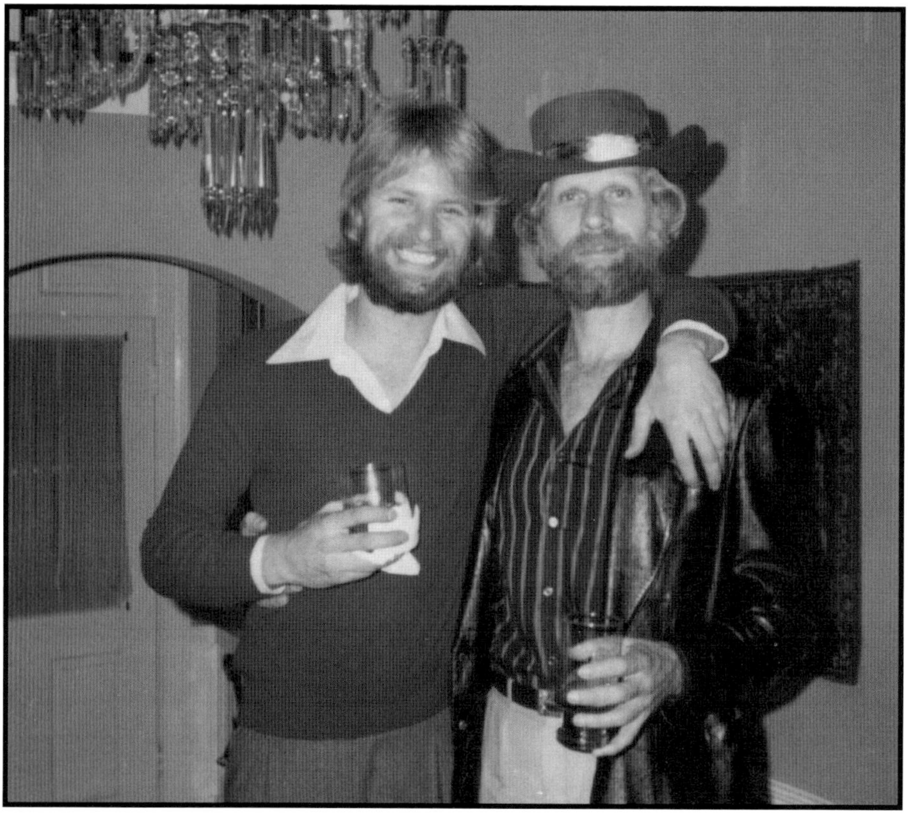

Jeff and I at my 50th birthday party

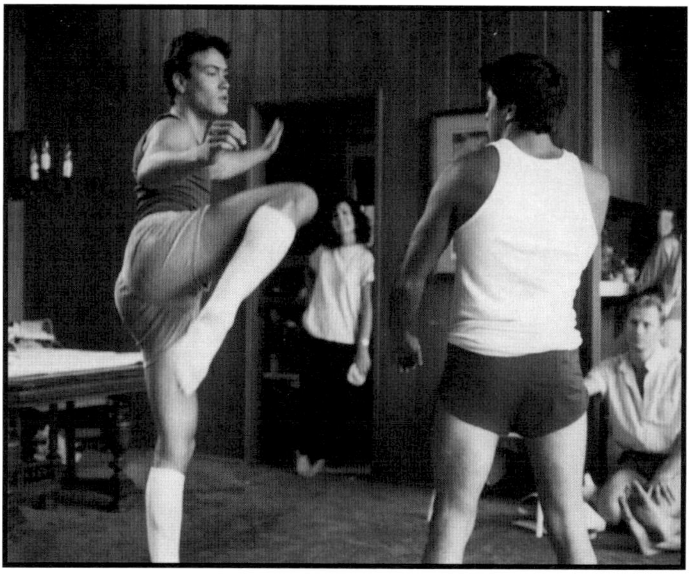

Brandon Lee demonstrating a martial-arts move
at a weekend workshop at my house in Lake Arrowhead

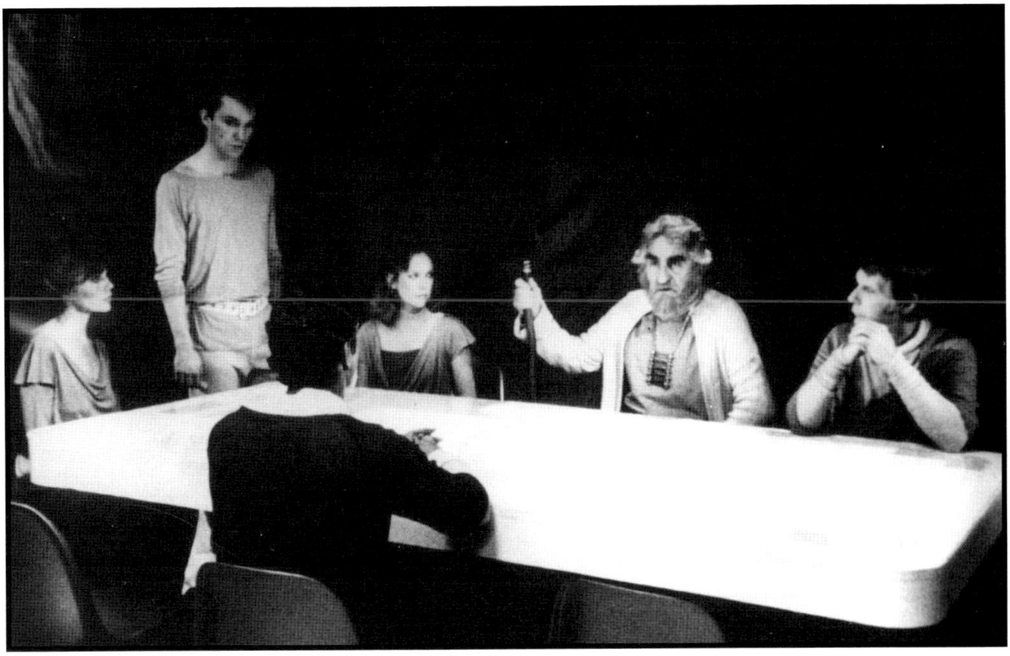

In *Battle beyond the Stars* I'm sitting to the left of Jeff Corey, and Richard Thomas is standing.

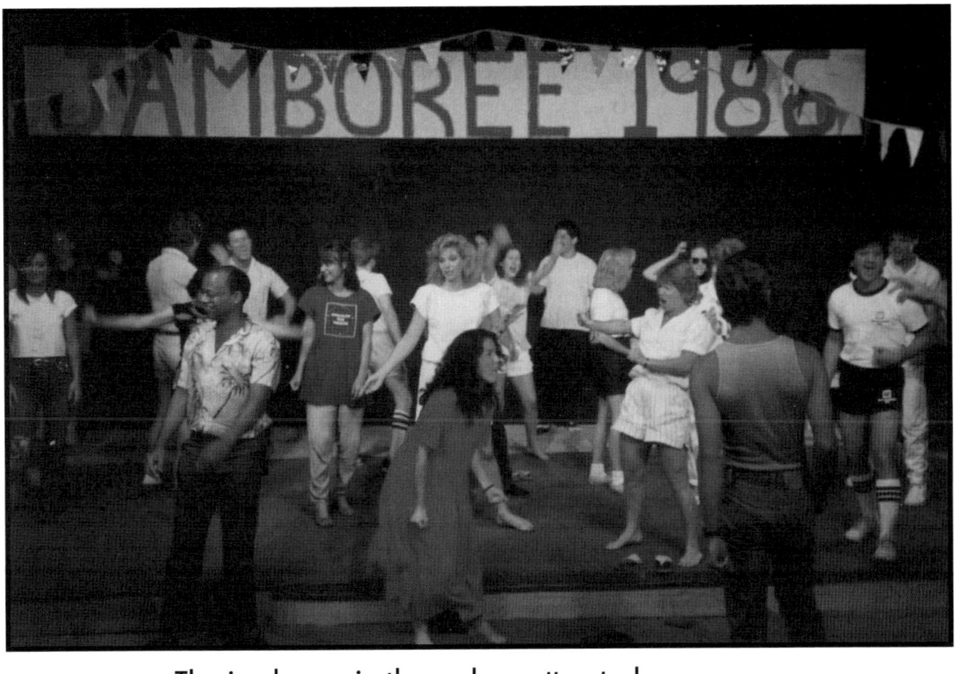

The jamboree in those days attracted as many as 80 or 90 people. My daughter, Suzy, is in the center on stage.

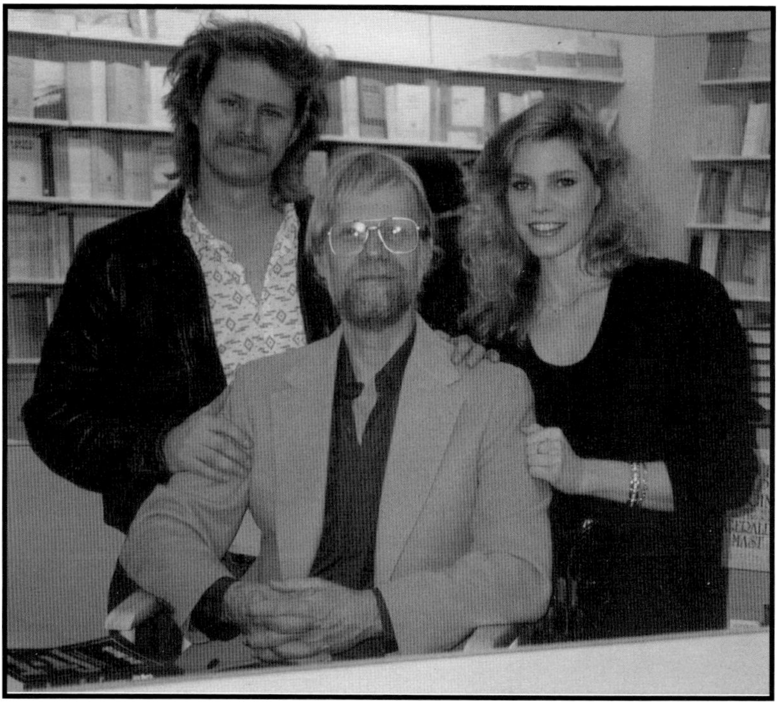

Jeff, Suzanne, and I at a book signing
for *Acting from the Ultimate Consciousness*

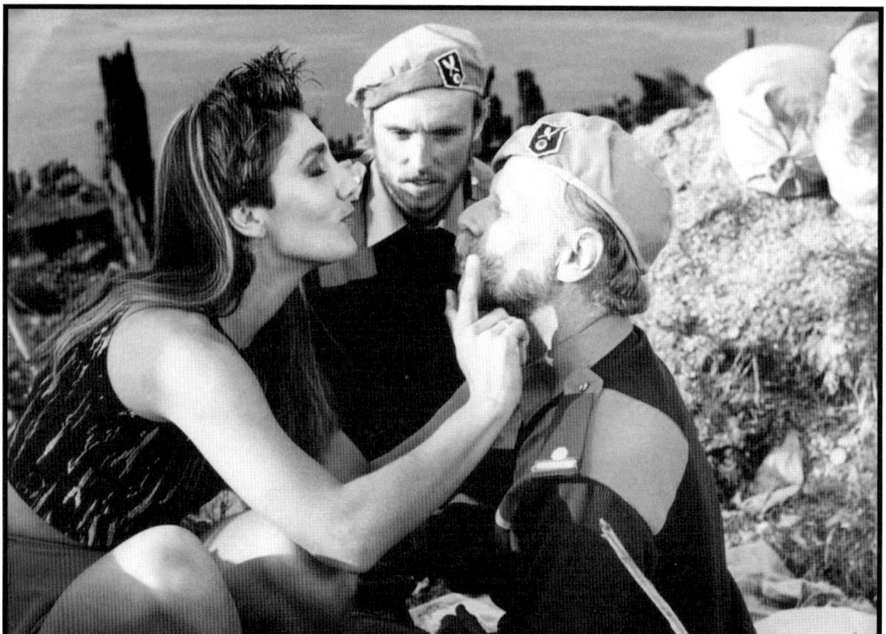

In *The Tango War,* which I did in Argentina,
I played an English colonel.

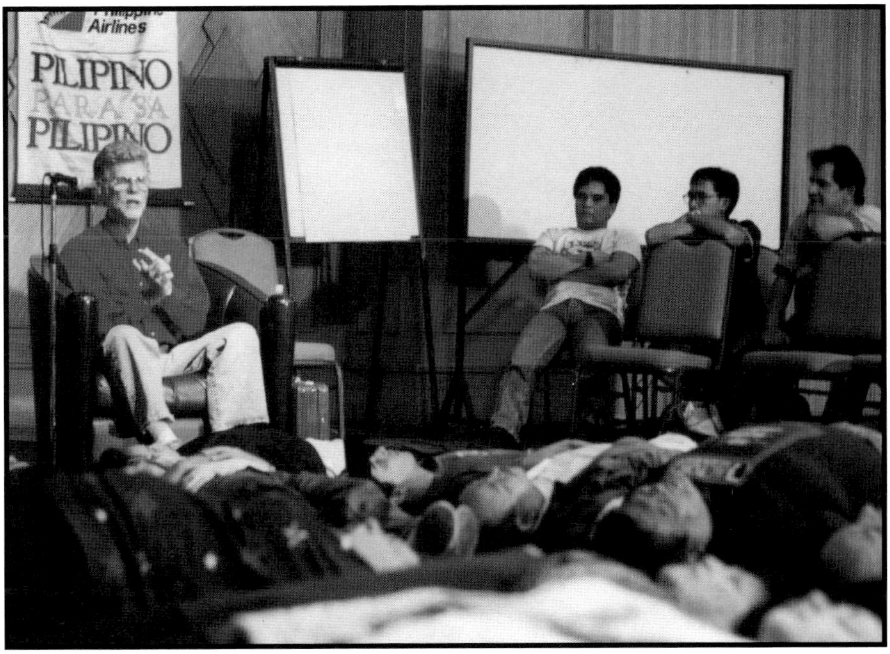

Teaching in the Philippines was magic.

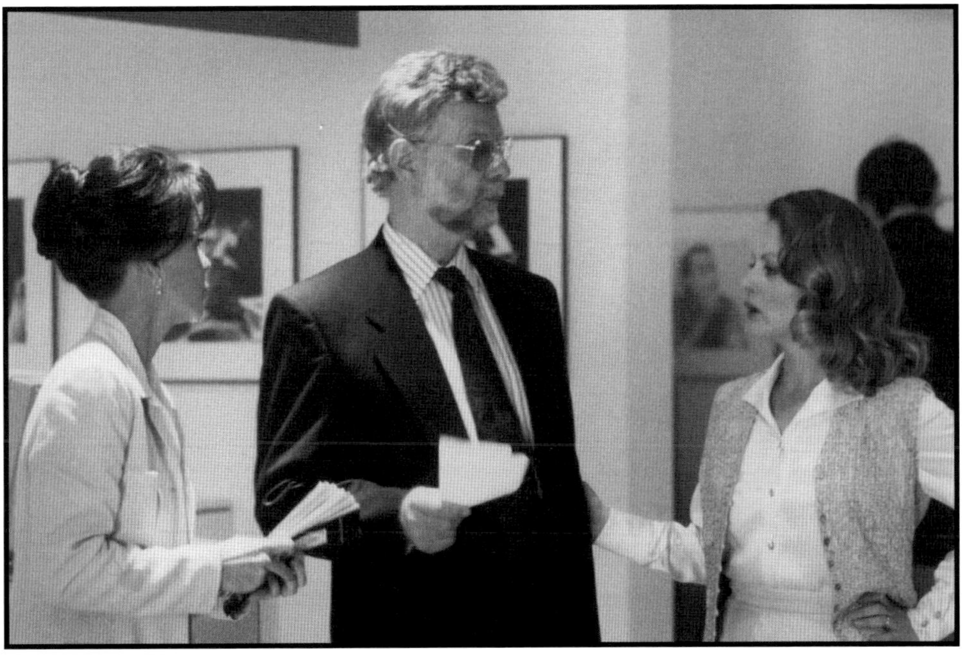

In *Eye for an Eye* with Sally Field and Beverly D'Angelo, I gave the character an officious and effete quality.

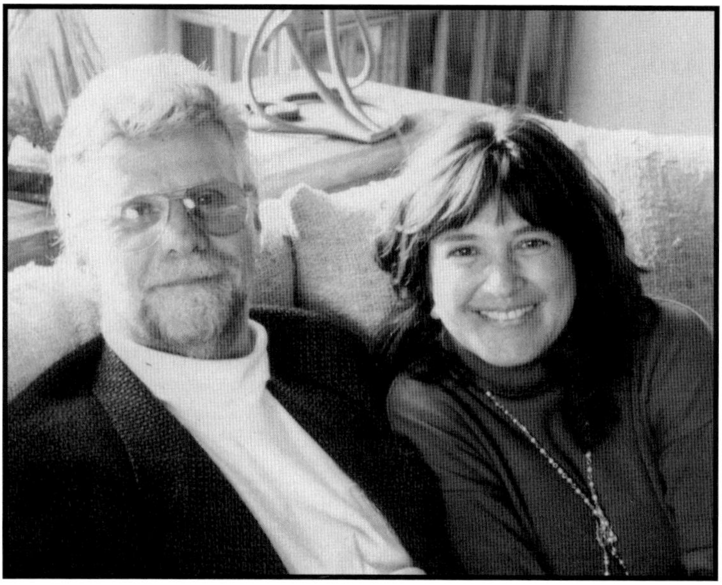

Susana and me

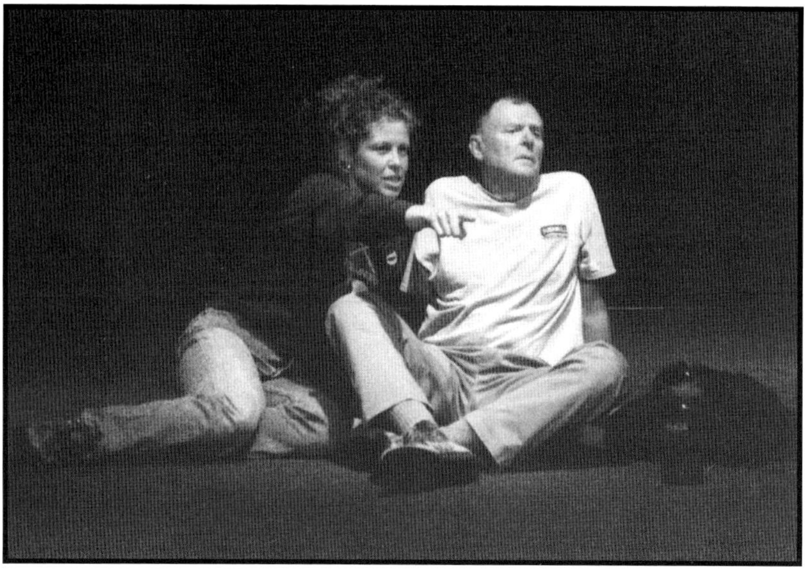

I directed Norman Crawford and Courtney Birch in *Love Always,* which was written by Norman and which played in the United States and Europe.

CHAPTER 7

THE TEACHING AND WORKING YEARS

The Early Years: The Sixties and Seventies

At the beginning of this chapter I have to say that I have been teaching for forty-five years and that it would be very difficult to document all those years in one chapter or maybe even in an entire book. Looking back at my lesson plans is like taking a trip into the twilight zone. The names, the faces of people, some of whom are now gone, bring back a special time to me. I love teaching, and I have learned much about myself and about life as a result of working so intimately with so many people. This life journey has been richer than it would have been in any other profession I could have chosen. I am still an actor, and I love acting, but if I had remained just an actor, I think that instead of seeing the panorama of the world I would have continued to see only my own reflection.

That fateful day when it all began, I was sitting in the breakfast nook at my house in Burbank. I heard Jean singing in the other room, and it warmed me. I was still without a class, however, and felt that I was losing ground with the craft. The things that I had learned and that had given me a security as an actor that I had never had before seemed to be slipping slowly from my memory—or maybe I was just scared and imagining it. I was killing time trying to put off getting dressed and going to that boiler room in Pacoima. It is incredible how much we do to stall and avoid doing distasteful things: I'll have just one more cup of coffee; I need to read more of the newspaper; I'll check on Jean—anything to keep from getting dressed and going to work. I leaned back, resting my head on the vinyl cushion of the booth, closed my eyes and began to daydream: What if someone I don't know died and left me a fortune? What if I got a lead in a successful television series?

After about ten minutes of wishing, I opened my eyes and found myself staring at the pastel beams of the ceiling. It seemed like *déjà vu.* It was not my habit to stare at that ceiling in the breakfast room, but there I was, looking at the same part of it, remembering when I had given myself up to that higher power. Well, I thought, it worked once. Why not try it again? I wasn't adept at prayer, and I didn't know if there was a specific protocol, so all I did was say, "Please, if you hear me, please help me find a teacher, a class, an acting job! I can't stand the thought of growing old with a telephone in my hand." Immediately after my strange prayer I felt really guilty: There I was, complaining about my life, when I had everything in the world to be thankful for. I was healthy, I had a wonderful wife and was about to have a new child, I ate three meals a day and we were paying our bills, I was driving a beautiful, almost new, red Corvette and living in a quaint and lovely house, so what was I "miserizing" about? I jumped up out of the booth and went to the shower, got dressed, kissed Jean, and was halfway out the door when the telephone rang. I stood there for a moment, deciding whether or not to answer it. It might be my agent. No, not at this hour. Go ahead, I thought. It will only take a minute.

"Hello?"

"Hi, this is Ann O'Hara. You remember me, right?"

"Yes, hi Ann, how are you?"

"I'm fine. I have been thinking about you recently, and I thought I would give you a call to see how you are doing."

It seemed strange that she would call me. I had done some exercises and a scene or two with her when we were in class, but I had never been really close to her.

"I'm doing O.K.," I replied, "working, getting ready to be a father."

"Well," she continued, "I'm wondering if you have found another class yet."

"No, I haven't, and I'm beginning to think there isn't one out there."

There was a moment of silence, and then she said, "Well, I was thinking that you might start one of your own."

I was surprised by her suggestion and for a moment was at a loss for a response. She continued: "I think that you would make a wonderful teacher. I learned as much or more from you in Marty's class than I did from him."

I was flattered by her statement but didn't know how to respond to a suggestion that seemed to come out of the blue. "I'm not a teacher, Ann," I finally said. "I'm an actor."

"Yes, I know that, Eric, and a damn fine one too! But you haven't found a place to continue your training, right?"

"Well, yes, that's true, but I'm still looking and hoping."

"Did you ever think that you could promote your own growth as an actor by teaching?"

Wow, I thought, she really said the magic words!

"Well," I responded, "I never thought of that. I guess by teaching the work, I will continue to be involved with it, and I suppose I could do some work myself."

"Exactly! That's what I thought too."

Was this the higher power responding to my strange prayer? I thought.

"O.K.," I said, "Where do we start?"

She told me that she would be honored to be my first student and that she knew a guy who would also take my class. I responded that I would get back to her in a day or two. On my way to work I felt excited and renewed and was actually looking forward to getting there and making my first call. I was going to sell a lot of ads today! It's funny how, when you have something to look forward to, life takes on different colors. Even that drab, uninspiring industrial room looked better. I saw things in it that I had never noticed before. My mind was racing with thoughts of what to do, where to start the work, how to structure it, and so on. I had to find a place where to teach the class. It was going to cost money to rent. I figured that two students would cover part of the cost and that I wasn't thinking of making money as an acting teacher. All I wanted was to keep growing as a craftsman.

The next morning I called Jed Duane, the guy who put together Marty's spaces. Jed was creative and had a good eye, so I figured he might already have a space that I could rent for one night a week. He told me that he did have a small one on McCadden Place just south of Sunset Boulevard. I called Ann, and we had our first class that week. It was a Monday night, the same night Marty had held his class on. Ann brought Marco, a young Hispanic man about twenty-five years old. We started by talking about what we were going to do, what kind of exercises I had planned, and what they both wanted out of the class. I was a little nervous about my position. While it was true that I felt comfortable commenting in Marty's class, this was an entirely new situation. I was the teacher, the leader, and that felt like a huge responsibility. We started with some relaxation exercises and then launched into a complete sense-memory workout. I explained the process to Marco and showed him how to work with and without an object. After that, I had both Ann and Marco do the singing exercise that we had done every week in Marty's class.

For quite a while after I started teaching, I followed the structure and exercises that I had learned. In the first few months the number of people seesawed. I began with two students, continued with three, then four, then back down to three. Even though my classes were small, I felt positive about the future.

The day finally arrived on March 3, 1962. We went to the hospital, where Jean gave birth to our first child, a boy about nine pounds and a few ounces. Just like me he had a full head of long blond hair that reached his shoulders. As I looked at him in the nursery, I filled with pride and a sense of accomplishment I had never felt before. There were about twenty infants there, and even if our name hadn't been on the crib, I would have been able to pick mine out from all the rest! On the way home I was so elated that I felt as if the car could leave the ground and as though I were the only person on the planet who had ever fathered a baby. We named him Jeffrey Eric Morris.

A short while later, I received a call from Curt Conway, who told me that he had heard I was teaching a class and that he was interested in coming down to observe it. He said that he hated working with people in the very beginning of their training and asked, if it worked out, whether I would be interested in teaching a beginners' class for him. I told him that I would. Meanwhile, the people Jed was renting from had other plans for the building, so we had to move from McCadden Place to another location. On the corner of

Highland and De Longpre Jed found an old house, which had probably been built in the late thirties or early forties. He rented me what had been its living room, which faced Highland Avenue. I guess it had been a tiny room, so whoever it was had wanted to enlarge it and had begun to tear down a wall between it and the adjoining room. Unfortunately, he or she hadn't completed the job, and the room I was to teach in was split in two by the framing of the wall that had originally been there. You could see the other space through the separated two-by-fours. Jed had had very little time to find another location, so he had taken this one, planning to finish the job and turn the room into as nice a place as he had arranged for Marty.

As promised, Curt came to see my class one evening. When he walked in, just as we had started our relaxation exercise, he informed me that he could only stay for a couple of hours and told me not to take it personally when he left. I nodded my understanding and went on with the class. I did most of what I was accustomed to in the first two hours. I wanted to make sure Curt got a sense of what the class and my teaching were like. At that time I had about seven students, so it looked more like a small acting class than a private session. When it came time for Curt to leave, he quietly passed me a note and left. I went on with the class, reserving a later time to read his note. When the class was over and people had finished with their departing questions and added need for attention, I read the note, which said:

> Eric, you are a born teacher! I would be honored to have you teach a class for me. Call me.
>
> Curt.

I was very moved by it. Even though I didn't relate to what Curt was teaching, I nonetheless respected the fact that he had spent a great deal of his life acting and teaching and had developed a respectable reputation.

Curt was teaching in a fairly large space on La Cienega, just about two hundred yards south of Santa Monica Boulevard. I taught the several people he sent me in the same place, which had a raised area that was used as a stage. He paid me 60 percent of the income from the class and kept 40 percent for himself, which I thought was quite fair, since he was taking care of the rent. He had been teaching for a while now and had attracted some working actors, whom I would run into in passing between classes. Since I had kept my own class separate from the one I was teaching for him, I was now teaching twice a week and really liking it, although I still wasn't making enough of an income to quit working for Victor Bloom.

By then Curt had started working again as an actor in Hollywood. The blacklist was a thing of the past, though it had left in its wake the ravages and destruction of many lives. One afternoon Curt called me to tell me that he was working on a film and that they were going to run overtime. He asked if I could start his class for him. I told him I would be there and not to worry. He had a much larger class than I at the time, and when everybody arrived, sat down, and saw me, there was a little bit of a dissatisfied murmur. I thought that I would skip the relaxation exercises and go directly to the individual work. Just as I was ready to start, Andrew Prine, who at that time was working fairly steadily as an actor, got up and started to leave, taking a couple of others with him; however, when he was halfway out, Harry Dean Stanton, who had been a fellow student in Marty's class, stopped him and told him quietly to give me a chance. I guess Andrew respected Harry Dean enough to return to his seat.

I pointed to a tall actor sitting in the first row and asked him to get up onstage. He sauntered up there and winked to the group, as if saying, Watch this! I'm going to put this asshole in his place. I picked up on it and smiled at him. He was good-looking, had a lot of hair and a decent body. I asked him to tell me his name. He hesitated, looked at the class, and smiled. "Hampton, Hampton Fancher," he said. He started to shtick and do a lot of numbers, repeating some of my questions in such a way that it was obvious he was mocking me. Some of the people in the class were laughing and subtly urging him on. I had a moment when I wished Curt would walk in and I could get the hell out of there, but I could see that wasn't going to happen, so I adjusted myself solidly in the chair I was sitting in and proceeded to dismantle Hampton Fancher. I called him on all his shticks and pointed out where his tension was and how he was redirecting all of what was really going on underneath his antics. I pointed out his insecurities and how he was compensating for them, and at the end of about ten minutes his left leg was shaking, he was perspiring, and he was exposing a lot of his emotional life and impulses, which he was not even aware of. I could see that he was making some discoveries about himself at the same time. I proceeded to point out his redirections and suppressed impulses. Every time he would attempt to save himself, I nailed him on what he was doing. Finally, when he got to a state of reality where he was not doing any of his numbers, I told him that at that moment he was ready to act. I asked him to do a piece of a monologue on a moment-to-moment basis. He started the words and became very vulnerable. His eyes filled with tears, his voice cracked with emotion, and when he was finished, you could have heard a pin drop in that room. Everyone was riveted on him and me. I could feel their shock at what they had just witnessed, and I felt pretty damned good. As an aside here, I must add that Hampton came to study with me, was in my class for years, and that we have remained very close friends.

I worked several more people in a similar instrumental way and achieved excellent results with all of them. When Curt finally came in, I felt that the rest of the people, whom I had not gotten to, were disappointed that I was leaving. After that evening several of the students in Curt's class also came to work with me, but I made it clear that they could only do so if they continued in Curt's class.

We were still in the early sixties. I had started teaching right before Christmas of 1961 and had been doing it for less than a year. Most of what I was doing was a carryover from Marty's class, but I had injected my own personality into my work and had added a number of exercises of my own. My classes were growing, and I felt that I could stop working for Victor. Jean was a bit insecure about my giving up that job, but I was making enough not to have to subject myself to it anymore. Some of Marty's people came to work with me, and it was for me a familiar environment. Harry Dean Stanton was there; Jack Nicholson camc in around 1962; Ann O'Hara, who had changed her name to Ann Raymond, was still there; Marco was long gone, but he had been replaced by many others. Hampton was living with Joan Blackman at the time. She was under contract to one of the major studios and at first was very resistant to what I was doing; however, after that night when I had replaced Curt, she encouraged Hampton to come to my class, if for no other reason than to see what the hell I was up to. She told Hampton that she thought I was too psychological and that what I was doing had nothing to do with acting but that she felt they should come and see if there was anything there.

Those early years were very productive. A lot of other talented people came to study with me: Hubert Cornfield, Maggie Blye, Michael Parks, Scott Wilson, Kayla Garren, Ulla Jones—Quincy Jones's wife—and many other exciting talents. Hubert was a director and took my class not as an actor, although he did some interesting acting work while there. Michael Parks was working and was a unique talent. Scott, whose real name was Bill Wilson, was brought into the class by Michael. Ulla was a Swede, with long, flowing, blond hair, and stood almost six feet in height. Quincy often came to class to sit in and watch, and on one occasion, after the class was over, he came up beside my chair and said, "Eric, you're a fucking genius!" I was very touched by that, since I thought then, and still do, that *he* is a genius in what he does.

Nineteen sixty-two and three were important years because I was learning how to relate in a different way. I was tough, demanding, sometimes harsh, and very direct. I developed the reputation of being very hard sometimes; for example, a couple of actors would get up to do a scene, and if within the first thirty seconds I could see that they were not organic or doing the work, I would shout, "Stop! What do you call what you are doing?" They would usually stand there speechless and, I guess, somewhat bewildered at my behavior. "If that's what you are going to do," I would continue, "then get the hell off the stage!" Usually at that point I would lead them into their choices and steer them into an organic state. Looking back on those early years when I was called "a holy terror," I realize that so much of that behavior, while well meant to achieve results, came from my own insecurities. A student from those early days came to visit my class a few years ago and was blown away at how mellow I had become. "Where's my Eric?" he exclaimed. "What happened to that guy? I must say I like this one better, but I was expecting to see Scrooge!" I don't want the reader to get the wrong idea here. I was always encouraging and supportive of all the people I taught. I had discovered that teaching was my calling, and I was dedicated to helping everyone become conversant with the craft.

A typical class was comprised of relaxation techniques, followed by a singing-and-movement exercise done by three or four people, then possibly a group sense-memory workout, a variety of individual "therapy" exercises, designed to address an area of obstacle or difficulty in an actor, maybe a monologue or two, and some scene work using the craft. Marty had used the singing exercise to identify blocks and obstacles and liberate them, but mostly to bring to the surface unexpressed emotional life. The actor had to sing a song, holding each note for a short period of time. Then, while still singing, he had to do four different movements: first, he had to bend forward and straighten back to an erect position; next, he was to move from side to side, feet planted in a fixed place; third, he would march in a circle; and in the fourth part, called jazz, he was to undulate his body as if dancing while standing in place. As I said before, the whole technique was designed to identify splits. When an actor is functioning as he should, all parts of his instrument work together as a unit—the mind, the body, the voice, and the emotions. When he is doing the movement part of the exercise, it becomes very clear when the voice and the emotions separate or when there is a physical split, where the body isn't connected to the other parts, and so on. The exercise came from Strasberg. Marty used it, and so did I for a number of years.

In addition, Marty did an exercise called "the original being," which was great for getting involved and discovering all of the things we take for granted. To do it you lie down and close your eyes. After four or five minutes—or longer if necessary—you wake up as if for the first time, becoming conscious of everything, seeing, hearing, and feeling things for the very first time, discovering your own body—how your fingers work, the movement of your head, the sounds you make, where they come from, and so on. It is a great exercise for discovery and for raising consciousness, and I sometimes still use it.

When an actor was really blocked, Marty would have him do an abandonment exercise, which involves lying down on one's back and with great abandon having a tantrum, expurgating very large vocal expressions, while at the same time the body is flailing in all directions: the arms are waving, and the legs violently moving up and down in the air. This exercise is fantastic for getting rid of tension and suppressed impulses. I also still use it. There may have been a few others that I can't remember, but as I continued to teach, I became aware of the lack of techniques and exercises to address each individual actor's obstacles. There are so many issues instrumentally that keep an actor from achieving a state of "being" and a readiness to act from an organic place: tension; insecurities; inhibitions of all kinds; compensational behaviors; vocal dependencies;

fear of judgment, of failure, or of rejection; fear of the unknown; concept and premeditation of expression; sexual and body-image issues; negative images of self or lack of awareness of self; a large variety of ego and self-esteem issues; a low level of consciousness, including being out of touch with internal impulses; emotional blocks that may exist in a wide variety of areas and conditioning; dependencies, which encourage the actor to depend on behavior he feels secure with, as opposed to allowing his impulses to flow freely without short-circuiting them; social obligations and the conditioning that makes people behave in a socially acceptable way; sexual fears and conditioning; religious taboos; and others. The list of those obstacles, blocks, and problems can go on into infinity. As I dealt with actors in my classes, I realized that the instrumental therapeutic training of the actor was extremely limited and even nonexistent in most training venues. So I invented exercises that would directly address specific problems and blocks. If it worked for one actor, it would surely work for others with similar issues. A lot of my exercises became standard and universally usable. I developed a theory that if you ask an actor to do the most difficult thing first and he succeeds, he no longer has a need to do exercises leading up to that difficulty. The list of my exercises topped two hundred at one point in my teaching. The results we were getting were fantastic. People's lifelong problems and blocks disappeared, and not only did that affect their acting, but it also changed their life. I have almost always felt that there isn't any separation between living and acting, and if there is, the acting doesn't come from an organic or authentic place. During the first few years and all the way into ten years of teaching, I inherited a reputation of being too psychological in my work. Worse than that, people accused me of practicing psychotherapy without a license. In fact I became the butt of jokes: "Oh, are you going to Eric Morris's couch class?" people would ask. "Is he going to have you lie down on the couch and talk about the way your mother abused you?" I heard all of the criticism and remained resolute in my approaches. Later, when some of the more famous people I had taught went on late-night talk shows and sang my praises, saying that they hadn't even known what real acting was until they took my class, that's when the jokes and the ridicule stopped.

I am, however, jumping ahead of myself here. We are still in the early sixties, I have my own class, and I'm teaching one for

Curt. We had to move from the space at La Cienega because Liberace had bought the building, so Curt found a very cute little studio theater on Robertson, just below Santa Monica Boulevard, which had a small stage and theater-type seats. It was not directly on the street but was recessed in the back of a building. I think it is still in operation. I moved there, so that we were both teaching all our classes in the same place.

One Monday evening Curt visited my class. He sat in the back for about half an hour and stormed out. I didn't think too much about it, figuring he had perhaps remembered an appointment he was late for. After class I went home and did some reading. I can't go to sleep directly after a class. I'm too stimulated. At about two in the morning my phone rang. It was Curt. He was obviously drunk and extremely belligerent. He called me every name under the sun, even some I had never heard before! He accused me of stealing his students. "Your whole goddamned class is full of my people, you rotten son of a bitch!" he exclaimed. He went on, getting uglier by the minute. I was flabbergasted. I couldn't get a word in edgewise. I was really being abused by him, and there was nothing I felt I could do about it. I tried to tell him that some of his people had been coming to my class for a long time and that I had told them that they could only attend if they were also in his class, but I could never get a full sentence out. I had never been exposed before to an ugly, mean drunk. It was a totally new experience for me. When he hung up, I was sure that he didn't want me to work for him anymore, and I didn't know if I wanted to either. I had trouble sleeping that night and in the morning told Jean the whole story. She said that she thought it was too soon for me to go on my own. I didn't have the reputation yet that would attract enough people to my classes. She felt that I needed Curt and encouraged me to wait until he was sober and work it out. "Tell him that you had no intention of stealing his people and that you want to continue the relationship," she advised. Marty Landau was back from Rome by then, so I called him and told him the whole story. I asked him to intercede for me, to talk to Curt and tell him what kind of person I was. I fully expected him to believe me, since I thought he knew me well and it was the truth. Instead he asked me if I had taken those people away from Curt. Did I know what I was doing? I was hurt and disappointed that a man I so admired, with whom I had had a relationship for three years, could even entertain those thoughts. I told him that I was hurt that he didn't believe me and that if he didn't want to talk to Curt it was O.K. I hung up the phone and had a really good cry.

I don't remember whether Marty called Curt or not, but at any rate I did. When he answered the phone, his voice sounded quite different. It wasn't as guttural, and his words weren't slurred. I figured that he would be more reasonable being sober, so I told him my side of the story. He listened quietly and then said that a number of those people weren't taking his class. I told him that I had been unaware of that and apologized. I asked him what he wanted to do. Did he want me to stop teaching for him? There was a long silence. "Why don't you come out and see me?" he finally said, "and we'll talk and see if we can resolve this situation. I'm renting a little house in the Malibu Movie Colony."

It was a long drive, which may have seemed a little longer because I was so nervous. The Movie Colony is right on the ocean, and it's called that because most of the people who live there are either actors or somehow involved with the film industry. Most of the houses are beach houses and sit right near the sand. Curt's house was small and cozy and smelled of the ocean. He invited me in, and I sat down on one of the overstuffed chairs, which had so many pillows on it that it was hard to find enough space for my butt! Curt was in a terrycloth robe and wore fleece-lined slippers. I thought it was rather unusual to still be in a bathrobe at two in the afternoon, but he seemed fairly relaxed and mellow, which made me feel better.

"How about a drink?" he asked.

I took a moment before responding, "Thanks, Curt, I don't drink."

The next moments were surreal: He stopped dead in his tracks, looked at me as though I were an alien from another world, and said, "You don't drink? Ever? His voice took on the quality of a comic's straight man setting up the punch line for the comic.

"No. Well, I sometimes have a beer on a hot day," I replied.

He poured himself a drink from a half-full bottle of Scotch, sat down in a wicker chair with a huge back, took a big swallow, looked at me intensely eye to eye, and said, "Eric, you don't know what you are missing. It is one of the greatest pleasures life has to offer."

I felt that I was batting zero at that point. I knew that if I drank with him it would make the problem between us less impacting, but I also knew that if I did I would probably pass out.

We sat quietly while Curt savored his drink. I broke the silence by saying, "I want you to believe me, Curt. I was unaware that the people from your class who were also in mine had stopped taking yours. I would never knowingly do something as unethical as that."

"I do believe you, Eric," he responded, "but you must admit that without knowing the real truth you would probably have come to the same conclusion."

I agreed that it was true and then told him that I had an idea how we could avoid any future misunderstandings: "Why don't I include my class with all the others, so that every class falls under the umbrella of the Curt Conway Actors' Workshop?"

He seemed surprised at my suggestion, but I could see he was pleased. The ends of his mouth curled up slightly in the promise of a smile, which he was careful to control. "I'll go you one better," he said. "Why don't we become full partners? Right now you are an associate."

I was taken aback by his proposal. I hadn't expected anything like that. "Gee, Curt," I replied, "I don't know what to say. I think that would be wonderful!"

"O.K. then, let's get a lawyer to draw up a contract and get going on this. Of course, you know that you will be the junior partner, right? We will, however, split all the income and expenses down the middle, fifty-fifty, O.K.?"

"Yes, that's fine with me."

I left, feeling great! It wasn't at all what I had expected would happen. When I got home, I told Jean about the proposition, and she was delighted. I guess it gave her the security she needed.

Our studio was still on Robertson, and we were feeling somewhat cramped for space. All the classes had grown in size, and we needed to have more room to move around without stumbling over each other. After signing our contracts, we started looking for a bigger and better space. Curt said that we should look for a small theater. We found one, the Circle Theater on the corner of Waring and El Centro, a theater in the round—or I should say in the square. It had a square stage surrounded on all four sides by over a hundred seats and was next door to a smaller proscenium theater, which seated about fifty people. It had been a very busy working theater for many years and had done some critically acclaimed productions. George Boroff owned it and had been operating it for a long time, having produced many of the plays that were done there. He had come to a time in his life when he had decided to step back from being directly involved, so he was willing to lease it to us. George was a character in every sense of the word. At that time he was in his middle fifties, perhaps a little older, and sported a crew-cut hairstyle that seemed too young for his years. He was a little paunchy and spoke very deliberately. His wife, Blanche, was Shelley Winters' sister. After we settled into the place, he would come around quite often, and if he happened to catch me unoccupied at any moment, he would take me on one of his famous walks around the block. He was known for doing that with everyone. He would talk about theater, the plays that had been there over the years, his love for it all, and so on. I indulged him frequently, excusing myself when I had to greet a private student.

Curt's mother, Claire Conway, became our collector. She was well into her seventies at the time and looked as though she had cloned Curt. They looked so much alike it was uncanny. It was my first experience teaching in a real theater environment, and it felt very professional, but as it turned out, the partnership wasn't such a good idea after all. I was teaching five classes each week to Curt's one. We were paying his mother a salary and splitting everything down the middle—the rent, the utilities, and the insurance. I was in that theater over thirty hours every week, while Curt sauntered in to do his one class and put in a total of five hours a week. I was making a living teaching, and I was very grateful to be able to pay all my personal bills doing something that I loved, so I said nothing about the arrangement. I was essentially at the beginning of my teaching career, while Curt had been teaching for at least ten years by then. What really got to me, however, was that he had a huge sign painted on the outside wall of the theater in bright yellow letters, which read: CURT CONWAY, ERIC MORRIS ACTORS' WORKSHOP. I hated it! It was crass and commercial and lowered what I thought we were involved with. This wasn't art; it was merchandizing! It made me feel as though we were selling produce on the other side of the entrance. Every time I arrived at the theater, I purposely avoided making eye contact with the sign.

My classes had grown in size. I was beginning to attract people on my own, had some really talented actors as students, and was doing really good work with everyone. When an actor would get up onstage to do an individual exercise, the first question I would ask him or her was, "How do you feel?" I asked it not because I wanted to know, but because I wanted the actor to know or find out. I was still doing all the things I had learned in Marty's class: the singing exercise, which I used all the way into the early seventies and probably beyond that, abandonment exercises, and a few others designed to liberate the actor from his problems and obstacles. It wasn't enough, however, and as I worked individually with each actor, I would often suggest that he or she try something that I might come up with at that moment. I wasn't always successful with the specific exercise, but quite often it worked. I found that encouraging each actor to expose his fears and inhibitions to the class eliminated his need to cover them up. They were out in the open and everyone knew they were there, so the actor could embrace them and move on.

With each class I learned more about how to address a problem or obstacle, and I created numerous exercises and techniques to antidote each issue. I invented a number of new and different relaxation techniques. Marty and Lee Strasberg were very big on relaxation, and when I started teaching, I used some of the exercises I had learned in class, but I later added many others that seemed to work for people who had resistance to the standard ones. I created an exercise I called "logy." I also used deep breathing, as well as "tense and relax," which consists in tensing each part of the body until one is totally rigid and then relaxing from the top of the head to the bottom of the feet. Tension is a large problem for actors, which is not confined to the young and inexperienced. I have seen, and worked with, actors who have been acting for forty years and still suffer from tension. They have found ways to disguise it and work in spite of it, but tension is the killer of creativity and keeps them from being organic. It acts like a cap on the instrument. It is the manifestation of bottled-up and unexpressed emotional impulses and therefore leaves the actor to act above the real life that exists below it. I found that an enemy to tension was selfless involvement. If the actor can get involved in something or someone other than himself, the tension just melts away. It was also clear to me that self-involvement was a humongous issue in crippling the actor, so I created a number of selfless-involvement exercises, such as "observe, perceive and wonder," which can be done in relation to another person or to the environment that surrounds the actor, and which liberates him from his self-involvement. Another way to antidote tension is to create a choice that is so involving and impacting that it takes precedence over everything. The actor gets so involved and affected by the choice that there isn't any room for self-involvement. I later defined it as making the stimulus or impetus more important than the event. In order to get each person to trust his or her impulses, I also created a large number of impulsivity exercises. Later in this chapter I will describe the specific exercises that I invented to address each and every one of the obstacles and blocks that an actor may have instrumentally.

More and more I felt that the missing link in the Method was the lack of consideration and attention to the actors' instrumental problems. Strasberg did deal with the actors' blocks and issues, but he did not go far enough, because he was afraid of crossing the line between acting and psychotherapy. All the other master teachers—Sanford Meisner, Uta Hagen, Stella Adler—weren't aware of the absolute necessity of working to free the actor of those often crippling blocks and obstacles, or they refused to address the issue. So if the actor needed serious attention to those areas, he was out of luck. In the *Tulane Drama Review* Strasberg wrote that only two percent of all the actors in the world used the Method and only about one percent used it with some success. It is no wonder that so few of them were successful, since their instrumental issues weren't dealt with! When I was at the Actors Studio—which I will go into later on when I write about the seventies—I often heard Lee admonish actors for talking about their choices in personal terms. He seemed almost paranoid about anyone exposing anything personal in the sessions. I find it somewhat amusing, since acting is one of the most personal of all the arts. At any rate I strongly felt that many very talented actors failed to do the kind of work they were capable of, because of this prejudice. I dedicated myself to addressing the instrumental problems of the actors who studied with me, and over the years I created hundreds of exercises to alleviate the blocks and walls that had been built up over a lifetime.

I was also adding to the craft process. Most of what I had learned from Marty about craft was largely dependent on creating choices using sense memory or affective memory. We also used what was there availably. In addition, we were told to go to the zoo and get a sense of an animal to use for characterization. Although those craft approaches were infinitely more than I had gotten in the previous ten years of my training, I found them to be limited in scope. Although I used sensory work predominantly in the first six years of my teaching, I became dissatisfied with the limitations of that incredible approach. I started to explore, invent, and work with, other approaches to create choices that would address and fulfill the material obligations. I called them CHOICE APPROACHES, because they were the approaches to creating the choice! I added them slowly over the years, starting with simple ones, such as imaginary monologues—which I originally called "steering-wheel monologues." I had come upon that one while driving down the street one day. I started talking to someone who was not there, and I had a heated conversation with that person, a real person I had been in conflict with, who wasn't present at the time. Not only was this a good craft technique, I thought, but it could also be used as an instrumental exercise. It could be quite liberating, and it had no consequence, since the person being addressed wasn't there. I also created a step-by-step blueprint on how to study an animal, get a sense of it, and translate it into human terms, so that it can be used to address a character in a scene. When Marty had taught us to work on animals, he had given us only two things to look for: the animal's overall rhythm and its limitations. That's how I got started with the externals choice approach, which later became a "megapproach." Over a period of time I added ten or more things to address when studying an animal—leading and secondary centers; centers of weight, power, and balance; mannerisms of the particular species, as well as individual mannerisms of the animal; tempo; the sounds the animal makes and the origin of those sounds; isolations; corresponding and contrasting rhythms; and so on. I also added people, insects, and inanimate objects and detailed a specific way to approach each of those areas. All of those techniques are described in great detail in my other books. I can't recall the chronology of how all of the different choice approaches came to be, but at the time of this writing there are thirty-one that are part of my system.

My classes would sometimes go into early morning. The work was so exciting that people would jump up on the stage full of energy and excitement at one in the morning. I also gave a number of private lessons each week. We would work on instrumental issues, craft, monologues, and audition preparations.

After teaching a little over two years and working very hard, I was making a fairly good living, so Jean and I decided to look for a house to buy. The Burbank house was fine, but it was old and needed work, and since it didn't belong to us, we weren't going to do any of the needed repairs. We found a three-bedroom brand-new house in Shadow Hills, in the San Fernando Valley not too far from Hollywood, in an area that is rural and ranchlike. Even though there is a lot of horse property in the area, boarding horses was not allowed on our street. What we paid in those days wouldn't even cover half the cost of a good automobile today. Jean was very happy in the new house. We had a pool put in and everything else to really make it a home.

I was working as an actor with some frequency then, even though my acting career had seemed to take a backseat to my teaching. I had become so involved with the work that I got lazy about calling my agent or reading the trade papers. I was excited and being extremely creative, and I guess my creative juices were being used. I did, however, have several auditions and some small parts in the early sixties. I was cast as a Union soldier on a television series called "The Americans." It was about two brothers, played by Darryl Hickman and Dick Davalos respectively, who were on opposite sides during the Civil War. I had a small but interesting role and was killed by Lee Marvin. I also played a doctor on "Doctor Kildare" and a critically ill patient on the "Ben Casey" series.

One of the people who had come to my class from Curt's was Evelyn Patrick Silvers, a very beautiful woman, who had been the Revlon spokeswoman for several years before marrying Phil Silvers of "Sergeant Bilko" fame. Of course, Phil Silvers had been very successful in vaudeville and on Broadway long before that show. At first, Evelyn's response to my teaching was similar to what some of the others, such as Hampton and Joan Blackman, had felt. She was appalled by how personal my approach was and openly angry at the way I manipulated people when they got onstage to do an exercise. I fully expected her to leave the class before I could show her the results of the work, but Harry Dean convinced her to stay and watch, and when she saw what happened to each person onstage, she calmed down and got involved. We became great friends after that. Jean and I were frequently invited over to the Silvers' home in Beverly Hills. Quite often we would go there on a Sunday. They had five daughters, including twins. Phil really liked Jean, me, and our son, Jeff, who was just an infant then and whom we brought with us sometimes. On certain evenings Phil would invite a group of his contemporaries, such as Groucho Marx, Jack Benny, Buddy Hackett, and a few other notable comics. They would sit around kibitzing, throwing one-liners back and forth and doing good-natured one-upmanships. I sat there, very quietly observing those giants of the entertainment industry, feeling totally out of my league. However, they all made an effort to make me feel included and would often direct something to me or ask me how I felt about something. Evelyn's friends included Polly Bergen and Barbara Rush, among other wives of the rich and famous of the Beverly Hills clan. Evelyn told me that they all bought original designer gowns and outfits that cost twenty-five hundred to three thousand dollars apiece and that they could only wear once or twice in the company of the same people. I know that today that amount of money doesn't seem so extravagant, but in 1962–1963 it was worth more, many thousands more by today's monetary standards, and for Jean and me, who were living on $150 a week, it seemed like all the money in the world.

Phil was now preparing to do "The New Phil Silvers Show." The original "Phil Silvers Show," filmed in New York, had been an overwhelming success. It had captured a large audience and had a wonderful cast, not to mention that it had made Phil very rich. This time, however, instead of being in the army, he was to be Harry Grafton, a foreman in a factory, surrounded by all of his working crew; and instead of the shenanigans he had pulled on the army brass, he was going to wheel and deal with the corporate structure that owned the factory. The producer-director was Rod Amateau, who had great success with shows such as "Gilligan's Island" and several other sitcoms of that period. Evelyn suggested to Phil that maybe I could audition to be a regular on the show, and he responded very positively. I was elated at the possibility of being a regular on a TV series. To that point I had done parts in films and a day or two on various TV shows, so the thought of being a regular on a network show was mind-boggling to me.

The audition took place in a large office at Twentieth Century Fox Studios. Phil was there with Rod Amateau and a bunch of other actors. There was no script yet, so we were given a circumstance and told to improvise the scene. We all jumped in, and it was mayhem. I jumped up on the desk and started doing what I thought was right for the circumstances and got some laughs for my audacity. When we were finished, Rod said, "Good! Let's try something else less energetic!" so we sat around trying to fulfill the next scene circumstance. Since I had done several seasons of summer-stock comedy, I instinctively knew that the behavior had to be animated and somewhat exaggerated, so I played a character like one of those I had done in stock. I could tell that Rod and Phil both related to what I was doing, and I was pleased. The audition lasted for about an hour, and when we finished, Phil thanked everyone and told us that we would be hearing from them in the next week and that if we didn't get on the show it wasn't because we hadn't done well, but because they had to balance the physical types so there would be the right contrast between characters. I left, feeling that we were being let down gently and that they were probably going to have half a dozen auditions like the one we had done. When I got home, Jean was standing in the doorway of the front door with a smile that seemed to go from ear to ear. "You got it!" was the first thing out of her mouth. They had called my agent while I was on my way home and had hired me for the series. I was elated! I thought that it was the beginning of a great acting career. I had done a lot of work up to that point, but to have a regular role on a network series that might run as long as "Bilko" seemed like an opportunity to become established in the industry, and I thought I'd be working steadily from then on.

I didn't know what kind of character I would be playing yet, but I figured it would be a comedy type of guy. The show had a staff of writers attached to it, one of whom was a good friend of my brother Ed, so I figured that when he wrote a show I would have good visibility in it. We had our first table-reading meeting in one of the conference rooms at Twentieth. I wasn't in the first show but decided that I was going to be there all of the time. I was assigned the character of Stanley the Computer, a character that was described as a human calculator. Whenever Phil would want to know something that had numbers involved, he would ask Stanley for the answer, and Stanley would give it to him in a matter of seconds. Of course, Stanley would have other functions in the factory, but that was one of his major responsibilities. I think that my debut was in the third show. I approached the character with an external. I worked to get a sense of a somewhat cerebral and uncoordinated guy who had been in Marty's class. His movements were very erratic, and he was somewhat of a dork. Not wanting to come across exactly that way, I made a few adjustments and only retained some of his less objectionable characteristics. At that time the externals choice approach was not yet developed. I had only been out of Marty's class for a couple of years, so my approach was limited to what I had learned there.

The antagonist in "The New Phil Silvers Show" was played by Steve Mitchell. His character was there to challenge, and be the obstacle to, all of Phil's schemes and to attempt to upset the con jobs Phil was into. Of course, he always failed to obstruct Phil's capers and would constantly be frustrated and bluster his way out of Phil's office. Another regular, Herbie Faye, was one of Phil's friends from the old days and a carryover from the "Bilko" years. He was about sixty-two at the time and not only a character in the show but a buffer for Phil. He ran interference when there was any need to protect Phil and was there to do anything Phil needed done. I became very close to Herbie, since we also spent time together socially at Phil's house.

I had the time of my life doing that show. I got up every morning, drove to the studio, waved at the guard at the front gate, and parked in the talent parking lot. I sauntered over to the soundstage, went to the dressing room that had my name on the door, changed into my factory uniform, which was made of a light blue, soft denim fabric, then reported to makeup and waited for everyone else to congregate on the set. I was always early, just as I was used to doing in summer stock. It was a three-camera setup: one was always on Phil, and the other two covered the close-ups and followed the action of a scene. Rod Amateau was a small guy, about five foot four or five, and a lot of his behavior compensated for his height. He was bald, wiry, and quite athletic. He was also a health nut and was always sucking on an apricot pit. Anytime one of the actors came up with a good idea for a scene, he would yell out, "Give him a bottle of champagne!" which he really did. While on the series, I got three or four bottles, which I gave to the actors who drank, since I didn't.

Besides the regular cast, we had guest actors on almost every show, some of whom were old character actors I had grown up watching in the movies. Sig Ruman, who always played comic Nazis in the forties and fifties films, played a waiter on our show and was very funny. He had a heavy German accent that seemed a little burlesque, and his mannerisms were very amusing. I had an opportunity to talk to him at lunch and told him how I had enjoyed him over the years, and he said that he was very happy to still be working. Another actor, Ludwig Stössel, also a German, had been so convincing as a staunch Nazi that I had thought maybe he really was one, until I found out he had barely escaped the Nazis by fleeing Germany in a speeding car, with them hot on his trail. Bernie Koppell, later a regular on "The Love Boat," played Stanislavski, an actor who was a visiting character on the show. I had known Bernie from around town before he appeared on one of the segments.

Since Phil's eyesight was not good, he didn't drive a lot, so on some mornings I would pick him up at his house and drive him to the studio. It was only about a twenty-minute drive, but in that time he would really open up and talk about his life, his dissatisfactions, and the things that made him unhappy. I listened and usually said nothing. Occasionally I would nod understanding of the things he talked about. It is peculiar that most comics seem to be unhappy or bitter people. When we got to the set, Phil's energy and demeanor changed, and he was a comic inspiration to all of us. I really liked Phil and over a period of years learned to love him. Quite a bit older than his wife, he loved Evelyn and his five daughters. He seemed to be of a different era, although I'm not sure what I mean by that. That whole period was an enchanted time for me. I was recognized on the street as one of the characters on the show, and at one point we were even on the cover of *TV Guide.* I was living the Hollywood life and really enjoying every minute of it.

The show had debuted on CBS on September 28, 1963. We did about fourteen or fifteen episodes, and then the ax fell. We were called into Rod's office and informed that the venue of the show needed to be changed. It wasn't working. What had clicked in an army setting didn't play in a civilian environment, and since it had been fashioned on the "Bilko" formula, it had failed. They were going to move the plot into Phil's character's home, thereby letting all the factory workers go. I was devastated! Of course, I had continued to teach all of the time I had been working on the show. While it was steady work, we were only paid minimum wage, and in those days that wasn't enough to live on, so I would leave the set and go teach my evening classes. I had had to give up my daytime private lessons but had never missed an evening of teaching. Every time I have worked as an actor while teaching, it has brought me an even greater understanding of an actor's working experiences. It has tempered my critiques and made my personality somewhat mellower.

My friendship with Phil and Evelyn continued for many years after the show ended, and as my children grew older, they would come along to the Silvers' house on weekends and play with the girls. During that period I continued to work in films and on TV, and my work as a teacher was also evolving. I felt that I had found my calling. When I had first started teaching, I had done so because I wanted to further my own training as an actor, but as the years went by, I became much more involved in teaching. I enjoyed creating exercises that helped the actors make breakthroughs instrumentally. Inventing dozens of exercises on the spot and experiencing the dynamics of their results were both exhilarating.

In November of 1963 I would have as many as ten private lessons a day. I had to rent space away from the Circle Theater because of class schedules, so I used the little house on Highland at the corner of De Longpre that Jed Duane was still in the process of building into a small studio. I was teaching an hour session to Maggie Blye, and we were in the middle of some exercise, when the guy who lived in the back of the house burst into our room and said, "The President has just been shot!" We all know where we were on the day Kennedy was assassinated. It was one of those moments one lives through after receiving shocking news. Everything seemed to stop or move at some kind of decelerated speed. The environment changed, and the colors in the room went from vivid to gray. The young man brought his radio into the room, and we listened to the mayhem that followed the shooting. Everything in our country changed that day, and it has never been the same. Up to then we were a country that seemed bonded together. We all liked each other, and the level of hope was tangible. It was truly Camelot!

I was still working as an associate to Curt Conway and teaching five classes a week. I used Hampton to help me affect other students when I wanted to get something from them during an exercise. He called himself my jack-in-the-box, because he would pop up and confront, insult, laugh at, or hug, a student onstage whenever that was what was necessary to stimulate the life I wanted the actor to experience. Recently I spoke with Hampton on the phone, and he reminded me that he had never paid a dime for Curt's classes or mine and that Mrs. Conway, our collector, had resented him openly. Hampton was incredibly talented on a number of levels. He was a really inventive actor, and he also understood film and had a feeling for directing. He recently told me that his only formal education had come from my classes. After his relationship with Joan Blackman ended, he had a string of liaisons with numerous women. He was extremely attractive to the opposite sex and took great advantage of that fact. He brought Sue Lyon to my class shortly after she played Lolita in the original film with James Mason. He was living with her and thought that the class would really help her grow as an actress. She did some very courageous work in class, really stretching herself. She worked on scenes about characters much older than she was and did *Hello from Bertha* and *The Death of Bessie Smith.* I worked with her on her role for *The Night of the Iguana* with Richard Burton, Ava Gardner, and Deborah Kerr. John Huston liked her work, but when Hampton went to visit the set, he kicked him out. When Hampton told me the story, I totally understood, since I knew that Hampton could be very outspoken and direct. After he and Sue split, he got involved with Teri Garr, who had come to my class right off a Saturday night dance show on television. She was a dancer who wanted to act, but in the two or three years she was in class she never did one comedy scene! Hampton was in class well into the eighties. Of course, he would occasionally leave to do a movie or TV show and would sometimes be gone for a couple of months, but he always came back to the class.

One of Curt's students was a very attractive woman named Joan Huntington, who was married to an Israeli, whose original name had been Zev Lahavre (I am not sure of the spelling). He had built a theater for his wife, I think, had called it the Princess Theater, and changed his name to Laurence Merrick so that people would associate him with the Broadway producer David Merrick. I must say here that he was the most despicable human being I had ever encountered. He had no ethics, scruples, or morals. He used and manipulated people for his own advantage and didn't care what the consequences would be as long as he got what he wanted from them. He came to watch one of my classes and from that moment on was on a crusade to get me away from Curt to teach for him. He was teaching classes at his own theater and most likely knew that his teaching qualifications were questionable, and he was so impressed with my talent that he probably thought he could make a lot of money from my work. I told him that I was committed to Curt and that I would never violate a trust or commitment. He kept at me for a long time, saying that he would handle Curt if I came and worked for him. His theater was on Highland and was a beautiful plant. It had a little house right behind it, which had a small room that was used as an office and a larger space suitable for classes. At that time I still had eight or nine private lessons a day and needed a place to teach them. I couldn't use the Circle, because I would have infringed upon classes and rehearsals, so I rented the room next to his office for my private lessons. After a short time I noticed that the top part of the mirror on the wall connecting to his office was separated from the rest. It looked as though someone had cut the mirror down from the top about eight or ten inches. It seemed peculiar to me, particularly because I hadn't noticed it before. I continued to teach my people, but every time someone came in to work, I would hear a chair being moved to the wall behind the mirror. One afternoon, when I was finished teaching, I heard Laurence leave the office, so I went to the mirror and put my face very close to the top part and looked into his office from my room. That son of a bitch had put in a two-way mirror to watch me work. I guess he thought he could steal all my secrets and use them for his classes. I walked out of that room, slammed the door, and left. In the years that followed, Merrick got into making adult and other low-budget independent films and obviously fucked someone over, because a person walked into his office and shot him to death. I wasn't in Schwab's the day someone came into the dining room to announce that Laurence Merrick had just been shot and killed, but I heard that the whole room exploded in spontaneous applause, yelling and screaming with approval. I thought that Merrick hadn't had to wait for the next life to experience karmic justice.

In 1964 or 1965 Francis Ford Coppola came to my class at the Circle. At the time he had done a film for Roger Corman, called *Dementia 13,* with Luana Anders, one of the people who hung around with our crowd at Jack's house. I'm not sure if he had done any other films by then. He approached me, saying that he wanted to come to my class and that he would pay full price to just sit and watch. He told me that he was a director and that he wanted to observe how I worked with actors. I agreed to let him do that, and he religiously came every week to one of my evening classes, where he sat in the back, high up on the risers. He was there for a couple of months, maybe slightly longer, but he never made a single comment. One night after class, he came and stood next to my chair as I was preparing to leave, and he said, "I want to thank you, Eric. I won't be coming back, but I got a lot from being here, and I think you are a great teacher." I shook his hand, and he left. The rest for him is film history.

I had been teaching for less than three years, and, while I was building my class, my income had been limited for the first year and a half. When I started working for Curt, my finances improved measurably, and the saying that a baby comes with its own loaf of bread seemed to prove true for us when on November 2, 1964, our second child was born, a girl whom we named Suzanne Leigh Morris. We chose that middle name because we thought that my wife, Jean, had a strong resemblance to Janet Leigh. Suzy was also born with blond hair, like Jeff, but not as long or as thick as his. From the very beginning of their life my children were as different as night and day. Jeff was always mellow, while Suzy seemed to be born with a type-A personality. As they grew older, they continued to develop different personalities. Jeff seemed more like Jean, while Suzy was very much like me in temperament.

By 1965 my acting jobs were fewer and farther between. I was still getting some work, but it was sparse. I was making a decent living as a teacher, but I had come to California to act, and that is what I wanted to do in addition to my classes. I began to think that I needed to diversify even further and do other things in the business, so I filled out an application to the film school at UCLA as a graduate student majoring in film directing. I thought that if I learned the mechanics of film making, coupled with my ability to facilitate actors, I could be the best combination of David Lean and Elia Kazan in a single person! I waited for a few weeks and finally received word from UCLA. I had been rejected! The reason they gave me was that I was overqualified and older than the average film student. I was very pissed off and ready to go down to Westwood and throw one of my famous tantrums, but my wife, Jean, talked me out of it. I contemplated applying to the University of Southern California, but the tuition was prohibitive, so I figured I would approach various production companies around town to see if I could work for them and learn about filming, editing, and all the various techniques for being a competent film maker.

I stumbled into a small office on the Sunset Strip because of the sign above the door, Steckler-Wester Productions. Sitting behind a small makeshift desk was a techie-looking, nerdy man with very thin hair and round eyeglasses, the kind that had probably gone out of style in the thirties. He was intently staring at some papers on the plywood table and did not acknowledge my presence. Finally, I cleared my throat, and he grudgingly looked up at me.

"Yeah, what can I do for you?" he asked.

For a moment I was at a loss for words, but finally I said, "I...I mean...I would like to work here."

He laughed, "Oh, yeah, doing what?"

I thought for a moment, wanting to say just the right thing: "Anything in production. I want to learn film making. I want to be a director."

He looked at me for a while—probably thinking, Another starry-eyed hopeful, right off the bus in Hollywood—and finally said, "Well, I tell you straight out, we can't pay you. We are barely making our salaries ourselves." And with that he dismissed me and went back to his plywood makeshift desk, which should have been a real clue from the beginning.

I stood there waiting for him to look up at me again, and when he finally did, it was obvious he was annoyed that I was still there. "I don't need to get paid," I said. "I just want to learn, and I'm willing to work for nothing."

He was stunned silent. I could read his thoughts on his face: What kind of schmuck has wandered in here? Finally he spoke: "You mean you will come here every day and do what David and I tell you to do around here and won't want any money in return?"

"Yes," I responded almost before he had finished speaking.

He was definitely puzzled. "How do you pay your bills? Are you a trust-fund brat?" he asked.

"No," I replied, "I teach acting, and I do pretty well financially and don't need any additional money, and if you're thinking that I'm really wet behind the ears, you're wrong. I am an actor and have also been earning a living at that. I do know something about film making, but I need to learn more before I start looking for a directing job."

He visibly softened his demeanor. "O.K.," he said, "you're hired! Come back tomorrow morning, and we will start editing a commercial that we filmed a week ago."

I worked there for about a year or so and got really close to Ray Steckler. He had a wife and two beautiful kids. He and David Wester had wanted to do their own thing, so they had started the company. I learned how to create a story board; sound and lighting became familiar, and camera setups were also a breeze. Ray's children were very endearing towheaded kids, who, whenever I visited their home, descended on me as if I were the Good Humor man, so I started bringing ice cream every time I visited. Ray wanted to do a TV series for children, entitled "The Lemon Grove Kids," using both his children as the stars of the show. He had filmed a couple of half-hour segments, when he asked me to act in the next ones. The project was completely on spec, but he had faith in it, and rain or shine, he was going to do it. The first segment I was in was about two kidnappers who came and took his kids. They were Damon-Runyon-type characters, very comical in their fumbling and stumbling antics. The other actor was a guy named Herb Robbins, who actually fit the description of the character. We did about three segments before Ray abandoned the project. All in all, it was a wonderful experience working there. I learned a lot and had a lot of fun. Ray was really a good soul. He would help street people and try to reform hookers. At any one time he had at least one "working girl" cooling out at his house.

I was, of course, still teaching during all that time, and my classes were exciting. The actors were inspired by the work and I guess by the times we lived in. It was quite different from the present day. We were all growing together, I as much as everyone else.

A Typical Class of That Period

I always started my classes with a relaxation workout. I explored a variety of relaxation techniques, a couple of which I got from Marty's class. We would do the rag doll, tense and relax, or deep breathing, to name a few. I'm not sure when I added the sensitizing and personal inventory as part of the preliminary group of relaxation preparations, but I do know from the lesson plans of that period that I had already been doing the three parts in 1967. After the relaxation, I would often do two-person workouts, which varied in content. I would choose different involvement exercises, where each of the persons would find ways to get involved with the other. This was not only a way to get ready to work with the other actor, but as a bonus also eliminated any residual tension. I might ask the actors to do an exercise I called "double exposure" or to get involved in an ego workout, designed for them to help each other get ready to act, where each person would validate the other, giving him or her compliments and support. We also did sense memory together. Sometimes, after the relaxation cluster, I would start the class with an improvisation. I would supply a circumstance, and then the actors would have to deal with the obligations of the situation by working for choices that would address them. After the two-person exercises, I would do the singing exercise with three or four actors, working with each one on individual issues that would surface during the process.

The next involvement included the individual-therapy exercises. In that section I worked individually with as many as ten or eleven people, dealing specifically with their personal instrumental issues and needs. I had an infinite number of exercises, usually designed or invented each for a particular person. All of them were meant to expose, liberate, or antidote a block, inhibition, or whatever stood in the way of the actor's freedom. Confronting people in areas of conflict for those who had difficulty in that area; large expurgation dumps; sexuality exercises of all kinds, done in good taste but aimed at making the particular actor more comfortable in sexual areas; antisocial exercises; silly-dilly workouts, which would stretch the actor's ability to risk making a fool of himself; expressing love and affection to people in the class and imaginary people; the *no* exercise, saying no to everyone and standing behind it even if we said yes—those arc just a few examples of the hundreds of exercises that have evolved over the years. Naturally there weren't a hundred in 1963, but there were quite a few that I was using at the time, discovering and inventing new ones in almost every class.

Sometimes, while working with an actor, I would come up with a new exercise that worked, and so I would name it after the actor for whom I had invented it. I had quite a few of them: the Durnie exercise, the Frontis exercise, the Dennis exercise, and so on. I might then use the same exercise on another actor. "Get up there and do the Dennis exercise," I would say. If I used the exercise often enough, the people in the class became familiar with what the specifics were and would jump into it. Actors have a lot of blocks and inhibitions in common, so the same exercise may work for many people.

After the individuals, we often did a scene or two and almost always ended the class with a group improv that had a specific theme or circumstance. I would whisper different obligations to some of the people, so that there would be a lot of surprises and unpredictable things that would come up and that they would have to deal with by making the necessary adjustments.

It was very rare that any two classes were the same. There were always surprises and new things that would come up every time. The greatest reward for me was to see the growth and the liberation of actors who had come from a place where they could hardly function to a place of freedom, which they carried over into their scene work. I think that was, and is, the greatest fulfillment that any teacher can experience.

In those beginning years, the early sixties, and without knowing it, I was laying the foundation for my system. The following is a list of exercises and techniques that had evolved by 1967. Many of them are detailed in my other books, so I won't go into the description of how each one is done.

Personal inventory: Probably one of the most important techniques an actor can employ, it makes him aware of what he is feeling and what the obstacles to his impulses and expressions are. Getting in touch with where he is in the moment allows him to address any obligation from a place of being.

Sense-memory inventory: I devised this as a way to explore how the senses work. It is done by isolating each sense and exploring where it is more accessible; for example, the tips of our fingers are less tactilely accessible than the pads, since there are more receptors in the pads.

Ego exercises of all kinds: They promote the elevation of ego and self-esteem.

Imaginary monologues: One of the great acting techniques that I used as an instrumental, this later became one of the most commonly used choice approaches.

Antisocial exercises: There are a great number and variety of these, which are designed to antidote socially obligated behavior.

Vulgarity workout: This technique is an extension of the antisocial area. However, it goes much further in allowing the actor to risk uglier behavior. It is designed to free him to be able to expose repulsive behavior in the framework of a character, where the demands would require that kind of life.

Impulsivity workouts: Here again there are ten or fifteen impulsivity techniques that I came up with and that are designed to encourage the actor to express his impulses rather than fall into the trap of concept or premeditating behavior.

Antiprivacy: While I never ask an actor to violate his privacy, this exercise encourages him to express more of his personal feelings in a stream-of-consciousness framework.

Relationship workouts: These are two-people encounters that stimulate involvement and relationship. There are several approaches to creating relationship onstage.

Intimacy workouts: Done onstage alone or with another person, these exercises encourage the actor to expose and deal with his intimate feelings about life and about other people and to talk about whom he loves and how he loves them.

Vulnerability techniques: In order to become more vulnerable and affectable, the actor talks to, or about, people and things that elevate his vulnerability.

Dealing with fears and exposing them: In a class setting and in a stream-of-consciousness approach, the actor progressively exposes what he fears about everything. As I've said before, the antidotal value of these exercises is infinite.

Exploring the kinesthetic sense: This is what I call the fifth and a half sense. It is part of the tactile sense but is also different from it. Blind people develop this sense to a very high degree. They can feel the presence of objects in front or in back of them without actually coming in contact with those objects. It is a sense that seeing people can develop and use to address specific choices.

Sexuality exercises: There are also many of these, which are used to antidote issues of sexuality and taboos people grow up with. Repeating these techniques in instrumental workouts liberates the actor from social, religious, and other kinds of inhibiting forces.

Sit onstage in front of the class and do nothing: By doing this exercise the actor discovers all of the demons, obstacles, and obligations that come up while he is sitting there without doing anything.

Method song: This is one I created to avoid concept as well as to have a framework for using the craft. The actor sings a song using various choices while singing, being irreverent to the meaning of the song.

Task inventory: This one is really a bonanza for the actor. So many times as an actor I had difficulty finding a choice for a specific scene or obligation. Most actors have the same problem, so I worked out what I believe is a foolproof technique for finding the right choices. I believe that the process is explained in *Irreverent Acting.*

Surrounding oneself with meaningful objects: By doing this the actor accomplishes a variety of things: He gets a sense of being someplace other than onstage, alleviates any tension or audience inclusion, and creates a changing emotional point of view by relating to the variety of objects that he creates.

Taking responsibility for helping other people: While onstage in a class, the actor encourages himself to get involved with the people in the audience and obligates himself to perceptively give each person feedback on how he or she can help him or herself grow and eliminate obstacles. Of course the actor should be somewhat familiar with the others in class.

Those are just a few of the exercises and techniques that had evolved by the late sixties. There are many more.

Since I was teaching five classes a week to Curt's one and we were splitting everything down the middle, feeling the inequities of our partnership became too much of a burden for me to carry. Around 1966 or 1967 I approached Curt and told him how I felt about the situation. It had taken me a long time to muster the courage to confront him, since he was extremely intimidating. He didn't hesitate to go on the attack whether he was drunk or sober, but much to my surprise he was very reasonable in his acknowledgement of the situation. I think part of the reason he was so accepting of the dissolution of our partnership was that he had been hired to be the talent coach at Twentieth Century Fox. I had been interviewed earlier for that position, but they had given it to him because he was older, had gray hair, had been in the business much longer, and would be respected by the actors under contract to the studio. Curt also became artistic director of Theater West at about the same time. After he left, I remained at the Circle Theater and kept his mother on as my collector, since she had been there for a number of years and knew the people. Besides, I had developed some affection for her and worried about what she might do if she didn't have the job. I knew Curt would support her financially, but if she had nothing to do but sit around in her studio apartment, I was worried that her health might deteriorate. The day after Curt left, I got some gray paint and painted over that awful sign in front of the theater, replacing it with a much smaller and more tasteful plaque over the entrance.

One evening as the class ended, Jack Nicholson came down from the risers to the right of where I sat to teach the class. He stopped at the side of my chair, threw his arms into the air and said, "What's this all for, Eric? What are we doing?" I could see how depressed he was. I knew that he was going through a divorce with Sandra and that his acting career wasn't doing well at that point either. He was writing a picture for someone at Columbia and making a living, but I had never seen him so down. I got up out of my chair, put my arm around him, and walked him out into the street.

We stood there for a couple of moments, and I said, "Jack, how long have you been pursuing your career as an actor?"

"You know, Eric. We both started at about the same time, sixteen or seventeen years ago."

"Well, I know that you're going through a hard time now, but you are never going to be happy or fulfilled unless you do it as an actor. Just hang in there. You're talented and you're going to make it!" I think I made him feel a little better. Eleven months later he got *Easy Rider.* Very recently he reminded me of what I had told him that night. I had forgotten.

In my telephone conversation with Hampton, he told me that he felt that the years from 1967 through 1969 had been the golden years. I asked him what he meant by that, and he said that the work had been incredible. The people there at the time, the amount of talent in the classes, and the scene work were inspiring. Since I have been teaching for over forty years, it seems as though classes have gone through many changes and there have been periods of great inspiration and growth and times of lethargy. The sixties, seventies, and even well into the eighties were very exciting years in the classes and the profession.

One afternoon I received a call from Sharon Tate. I knew who she was, having seen her in a few films. She asked me if I could give her a private lesson. She was preparing to do a film and needed some help. She told me that Jack Nicholson had recommended me and that she needed to see me soon. When she walked into the theater, standing in the doorway with the light framing her from behind, she looked like a saint in a religious icon from the Middle Ages. As she came into the room, it was as if she radiated her own light. She was startlingly beautiful. She told me that she was having trouble being terrified and that it was an important obligation in one of the scenes in the film. I asked her what frightened her, but she had a difficult time coming up with any real fears large enough to address the scene. I suggested a number of possibilities, which I frankly don't remember thirty-seven years later. At any rate, none of my suggestions worked. I finally told her she was beautiful and had the face of an angel, and I asked how she would feel if someone cut her face to pieces. At this point I must say that for all these years, in light of the events that followed in that poor woman's life, I have regretted what happened next. I told her that I had a very sharp knife in my pocket and that I was going to disfigure her for life. I put my hand in my pocket, where there was no knife, and began to advance towards her. Her face went white, all the blood drained from her head, and she started to scream with the most terrifying terror I had ever seen. I quickly removed my hand from my pocket, threw both hands in the air and embraced her, whispering into her ear that I would never hurt her and that I had just been exploring a choice she might use for the film. She calmed down but held on to me for several minutes. When she broke the embrace, she smiled at me with gratitude and affection and said that she now knew what to do. On the way out she turned and said that I had not been oversold and that she would be back to work with me. That was the last I ever saw of her. A while after that encounter, I heard the news about her death and was very sad. Besides being physically beautiful, she was also beautiful inside, very soft-spoken and warm. I think she was probably in the early stages of pregnancy but hadn't yet begun to show.

Besides Sharon, I knew Jay Sebring, one of the other people killed at that house. Jay was the ex-husband of a student of mine, Cami, who I thought was one of the ten most beautiful women in the world. When she started my class, she had been divorced from Jay for a while but spoke of him often in her private lessons with me. He was a very famous hairstylist, who had innovated a revolutionary haircutting technique and was riding on the crest of a

Hollywood wave. Very much in demand by the Hollywood elite, he became very involved with the A list. I had met him at a very trendy disco, called the Factory, and had had a number of conversations with him about Cami, acting, and the business. He was there the night the Manson gang broke into the house and killed all the people. For some unexplainable reason I have been somehow connected to people who were involved in horrendous happenings. In addition to Sharon Tate and Jay Sebring, I also knew the house Roman Polanski and Sharon were renting. Located on Cielo Drive, it was quite secluded and mostly off by itself. The owner, Rudy Altabelli, was in Europe at the time. Rudy, an actors' manager, handled a number of my students and came around to the class occasionally. He was quite successful managing big name actors and had a few whom he felt he could usher to stardom.

During the week of the Tate-Labianca murders Los Angeles was the tensest city in the United States. Everyone was on edge and frightened. It was before the Manson family was apprehended, and everyone was looking over his shoulder. It was a hot July afternoon. The Circle Theater didn't have air conditioning, or maybe it just wasn't working that day, so I had opened the doors to the outside to get a little air into the place. The entire class was lying on the floor doing a relaxation exercise, while I was sitting in my usual chair. Suddenly, out of the corner of my left eye I saw a black-and-white pass on the street. I thought nothing of it until moments later, when two police officers coming in from opposite directions, guns drawn, entered the room and stopped in their tracks as everyone on the ground sat bolt upright. The officer who had come in from the front door lowered his pistol and said, "Well, you must admit that it looked very strange from out on the street." Both policemen were embarrassed, but that is exactly the way it was in our town that week.

In 1969 I landed a very nice role on a two-part "Kraft Suspense Theater." It was called "Strategy of Terror" and was about two Middle-European assassins who had come over to America to kill a high official in the U.N. I was to play one of the assassins, while an actor named Jan Merlin was the other one. The show had a very good cast and was directed by Jack Smight. Hugh O'Brian and Barbara Rush were playing the leading roles. I knew Barbara from the Phil Silvers crowd, and while we didn't have any scenes together, it was comforting to know and have a relationship with one of the leading actors. The show was to air on consecutive weeks and be put together as a feature-length movie to be released in Europe. My character's name was Tippo. In the dialogue he was referred to as "silent and moving with stealth." One of Jan Merlin's lines to me was, "You know, Tippo, that no one knows when you enter or leave a room!" I took it as a clue for working on a choice that would address and fulfill that character element. I chose to work for a leopard, since large cats move with a quiet and fluid gate. I had some time before the shooting started, so I spent a number of hours observing the leopard at the zoo in Griffith Park. I worked there and on my living-room floor at home, going back and forth from being on all fours to standing up and translating the sense of the animal into a human state. When we started filming, I had a pretty good sense of the animal and felt that it really inhabited me physically and also had an impact on me emotionally. After a few days of shooting, however, I decided that I had to reinvest in working for the animal on all fours, so I found a place on the set that was separated from the active area, got on the floor, and started to work to get a sense of the leopard in the animal position. I was so involved in my exploration that I didn't notice that the stage crew had moved one of the walls of the set I was working in, exposing me on all fours to about forty people! As I turned my head and saw all of them frozen in place and staring at me, I slowly stood up, turned my back on them, and sauntered off the soundstage. I was so embarrassed I could hardly speak. When I returned to the set, I fully expected someone to say something to me, but no one did.

It was a great experience working on that film. It was a large role and had many scenes, some of them very physically exhausting. Hugh O'Brian was playing a detective hot on our trail, and watching him work was a real education. In my opinion he has questionable talent. In every scene he leaned on something: the wall, a desk, the back of a chair. I understood why he needed to do that. It was his way of looking relaxed, cool, and in control and was, of course, compensational for his tension and discomfort. I don't think anyone else knew that, but since I dealt with actors and their redirections sixty hours a week, it was easy for me to see it. After a full week of watching him lean on everything available, I went up to the director and said, "We would all be in trouble if you decided to shoot a scene in an open field." He looked at me, totally confused about my statement, and was still standing there as I walked away. In one scene O'Brian was supposed to be having a fight with one of the other characters, and he really hit the actor several times and hurt him. I know that he was being macho and figured it would make him look good, and I believe the other actor, a day player with no lines, was much too intimidated to make a thing out of it. I saw him walking off the set wiping some blood from his nose. There is no excuse for that ever! It reminded me of a story told to me by Larry Dobkin, a well-known character actor who had been in films for forty years. We were working together in a play at the Players' Ring Theatre at the time. He told me that he had been doing a film with Pat O'Brien, a character star in Hollywood in the forties, fifties, and into the sixties. In a fight scene O'Brien had hit him so hard in the stomach that he had almost passed out. I asked him if it was an accident, and he said that he knew it had been done on purpose, because O'Brien was a staunch anti-Semite. I don't know if that was the reason, but Larry was convinced that it was. There were a few other actors I knew on that show: Vic Tayback, who had been responsible for my getting into the Angels Company, and a couple of others whose names have escaped my memory.

I continued my classes at the Circle Theater until George Boroff died, which was about 1970. His wife, Blanche, sold the theater, and I had to move. I was sad to leave. The place I moved to wasn't nearly as nice.

A short while before I left the Circle Theater I received a call from Shelley Winters, who told me that she wanted her boyfriend, Richard, to come and study with me. The reason she had called me, she said, was that since she had been on the audition committee at the Actors Studio, all of the people auditioning who claimed they had trained with me were "the most impressive and seemed to really know what they were doing." Over the years almost 95 percent of all the actors auditioning for the Studio who had been in my classes for a couple of years have passed both auditions and become members of the Actors Studio.

It was the beginning of the seventies, and I had already been teaching for almost a decade. The next one, probably the most incredible of the four, was going to be filled with many dynamic things and possibly be one of the most impacting and formative times in my life. So much happened in those years that I wonder how I dealt with all the changes and events.

I moved to Fountain Avenue near the corner of Vine Street. I bought some theater seats, hung some drapes around the stage, carpeted the floor, and made it as much of a studio theater as possible. It was a come down from the Circle Theater, but after an exhaustive search, I settled on that space because it was the best of the worst. It sat adjacent to a parking lot, but the only good thing about that was that I had a regular parking space.

Shortly after, I started what I originally called "marathons." At first, they were long twenty-four-hour workshops, which lasted from ten in the morning to ten the following morning. We would take eating and toilet breaks but would continue to work straight through. No one slept. I did about four or five of those and finally decided that they had diminishing returns. My original idea had been that if the actors were really tired they would not be able to hang on to tension, and when they reached that relaxed state they would be open to making some important discoveries; however, by early morning they were so punchy that they really couldn't focus on anything. After that, I started to do two-day weekend workshops, which went on from 10:00 A.M. to 6:00 or 7:00 P.M. each day. At first they were exclusive to Los Angeles, but later I started to do them in Lake Arrowhead and then ultimately branched out to thirteen cities in the United States.

In 1972 my life was turned upside down. I fell in love with one of my students and had a romantic affair for two years before telling my wife about it. What followed was one of the most traumatic periods in my entire life. While my productivity was high, my personal life crashed. I don't excuse what happened. I had been married to Jean for nineteen years, but from the time she had gotten pregnant with our first child, my existence had seemed to evaporate. I didn't exist for her. She had waited so long to have a child that when it happened it seemed to take over her entire life. I was working a lot and was seldom home. I found excuses not to be there. Of course, I came home for dinner and was there every evening I wasn't teaching, but my interests in other women grew strong. I wasn't getting what I needed at home, so I began to look elsewhere.

In 1972 Joy King appeared in my class on Fountain Avenue. She was a small, very pretty brunette Southerner from Oakridge,

Tennessee. I was sitting in my chair waiting for the students to arrive when she walked up to me and in a very thick Southern accent said, "Hi, my name is Joy King, and Nathaniel Brandon recommended that I come and take your class." She had come to Los Angeles to get into therapy with Nathan, who was a devotee of Ayn Rand and also an objectivist. In the dedication page of *Atlas Shrugged,* Rand wrote that Nathan was her "intellectual heir." He had been involved with her for many years and in fact had had a romantic relationship with her, which ended badly when he got involved with Patricia, his wife at the time I met him. Patricia was taking my class because she wanted to be an actress. That is how and why Nathan had sent Joy to me. He had said that after he had worked with her in therapy, she needed "emotional release."

At the end of the class Joy walked over to my chair, said, "Good night, I'll be back," and left. She had come to Los Angeles with a girlfriend, Libby, also from the South, whose husband was serving as a pilot in the air force. Joy later told me that when she got home that night she told Libby that I was "a strange little guy"! The following week, she returned, joined the class, and did her first instrumental, which I think was some kind of antisocial exercise. After the class she came over to thank me. I stood up, and she backed away, looking up at me as if I were Gulliver. "My God," she said, "You're *big!*" (I, of course, towered over her, since she is barely five feet in height and I am six feet tall.) "I thought you were a little thing, sitting in that chair."

I was instantly attracted to her but did nothing to betray my feelings, at least in the beginning. She had a small trust fund left to her from her father, which she was using for her therapy and acting classes. She began taking private lessons each week, and in one of those I expressed my attraction to her. She was surprised and somewhat taken aback by my overture, but after a few moments she stood up from her chair and came towards me, standing very close to me, and I kissed her. At a later time she told me that it was that kiss that had done it for her. "I think I fell in love with you at that moment," she said. We started an affair that lasted two years. It was extremely intense on every level, particularly sexually. At the time Joy lived in an apartment in the San Fernando Valley with her two children—a boy, twelve, and a girl, eleven.

A big part of the attraction I felt for her, beyond the physical aspect, was that I really believed she saw who I was, what my essence was. She related to my approach to life and to acting and almost immediately seemed to understand the uniqueness of my work and to totally relate to my emphasis on individuality. It resonated with her involvement with the philosophy and work of Ayn Rand. At that point in my life I hadn't read any of Rand's books but had come to some of the same conclusions on my own, which were later validated by our therapist, Roger Callahan, after he visited one of my classes. In the beginning I was mostly interested in Joy sexually, and I believe she knew that. I arranged to get away for a weekend, and we went to Desert Hot Springs. It was on that trip that I fell madly in love with her, and the roller-coaster ride began. My double life started. For two years I was a married man, husband, and father, counting the hours until I could be with Joy again. We spent every Friday evening together. She would cook a great dinner for me, and we would spend the next three hours in bed making love. I also saw her during the day for lunch and other things.

However, this "captain's paradise" is not all that it is cracked up to be! I suffered a lot during those two years, feeling guilty and split all the time. I loved Jean. We had a long history and two children, but as I said before, I felt she was no longer interested in me. She was so devoted to her children that I had become the breadwinner and not much more. Joy had sent both her children to Tennessee to live with their father—I believe purposely, so that I would not be put off by their presence and also so that we could be totally and exclusively involved.

At the end of two years, one morning before I left my home, Jean stopped me and asked me what was going on.

"We haven't made love in months, and you are away all the time," she said.

I sat down and choked out the words: "I'm involved with another woman."

It was as if the room turned gray and all of the colors muted. There was a long silence, and finally Jean asked me with whom I was involved. I told her as much as I could, trying to keep the pain level to a minimum.

The next few weeks were a nightmare. I felt horrific guilt and pain in relation to my two children. I moved out of the house on April 1, 1974, April Fools' Day! It was the beginning of the most traumatic period of my life. I settled into the Magic Hotel, which at that time was both an apartment building and a hotel. One of my students, Charles Gorgano, had informed me that he was moving into Hollywood from Alhambra in order to be closer to the classes and the industry. Charles had been working as a sheet-metal layout man for many years and was also pursuing an acting career. We spoke about my situation and decided that it would be convenient to share a two-bedroom apartment in the hotel.

Jean thought that I had gone off the deep end and would desert my children, but of course she was more than wrong. I saw them every weekend, and sometimes in the middle of the week too. It was a hard time, because they had to adjust, not only to the separation, but also to my relationship with Joy. When the four of us were together, Suzy was very rude to Joy, and her resentment came out in a variety of other ways.

Joy had an apartment off Fountain Avenue near La Cienega, but after a few months she moved into our place at the Magic Hotel. The three of us lived there for almost a year. Charles had one of the bedrooms, and Joy and I shared the other one. It worked very nicely, since we all got along very well. I must add here that Charles continued in my class for a number of years and that we became very good friends. That friendship has lasted for many years and is still going on today.

I was in love with Joy but felt like a displaced person for much of that first year. I threw myself into teaching and found it a haven from my angst and depression. That year was the toughest, and things got only slightly better each following year.

I was teaching four classes a week, and my energy had never been at a higher level. As I worked with actors, I became more and more courageous in designing exercises to liberate them. I continued adding craft elements and choice approaches, while at the same time addressing each scene in terms of the author's intentions. Almost since the very beginning of my teaching I related to the class as a laboratory, and in the process of addressing a scene I encouraged the actors to explore choices and impulses that they thought might fulfill the material, all the while having permission to go in any direction their choices led them. Even as late as the seventies I was dealing with a controversial reputation, still hearing from people who had no idea what I was doing that I crossed the line between acting and psychotherapy. Undaunted, I proceeded to explore a multitude of possibilities that would take the actor into new and exciting areas of behavior.

Early in the seventies I started weekend workshops in Lake Gregory, which is located in the San Bernardino Mountains about eight miles west of Lake Arrowhead. About every two to three months I would do a two-day marathon. The family of one of my students owned a house above the lake, which I was able to rent periodically for the workshops. A couple of my female students did all the cooking, and we worked ten hours each day. Because I had so much time, I was able to get deeper into the work. I was dealing with people who were already in my weekly classes, so they had some understanding of the system. I split the time between instrumental work and the craft. We did scenes and monologues and explored a variety of choice approaches. This went on for a number of years.

At the beginning of the decade Lonnie Chapman invited me to be an observer at the Actors Studio West. Lonnie is a man of the theater. I have never known anyone so committed to theater and to the creative process who is at the same time so open to experimentation and individual statement. Lonnie had been in partnership with Curt Conway in a summer theater back East but was as different from Curt as night is from day. The experience at the Actors Studio lasted for at least seven years and was probably one of the most important periods in my life.

The first evening I sat in on a session was mind-boggling, however. For so many years in Marty's class we had sat around at Jack's house talking about getting into "the Studio." We thought that it would be an important event in our acting careers. It was like the temple where the great actors went to worship Lee, learn the process from the horse's mouth, and rub elbows with the likes of Marlon Brando, Marilyn Monroe, and all the other legends we watched in the movies; but sitting there watching the work and then listening to the actors talk about what they had done to arrive at the behavior we saw was in some cases embarrassing, not because their acting was bad, but because for the most part they misstated or misinterpreted or blatantly did not understand the craft.

There were various moderators for each session, since Lee at that time was still working in New York and would just come out in the summer to conduct the session only for about eight weeks.

That started around 1973 or 1974. Until that time Studio members did the moderating. Let us say, for example, that Lee Grant or Bruce Dern was the moderator on that first evening. To the best of my recall, he or she said to the actors onstage who had completed a scene, "O.K., what did you do or what do you want to tell us?" The actors then talked about what choices and approaches they had explored to address the specific elements of the material. One of the actors may have said, "I did an affective-memory thing to take me back to a place and time in my life." On the surface that may sound like an intelligent choice and approach for the obligation of the scene, but that actor hadn't had or taken the necessary time to do an affective memory, and I was in serious doubt whether he even knew what affective memory was! The other actor may have explained, "I was working for another person, instead of him, whom I feel that way about." Again that sounds like an intelligent choice, but she couldn't explain *how* she had done that. I sat quietly through about four scenes. After all, it was my first night as an observer, and I was visiting. When I could not take any more of this generality, and maybe because I was so disappointed in the expectations I had created over a fifteen-year period—that I would see the same kind of work I had been doing in my classes—I raised my hand, and the moderator acknowledged me. I don't remember exactly what I said, but I was surgically specific in my comments about the scene I had just watched and all the others before it. I directly addressed the process of the actors and what they had said they were doing, as opposed to the specificity of what they might have done. My comments were succinct, specific, and right on. The moderator let me finish before asking who I was. Several of the people sitting in front of me turned around to see who was making all those comments about process and craft. I could tell that they resented "the new kid on the block" for being audacious and for commenting at all. Red Buttons, who was sitting directly in front of me, turned to look at me and related to me as if I had just spoken in Greek. It was obvious that he didn't understand a thing I was saying and that he was completely unfamiliar with the terminology I was using. Red Buttons, a successful actor and comedian, had done very well in the movies, winning an Academy Award for his performance in *Sayonara.* I think he was a member of the Studio, but I had no idea how he had gotten in and what his audition had been like. It wasn't that he wasn't quite talented, but he was completely in the dark about craft and process. It was later that I learned that Lee Strasberg was incredibly impressed by movie stars and name actors, and that in itself seemed to be enough to gain entrance into the Studio. The average unknown actors, on the other hand, had to go through several auditions to get in. The first one took place in front of an audition committee, usually comprised of senior Studio members, and if the applicants passed it, then they would audition for Lee, usually several times before he would accept or reject them.

That first evening was quite an eye opener for me. I had already been teaching for ten or eleven years and was in this cave or monastery of creativity, with an intense concentration on process, exploring *how* an actor addresses and fulfills dramatic material. The ignorance and generality of what I had witnessed were very disconcerting. There were, and I am sure there still are, a lot of very talented actors at the Studio on both coasts, since one of the main ingredients an actor has to have to be invited to be a member is talent. However, the Studio purports to be a workshop where actors can explore a craft and grow.

After that first night, I began to attend the sessions regularly. At first, if my memory serves me, there was only an actors' unit, but shortly after I was invited to be an observer, Lonnie started a directors' unit, and I became a participant in it. I think that almost simultaneously a writers' unit was also formed. Both units functioned independently of each other, but the writers were welcome to attend the directors' unit and often employed one of the directors to work on a project they had been writing. I jumped in and started to work with the actors from the actors' unit and usually had something on the stage every week. My work was specific, the actors were very articulate about what they were doing, and the results reflected that. Lonnie had done most of the moderating as head of the unit, but after about six months he asked me if I would moderate some of the sessions. I was flattered by his request and agreed to do it. I was still able to bring in material while moderating. One might think that all of that responsibility would have affected my own classes, but the opposite was true. I had more energy and excitement to bring to them. Because my work was so specific and the results so impressive, I was asked to moderate some of the actors' sessions. I think that may have been the first time an observer was asked to do such a thing.

The Actors Studio was housed in a building that was originally the William S. Hart estate. Hart had been a cowboy actor in the silent movies, and when sound came in, he continued to do Westerns. He had a long face and extremely piercing eyes, and of course, as was the style in those days, he overacted terribly. I believe the estate had been given to, or taken over by, the city and donated to the Studio. They are still there today. It was a fairly nice space, which must at one time have been part of the living quarters and was large enough to accommodate sixty or seventy people in the audience. It had a high A-frame ceiling and a large stage with some backstage facilities. In another part of the building there were a couple of rooms that served as offices, a small kitchen, and an entry hall, which led to a room that must have once been a living room. There was also a second level, where actors could rehearse or prepare before an audition. All in all it was a good plant. The Studio was probably paying a dollar a year for the privilege of being there, while the city was congratulating itself for contributing to the arts, so everybody was happy.

After I had been there for about a year, Lonnie, who wanted to move on to other involvements, suggested that the membership elect someone to head the directors' unit, and he nominated me. There were no other nominations, so I was unanimously approved by the membership. The politics of the Studio, or for that matter that of any other group, never appealed to me, so I ran the unit very democratically, asking for suggestions and input from anyone who wanted to contribute. I held that post for about three years, during which there was a lot of work done.

It was there that in February of 1970 I met Joan Hotchkis and began to work with her. She was about forty at the time and was very attractive, with reddish brown hair and patrician features. Her ancestors dated back to Plymouth Rock and had come west during the Gold Rush. Joan had spent the past fifteen years studying in New York and acting both on and off Broadway and also in live television. In 1968 she had moved back to California, her home state, and right away had been cast as William Windom's co-star in the Emmy-winning series, "My World and Welcome to It," and soon after in the recurring role of Jack Klugman's girlfriend in "The Odd Couple."

Joan was a lifetime member of the Actors Studio in New York and was continuing her involvement at the Actors Studio West. In the scene class one day, I had watched an actress perform part of a solo play that she was writing and afterwards had added my comments to the discussion about her work. The next day the actress, Joan, phoned me to thank me for my insights and to say that she wanted to study in my acting classes and would also like to talk with me about something else. We met at a coffee shop and immediately bonded, each attracted to the other's talent. She asked if I would direct her in *Legacy,* the first play she had ever written. She planned to produce it at the Actors Studio and other venues.

I said I'd be glad to direct her if she would help me write my first book. I explained that I had grown up in the shadow of an older brother, a professional writer, who had enjoyed putting me down for most of my life. In addition, when I had recently told Curt that I wanted to write a book about acting, detailing my discoveries, he had laughed and said, "What is it that you think you have to say about acting that hasn't already been said by more experienced and knowledgeable people than you?" That was why I had zero confidence in my ability to write and needed Joan to co-write this book with me.

Joan liked the idea of this creative exchange. "It's a deal," she said. "If you help me birth my baby, I'll help deliver yours." And so we began a five-year journey together. We worked two days a week on Joan's play and two days a week on my book. All through that time Joan was taking a five-hour acting class from me twice a week, plus numerous private lessons. She also attended a weekend marathon, steeping herself in the many exercises that we were describing in the book.

Since she had studied two years with Lee Strasberg in New York, she was familiar with a lot of what I was doing in my classes. However, I saw that she had some instrumental problems that needed attention. For instance, she was so consciously focused on what she was doing onstage that her acting was over intense at times, and this intensity caused tension in her work and a kind of pushing for certain results, all indications that she needed to develop more trust in her talent and her instrument. So I invented a cluster of exercises, which I labeled "wheat-in-the-wind," to develop in her a state of behavioral permissiveness. I still use those exercises in my classes now, especially "allow, permit, accept, and include," which is done in a stream-of-consciousness framework, where the actor continually adds, "I allow that...I permit myself to feel that way...I accept it...I include it..." and so on. There are four or five exercises within the wheat-in-the-wind cluster. Over a period of time they worked wonders for Joan.

One evening in class she was doing the bathtub monologue from her play. In order to address the requirements of the scene, she needed to be naked, so she took off all her clothes and began to work for her choices, then moved into the written lines. While she was just about a third of the way through, a late-arriving student walked into the theater, and seeing Joan in her birthday suit, he froze, just like a stop-action cartoon. He got some laughter from those students who saw him, but none of that distracted Joan, who continued undaunted.

After being in my class for about a year, Joan got a role in a feature film, *The Late Liz,* in which she played a middle-aged society woman who was always tipsy—not falling down drunk, just giddy and prone to constant giggling. She decided to create a physical sense of a freshly opened bottle of Cold Duck, an inexpensive carbonated wine, as a character choice, with essences and abstracts as her choice approach. Later, when I saw the film, I was extremely impressed with her work. She was able to inhabit the choice physically, which in turn impelled the character's emotional behavior.

She told me that she believed her steady progress as an actor was due to her double exposure outside my class, those four days a week when she was either helping me define and explain my exercises in the book or working as an actor with those same exercises in our rehearsals for *Legacy.* Twice a week I would drive out to her house in North Hollywood, where she sat at her Olivetti portable typewriter while we talked about the work. During the first six months we went through all of my class lesson plans, culling information and getting ideas about the structure of the book. Then I began to dictate. Frequently Joan would question me on certain points and challenge me when what I dictated wasn't clear or understandable.

I would often get frustrated with her and say, "Oh, for God's sake, Joan, you know exactly what I mean!"

"Maybe so, Eric, but what about someone who isn't familiar with your work, would he or she understand what you just said?"

Of course, most of the time she was right. I could not have written my first book without her help, and I'm very grateful. The whole experience gave me the confidence to write four more books on my own.

One day, about two years into our collaboration, Joan and I were sitting at her dining table, when we looked at each other and almost in unison said, "I think we should stop here and call it a book." A great wave of relief washed over me. I felt twenty pounds lighter. Elated, we hugged and shook hands vigorously. Then we discussed what to title the book. I remembered a wooden plaque given to me by one of my students. It had hung for years over the entrance of the Circle Theater, and I had taken it with me when I moved. Carved into the beautifully stained wood, it said NO ACTING PLEASE. I decided that was a good title, and Joan agreed.

If anyone had told me that it would take five years to publish my first book, I would not have believed him. Joan had a friend, Val Avery, who knew a literary agent in New York. We sent our manuscript to her, and she submitted it to a number of publishers; but two years later all we had were some very nice, polite rejection letters. I was about ready to throw the thing into a drawer and forget about writing any more books. I had given copies of the manuscript to a few friends to get their response. One of them was Paul Whitehouse, a diverse individual, who has a variety of businesses and a number of interests. Though not an actor, he is a patron of the arts and has a great deal of respect for me.

We were having lunch together at Canter's, the Jewish deli on Fairfax Avenue, and I was crying the blues about my unpublished book: "Two years' work and a lot of excitement went into this project, Paul, and I'm really depressed about how it turned out."

We sat a while without talking, eating our pastrami sandwiches. Then Paul broke the silence: "You know, Eric, this is a good book. It would be invaluable for actors struggling with how to approach a part. It's filled with information that I haven't seen in any other acting book. Why don't you publish it yourself?"

My answer was defensive: "I am not a vanity writer, someone who publishes his work because no one else will!"

His reply was just as adamant: "This isn't vanity, Eric. It's a very good book and a hell of a contribution to your field, and you can afford to publish it yourself. I'll go one step further: If you do self-publish it, I will promote it and get it out there, even if I have to hand carry it to every bookstore in Los Angeles and New York."

I was very moved by his enthusiasm and agreed to publish the book myself. I asked Bronwyn, a student in one of my classes, to format and type the entire book, and I then had it offset printed. Paul designed the cover, as well as some of the art inside, and as promised, he began to "get it out there." With another of my students, Danny Spelling, he formed a company called Whitehouse/ Spelling Publications. For about six months they promoted the book in every way possible, short of spending any money on advertising. They hand carried it to bookstores and sold it to a number of them.

The first printing of the book was three thousand copies, which cost me slightly over four thousand dollars. Almost the entire run sold in about a year. Danny attended the convention of the ABA, the American Booksellers Association, in New York City and successfully sold the book to Quick Fox Publishing, a company that specialized in music but also had a small backlist of different titles that they published and distributed. I was ecstatic, and so were Paul and Danny. I was amazed that Danny had sold the book on the strength of that first edition, which in later years I called "the Mickey Mouse edition." The book was priced at seven dollars, and the authors' share was seven percent of the cover price. I didn't care one way or another, since I hadn't written the book with money as the goal. I just wanted to "get it out there." Today, thirty years later, *No Acting Please* and my four other books are still being used in colleges and conservatories throughout the United States and abroad.

While all of this was going on, I was directing Joan in her play, which we rehearsed at least twice a week. Because *Legacy* was Joan's first play, she was having difficulty avoiding the writer's trap of wanting the audience to hear every single word she had written, and this made her acting too conscious, too deliberate. So I taught her an antidote, in this case a nonverbal exercise, and suggested she use it the next time we presented the play. We decided to bring the work into the directors' unit at the Actors Studio and to show them only the section we were working on at the moment.

That evening, Joan got up on the stage and began to create sensorially the objects, the environment, and the specific people, letting herself be affected by her choices; but instead of speaking the lines, she expressed all her feelings in gibberish and nonverbal sounds, as I had taught her to do. This went on for about twenty minutes. When she finished, she sat down in a chair onstage, facing the audience, ready to discuss her process.

I happened to be the moderator that evening, but before I could open the floor to discussion, one of the writers yelled out, "Eric, what the fuck was that?"

His question sent a rumble through the room. Obviously, there were others who felt exactly the same way. I waited until the room settled down, and then explained exactly what was going on: "First of all, I want to say that I am in the fortunate or unfortunate position of being both the moderator for this session and the director of this play. We presented only a small part of it, and this was a rehearsal or, as we say here at the Actors Studio, a 'work in progress.' The play is about a day in the life of a Pasadena society matron, who is married with two children. She's desperate because she feels she is dying, suffocated by meaningless minutiae and empty social obligations. She thinks about suicide but can't figure out an effective way to kill herself. Since Joan is also the playwright, she is naturally attached to the lines she wrote. Her attachment was hampering her freedom as an actor, preventing unconscious impulses from being expressed. I directed her tonight to work sensorially for her choices and, instead of saying the written words, to use gibberish and nonverbal sounds. Later she'll start including some of the lines. Isn't the Actors Studio a laboratory, a place where actors can experiment?"

Then Joan spoke about her process, and I saw the light beginning to dawn in the eyes of some of the people out there. Throughout that year we brought *Legacy* into the Studio several more times, slowly adding the lines as Joan's acting became more spontaneous. One evening when I was again the moderator in a session that was open to all the units—writers', directors', and actors'—Joan and I presented a section from the middle of the play, a phone call to the character's psychiatrist, in which she asks if she can see him that day to talk about her wanting to swallow a bottle of sleeping pills and wash them all down with a quart of fresh orange juice. It is apparent that her psychiatrist is less than interested and does not have time to see her.

Joan sat there for a moment, motionless, the phone in her hand. She let out a scream of frustration so loud and so long it was shocking, and then finished the scene with her psychiatrist.

I opened the floor to discussion, and one of the playwrights raised his hand. Somewhat agitated, he asked, "Was that scream written in the scene?"

"No," I replied, "it wasn't."

"Then tell me," he said, "how can you as a director allow the actress to do such a thing?"

"First off," I responded, "let me say that as the director of this piece I do not allow or disallow anything that the actress is feeling, and moreover, who is to say that the character in that moment couldn't respond that way?"

Well, that statement sparked a revolution in the room! Writers were yelling that actors couldn't take that kind of liberty with their material. Some directors shouted their agreement with me, while somebody else kicked a chair over and ranted at me, at Joan, and at the directors who agreed with me.

Admittedly, Joan's scream had come out of her own frustration with herself in that moment, but she had *included* it in what the character was feeling, having learned to "allow, permit, accept, and include." When the room settled down, something wonderful came out of the chaos. Many of the people there that night began to understand that the truth in any given moment onstage can be totally included in the actor's behavior and no writer can honestly say that it is impossible for the character to behave that way. If an actor is working for choices that address the author's intentions, then he or she is in the arena of the text and by including unpredictable impulses discovers the next moment in the next moment and exactly at the same moment as the audience. This experiential approach to acting produces truth that is totally authentic and often electrifying.

Joan and I spent two years rehearsing and developing *Legacy* until we both felt ready to produce it. The Actors Studio gave us permission to use their theater and offer a full production to the public on a series of weekends, which were very successful. During one of our post-play Q and A with the audience, Vic Tayback, who was also a Studio member, spoke positively about our work, then said with genuine anger that he hated the character's husband and thought he was a complete jerk. Half laughing, I asked him what the husband looked like, since there were no other actors on the stage with Joan! Vic was quite embarrassed when he realized that he had created a person from his imagination, but I applauded him for it. His anger at the husband made a wonderful statement about how successful Joan had been in creating the presence of other characters in the story.

We also took *Legacy* to Theater East and then presented it for several weekends at Continuum, Emilie Conrad's dance studio. One of those evenings at Continuum, Joan's performance was seen by a young filmmaker, Karen Arthur, who, fresh out of the UCLA film school, was looking for her first feature. Joan adapted the play for film, and Karen directed and produced it on a total budget of forty-six thousand dollars and a twelve-day shooting schedule. Joan said to me, "Yeah, Eric, we shot it in twelve days after two years of rehearsals." *Legacy* won several awards in film festivals around the world and was distributed in eighteen countries, including the United States.

Later I had the pleasure of directing Joan, with three of my other students, in a local production of *The Glass Menagerie,* in which she was brilliant as Amanda. To this day, Joan and I are grateful for those five collaborative years, when we learned so much and achieved far more than either of us could have done alone.

During that period at the Actors Studio I directed two other projects that were ultimately presented to the public. The first one was *Knock, Knock,* a two-person play written by Richard Link, a very successful television producer at Universal Studios. It starred Lorraine Gary and Bill Joyce. Lorraine, a member of the Actors Studio, was the wife of Sid Sheinberg, who ran Universal. Bill was a tall, handsome actor, who looked as though he would conquer the world doing commercials. Since the play was a relationship play, I worked with both actors, attempting to establish an intimacy between them. I did a lot of relationship exercises and asked the actors to explore and share meaningful personal things about their life that paralleled the play. I felt that we were succeeding, in spite of the fact that Bill resented my approaches. He thought that I was asking too much in the personal area, even though I explained that this play was about two people in a very personal relationship! We worked on the play for several months and finally presented it publicly.

The next project I got involved with was also a play written by the actor himself. Called *People of the Shadows,* it took place sometime in the late thirties and was, among other things, about the Triangle Shirt Company fire in New York. Many people had died in that fire because they had not had a union to protect them from ruthless businessmen only interested in making money, even at the cost of safety. Harry Davis, the author, was perhaps about sixty-two or sixty-three years old at the time and was married to a successful mystery writer, whose books were very popular. I think he lived in the shadow of his wife's success. He was from the generation that thought Communism might be the answer to our social and political problems. Though he was certainly not a Communist, he may have been a little bit of a socialist. I liked him very much and invited him to my house for dinner on a number of occasions. His play was also a one-person piece, which he had performed in various places in New York over a number of years. He was easy to work with, and he took my suggestions and direction well. He told me a story about an experience he had had with Elia Kazan. When Kazan was casting *America, America,* he had called Harry and asked to see him about the part of the lead boy's father. He had instructed Harry to meet him in the lobby of a New York hotel at noon. Harry went there and waited two hours, but Kazan never showed. Thinking that Kazan had changed his mind and hadn't had the courtesy to call him, Harry finally went home. A day or two later, Kazan called him and told him he had the part. When Harry asked him why he hadn't shown up at the hotel, Kazan said that he had been there, out of sight, and that he had just wanted to see Harry walk. The funny thing about it is that in the film I mostly remember Harry sitting, not walking!

Another person who approached me to work on a project was Marc Lawrence, a recognizable character actor, who often played gangsters and Italian mafiosi. His dark, swarthy look and complexion were ominous and accounted for his success as a villain in many films. Along with Jeff Corey, he had been a victim of the House Un-American Activities Committee and had been blacklisted during that awful period in Hollywood. I'm not sure who had named whom, but he and Jeff never spoke to each other again.

Marc asked me if I would work with him on a film he was going to do. I'm not sure whether he had written it or was just going to produce and direct it, but I believe he was using his own money. It was a kind of horror film, called *The Thirteen Pigs.* His daughter was playing the female lead, and the rest of the cast came from Studio actors, with the exception of Erik Holland, a good friend of mine and former student, for whom I was able to get a part in the film. I was there to work with the actors and get the best possible performance from them. As I was involved with Joy at the time and she owned a top-of-the-line Nikon camera—since one of her many career choices was to be a photographer—I got her to be the still photographer on the film.

The plot involved a coffee shop run by the character Marc played. His daughter, Toni, had escaped from a mental institution and somehow ended up at that restaurant. Marc was killing the customers and feeding their bodies to his pigs. I only worked on the film for about a week and did the best I could to make that outrageous plot real for the actors, who all knew the process and techniques I used. Toni Lawrence was a different issue though. Since she wasn't familiar with my exercises or craft, I had to invent a completely new terminology for her; but because I quite often had to do the same in my classes each time I worked with a new student, it wasn't that difficult for me to get her to go where I was leading her. Later I heard that Marc had sold the film to Rod Amateau for a healthy profit. It ended up having a dozen different titles and became available on video, but I am not sure it ever had a theatrical distribution.

I was enjoying my tenure at the Studio. I got a lot from being there. When Lee would come in the summer and conduct the actors' sessions, I never missed one. He was extremely perceptive and would give great suggestions to the actors, but he didn't want them to reveal the personal contents of the choices they worked on. Whenever an actor would begin an explanation about his choice—he might say, for example, "I worked for a heavy conflict I had with my mother"—Lee would immediately cut him off, throwing his hands into the air and saying, "I don't want to hear that. Save it for your therapist!" His responses seemed a little over the top. It wasn't as if he was protecting the actor's privacy, but it seemed that he was affected by the personal nature of what the actor was exposing. I have always had the awareness that Lee, who ostensibly was teaching actors to be emotional and to express those emotions, was himself terrified by his own emotions. I hadn't put that together when I had first encountered him at the Lake Arrowhead theater conference in 1958.

One summer, on the first day Lee arrived at the Studio in L.A., he heard my name come up quite a number of times, and since he did not know me personally, he freaked out. In the living room at the Studio he called several people in to talk about who this Eric Morris was and why he was representing the Studio. He got quite excited, and as it was told to me by people who were in the room with him, his face turned bright red, the veins in his neck bulged out, and he started yelling at the top of his voice, asking about me: "Who is he? What has he directed? Why is he heading the directors' unit?" and so on. I know that Marty Landau was in the room. I think that Lou Antonio was also there and Lonnie Chapman, who went to bat for me, telling Lee that *he* had brought me in and that I was doing great work at the Studio. Alejandro Rey, a student of mine and a member of the Studio, also really stood up for me, telling Lee that he had been studying with me for a couple of years, that my work had changed his life, that I wanted exactly what Lee wanted, and that the work I had been doing at the Studio was exemplary. At that time Alejandro was in very good standing with Lee and at the Studio, because he had been able to get a new place for it, the Merle Oberon Theater. He knew Merle and had talked her into letting the Studio use her theater—which somehow they finally never did! Marty said nothing. As far as I know, that was the second time he wasn't there for me. The next day Lee dissolved the directors' unit and the writers' unit, and I know that the move was designed to get rid of me, as he had no other reason to ask me to leave. I know that someone reading this will probably think that my reaction is paranoid, but a lot of the people in that room agreed with me, and it is a fact. Lee was a frightened little man, who was intimidated by anyone who had new or different ideas or threatened his authority or leadership, although that was not the case with me. I respected his contribution to the theater, most particularly what he did for actors in helping them to achieve craftsmanship, but I truly believe that his impact would have been far greater if he had been open to the input and ideas of his contemporaries. It was, however, a personality flaw of his, which stemmed from his deep-seated insecurities. In one of the sessions Orson Welles' name came up, and Lee said, and I quote: "Orson forgot that there were other people out there who had eyes and perceptions besides his." Well, it is really unfortunate that Lee, who suffered from what he was accusing Welles of, didn't have the insight to look to himself. What I learned from Marty in some part came directly from Lee, and I was grateful for that. I have always said that if not for Lee and Marty, there would be no Eric Morris or the system I have created.

Another interesting experience I indirectly had with Lee was related to a scene I had been directing for a couple of months. It had been written by Jack Guss, the husband of Maggie Fairchild, a Studio member and actress, who was also studying with me at the time. She was doing the scene with Mark Leonard, quite an accomplished character actor, also a member of the Studio. The work we did together was deep, personal, and impacting. I put both of them through exercises and techniques that reached deep into their very being, and the results were amazing. When they finally felt ready to do the scene at an actors' session in front of Lee, Maggie, knowing how he felt about me, did not mention that I had directed it.

I was having lunch at Schwab's on the day they were presenting the scene, when Steve Gravers came in and sat down in the booth with me. Steve was a longtime member of the Studio and had just come from there. He had a big smile on his face but for some minutes said nothing. I looked at him, curious about the smile, since Steve was usually very surly, critical by nature, and not prone to smiling, and I said, "What? What?" He told me that he had just come from the Studio and had watched the scene between Maggie and Mark. He started speaking very deliberately, like a person who has something impacting to say: "Well, Eric, I know that you have been directing them for some time now. I've talked to Maggie about what you were all doing in your rehearsals; so let me tell you the incredible thing that happened when they had finished the scene. Without asking the actors anything, Lee turned to the audience—something I have never seen in all the years I have been there—and said, 'THIS IS THE KIND OF WORK THAT THE ACTORS STUDIO WAS CREATED TO DO!' I had never seen Lee so moved or impressed by the work in any session, so you should be very proud of where you took those actors." I was very affected by what he had just told me, but instead of being elated, I was very sad. I know that if Lee had realized I was involved, he would probably not have said what he did, and the fact that he had dissolved the units to get me out of there was impactingly ironic.

When Rob, one of my students, had his final audition for Lee, to gain entrance into the Studio, Lee asked him with whom he had studied, and Rob said, "Eric Morris, who has been my only teacher to date."

Lee stared at him for a moment or two and then said, "Oh yes, isn't he the guy who wrote that book, *No Acting* or something?"

Rob replied, "Yes, that's right, *No Acting Please.*"

"Well," Lee continued, "if there is no acting, then there is no acting!" It is so obvious that he had never read the book or never even knew that everything in it reflected ideas he had spent his life working with!

I had profited a lot by being at the Studio, though, and had no regrets. I had met Joan, had written a book with her, made a lot of new friends, and been able to apply most of the things I had been teaching for the previous ten years and to put them into practice with actors who had not studied with me. It was a perfect situation. I was able to take my process and the exercises and techniques I was using in my classes into the work I was doing at the Studio, and I was bringing into my classes discoveries I was making while working with actors at the Studio. I had directed three public projects during my tenure there and met Roger Corman, the biggest independent film producer at the time. He had seen me work with some of the actors in the directors' unit, and obviously impressed by what he saw, he hired me to be the dubbing director on a film he and his brother had done in Ireland, *Von Richthofen and Brown,* which was about the World War I German ace who had shot down numerous Allied planes, and his rival, Brown, who was finally victorious in shooting the Red Baron down. The film was going to be released by Allied Artists, but they refused to do it because the Germans spoke with American accents and the actor playing Major Boelke had a decidedly Texas accent. I therefore had the job of casting the actors who would dub the film with German accents. I called all the original actors in to see if they were able to effect a German accent and found that most of them could but that a small number were unable to, so I had to recast those parts, which was very upsetting to the original actors. I felt terrible about it, because, being an actor, I knew exactly how they felt. We did the dubbing sessions at Glen Glenn Sound, and I ended up having to supply about eight different voices, including those of children. I worked for Roger and his brother a few more times as a dubbing director and in the eighties was hired to back up Jimmy Murikami, a director Roger had hired, who was a great effects director but had little experience with actors. The film was *Battle beyond the Stars,* and besides a nominal salary—all salaries for people who worked for

Roger were nominal—Roger also gave me a part in the film, I guess to get me to agree to the other job.

In 1975 one of my students, Jim Davidson, who was studying film making at the University of Southern California, approached me and asked if I would be interested in teaching a class there at the film school. He told me that it was a fantastic school technically but that no one there at the time could teach young directors how to work with actors or direct them. He had spoken about me to the head of the film school, who invited me to have lunch with him at USC. His name was Bernie Kantor, and he had been there for some time. He was in his fifties, I guess, and was very soft-spoken and deferential. We had a good lunch and some interesting conversation. He told me about the school and what they wanted to accomplish, which was to supply future directors to the film industry. He asked a few questions about me, my workshop and what I taught, and he seemed satisfied with my answers. I got the job of teaching one directing class twice a week. I was a part-time teacher, free to structure my class anyway I wanted.

My first class was full. I had been given a small soundstage to work on and some equipment, such as lights, light stands, and a camera mounted on a tripod. Since USC was on the semester system, I only had five months with those students, and I knew that it wasn't enough time to teach them what they needed to know about working with actors. I therefore invited all of them to attend my classes in Hollywood as observers, in order to get an idea what actors go through to reach a level of performance. I also felt, and still do, that every director should spend time acting, if not professionally, at least in a class. I feel very strongly about teaching a director what actors feel, what blocks, tension, and insecurities they experience while attempting to fulfill a scene; and the only way he can truly understand that is to experience it for himself.

David Anspaugh, one of my students at USC, showed up at my Hollywood workshop the night after he attended my first class at the university. Instead of observing the class, he joined it as a participant and began working as an actor. I particularly single David out because he stayed in my personal classes for many years after our first encounter. Since leaving USC, David has become a successful director and has also written and produced. To this day, some thirty years later, he occasionally pops in on one of my classes and watches the work.

There were others from the film school who went on to make movies. One of them hired me to coach the actors on *American Anthem,* a film about gymnasts that he was doing in Arizona. Al Magnoli, the director, had also worked with me for a period of time before entering the job market. I was on that film for many weeks, flying back and forth from L.A. to Flagstaff, where they were doing most of the gymnastics in a college gymnasium furnished with all the athletic equipment necessary for the various gymnastic styles. I also got Joy to coach the actors, who were mostly real gymnasts. The lead was played by Mitch Gaylord, an Olympic champion and, as it turned out, not a bad actor. The female lead opposite him was a very beautiful blond woman, who had also had some athletic training. Her name was Janet Jones. She later married Wayne Gretsky and had a couple of children with him.

At USC I set the classes up so that each of the directing students had to present a scene, using actors from the theater department or from my personal classes in Hollywood. They were told to rehearse the scenes outside of class, and then to bring them in and treat their work in class as an additional rehearsal. I did not want them to fall into the trap of obligating themselves to results or performance. Then, as today, the lesson was the only goal of the class, which had to be approached as a laboratory. At any one time I would see six or seven scenes, and then I would ask the director what task he had set for himself—what he had intended to address in that rehearsal. After sharing that with us, he was asked to talk about what techniques he had used to encourage the actors to stimulate the desired behavior. As the semester wore on, all of the students became familiar with the terminology and the techniques I was teaching them, and they were able to use those techniques to creatively manipulate the actors. After the director-student finished sharing his process, I would ask the actors to comment on the director: Did he communicate well? Was he able to suggest techniques and choices that the actors could use? Was he sensitive to their problems and needs? Did he give them the freedom to explore their choices without demanding results? Did he suggest or use techniques to stimulate and support their relationships in terms of the character obligations? It was very important for the directing student to get feedback from the actors. Hearing their responses would certainly make him aware of what adjustments he had to make to be able to achieve creative results. The techniques I used were extremely successful in teaching those fledgling directors how to relate to actors and get what they needed. I told them that when I was directing at the Actors Studio I could get anything I wanted from the actors I was working with because I was willing to do anything I asked them to do. I too was an actor, who understood their issues. I never made a separation between "management" and "workers." I always addressed issues with "we," not "you."

None of the faculty, including Dr. Kantor, ever visited my class at USC. I was totally left alone. The woman who was the administrative assistant for the film school, Dari, resented me and was quoted by some of the people she talked to as calling me "the fair-haired boy." At one point, I got tired of driving downtown to the USC campus, so I told my students to come into Hollywood and work in my studio, which they did, and no one complained. After about a year or so, I began to wonder why no one ever visited my class or checked up on me in any way. I wondered if they cared about what I was doing on that soundstage. I asked Bernie Kantor to have lunch with me, telling him it had been a while since we had communicated, and he was delighted. During our lunch I asked him why no one had ever been to my class. He smiled and responded, "We know exactly what you are doing in there. It is so obvious in all of the 480s." The 480s were sync-sound sixteen-millimeter films done by the more advanced students and presented for a final grade. He continued, "You know, Eric, I have been here for many years and have seen hundreds of 480 films, and I must tell you that since you have been here, the level and quality of the work in those films has elevated considerably, and not just the acting, which I guess is to be expected, but the visuals too; and the directors' influence on the actors and the dramatic content of the scenes have become more dimensional. Yes, Eric, we know what you are doing, and we don't have to watch you do it. We just need to experience the results." I was very flattered.

I taught at USC from 1975 well into the early eighties and only gave it up because I got bored with starting at square one every semester. All of the new people in class had to be taught from the beginning, and after seven or eight years it got to be frustrating for me. I replaced myself with one of my students, Tony Morina, who taught there for several years and turned his position over to another one of my students, Laurie Burton, who is still there and has become a full-time professor with tenure.

Around the same time I started working at USC I received a call from Bob Rafelson, a fine director, who had directed several memorable films, such as *Five Easy Pieces, The King of Marvin Gardens,* and other notable ones. "Hi, Eric," he said, "this is Bob Rafelson. I'm directing a film called *Stay Hungry,* which in large part is about weightlifters, bodybuilders, and the Mr. Universe contest. Jack Nicholson recommended that I call you, since I need your help with one of the people I intend to use in the film. He's perfect for the role. He is a famous bodybuilder, who has already won the Mr. Universe contest more than once; however, he has no acting experience at all, and his part is very large. Jack speaks highly of you. Can you help me?"

I was immediately intrigued, so I asked him, "How long do I have to work with him before you start filming?"

He told me, "Twelve weeks."

"Well, Bob," I replied, "I really would like to help you, but I might succeed in confusing him more than helping him in that short a time. I mean, if he was an experienced actor, twelve weeks would be more than enough time, but—"

He interrupted me before I could finish: "I like your honesty, and you come highly recommended, so would you at least meet with him and then decide whether you can work with him?"

I agreed to do that and asked, "What's his name, and how will I recognize him?"

There was a long silence before he responded. I thought I had lost the telephone connection. Finally, he said, "His name is Arnold Schwarzenegger, and you won't have any problem recognizing him, because he is about as wide as he is tall."

I agreed to meet him the next day. I gave Bob my theater address on Fountain and the following day waited in the parking lot next to the theater. Exactly at noon a silver BMW drove in, and out came Arnold, wearing a white turtleneck shirt and looking as big as a house. As he walked towards me, he flashed a big smile, extended his right hand, and said, "Hi, I'm Arnold. Are you Eric?" I nodded and shook his hand with trepidation, thinking that anyone who looked like that could shatter every bone in my hand with a simple handshake. To my surprise his handshake was firm, yet gentle. We took to each other immediately. We sat in my theater talking for a couple of hours. He told me about himself, and I tried to explain to him what I did. We liked each other from the start, which I felt was a good beginning for collaboration. I worked with him for two or three hours three times a week. I had read the script and knew what his responsibilities were but decided not to address the material directly, at least not right away. As a matter of fact, we worked for nine weeks without opening the script. I had him specifically talking about his life, his youth, his background, and so on. We spoke about Austria, how he felt about America, and just about everything else. As we proceeded with each session, I began to point out experiences and relationships he had had that could be used for each scene in the script. By the time we got to the material, he seemed to understand everything that we had been doing in those nine weeks. I must say here that Arnold is one of the most intelligent people I have ever known. We spent three weeks on the script, using all of the choices from his life that paralleled the character's experiences.

The film was being shot in Birmingham, Alabama. About two weeks after I finished working with Arnold, I got a telephone call at five in the morning. It woke me out of a nice dream I was having and scared the shit out of me. I thought, Who would call at this hour with anything but bad news? It was Bob Rafelson.

My first response was, "What's wrong?"

He must have suddenly realized that there was a time difference, because he said, "Oh God, I'm sorry! It must be very early there, but I had to call and thank you. Arnold is doing great! I owe you."

I told him that I appreciated the call and was delighted that Arnold was doing good work. "You don't owe me," I added. "You paid me." He told me that what I had done went beyond payment.

When Arnold finished the movie, he enrolled in my class, which was now on La Brea. He was there for at least eight months, attending every week. I had him doing instrumental exercises to elevate his vulnerability and stimulate behavior that went in the direction opposite his size and persona. In one class I asked him to do an "I care" exercise, sharing all of his feelings about the things and people he really cared about. He spoke of how much he loved his mother and some of his friends, past and present. Doing exercises of that kind elevated his vulnerability and softness, which created an incredible contrast between what was visually there and this compelling affectability.

Around that time, Joy and I broke up, probably for the second time—I'm not sure. I was incredibly depressed, and it showed in every part of my body. Arnold walked into the class and stopped short when he saw me. He paused and slowly walked towards me, saying, "What de matter, Eric? You look like your dog just died!"

I responded, "No, Arnold, not my dog, my relationship. We broke up, and I am devastated."

Arnold knew Joy, and I think he liked her. He threw his arms around me, and I disappeared into the cavern of his humongous chest, "Don't worry! I take you on the road with me, and we find you a new lady," he said.

Well, I didn't go on the road, and shortly after that evening I reconciled with Joy. The reason I tell of this experience is so the reader will know what a kind, loving, and sensitive man Arnold is. If he likes you, he will probably do anything for you, but if he doesn't, look out!

I recently had lunch with David Anspaugh, and we were talking about the old days and the class. I asked him what he remembered specifically about any of the people there. After a short pause to swallow his buffalo burger, he said that he remembered an exercise I had given Arnold and that the memory of the event had stuck with him over the years. I asked him to talk about it, and he started by saying that I had asked Arnold to sit in the center of the stage—which was surrounded on three sides by the members of the class—and to sensorially create the living room of his home in Austria when he was a little boy—the color of the walls, the sounds and smells indigenous to that place, all of the objects and where they were in the room. I had worked with Arnold long enough for him to have developed some sensorial facility. Then I added that it was Christmas morning and that he was playing with his favorite toy. He took several minutes to create the room and then the toy, which was a metal locomotive. He proceeded to run it along the floor, slowly making train and whistle sounds. There was this hulk of a man, transformed in every way to being a little boy, surrounded by his family and exulting over his new toy. After David reminded me of that exercise, it all came flooding back, and I remembered that its impact, which had affected everyone in the room, had also stayed with Arnold long after he had gone back to his seat.

Arnold also did some scene work in class. He did a scene with Kayla Garren from *Sweet Bird of Youth.* Kayla played the aging asthmatic actress, Arnold was her young gigolo, and as I remember, they were both wonderful. Arnold used his charm and sexuality to seduce Alexandra Del Lago and get what he wanted from her. I have always felt that if Arnold had continued to pursue dramatic acting, he would have been a wonderful actor. As a matter of fact, sometime after he left class, in the mid eighties, he came back to visit. I was on Cahuenga at the time. After the class a bunch of us went to a Mexican restaurant on Sunset. Arnold had already done one, or maybe two, action-adventure films by then. He said that he had enjoyed the class and that I was a brilliant teacher but that it was not the kind of acting he wanted to do. He wanted to be an action-and-adventure actor and enjoyed the physicality of that kind of work. I told him that I understood and wished him the best of luck, adding that I knew he was going to be very successful. However, it wasn't always like that for Arnold, at least not in the beginning. After he had finished *Stay Hungry,* there was a period of time when he wasn't working and wasn't getting auditions, and I believe he was having a difficult time. One night he walked into class and sat down directly across from me. I could see that he was very upset. I figured I had better get him up onstage to ventilate whatever was disturbing him, so immediately after the relaxation exercises I called him up there.

"O.K., Arnold, what's bothering you?" I asked.

He stood there for a moment and then exploded, "Dey don't like my body, dey don't like my name, and dey don't like my accent! So fuck dem! I'm going to be a superstar!"

The outburst drew applause from everyone in the class. He felt better after purging that, and of course he did become a superstar.

As I said earlier, the seventies were jam-packed with all kinds of creative activity. I was on the job market and would occasionally book a part in a movie or on television. The time frames run together, so it is hard to know when I did what. I was so busy doing so many things it was hard to squeeze in even a day's work, but I was always willing to move things around or cancel a class if a part came up.

In 1976 two of my students, Greg Mullavy and Meredith MacRae, recommended me for a film they were doing, originally called *Echo of a Massacre,* but later retitled *My Friends Need Killing.* It was about a Vietnam War veteran who had returned to society and was unable to adjust because of his involvement in a massacre in Vietnam. I played his psychiatrist. It was an interesting experience working with my own students. It was directed by Paul Leder, whose daughter, Mimi Leder, became a very successful director a couple of decades later. A little while after that, I played a ghost on "Fantasy Island."

Then, around 1977, a young Asian woman named Tiana came to my class. She was the wife of Stirling Silliphant, a famous screenwriter, and she seemed serious about acting and becoming a craftsperson. About a year later, her husband was hired to write a miniseries called "Pearl," which told the story of the attack on Pearl Harbor, what had led up to it and its aftermath. It included the role of an attractive Japanese-American woman who falls in love with a naval officer who is tragically killed during the attack. It was a very juicy role filled with impacting emotional scenes, and Tiana wanted to audition for it, but, as I remember, there was some reluctance on the part of the producers and casting people. Since she was the writer's wife, I imagine, they finally acquiesced and scheduled an audition, probably as a courtesy to Stirling.

Tiana and I had a number of private lessons to prepare for the audition. There was a scene after her lover is killed where she talks to his dead body and completely falls apart. We worked diligently using "coffin monologues" and pulling up all the grief she had ever experienced, and when she auditioned, she blew them away and got the part.

She wanted me to come to Hawaii to coach her, so she arranged for Joy and me to go there for a week and stay in a beautiful hotel facing the ocean. I was on the set almost every day and was invited by Stirling and Tiana to cocktails and dinner with Robert Wagner and Natalie Wood. Robert was playing one of the leads in the miniseries, and Natalie accompanied him. She was extremely shy and spoke very little. He was very verbal, however, and was an extremely nice man, very polite and accepting. Joy and Natalie appeared to have a quiet affinity for each other, since there was a strong resemblance between them, not only physically but in essence and spirit too.

I worked with Tiana every day in her hotel room and on the set, and she did incredibly good work on the show. Both she and Stirling took a weekend workshop with me in Lake Gregory.

Robert Wagner and Natalie had a boat in the same marina where I docked my boat, and on one weekend the four of us ran into each other on Catalina. Robert affably said with a big smile that we would "have to stop running into each other on islands." We spoke for a few minutes, while Natalie hung back, not saying anything. Then we said good-bye and went our separate ways.

In 1978 Kayla Garren approached me to be the host and moderator for a series she was producing with her partner, Fred Thorne. It was being funded by the Mormons, who were somehow being represented by a Catholic priest, Father Banahan, who was a real trip. He was as Irish as Paddy's pig. As a matter of fact, his picture appears under *Irish* in the dictionary! His job for the church was media. He was in charge of anything to do with the media, propaganda, or show business. He had a reputation that traveled throughout the entire Catholic Church, at least in this country. He had been asked to leave Chicago by the cardinal, who didn't approve of him at all, but then, when that cardinal was replaced, Banahan was invited back. He had a mistress, who was present on the set every time we shot a show. She followed him around like an obedient dog.

The show was called "Eyewitness to the Past." Thirty-nine episodes had been planned, each to last half an hour. I was to be the interviewer and moderator, interviewing famous people from history, such as Napoleon, George Washington, and others. We were scheduled to shoot four shows per weekend. Father Banahan was in charge of researching and supplying the historical figures. There wasn't an actual script. The way it worked was that the actor would get a background on the character he or she was to play, filled with many of the details the interview would cover. I was given similar material, and it was my job to structure an interview that would draw the historical character out in the most dramatic and theatrical way. I got work for many of my students and even had my brother Ed play two characters: Junípero Serra and Lenin. He was great in both shows. Erik Holland did Hitler; Michael Green, Jefferson; and Joan Hotchkis, Mrs. Lincoln; an actor I knew from Schwab's Drugstore played Mussolini, and Father Banahan did King John of the Magna Charta. Some of the shows were really heated and theatrical. Besides having the pleasure of hosting a thirty-nine-episodes syndicated show, I felt as if I were taking a two-year history course in college. Because of all the material that was supplied and all the information on each character, I found out things about those people that I hadn't learned in school. It was one of the highlights of the seventies, and it afforded me the opportunity to do a lot of acting—not to mention that everyone was paid for his or her work.

My personal life wasn't as fulfilling as my creative life though. Joy and I had an intense relationship and were doing a takeoff on *The War of the Roses*. The first two years had been great, but after I had told Jean about the affair and left, the relationship started to go downhill for the next thirteen years. Joy's kids were one of the problems, and her own personal dissatisfaction with herself, another. We went to therapy for several years—group and individual. We really tried to work at the relationship, but there were too many issues, and therapy wasn't doing much to change things.

I was in a private lesson with Anna Ivara, an actress and student, and I guess I was really distraught, so she asked me what was going on. I told her about the problems I was having at home, and she asked me whether I was getting any help. I told her about my therapy with Roger Callahan, and when I said I had been working with him for about eight years, she was shocked.

"So how long are you going to give this guy before you decide that he isn't helping you or Joy?" she asked.

I didn't know how to respond to her question, but it made me think. I finally said, "Well, do you have any suggestions?"

She shook her head and responded, "Yes, I certainly do. I work with a therapist who uses techniques that make therapy a short-term proposition. His name is Hal Stone, and I'll give you his number if you're interested."

"Are you kidding? Short-term therapy? I'm *very* interested."

I called and made an appointment. Hal worked out of his home, a typical California ranch-style house in North Hollywood. He greeted me with a warm smile and a handshake and ushered me into a smallish room that looked like a den or small library. There were a leather loveseat, a chair, and a stool. He sat on the loveseat facing the chair and invited me to sit down.

He started the conversation: "So tell me why you are here."

I began to talk about what was happening in my relationship and was about two minutes into it when he stopped me and said, "I would like you to move over and sit on the stool and let me talk to that voice I just heard."

I stared at him blankly, because I didn't have a clue what he was saying. "All right then," he continued, "go on with what you were saying, and when I hear that other voice, I'll ask you to move, and I will talk to that part of you."

I continued on the subject I was talking about, and again he asked me to move over, which I did. He started to speak to what he said was another "subpersonality," and all hell broke loose! I moved from one emotional state of being to a completely opposite one. When I had first started to speak, there had been a complainer doing all the talking, and what had happened was that another part of me had broken through, and Hal had heard it and facilitated it. The second voice was a much stronger and objective self and seemed to know how to handle things, but at the same time it was very critical of the first voice. Hal moved me up and back and in the hour session facilitated four or five different subparts. It was my first exposure to subpersonality and voice-dialogue work, but I was blown away by the experience. Not only did I feel I had learned something and become conscious about the other energies that were there, but I also thought that this would be an incredible acting tool. I asked Hal if he did groups, and he said yes, so I enrolled in one that met twice a week at his house in the larger room. I went there every Monday and Wednesday, and later every Wednesday and Friday, and we did voice dialogue with Hal and then with each other. After a while, I started using subpersonality work in my class—at first as instrumental therapy, but soon I translated the process into a craft tool, which later became one of my megapproaches, one of the most powerful tools in my system. One of my future books is going to be exclusively about using subpersonalities as a major acting tool.

I had started to work with Hal on the cusp of the eighties and continued to see him well into that decade. Joy also began to work with Hal privately, and for a while things seemed to get better for us.

The Eighties and Nineties

The eighties were a time of travel. I logged two million air miles from the beginning of that decade until the mid nineties. I had already been doing weekend workshops in Los Angeles in the late sixties and seventies, but around 1981 I began teaching out of town also. I had somehow contacted, or been contacted by, various people in over a dozen cities all over the country, who became my administrators for setting up marathons. It was not unusual for me to have a workshop every other weekend during those years.

In 1980 and 1981, I was teaching in Los Angeles on Mondays, Tuesdays, Wednesdays, and Thursdays—four classes, plus a Saturday craft class. Since my work doesn't separate acting from living, and so many of the exercises are very helpful in liberating people from their fears, obstacles, and inhibitions, I decided to open up one class to people who had no ambition to act but really wanted their lives to be fuller, freer, and less restricted. My Monday class included nonactors and was called a being class. My Wednesday class, on the other hand, was an advanced class for actors who had been with me for a longer time. Many working actors were in it.

I started each of the classes with a four-part preparation that consisted of relaxation, sensitizing, personal inventory, and sensuality. I then had the students do an "I want, I need, I am, I feel" workout, and I continued with a two-person sharing exercise, followed by some kind of craft workout. After the group exercises, I usually went into individual instrumental work and then scenes and monologues. At the end of every class the students would sit in a circle, so they could all see each other, and I would do a "round," which was divided into four parts. In the first part, "reluctancy," anyone who had anything he was reluctant to say about himself or to others would express it, thus purging feelings and impulses that he might be incubating. The second part, "ego reconstruction," was designed to communicate observations one actor might have about another that could be insightful and helpful to the other's growth. The third part, called "feedback," included two kinds of feedback and was the only time a two-way conversation was allowed. In the mind-reading kind one actor would encounter another and say, for example, "I think you don't like me or my work. Is that the way you feel?" at which point the other actor might respond with, "No, I do like you, and I think your work is good and you are growing!" In direct feedback, one actor might ask, "What did you think of the scene I did tonight?" and the other would respond to the question. In the last of the four parts, "validation," the actors would validate one another in specific areas. Doing rounds at the end of each class allowed the students to express their thoughts and emotions and to leave the room without incubated feelings that might fester between one week and the next. It also encouraged them to express and expose things that they might not have if there hadn't been a venue for it.

The exercises I used in all my classes included several large commitment expurgations, such as Vesuvius or exorcism, and a variety of vulnerability workouts, such as the deathbed exercise, coffin monologues, talking to or about impacting things, and so on. We also did a group of silly-dilly, go-crazy exercises—including distorting the body and the voice and doing a monologue from there—as well as impulsivity explorations, slot-machine exercises, and other anti-concept workouts. In addition, I was still creating techniques to liberate the actors' instrument and antidote inhibitions and dependencies: anti-privacy sharing exercises, sexuality workouts, which elevated the actors' use of their sensuality, blatant-sexuality workouts, and dozens more. For about a year or so, I even used *batacas,* so that the actors could vent anger, frustration, and hostility. A bataca was a round, heavily padded instrument with a handle, with which two actors would beat each other. It was so heavily padded and soft that it inflicted no pain or injury. Besides, the rules prohibited the actors from hitting each other on the head or face. Only body blows were allowed. The batacas worked for people who had difficulty being aggressive and expressing their anger. I had learned about them from George Bach, a psychologist introduced to me by Joan Hotchkis, a unique and complicated man, who had written several books and was quite an innovator in the field of psychology. His books entitled *The Intimate Enemy* and *Fighting Fair* were very popular. George used batacas in his therapy, and I learned about them when I acted on a television show about a group-therapy session George was conducting, in which each of his supposed patients would tell his story, just as in a reality show. I played a recently divorced young man who was shattered by the loss of his wife and easily broke down. I was very successful in the role, using my relationship with my own wife, Joy. George approached me after the filming and asked me why I wasn't working as an actor every day.

Another of the exercises I later stopped using was one I called "standing up under a barrage." To do it an actor would stand on the stage silently, while people in the class barraged him with criticism and orders to do certain things or be a certain way. He would have to be able to take the barrage and deal with his emotional responses without saying anything. In some cases it was a wonderful way to build strength, power, and ego. I felt, however, that the negative elements outweighed the positive, and a few years later I stopped using the exercise as a therapy tool.

Around that time, both my children came to my classes to study with me. Jeff watched for a while and then did some work onstage. He had a scene with Michael Bowen, a seasoned professional, and I thought he did quite well in it. I could see that he was not enchanted with acting but that he really liked the process. He stayed in the class for quite some time and later started his own class. He turned out to be a very good teacher, who taught a couple of classes each week.

Suzy also worked on some scenes, one of which was from *Ladies of Manhattan.* I was very impressed with her natural talent for acting and felt that she could have a good career in the business. She even got her SAG card after doing a few film projects, but she decided that she didn't like the field and stopped pursuing acting as a career. She came to a number of my jamborees, however, and seemed to like the work, the people, and the activity. Later on, she went to college, where she earned a master's degree in psychology. She worked for a while as a management consultant for actors, teaching a class on the business and how to market oneself.

In the early eighties several other people came into my classes who were significant to my work and my books. One of them was an attractive, petite woman in her thirties, named Scarlett Gani, who had a French accent and, especially in the beginning, always seemed terrified. Watching her watch people work was a show in itself. She later told me that she was so frightened about being called up to work that she shook in her seat. Once I told her what exercise I wanted her to do, however, she settled down and did it. She taught French at one of the colleges and wanted to act avocationally. What was very interesting and something I found out much later was that she had a better understanding of the English language, grammar, and sentence structure than I do. As a result, I asked her to edit my third book, and over the years she has worked in that capacity on my later books. She did much more than correcting spelling—which I have always had problems with—or making sure that the grammar was right. She spent a lot of time researching specific events and the times and places where they occurred. I also depended on her to help me outline and structure the material so that it flowed well. I will always be grateful to her for her contribution to my work. She was in class until the early nineties and was very involved in the initial work of the American New Theater in Los Angeles.

Sometime in the eighties Brandon Lee, who was a student at Emerson College in Boston at the time, started to attend my New York weekend workshops. After a number of them, he finally moved to Los Angeles and joined one of my weekly classes. I advised him to be his own man and not to live in the shadow of his famous father, Bruce Lee. I knew that there would be people who would attempt to capitalize on his name and the connection with his father. Brandon was accomplished in the martial arts, and while nowhere near as good as Bruce Lee, he was more than competent. While in my class, he did scenes and monologues and applied the work he had learned. I thought he was talented and encouraged him to pursue a career in the industry, but I cautioned him to avoid slap-and-kick movies and to look instead for roles with depth. Unfortunately, my words fell on deaf ears. When I was in the Philippines a few years later, I saw a giant billboard on the side of a building ten stories high, advertising a film Brandon was in. He was billed as the son of Bruce Lee. It saddened me. A number of years later, while making the movie *The Crow,* he was tragically killed.

Around 1980 I was once again approached by Roger Corman, this time to back up a director on a very big movie Roger was preparing to do, a co-production with Orion Films. As I mentioned before, the director, Jimmy Murikami, was an effects director, who had no experience working with actors but was quite respected for his expertise in special effects. In order to entice me to work on the film, which had a four- or five-week schedule, Roger gave me a small part in it. Of course, I was paid SAG minimum for the acting job plus five hundred dollars a week to be there for the actors. Meanwhile, I was losing five thousand a week in teaching income! Roger Corman is a phenomenon, probably the most successful independent film producer in the world. He started doing low-budget films in the fifties and to date is still active in making movies. There is good news about Roger, and there is bad news. First, the good news: He has started the careers of many notable directors and actors, such as Francis Ford Coppola and Jack Nicholson, has contributed to the production of dozens of movies, and continues to make films. Now for the bad news: He does not like to spend money!

At the start of filming he called me aside and said, "Eric, you are here to work with the actors and help them. Jimmy doesn't have the experience to direct actors, so I'm counting on you. But I want you to do it so that nobody knows what you are doing. It must be very unobtrusive."

For a moment I was speechless. I didn't know how to respond to that, but when I got my voice back, I said, "Oh, O.K., Roger, I can do that!"

I don't think he picked up on the sarcasm of my response. He nodded, said, "O.K., that's fine," and walked away.

The film was *Battle beyond the Stars,* a science-fiction movie about a planet in another galaxy that was being attacked by another planet's superior force, which was attempting to conquer and occupy it. The cast included George Peppard, John Saxon, Jeff Corey, Robert Vaughn, Sybil Danning, Sam Jaffe—the original Gunga Din, in what was probably his last appearance in films before he passed on—Richard Thomas, Darlanne Fleugel, and some other recognizable character actors. The character I was to play was named Feh. Because, I believe, the script had been written by one or more Jewish screenwriters, they had named him after a Jewish expression of distaste. When something tastes bad or if you don't like another person or you disapprove of anything, you say, "Feh." My character was rather unheroic. When the people of our planet were given the ultimatum to surrender or be destroyed, all the others decided to fight with ancient spaceships and little war material, whereas Feh was in favor of surrendering to the superior power. In other words, his name somehow fit, if indeed you understood the expression. It is quite possible, however, that the only people who did were the writers and I.

The film is a remake of a remake of *The Magnificent Seven* and has elements of *Star Wars* weaved into it. Seven futuristic mercenaries are assembled to defend a helpless farm colony of peaceful inhabitants against Sador, an evil overlord played by John Saxon. Because of their tiny planet's lack of aggressive resources, its residents enlist the help of this motley crew of space travelers in a variety of spaceships that are only somewhat equipped with the capabilities of fighting a space war against such a powerful force as Sador. Among the seven is Robert Vaughn, a man with an enormous appetite for riches, who has a ship capable of engaging Sador in battle. Vaughn's character is named Gelt, another Jewish reference, since *gelt* in Yiddish means "money." The character is modeled very closely after Lee in *The Magnificent Seven*—in which Vaughn also played—so closely in fact that Gelt's dialogue is lifted almost verbatim from that film. Another mercenary is Cowboy, played by George Peppard, who runs an ancient spaceship from earth that carries a variety of cargo, which he sells to distant planets. His ship is like a galaxy-roaming barge and is ill-equipped to fight in a space war, even if it does have some defensive capacities. Cowboy is a colorful character, dressed in traditional western garb topped off by a John Wayne cowboy hat. He wears a special belt around his waist, which dispenses liquor into a hand-held glass whenever he wants a drink. He listens to modern earth music, drinking and lounging in the strange control room of this misbegotten spaceship. Also enlisted to help defend this hapless planet is Sybil Danning, who, outfitted in a costume that emphasizes her voluptuous bosom, and sporting a headdress reminiscent of a Valkyrie's, flits around the universe in a sports-car type of spaceship equipped with adequate firepower. Then there are the Nestor, a group of beings all totally white, whose leader, played by Earl Boen, speaks what they all think in unison and who have come to the planet to aid in the fight against the aggressor. All those characters and a few others are part of the "magnificent seven," although they are never referred to as that. Finally, an inhabitant of the small planet, Zed, played by Jeff Corey, loans his ancient and dilapidated ship, which is normally used for weather exploration, to Shad, played by Richard Thomas, whose character totally resembles Luke Skywalker from *Star Wars*.

As in *The Magnificent Seven,* most of the mercenaries are killed in the various battles with Sador, and, of course, Sador is defeated, his magnificent space fortress destroyed, and the tiny planet is saved.

Doing my job on the film meant watching every take, every scene that was being shot, and looking like an innocent bystander interested in learning about movie making. If there was a problem with an actor, I had to unobtrusively walk over close to him and pretend I was talking about something innocuous, such as what he wanted for lunch, while giving him some direction about what he was doing, how to make it more real, and so on.

It was Darlanne Fluegel's first day on the film. A young, beautiful blond woman with a wonderful smile and sparkling white teeth, she was one of the female leads in the film and was obviously nervous. She blew the first takes of her first scene, while Roger was there at my elbow watching. I could feel his anxiety like a tangible veil washing over him, me, and probably the cameraman.

He leaned over and whispered in my ear, "Eric, I'm going to the office and get someone over here right away to replace her. I can't afford this!"

I knew I had to say something quickly, or she would be gone. Being an actor, I not only understood what was happening to her, but I had also been there more times than I could count. I backed up out of earshot and said, "Look, Roger, it's almost lunchtime. Give me an hour with her, and I know I can get her calmed down and focused."

He took a moment and then said, "O.K., but all you have is the lunch break. Do your miracles or she's gone!"

We went to her dressing room, and the first thing I did was elevate her ego state. I told her how beautiful she was and that I instinctively knew how talented she was. We talked for about fifteen minutes. All the while I was attempting to raise her confidence and self-esteem. She had no idea that Roger was thinking of replacing her. That would have only exacerbated her tension. I had her do some of the relaxation exercises I do in my classes, and then I led her through a selfless-involvement exercise, "observe, perceive, and wonder." She did it about the room, me, and everything else she felt curious about, which totally took her out of herself. At the end of the lunch break, just before she was going to do the scene she had had difficulty with, I told her to do the selfless-involvement exercise silently with the other actor in the scene. They were setting the lights and getting ready to do a rehearsal, when Roger appeared like a hawk high on a limb watching the proceedings. The director said, "O.K., let's make one," the camera started to roll, the action began, and Darlanne was terrific—letter perfect, involved, and with a wonderful quality. They printed the first take and were ready to move in for coverage. Roger came over, looked into my eyes, and said, "Well, that's what you're here for!" His attitude was, Well, what do you expect me to say, thanks? After that first take and our work, Darlanne was absolutely wonderful in the film. I worked with her a few more times on specific scenes, helping her to find the right choices. I was also able to get a number of my students on the film as extras and a couple of them in speaking roles.

I enjoyed acting in the film and liked having an antagonistic role. The fact that the character was not at all attractive in his behavior set me apart from the others. In that pivotal scene when the group was gathered around a large table discussing what to do about Sador's threat to the planet and all agreed to resist and fight him with enlisted outside help, my character objected and wanted to surrender to Sador's overwhelming power, reasoning that it would be suicide to resist. Before we were scheduled to film the scene, and while they were setting the lights, we were all in a motor home waiting to be called onto the set. I thought that it would be a wonderful opportunity to do some preparation for the scene, but I knew better than to suggest such a thing to all those *seasoned professionals*. Everyone was sitting around talking about a myriad of different things. Richard Thomas was extolling the joys of reading and writing poetry, Jeff Corey was talking about politics and some of what was happening in the world at the time, and the women were discussing their opinions about their costumes. I decided to use whatever *available stimuli* I could find to service the realities of the scene we were about to do. My character had an adversarial relationship with Richard's and thought he was a young boy without the knowledge or experience to go into battle. The reality was that I thought Richard was a pompous ass. I could totally use that available choice, and I also took advantage of my antithetical opinion about poetry by really criticizing amateurs who thought they could write poetry. I confronted Richard and some of the others, taking an opposite point of view to everything they believed in. Jeff was an acting teacher, as well as an actor, and had been the most recognized teacher of acting when I had started my career in Hollywood. He was very well respected, and I liked and respected him too, even though our individual approaches to teaching acting were very different. To parallel Feh's feelings for Zed, I chose to use as *available realities* what respect I had for Jeff's character on the one hand and, on the other, the fact that I thought he was too intellectual in his attitudes and conversations about almost everything. I also took exception to his political views, even if in reality I agreed with him. All in all, I didn't win any friends or influence the other actors except negatively towards me, which was exactly what the scene was about. They never knew what I was doing or why, but when we shot the scene, it all worked, for them and for me. I had about five scenes in the film, and I approached each of them, no matter how big or small, with preparations and specific choices that addressed the obligations in them. In the one where I got killed, zapped in the back by one of Sador's ray guns, I fell in George Peppard's arms, and he turned my body towards the camera so my face could be on the screen. I knew what he was doing, and after the scene was over, I thanked him, and he very graciously said, "We have to look out for each other." I worked for more than six weeks on the film and was quite relieved when it was over and I could return to my classes.

Shortly after that, in July of 1981, I started to work on my concept of the "ultimate consciousness." I had heard Lee say many times that the bulk of an actor's talent existed in the unconscious, and over the years, as I taught my classes, I had discovered that more and more exciting moments on the stage came from the unconscious. I had had several ultimate-consciousness experiences while in Marty's class, not knowing at the time that that was what they were. I began to develop exercises and approaches that were designed to pique unconscious responses. Over a period of time more than a dozen techniques evolved, which you can read about in my book *Acting from the Ultimate Consciousness.*

I was still considered a holy terror in that chair, even though I had mellowed somewhat from the sixties and seventies. I still yelled and screamed at actors when they were doing bullshit onstage, but I guided them into the arenas of reality. I wasn't ugly. I was very passionately involved in truth and organic life onstage.

As I said earlier, I traveled a lot in those days. In 1981 I went to New York four times; Austin, Texas, once; Houston three times; Salt Lake City once; and Park City, Utah, once also. I remember working in a variety of places in New York City, but I don't remember who was setting up the workshops for me at the time. In Austin, Mona Fultz contacted me and was responsible for setting up the weekends. An acting teacher, who had taught at the university there and had read my book, she was a real character with a bombastic personality. About forty years old, with frizzy, wild hair looking for a describable color, she was a little broad in the beam but otherwise somewhat attractive. Every time I appeared there, she told me, "You look tired and spent. Drop your pants, and I'll give you a vitamin B12 shot in the ass!" I never dropped my pants, not because I was shy, but because I hate needles and shots of any kind.

I don't recall who administrated the weekends in Houston, but I do remember that I held them in a space used by comedians as a standup venue. The owner was an actor, who was very happy to have me come there to teach. In Salt Lake City my administrator was Phyllis Guerini Moore. She called me and said that she had seen *No Acting Please* in a bookstore and that the title had intrigued her. She later told me it was like a book on losing weight without dieting! That had prompted her to call my number to ask me if I would come to Salt Lake to do a workshop. I did, and it started a long friendship. Phyllis was a trip in every sense of the word. A live wire, with curly brown hair, she was short and a little plump, but very well endowed, sexy, outspoken, and very funny. Her sense of humor was legendary. She had attended the professional acting school in New York on which the television series "Fame" was based, and she was living in Salt Lake with her tall, good-looking, very conservative husband, who was selling oilrig drills. A more unlikely pair I had never seen. How those two people had found each other will remain one of the mysteries in my life. Phyllis later came to L.A. and started taking my classes.

At the same time, I continued doing marathons in Lake Gregory. Over the years I must have done fifteen or more of those. I had one in February and another in July, entitled a "craft-and-being marathon." I also did a one-day sense-memory workshop on La Brea. All in all in 1981 I did a dozen weekend marathons, in addition to teaching four classes a week and about twenty-five private lessons.

Whenever I would come to a new city or even if I had been there once or twice, I would have to work with people I had never seen before, so I would ask them to introduce themselves, and pretty soon I would pick up on their tension, fears, and other issues and would ask them to do one of my exercises that addressed the problem. After a short time I got quite good at zeroing in exactly on what each person needed. The results were incredible. I would also have each person do a monologue and/or a scene and teach him or her how to use the craft. I did instrumental and craft exercises at each workshop. After I had worked in a specific city several times, the repeat actors began to do the work and carry it out into their professional involvements.

It was on one of those interminably long flights to and from New York that I discovered that article in *USA Today* which I talk about in my fifth book, and which so intrigued me that I started on a twenty-year journey to explore, experiment with, and create, new imaging approaches that could be used as acting tools. All of the materials I subsequently investigated dealt with mental imaging, and as effective as they were, I felt that imaging could be even more valuable if sensory work was included in the process. In my classes I did exercises using imaging as a choice approach, adding all five senses to the procedure. The results were amazing! In addition, I began to discover that imaging was *an incredible conduit to the unconscious.* Since Jung had said that "images are the language of the unconscious," it seemed perfectly natural to use imaging as a way to pique unconscious life. I began to explore its use in dreams and attempted to re-create elements of those dreams by imaging the objects and people in them. I figured that if those images came directly from the unconscious, I could appeal to the unconscious by re-creating the images. It didn't work all the time, but quite often it did. After many years and much exploration, the imaging process elevated to a megapproach. I wrote an entire book about it, entitled *Acting, Imaging and the Unconscious.* It includes an avant-garde section on programming the unconscious to do the acting.

In 1981 my second book, *Being & Doing,* was published by Quick Fox. Actually, it was a compilation of articles I had written for the *Dramalogue,* an acting trade paper in Los Angeles. I had started a column I called "The Craft Corner" and for more than two years had written one article a week on acting and my system. For the book, I separated the articles into three categories: "The Instrument," "The Craft," and "The Business." *Being & Doing* is a workbook for actors, which has blank pages for them to make notes on. They can open the book on any page and do the suggested exercises on that page that day.

At the end of that year and well into 1982 I directed *The Glass Menagerie.* I mentioned in chapter 3 how I had worked on the tech crew of that play at Northwestern, had fallen in love with it and decided that some day I was going to direct it. Joan Hotchkis assumed the role of Amanda; Erin Nico was Laura; Tony Morina started as Tom but later had to drop out and was replaced by Richard Hatch; and finally, to round out the cast, Billy Hayes played the "gentleman caller." Billy had been in class for less than two years, fresh from his escape from a Turkish prison. It had taken the better part of those years for him to recover from that traumatic ordeal.

We rehearsed at the La Brea location, marking off the set with tape on the floor to indicate the various rooms of the apartment. The rehearsal lasted for about eight months and I believe was the most important learning experience of the whole project in terms of craft. It was quite a long rehearsal period, filled with incredibly creative explorations. There was a heavy responsibility to the historic obligation, so we got the Time-Life books of that period, the thirties, and we read all of the historical information out loud, assimilating what was happening in the midst of the Great Depression and the war in Spain. We listened to President Roosevelt's speeches on recordings and discussed the events taking place in America at the time.

Erin Nico had to visit many curio shops in Hollywood and select her own collection of glass animals, making up stories and fantasies regarding each one. Sometimes she shared her stories with Richard, who played Tom. I encouraged Richard to write poetry and read it out loud to Erin. Joan, who, as the character, had to sell magazine subscriptions on the telephone, actually did that. She would call people and sell subscriptions to imaginary magazines. I also had her tell the others about her courtship years, which paralleled Amanda's experiences. I encouraged a natural animosity to build between Joan and Richard, while at the same time elevating Erin's insecurities so that she would become more and more dependent on Joan. Billy Hayes, who was eager to make up for those lost years in the Turkish prison, wanted to do things with his freedom and to accomplish things in his life. As the gentleman caller talks about his ambition to be on the ground floor of the new television industry and become successful, I encouraged Billy to use available-reality parallels from his own life. I feel that we were quite successful in establishing a familial ensemble between Amanda, Laura, and Tom, while Billy remained an outsider and created a very nice contrast to the others. So many of the obligations of the material became the realities of the actors that it was hard to distinguish between their emotional lives and the play—which was exactly my intention. Everyone in the cast was, or had been, my student, so we had a common language and worked with the same tools. Besides using available stimulus and parallel available realities, the actors also worked for choices that addressed the time-and-place obligations, as well as the relationship and emotional ones. They used endowments, imaginary dialogues, believability, sense memory, and in a few cases affective memory, as choices and choice approaches.

We rented the Callboard Theater, which was very nicely located on Little Melrose near La Cienega, and Erik White, one of my students and an excellent builder and carpenter, built the set for the play. It was an incredible set, replete with a wrought-iron fire-escape stairwell. My brother Phil, the stage manager, was assisted by his wife, Patricia—which turned out to be a blessing. Phil had been a Broadway stage manager for many years, had worked on many top Broadway shows, and had developed a reputation for being one of the best in the business, so it seemed rather strange that he had a lot of trouble remembering light and sound cues. Patricia often ran the board and took over some of the other duties of a stage manager as well. I didn't know it at the time, but my brother was already in the first stages of Alzheimer's then.

We had rented the theater for a specified number of weeks and were supposed to open at a certain time but were unable to do so because of set difficulties. I didn't feel we were technically ready to open. We therefore used three of those weeks as additional rehearsal time, for which we were paying theater rates. Unfortunately, this backfired on us later, when we wanted to continue a successful run but had to leave the Callboard Theater because another play had been scheduled there.

Another near tragedy happened just before we opened: We received a letter from Samuel French, informing us that there was some activity regarding the play and that we could not have the rights to do it. We already had thousands of dollars invested in the production, so we were crestfallen. Billy Hayes, who somehow knew Williams, jumped on a plane and went to the Florida Keys to see him. After a day or two, Williams told him, "It's my play, and I'm giving you the rights to do it!" So we were saved. We continued to prepare to open and finally did.

One evening during the run, just before we were about to go up, a middle-aged man appeared in the lobby of the theater and asked if he could see our production. I told him that we were sold out and that as an Equity-waiver theater we were only allowed ninety-nine seats. He replied that he was a neighbor and very close friend of Tennessee Williams and would very much like to see the play again after all those years. I immediately put up a folding chair for him. After the play was over, he came into the lobby and asked if he could use the telephone on the wall. "I want to call Tom and tell him what I just saw," he said. I was standing next to him when he spoke to Williams: "Tom, I just saw a production of *The Glass Menagerie* at a theater in Hollywood, and Tom, it was fantastic! You know I was there at the opening of the play on Broadway, and I'm telling you that this was better." I stood there in awe, probably with my mouth hanging open. "Tom," he continued, "you must jump on a plane and come to see this show!" Williams didn't come, I think because he was ill at the time.

We received wonderful reviews and had full houses for the most part, so we wanted to continue the run of the play. We scurried around Hollywood looking for another theater and luckily found that the Fountain Theater was available. It was not in as nice a location as the Callboard, and because the ceiling was too low for our set, Erik White had to cut the set down to fit the stage; but he did such a great job that it looked as if the set had been built for that theater. The cast was wonderful. Joan inhabited the character of Amanda. Since she and I had worked together for several years, we had developed a wonderful rapport. Erin Nico was also quite good as Laura. She was small and seemed fragile, which really worked physically as well as in craft terms. Richard was probably better than in anything he had done on television and made a better Tom than I had seen in any other production over the years. Billy was truly the gentleman caller. Most of our craft explorations had taken place in the rehearsal stages, so that by the time we opened the play the experiential realities had already been established. All in all, the experience was incredible for all of us. To this day, twenty-five years later, I still run into people who talk about how wonderful the play was.

My classes remained the same throughout 1982. I started working on subpersonalities a lot during that year. At first, I used the voice-dialogue system as an instrumental-therapy tool, another way of identifying and antidoting the actors' obstacles and blocks. Quite often and without consciousness, an actor is being run by a subpart that does not allow him the freedom to act. By becoming conscious of it, he establishes an awareness of the situation and can then move that subpersonality out of the driver's seat. The "protector-controller" is usually one of the subpersonalities that run interference for the actor, as it attempts to protect him from injury. While being an important subpart, it totally keeps him from being impulsive and expressive on a moment-to-moment basis. Of course, other subpersonalities also create obstacles. By doing voice dialogue in my classes, I was able to help my students establish an "aware ego" in relation to those parts. However, since I had not completely overcome the notion that my work with actors was too psychological, even though I had already been teaching for more than twenty years, after a very short time I stopped using subpersonalities as an instrumental tool and instead began structuring the technique as a megapproach for use in dealing with dramatic material.

Early in that year I received a call from my agent, who told me that the series "Fame" was looking for an acting teacher as a running regular on the show. He wanted me to stay by the telephone in case they called and asked me to come in for an audition. I was very excited. The show, which was based on the New York professional performing-arts school, was very popular and would be a very important step in my acting career. I waited by the phone for most of the day, until my agent finally called. "Hi, Eric," he began, "it's Harry Gold. Well, they saw your picture, and when I told them that you had been teaching for twenty years, they said, 'He doesn't look like an acting teacher!' "

Instead of being shattered I started to laugh. All those stories about Hollywood that had been bouncing around in my head for years all of a sudden seemed hilarious. However, I did get a part on the show much later that year. In an episode entitled "Teachers," I played a visiting teacher who was coming from another theater-arts school to compete in an acting contest at the "Fame" school. My big scene was with the man who was playing the music teacher on the series. He was a man in his sixties, who was actually a music teacher from a real school. According to the story, he had done something to sabotage my students and prevent them from winning the dramatic competition. My character was outraged and confronted him with a great deal of anger and rage. I worked for a specific choice related to the actor and used a variety of available realities to really attack him verbally in the scene. Midway through my tirade he backed out of the frame, and the director stopped shooting the scene.

The old actor looked at me, a little pale, and said, "Are you angry with me?"

At first I was taken aback by the question, but then I replied, "Yes, I am angry with you, and I'm supposed to be!"

At that point the director pulled me aside and said, "Listen, Eric, he's not really an actor, and he is taking your anger very personally."

"Isn't that what he should be doing?" I asked.

"Well, yes, but he doesn't understand it, so would you lighten up a little with him?"

"Sure, but I still have a responsibility to the scene."

We did another take, and I toned it down some, but I was even angrier than I had been originally. I recalled that several months earlier they had said I didn't look like an acting teacher, and so they had hired a music teacher who wasn't an actor! The director printed the second take, which I felt didn't serve the scene as well as the first one.

I continued to do weekend workshops all over the country and in that year managed to do eighteen marathons, only three of them in Los Angeles. I had established relationships with people who became my administrators in each of the cities. Most of them were actors eager to be taught by me, so they were happy to set up the weekends. I did three in New York, two in Austin, three in Houston, two in Seattle, two in Atlanta, two in Salt Lake City, and one in Miami. I was flying all over the country, while still teaching four classes a week and quite a number of private lessons in Los Angeles. My relationship with the various administrators was ongoing and in some cases lasted several years. In Seattle Ann Graham, who had a school there, the Northwest Actors Studio, contacted me. I recently spoke to her on the telephone and asked her how we had gotten together, and she said, "I was doing Strasberg techniques in my classes at the time and was not satisfied with all of the gaps in the approach. I stumbled upon *No Acting Please* and was blown away by it, so I called you!" I started doing weekend workshops at her studio a couple of times each year and sometimes more often than that. Ann, who was the artistic director, and Meg, her associate artistic director, both taught classes. About a year after I started flying up there, they came to Los Angeles and took my classes for two weeks. I thought it was quite courageous of them to close down the school to come and observe my work. Ann got so deeply involved with it that she named a rehearsal room at her studio after me. It is still called the Morris Room.

Traveling to the various cities to do workshops was a meaningful component in the evolution of my system. I have often thought that we are one country divided by many regions, levels of consciousness, cultural involvements, priorities, religious influences, language, colloquialisms, and environmental inhibitions and taboos. Well, when working outside urban areas such as New York and Los Angeles, I encountered many behavioral issues that I had to address and in most cases antidote so that the actor I was working with could be emotionally free to act. I found that most of the people had social blocks and dependencies. Many new exercises were added to my repertoire of techniques for liberating the actors. I depended heavily on personal inventories of various kinds, stressing that the actor really get in touch with what he or she was truly feeling. I did antisocial workouts, conflict encounters with real and imaginary people, "You never gave me" tantrums, raunch-and-sleaze workouts, and so on. I realized that there were problems all people have in common, but as I traveled around, it became quite clear that there are also enormous differences in people from different areas of the country and world. Those experiences were responsible for dimensionalizing my process in instrumental as well as in craft areas. I was working with people I didn't know, and when I asked them to do a monologue, I was amazed at how representational they were. Most of the time I used exercises and techniques I had created for my own classes, but quite frequently I had to invent new approaches, because the students would not have understood those I had been using in Los Angeles. No matter where I went, with few exceptions, the actors I worked with had no process or craft. When I asked them how they had approached the monologue they had just done, they couldn't answer that question except in the most general, cerebral way. My emphasis with each of them was to establish reality to express what they really felt in the moment. I used a variety of instrumental exercises, ranging from expurgatives to intimate emotional sharing and different vulnerability techniques. To address the monologues, I asked them to do imaginary monologues with real people in their lives, as well as sharing monologues about things that really affected them. At the point where they were the most involved with real impulses, I would direct them to do the words of the monologue. The difference between what they had started doing and what they experienced from a place of reality was magical. It is a strange thing that happens to actors when they feel the difference between reality and impositional acting. They may not immediately be able to repeat the experience, but they are never again content with the lack of reality in their work.

In the early eighties, a student of mine in San Francisco told me that she had worked with Warren Robertson in New York and that his work was very similar to mine. That intrigued me, so on one of my weekends in New York I called him, and we had lunch. We hit it off immediately. We spoke for hours about acting and our classes, sharing ideas and discoveries about actors. Warren was tall and good-looking, seemed spiritual and somewhat mystical, and had a charismatic way about him. He was teaching a number of classes in a four-story building on Forty-fourth Street, within a few blocks of the United Nations building. It was a very nice space, which could accommodate several classes going on at the same time. Larry Moss was teaching for Warren at the time—a musical acting class, as I recall. Larry's ex-wife, whose name escapes me, was taking my classes and was also teaching acting somewhere in New York. Warren and I got really close over a period of time. We would get together every time I was in New York. At one of our lunch meetings he even asked me to move to New York, remarking, "Together we could take over the whole city as teachers of acting!" I was very flattered that he felt that way, but I told him that I couldn't live in New York. The New York energy was quite different from life in California, and the weather would kill me. Having grown up in Chicago, I had had enough winter snow and cold to last me two lifetimes.

I had never seen Warren teach, and he had never seen any of my classes either, but we decided to teach each other's classes. For two weeks he would teach in L.A. while I took over his classes in New York. However, when I told him that my Monday class was not an acting class, he freaked: "I don't do psychology! I'm an acting teacher. I teach actors and professionals!" I tried to explain it to him, but he didn't get it, so I cancelled the Monday class for the time I was in New York. It has been my experience that most of the New York teachers and coaches are paranoid about the personal nature of my work. I have already explained how Lee Strasberg would not let an actor expose anything personal when he talked about what he worked for in a scene. I stayed in Warren's apartment off Madison Avenue, and he stayed in my house in the Hollywood Hills. I took Joy with me on that trip, since I was going to be gone for two weeks. I thought that she could enjoy New York and have a little vacation at the same time.

Teaching the first of Warren's classes for the first time was a really unsettling experience. The first woman got up on the stage and did a monologue, supposedly staring out of a window. She was looking directly at a blank wall! After she finished the monologue, I asked her what she had done, how she had approached the material. Why was she staring at a blank wall, two feet away from her? She had no real answer about how she had stimulated the emotional life of the character, and she said that she had imagined there was a window there. When I suggested any kind of technique or craft process, she became very defensive. It was the same for the next three people. They all had general and vague responses to my question of how they had approached their scene or monologue. Joy leaned forward and whispered in my ear, "We are in trouble here!" And I was! From teaching Warren's classes I learned that the only similarity in our work was that he did some large expurgative release preparations to free the actors from their tension, but that was as far as the similarities went. I got through the two weeks as well as I could and had some success in unlocking a few craft doors for the people who were open to my approach.

Sometime in 1982 I was invited to watch a videotape of a show about lie detectors. It was a semi-documentary and was being considered by Sandy Frank, a very successful syndicator of what I believe was "schlock" television: innocuous game shows and the like. Sandy was dating Gayle, a friend of Joy's and mine. To describe Sandy one would say that if he were an actor he would be cast as a Jewish vampire in that kind of film, or you might say that he was the member of the Addams family who never appeared on camera! He was tall, very pale, with dark black hair and deep-set eyes that seemed to be searching for something. On various occasions Joy and I would meet him and Gayle for dinner. Watching Sandy eat was like a bonus floor show. Whatever was on his plate—fish, foul, or meat—he would violently stick it with his fork as if he thought he had to kill it before putting it into his mouth. On one of those evenings out he invited Joy and me to watch a videotape that had been done a few years earlier. The show was about people taking lie-detector tests, and for whatever reason Sandy was interested in developing a new show based on the premise. After watching the tape, I gave him a critique that so obviously impressed him that he asked me if I would sign on as creative consultant. He had contracted F. Lee Bailey to be the moderator of the show. Bailey was a famous lawyer with a wild reputation, who had defended Patty Hearst, among other notorious people, and who many years later would become part of "the dream team" at O.J. Simpson's murder trial. Bailey was officiating at a boat show in Chicago at the time, and Sandy wanted me to fly there and introduce myself to him as someone who was going to work with him, coach him, and so on.

I checked into a hotel in Chicago pretty late at night. I was exhausted, so I went directly to sleep. I woke up fairly early the next morning and made my way down to the convention center where the boat show was. It was fairly easy spotting Bailey. He had a group of people gathered around him and was speaking to them about anything but boats. I went over to him, hanging a little bit behind the others, and I waited for an opening in the crowd to get closer to him. F. Lee Bailey is a compact man, with wide shoulders and a square body. He exudes confidence, and his sense of himself is larger than his body. I caught his eye and said, "I am Eric Morris, and Sandy Frank sent me here to meet you and work with you." I should have stopped with "meet you," because when I said "work with you," he looked at me with an oh-yeah-what-the-hell-are-you-going-to-do-for-me look. We spoke for a few moments, and I pulled up all of my charm and creative-manipulation abilities and did the best I could to ingratiate myself with him. I told him how honored I was to be associated with him on this project and that I had been a fan of his work over the years.

We flew back to Los Angeles together that afternoon and bonded quite well. He asked me what I did and how I had gotten involved with the project. I told him about the books I had written and about my take on acting and reality. He seemed impressed. He spoke about his work, and I asked him specific questions about Patty Hearst and some of his other clients. He seemed very open to talking about them. He told me about a client he had gotten off, who had killed his wife and claimed that it was an accident. They had been arguing, and while he was working with his 30-30 Winchester lever-action rifle or cleaning it, she had grabbed its barrel and pulled on it, and it had gone off, hitting her squarely in the chest and killing her almost immediately. The man had claimed that the hammer had been at a half-cocked position, that the gun should not have fired in that position, but that it had. Bailey had brought in an expert from the Winchester firm to testify that the rifle was faulty because it had fired the bullet from that position.

I listened to the story intently, and when he was finished I said, "You know, Lee, I am a gun collector. I have two Winchesters just like that one, and it isn't a half-cocked position the hammer is in, it is a quarter-cocked position, and I'm pretty sure that from that place the hammer does not have a full-throw capability to drive the firing pin into the primer of the cartridge." He looked at me with a look I cannot describe. I continued: "If I had been on that jury, I would have asked that the rifle demonstrate its ability to fire off a round from a quarter-cocked position."

He took a moment to respond and then said, "You son of a bitch, I'm glad you weren't on that jury." I guess, as we moved closer to Los Angeles, he and I established more of a relationship and a greater sense of mutual respect.

The show was shot at a studio in Hollywood and was going to be distributed by ABC Television in syndication. A series of people who had been accused of a crime, or been somehow connected to one, were interviewed and then given a lie detector test. As the narrator-moderator, Lee would introduce the subject and give legal commentary on each of the tests and the results. Sandy was able to get some famous or infamous people to be interviewed and tested: the wife of Bruno Richard Hauptmann, the man who had been convicted of kidnapping the Lindbergh baby and had been tried and executed in the thirties; the security guard who had spotted the break-in at the Watergate Hotel and had been arrested later for stealing some sneakers at a K-mart; Zsa Zsa Gabor; and others I don't remember, but in order for the show to be interesting, each person had some visibility. The man who was giving the tests was a professional lie-detector expert and would interpret the results immediately following the interview. The production staff was comprised of some of the producers of the original show that had been done several years before, and the asshole franchise was rampant! They were typical business techie types, who would have been appalled at having a single cell of creativity inhabit their person. After giving the test to Mrs. Hauptmann, they concluded that she had not passed it, but because she was such an old lady, they decided not to use it on the air. I personally thought that was a humane decision. For heaven's sake, how could she remember all the details of what had happened fifty years before?

I was there to assist, coach Lee, and generally give creative input to Sandy and the entire project. Between interviews Sandy would come over to me and ask for any suggestions I had. I made some helpful comments, but it wasn't as though I was dealing with acting or the techniques involved in drama. I was able to stay close enough to Lee to give him some creative input on his presentation, but for the most part he did what he was very expert at doing. He and I developed a warm relationship, and he even invited me to his wedding, which I was unable to attend because I was off somewhere teaching a weekend workshop.

In 1983 I again traveled a lot. I started going to New York more often—seven times that year. I cancelled the Monday class in L.A., as my New York weekends were extended to three days, the third day being a master class, where we did scenes and monologues exclusively. In June I also started a master class in L.A. on Tuesdays, it too exclusively for scenes and monologues, by invitation only. I chose the most advanced people from my other two classes, so that we could approach material with some higher knowledge of the process. My personal goal was to ultimately produce projects and plays that represented my system. I was also still doing weekend workshops in other parts of the country besides New York. I spent so much time on planes that I received free flights and numerous upgrades to first class. I had been teaching for twenty-three years, and my work had become more dimensional thanks to the intense number of workshops and people I was working with. Besides the vast quantity of instrumental exercises I was inventing, I was adding new choice approaches and other craft techniques. I really think that had it not been for my travels I would not have been able to create such a complete system of acting. It is entirely true that necessity is the mother of invention.

That year Hal Stone and I did a two-day workshop in Houston. I don't remember how it came about, but Hal took the first day to do voice dialogue and other subpersonality techniques with all of the people, and I took the second day to translate subpersonalities to acting. It was a very successful weekend. The most amazing thing was that Hal had all the students doing voice dialogue with each other within the first half hour of the workshop. I asked him if he thought that might be dangerous, but he said that there was no danger at all, because the "protector-controller" of the person being facilitated would keep that person from going into areas in which he or she didn't feel safe. At that point I had already been working with Hal for a number of years and felt totally comfortable with the subpersonality process.

Around that time, I received another call from Roger Corman, this time informing me that he was going to do a film called *Space Raiders* and that the author, Howard R. Cohen, who was to direct it, had not had a lot of film-directing experience and needed someone to help him set up all the shots. So would I come and camera block the film with him? Roger had bought an old lumber company in Venice and turned it into a movie studio, where we had already done *Battle beyond the Stars.* When I arrived on the set, it looked oddly familiar, and that's because for the most part it was the same one that had been used for *Battle!* There were some modifications, subtractions and additions, but it was the same set. Roger is a master at getting the most out of everything and everyone. While in Ireland, he and his brother had spotted a group of World War I double-winged biplanes and decided to make the film about Von Richthofen that I mentioned earlier.

Space Raiders starred Vince Edwards and a number of other actors whose names it would be hard to put a face to. I worked with Howard on structuring the camera angles on every scene. Whenever we didn't agree, we would discuss it and come up with a suitable compromise. He was easy to work with and very open to my input. I think we did the entire job in about a week, before shooting began. I was able to get some of my people on the film as extras and atmosphere: Brooks Clift was in most of the group scenes, and my brother Phil also worked on the film. Life is funny! It was Phil who had gotten me my first job in summer stock in 1951, and now, in 1983, I was able to get him work, which he needed not only for the money, but also for his morale. As I said before, Phil had had a pretty good career as a stage manager on Broadway. He had later gotten involved with Harry Belafonte as his producer and partner and had enjoyed a very successful eleven years with him; but when they parted, Phil tried a number of projects, all of which failed in one way or another. When he moved to Los Angeles, he couldn't find a niche and became quite depressed.

He had been a wonderful brother to me when I was growing up. He had spent many Saturdays with me at the movies, had taken me to plays and was responsible for my classical-music education. He had bought me recording devices and movie projectors and had always been willing to listen to anything I had to say. He had been very instrumental in my growth and evolution as a youngster and an early teenager. He had then gone to New York to pursue his career, and we had lost that connection, until he moved to Los Angeles almost twenty years later. So I was very happy to do anything I could to help him at that time. He had already helped me with some of the business aspects of my classes, and I had hired him to stage-manage *The Glass Menagerie* a couple of years earlier.

That same year one of my students, Michael Green, who incidentally is the one on the cover of *Being & Doing*, recommended me for a part on a movie called *Wavelength,* a science-fiction film in which aliens land at a facility in Laurel Canyon. It was the part of a naval captain, who was also a doctor and who had been called in to examine the body of one of the crashed dead aliens. It was a very good part with many scenes, including a terrific death scene. As I've mentioned before, I love playing death scenes. I probably won't do as good a job with the real thing when I die! I had a full beard, as I still do, and the writer-director, Mike Gray, really liked its look for the role, since in the navy it is legal for an officer to have a beard. I auditioned in a small office and read with Bobby Carradine, the half-brother of one of my students, Michael Bowen. Bobby was playing the leading role in the film and had heard really good things about me, so he was very anxious to work with me.

We filmed almost the entire film at a closed military installation in San Pedro. I am very demanding about my work and somewhat critical also, but I must say that I thought I did pretty good work on that film. I used my military experience to approach the role and found various parallels from my own life that addressed the character; for example, by that time I had been pursuing an acting and teaching career for more than twenty years, while the character had been a doctor and naval officer for an equivalent amount of time and was equally passionate about his work. I was also able to carry my knowledge of military protocol and the power of my rank into the work. In one of the scenes, I was supposed to be operating on one of the dead aliens. Since the actor assisting me was a real surgeon, named Milt Cogan, he took me through all the procedures for holding the scalpel and making the incision into the chest of the alien. I called the coroner's office and asked if I could observe an autopsy, explaining why I needed to do it, but of course they turned me down. I did other research on the obligations of the character, but after all this time it is somewhat vague.

Shortly after that, my agent set me up for an audition for "Days of Our Lives," a daily soap. I had never before seen myself as acting in a soap opera or doing commercials—not that I think it is a bad thing for actors to do, since we all have to pay our bills and make a living. In any case, I went to the audition and got the part of a psychiatrist who worked at a state institution. I had one scene, but a solid one, with the woman playing the lead on the show. She wanted to know my impressions of the mental state of a patient we had both been working with.

I walked into her office on the set, looked around the room, and sat down. She started to speak to me; I responded; and she went blank. We did the scene again and again, but to no avail. She couldn't come up with the next line. Embarrassed, she explained that she was getting so involved with listening to me that she kept going up. They finally had to put her lines on a board so she could read them while relating to me. After we did the scene, the producer approached me and told me that I had been so real and so unlike a soap-opera actor in behavior and style that I had thrown her. He congratulated me on a fine performance and said he hoped to work with me again. That was my one and only soap-opera experience!

By 1984 I had started going back and forth to New York every other weekend, while continuing to travel to Washington, Houston, and San Francisco. Looking back on all of that, I wonder where my energy came from. I suspect it was the inspiration and excitement I felt for the work.

My administrator for the Washington, D.C., workshops was a guy by the name of Mike Barbary. I mention him because he was a real character. A representative for a pharmaceutical company, he was supposed to go out each day to visit doctors and give them free samples of drugs, so that they would write prescriptions for their patients. When I was teaching in Washington, I stayed at his apartment, and in all that time I never once saw him go out and do his job. He would sit at the dining-room table and memorize lines for scenes he was going to do in the workshop. Acting was his major love, and he was willing to do anything to promote himself as an actor. In spite of a legion of shortcomings, he was a good administrator. He became quite involved with the work, even moving to New York later and also attending jamborees in Los Angeles.

In my Tuesday master class in Los Angeles people started to develop projects. In February, Dutch Schultz (not the notorious gangster!) and Kent De Marche started working on *Lunchtime,* which they presented as a work in progress later and at the jamboree in July. Alice Champlain and Fran Cobb Vincent were working on *'night, Mother,* and in May, Tony Lani and Byron Teegarten started to work on *Mass Appeal.* All of those projects were ultimately to be produced as plays. The first time I directed *'night, Mother,* therefore, came out of the class. Both actresses were my students. Fran Cobb played the mother, and Alice Champlain, her daughter, and the two worked for several months on various scenes from the play. After each scene, as was the protocol of the class, they would discuss their process, and I would critique the work and tell them where I thought they should go next. They approached every scene that way. When I thought they were ready to put it all together, I asked them to do the whole play in class. It was lovely! It had evolved in the workshop and was truly a work in progress that had progressed. We presented it the following year to all the classes in L.A. on April 2 and at a jamboree in New York in May. It was received with raves from the students. Eight to ten years later I actually directed and mounted the play with a different cast as part of the American New Theater at the Cahuenga space.

The first bicoastal jamboree had actually taken place from July 9 through 13, 1984. New York and other out-of-town students stayed with L.A. students. This was the way we had designed the bicoastal thing: When we had a jamboree in New York, the L.A. people would stay with the New York students, and vice versa. The host city would alternate between the East and West coasts. I called them jamborees because they started attracting people from all over the United States and even other parts of the world. I had taken the name from the Boy Scouts. Once a year all the troops from all over the United States get together in a single place for a week, exchange information, and share stories and games. Those meetings are called jamborees.

The '84 jamboree was also the unofficial start of the American New Theater, which, however, did not become official until 1986. I was the artistic director, and my associate and assistant artistic director was Michele Martin, a talented actress, who had been working in New York and was now here. Even though we hadn't officially launched the group, we started a newsletter on both coasts. The American New Theater was to be a bicoastal theater dedicated to doing 50 percent new material and the rest plays that were established. That, however, never panned out. We did have play-reading committees, which read a number of original plays and sometimes had staged readings of those plays. In fact, one of my brother Ed's plays was later read by the New York contingent. It was cast right out of the membership, and we invited some outside people to watch it, but it was never mounted into a full production. Later, we established a writers' unit on both coasts to bring in original material, and in 1986 the writers in the group were even invited to sit in on the acting classes to get a better idea of the process and the goal of the plays. The original plan was to do plays in both cities and then switch. The New York play would move to a venue in Los Angeles, and the Los Angeles play would perform in New York. Somehow that never happened, though. I really don't know why, since it was such a great idea.

All of the students in the master class were encouraged to work on projects and to develop them as works in progress. Those particular projects that cried out to be productions were supposed to achieve that status. The thrust of the American New Theater was to do the work. Being, irreverence, reality, and organic life were the goals of every project and play. At that time I had not yet begun to use the expression "professional experiencer," but it was indigenous to everything we did. As the years progressed, not only did the meaning become more specific, but the ingredients of experiential acting developed also. Everyone was excited about the American New Theater and the work. Some of the best work we did evolved during those years.

Nineteen eighty-five was a banner year for me. Not only was I traveling all over the country, doing plays and projects, but I also had *Irreverent Acting* published. Putnam distributed the book, but I was responsible for its printing and production work. Danny Spelling and Scarlett Gani put it together. Even though Putnam had acquired the rights to *No Acting Please* and *Being & Doing,* I didn't trust them to control the rights to this, my third book. They never told me when or whether they were going to reprint the books or take them out of print, so I felt that I had no control over them.

Irreverent Acting was the craft book. It was totally dedicated to the craft process and my system. At the time of its publication in 1985 there were twenty-two choice approaches, but since then I have added nine more over the years. That summer I also recorded five ninety-minute audiotapes called *The Craft of Acting,* which included all of the twenty-two choice approaches plus dozens of preparation exercises, as well as a complete exploration and definition of the seven material obligations. I also listed dozens of choices to give examples of what choices were.

In the middle of the year I had the La Brea studio remodeled from a rectangle shape to a proscenium-type theater in order to present plays in the venue. As a result, I stopped doing rounds at the end of each class. I also ceased using sensuality as part of the preparation cluster, I'm not sure why. My involvement with the American New Theater did not deter my specificity in teaching my classes. If anything, I was more demanding of craft specificity. In addition to a very busy schedule in New York, I was able to do three weekend marathons in San Francisco, two in D.C., one in Lake Arrowhead, and a one-day workshop in Sacramento.

At the end of 1985 we mounted a production of *Mass Appeal.* As was my style, we had worked on it for about a year. Several projects started as scenes in class. The actors would bring in a scene from a given play, and I would critique it afterwards, often working with them to create a greater organic reality. I was famous for saying, "I didn't believe it! What were you working for?" Quite frequently I would tell the actors to forget the lines and talk about their experience or the content of their choices. That technique worked almost every time. Sometimes the actors would bring in successive scenes from the same play and work on them. Ultimately, after many months, they had worked on the whole play, and that is how some of the projects were mounted.

There were only two characters in *Mass Appeal,* the older priest and the young Jesuit student. As memory serves me, the young student had been having sexual-identity issues and had somehow come into conflict with the head priest of the school, who didn't like him at all. Byron Teegarten, who was playing the older priest, took the young student under his wing and attempted to help him. Since it is a relationship play, I had the actors spend as much time together as was possible. At that point in time I hadn't started doing scene parallels yet (I'll talk about that later), but I would ask the actors to talk to each other about their personal lives, including the elements that somehow paralleled the contents of the play. I told Byron that Tony, like the character, had issues with his sexual identity and that he too had had some homosexual encounters in the past. That wasn't at all true, but I felt that with this information Byron would have a strong empathy for Tony, which was right for their relationship. I instructed Byron not to tell Tony what I had told him and never to let Tony know that he knew about it. It worked! Byron's attitude towards Tony became much more sympathetic, and there was a real concern that translated into the play. They started to accomplish an ensemble relationship, and by the time we opened, the work was wonderful. We ran the play for several weeks, and I believe it was the last one we did in the La Brea venue. On the evening of the last performance I took Byron and Tony aside and confessed to them what I had told Byron. I expected them to be angry with me, but the response was quite positive, and they both laughed. I don't usually direct actors in that way. I was always angry at Kazan for doing things like that, so it was unusual for me to have planted that lie in Byron's mind, even though it worked and I believe was almost totally responsible for the success of their relationship.

Late in '85 or early in '86 I received a call from a government organization that was conducting a third-world tour of the United States, primarily the theater and movie centers, such as New York and Los Angeles. The man I spoke to said that groups from Africa, the Philippines, and other small third-world countries were involved and that a woman film director from the Philippines had requested an interview with me. He asked if I would make time to see her. My initial response was, "O.K., but I don't know anyone in the Philippines, and I can't imagine what she wants to see me about." A few days later, this small, attractive Filipino woman in her early forties walked up the stairs to my studio on La Brea. She sat down, seemed quite nervous, and started to speak in very good English.

"I imagine that you are wondering why I requested to meet with you," she said.

"Well, yes," I responded, "I am a little confused."

After a short pause she continued, "Well, I know that you don't know me, but we know you. You see, we have been doing your work for a number of years now. We have been using it in the classes we teach and in the films we make, and we have had incredible results with your process. We think of you as the Stanislavski of the Philippines."

I was speechless for several minutes. I finally replied, "I'm not sure what to say, since I was totally ignorant of this whole thing. Of course, I'm very flattered!"

We spoke for about half an hour. She continued telling me about the actors and directors who were using the work and how their acting had improved and grown. Then she came to the reason she was here: "Would you consider coming to the Philippines and teaching at our workshop for a couple of weeks? Your government will arrange everything, including your salary."

I told her that I would have to work out my teaching schedule but that I was interested. The arrangements were later made for me to go there, but as a revolution was taking place, I opted not to go until the following year—which I'll get into later.

In February of 1986 the American New Theater opening ceremonies were held at the La Brea theater. An ANT charter and articles of incorporation were written, and we received tax-exempt status as a nonprofit organization. At the same time the New York people started ANT New York and were immediately well organized. A group of actors from the workshops assumed the positions of running the company and created a charter based on the one we had drawn up in Los Angeles. Katie Bull, whom I had originally met when, at eighteen, her aunt had brought her to one of my Los Angeles classes, was now permanently in New York and several years older. She held the ANT meetings and took copious notes at every session. She was also very instrumental in choosing the material to be read and passed on for staged readings and future performances. At a recent weekend workshop I did in New York, Katie dropped by with her little girl, who is as beautiful as she is. Leann Enos was another very important part of the ANT group. She and her husband, Randy, an artist who regularly attended the workshops, worked very hard to establish ANT and our theater activities in New York. It was a family thing, since Randy and Leann had two sons who also took my weekend workshops and appeared in projects. Randy designed the imaginative ANT logo on our stationery and business cards. There were many others who contributed their time and energies to making ANT work. I had many administrators, all from the classes, who set up the bimonthly workshops. Bob Walsh was probably the one I most counted on.

In Los Angeles we jumped right in and started to do one-act plays and staged readings. After *Mass Appeal,* one of the first things we did was *It's Called the Sugar Plum,* with Tony Lani and Linda Ewing, followed by *Sister Mary Ignatius Explains It All for You,* directed by one of my students, Ron Salley. We had a dress rehearsal for an invited audience March 7 and 8, and the plays were scheduled to open on March 14 and run through May. Unfortunately, my theater burned down on Easter Sunday. I received a call from the owner of the building, telling me that the kitchen store next door had had an electrical fire, which had burned right through the walls of my theater and destroyed almost everything, and that what hadn't been destroyed by the fire had been waterlogged by the firemen who were putting it out. I was essentially theaterless.

I had to scurry around Hollywood looking for a suitable place to start an Equity-waiver theater. I contacted rental agencies, drove all over Hollywood looking for lease signs, frantic to get a place where I could continue to teach my classes. One of the agencies I talked to found a place, the one on Cahuenga, which must have been a storage facility, since it was just an open space with no plumbing and one electric light bulb hanging on a frayed wire in the middle of the room. The walls were just wooden planks, and the floor was pockmarked and discolored cement. Sal and Alba Morino, who owned the property, also had an Italian restaurant on the other side of the street towards the corner of Sunset Boulevard. Called Martoni's, it was a very popular place for the show-business crowd and certainly in a lot better shape than the storage facility where they kept their old kitchen equipment. I made a deal with Alba to take the place "as is," knowing that it would take a lot of money and time to make it into a theater. However, after immediately installing a toilet, I was able to teach my classes there. I took a second mortgage on my house and enlisted a few of my students who had some construction ability. Erik White, who had many talents in construction, electrical work, and plumbing and who was also a member of the American New Theater, started building the theater with the help of a dozen or so others who volunteered to work with him. The space had eight four-by-four wooden columns running through the center of the room, which were there to hold up the roof. Of course, they had to go, and fifteen thousand dollars later they were gone! It took the better part of two years, at a cost of over one hundred thousand dollars, to finish the project. We did, however, work in the space at every stage of development. We had a company. At completion the theater was beautiful. I had purchased all the lights, light board, sound equipment, and theater seats from a theater in Hollywood that was closing. We painted the walls a dark maroon and carpeted the entire place, except for the stage, in a contrasting dark blue color. The stage built by Erik White was huge, probably the largest of any Equity-waiver theater in Los Angeles.

That same year I started doing weekend workshops in Tampa. Kathy Laughlin, a casting director, contacted me and began to bring me there about three or four times a year. Her office was in a house in the Hyde Park district of the city. I taught the workshops in the living room of that house, a two-story frame house probably built in the early forties, with a lot of rococo wood scattered around the walls and entrances to the rooms, which did nothing but obstruct easy access to the living room. Kathy had a partner named Lillian, and what it was that Lillian did I never knew, but she was always sitting on the stairs with Kathy, watching me teach the workshops. This went on for a couple of years. I recently learned that Kathy had started teaching classes the year I came to Tampa. There were a lot of interesting people in the workshops. Some of them were actors who worked in and around Florida, as did Debbie Barone, who came to every workshop, did instrumental exercises as well as scenes, and later taught for Kathy. Kathy later moved out of that house to a larger space in the Town-and-Country area of Tampa. That space had more of a theater structure, with a stage of sorts and director's chairs in the audience section. I continued going to Tampa three or four times a year into 1993 and then dropped down to once a year until 1997.

On June 17 and 18 in New York we did a staged reading for invited audiences of Saroyan/Inge one acts, *Bus Riley's Back in Town* and *Hello Out There,* directed by Ron Orbach at the Cubiculo Theater. I felt split between two families, my New York people and my L.A. people. We did come together in jamborees, and there was communication between the people on opposite coasts, but the energy was different. I attempted to bring to L.A. some of the serious theater energy that emanated from New York, and I tried to get the

New York people to temper their energy with a little more of a Los Angeles kickback attitude. I figured they could learn something from each other.

The New York workshops on alternate weekends were incredible! The work and the involvement of the students were inspiring. I had already taught in a number of different places there. I had started on Eighth Avenue between Forty-second and Forty-third Streets, in a kind of dingy place as I remember. From there I had moved to the Harold Clurman Theater on Forty-second and Ninth Avenue. I liked that place the best. The acting studios were upstairs, and downstairs was the Samuel Beckett Theatre. That whole street is called Theatre Row because it is home to a dozen off-Broadway types of theaters. Sally Kirkland was teaching a class directly across from me. Our breaks seemed to coincide with each other, so we would stand in the hallway and talk about the work we were doing. Then I moved to a union building on Fifteenth Street, which had a small theater space in the basement. Another acting teacher sublet the space to me on my visits to New York. He taught a combination of British and American acting, and his wife, Eva Meckler, interviewed me for a book she was writing, called *The New Generation of Acting Teachers.* It contained about fifteen, possibly twenty, interviews—mostly New York teachers with a smattering of L.A. and college teachers. Later, the union building was sold and we had to move again. I found a place on Eighteenth Street, also in the basement, with several apartments right above the theater space. Every time we had a large or loud exercise the tenants above would pound on their floor and yell at us to be quiet. To say the least it was quite a nightmare being there.

A lot of people from the eighties are still in my life and still involved with the work. Anthony Vincent Bova has become a teacher of my system and represents it in New York. He had originally appeared at one of my weekend workshops in 1986. A dancer performing on Broadway in *Cats,* he was a short, wiry guy with black, curly hair, and an incredibly winning smile. Ron Orbach is a busy New York actor, who frequently appears on Broadway. Elkanah Burns, a lawyer who had a successful law firm in D.C. at the time, came to a workshop there, got hooked on the work, and took a train to New York every time I was there. He became so involved with acting and the work that he eventually moved to Los Angeles to pursue an acting career. I see him frequently.

One evening in 1986, I was standing in the parking lot of my theater on Cahuenga, preparing to do my class, when in drives who I thought was Willie Nelson in a 1950 rust-colored Chevy coupe. I was sure it was Willie, until he came closer to me, flashing a set of bright white teeth. He had long hair, braided like Willie's, and similar facial features. He extended his hand and said, "Hi, I'm Lobo, and I would like to study with you." He told me that his real name was Welmon Nelson but that he was not related to Willie. He had recently given up being an "outlaw motorcycle dude" and had decided to pursue a different career. Lobo was a nickname that I think he had acquired while hanging out with all those other Harley outlaws. They are referred to as *outlaws,* but they are not really bank robbers, or criminals of any other kind. They ride around, drink, party, and sometimes get into conflict with each other or with rival motorcycle gangs.

Lobo had been married and been a member of the corporate world for a number of years. As such, he had probably worn a suit and tie. After his marriage had failed, however, he had given up that world and gone in a totally different direction. For a while, he had lived in a sort of shack in the wilderness of Arizona, before coming to Los Angeles, where he lodged in a trailer on the beach.

He started my class, cut his hair after a while, and did some very good work in exercises and scenes. I thought that he was quite talented and seemed motivated. He was in class for several years, and we became very close friends. He is now married to a wonderful woman, continues to pursue his acting career, and is quite busy doing commercials. Lobo has been like a brother to me. His heart is bigger than the chest that houses it, and I truly love him.

On June 25, 1986, I received a beautiful citation in a framed plaque from the then mayor of Los Angeles, Thomas Bradley, and the L.A. City Council for my "contribution to the arts in L.A." It was a big surprise and one that genuinely moved me. You never know who's watching what you do!

In New York Pam Shaw and Bob Walsh decided to do the play *Split* by Michael Weller, and since they wanted me to direct it, a couple of times each month they flew into L.A. and we worked at the Cahuenga theater. I don't remember what our intentions were in relation to mounting it, but we did present it at the L.A.

jamboree from July 14 to 18. The L.A. contribution that year was *Laundry and Bourbon* with Debra Brown, Cynthia Sanders, and Megan Welsh. We also did *Lone Star* on the same program. Both plays were directed by Michele Martin.

I was still with Joy, and our relationship seemed more difficult than ever. Recently, interviewing some of the people from New York who were there at the time reminded me of the stress I had been under and how it had contributed to how short fused and harsh I was at times while teaching the classes. Anthony told me that he was terrified of me and that when he got up on the stage his legs would shake in anticipation of what mood I would be in that day. In '87 Joy and I finally separated. She went back to Tennessee, and I went through a period of serious depression. We had been together for fifteen years in the most intense and tumultuous relationship I had ever experienced. At times we argued and fought for ten hours a day. We lost many of our friends during this combat period. They just could not be around us at those times. Every weekend I was not teaching, I was going up to my house in Lake Arrowhead in order to write my fourth book, *Acting from the Ultimate Consciousness*. I finished it in May of '87 and sent a manuscript copy to Joy in Tennessee. The next weekend she called me, crying, and said, "Eric, it's wonderful! I don't understand how you were able to write such a beautiful book when I know what you were going through all that time."

We had a jamboree in New York from June 22 through 26 at the Susan Bloch Theater on Twenty-sixth Street. Some of the actors from my Washington, D.C., group would come to New York for some weekends and definitely for the weeklong jamborees. The jamborees in those years attracted as many as eighty or ninety people, and we worked for twelve or fourteen hours each day. We did instrumentals, scenes, monologues and went out on trips to the zoo to study animals, and to various museums to observe historical periods so that we could address those obligations that dealt with times in the past. In those years I did jamborees in New York, Los Angeles, and D.C. The Washington contingent, comprised of about six or seven people headed by Ramona Rhoades, said that they were interested in creating a branch of ANT in D.C. We agreed to sanction them as such, and they got to work immediately on a project. They opened with Mario Vargas Llosa's *The Spinster from Tacna* at the Source's Summer Theater Festival, August 1 through 4. The project was directed by Raoul Rizik, a Washington, D.C., member. It won several awards at the festival. Raoul got the best director award; Ramona Rhoades, the best actress award; and some of the other members of the cast received supporting awards. Shortly after the festival, I received a call from Raoul. He was very excited and told me, "We won all those awards at the festival because of your work, Eric, and our acting was far above the rest of the entries in the nature of how organic and real we were. Thank you!"

I was getting a little burned out with all the traveling I had been doing for so many years, so I cut back a little. Ramona and Patty Hardee were doing craft workshops, and Joy started doing the weekend workshops in D.C. Joy had been teaching classes for some years in L.A. before we separated, so she had a lot of experience with the work and was a very good teacher with uncanny perception.

It was nearing the end of '87, and we were very busy in L.A. doing projects and planning for others to start the next year off. Michele Martin started a directors' workshop, using people from ANT and my classes to promote new directors for future projects. They did a directors' showcase for ANT members on September 25 and 26. A lot of work was also being done in rehearsals, and some of it was brought into the classes. We were working on *Cabin 12* to be presented sometime in '88, *The Pokey, Say Goodnight Gracie,* and some other original works, which were in various stages of development.

In New York from December 11 through 16, in a small Equity-waiver theater, ANT mounted a production of *Bus Riley's Back in Town,* which had been done as a staged reading before. Ron Orbach, who had directed the reading, also directed the play, which was produced by Leann Enos. I was there that weekend for a workshop, so I was able to see the play and participate in the discussion afterwards.

At that point I dropped down to one workshop a month in New York. I felt that the group was functioning quite well and that the projects were being produced and directed without the necessity of my input. I was, however, still doing many weekend workshops all over the map. I did four in Lake Arrowhead, two in San Francisco, and three in D.C., alternating with Joy. One of those in D.C. lasted three days, so I called it a *mini-jamboree.* I believe that was the first time I used that term. I also did a weekend in Miami, one at

Cypress College outside Los Angeles, and a one-day workshop in Fresno.

The second time I received a call from Jim Callahan asking me if I would consider going to the Philippines to do a weeklong workshop, he assured me that the country was quiet and that Gringo Honason, who had led the previous year's revolution, was not active in the country. Gringo was a former colonel in the Philippine army, who had possibly gotten his nose bent out of shape by the government and had decided to stage a coup; but by that time he had gone back into the hills and was probably hibernating. I agreed to go and received the tickets. They included a twenty-four-hour stopover in Tokyo, which really excited me, since I had never been to that part of the world before. I stayed in a hotel in Tokyo that had been there during the Second World War. It was a strange feeling to imagine the Japanese soldiers walking around in the hotel lobby where I was sitting. I decided that since this was my first time in Tokyo, I would stay up for the twenty-four hours I was to be there and take a bus tour of the entire city. Another reason I elected to do that was that the bed in my hotel room was only long enough to accommodate a midget! I arranged for a bus tour early that morning and was taken all around the city. Of course, the guide only spoke Japanese, so I told myself just to enjoy the sights, which I did. We saw towers, Buddhist temples, outdoor markets, and the *Ginza.* It was a lovely day and evening. I walked the streets feeling perfectly safe, since the people were very polite, even though I sensed that they really didn't like "round-eyed people." I was totally impressed at how clean the city was. There were no animals lurking in alleys, and there wasn't even a cigarette butt in the gutters. It was the cleanest city I had ever been in.

I left the next morning for Manila and was greeted by a throng of people, who seemed to be anxiously awaiting my arrival. When I walked into the terminal, there were reporters and photographers snapping endless pictures. I was ushered into a VIP lounge and interviewed by at least four different publications. When the interviews were over, I was taken to one of the oldest and most historical hotels in Manila, the hotel where General MacArthur had stayed before, during, and after the war. I was told that we would not start the workshop until the next day so I could deal with overcoming my jetlag.

The group I was to work with included mostly members of the Actors Workshop of the Philippines. The three people running it were Johnny Delgado, Laurice Guilian—Johnny's wife—and Leo Martinez. All three were famous actors in the country and, as I found out in the succeeding days, were pounced on by adoring fans everywhere we went. The workshop was held in a building with a very large room and many chairs. There were about forty or fifty participants, all very eager. When I walked into the room for the first time, they all stood up to honor me, which was quite embarrassing. I signaled them to be seated and introduced myself, which was totally unnecessary, since they all had my books and had read them several times. I did an hour into the system and then asked all the participants to introduce themselves, if not to each other at least to me. I get a pretty good "hit" on where people are coming from when they talk about themselves in an introduction. I was aware that they had been doing my work for some time, but I was not prepared for how much they knew. I did a slew of instrumental exercises, about ten in all, and realized that their commitment and attitude were far different from what I experienced from new people in my Los Angeles classes. Almost every person I worked with knew why I was giving him or her a specific exercise—what issue it was meant to address. I started each person with a personal-inventory involvement and then moved into areas that would be antidotal to what I perceived might be blocks or inhibitions.

One of the overall issues seemed to be their concern with respect and politeness, particularly in relation to me, so I had some of them confront me or do antisocial workouts. The ones who seemed physically inhibited I asked for large freedom workouts, where they would stretch their bodies into large and exaggerated movements, while making very big sounds of all kinds. I have a great time teaching and can be very funny telling stories and jokes, which I did almost immediately, but no one laughed. I felt like a stand-up comedian in a lounge in Las Vegas whose jokes no one was getting! Finally I said, "It's a joke!" and they all cracked up. Out of respect for me they had not been laughing, but when I told them it was funny, they responded.

We also worked on monologues and scenes, and the work was quite impressive. They understood what obligations, choices, and choice approaches were. Of course, they had some confusion, but when I worked with them in creatively manipulating their choices and emotional responses, many things were better understood. I don't believe that I was dealing with the concept or phenomenon of becoming a "professional experiencer" at the time. Even though the work was very much the same, in the succeeding years I clarified the goals of the actor's responsibilities. I made it very clear that the actor must *experience* the same life as the character from his or her own real experiences (choices). That had always been there; however, my giving it a title, a handle, separated acting from being and truly experiencing all the varied emotional life of a given character.

My time in the Philippines was magic! I loved the people, who are the most giving and generous people on the planet. Every evening after the workshop, I was hosted at a dinner party in a different home. The houses were lavish and richly furnished, and the food was presented as a huge banquet—long tables with many kinds of food. I had never felt like such a celebrity, and at first it was a little unnerving. I met senators and people high up in the government, who were very eager to talk about American politics with me. Being careful not to say the wrong thing, I pleaded ignorance about the political world, announcing repeatedly that artists couldn't get involved with politics because we are too right-brained! I also very quickly learned not to admire anything, because they would immediately give it to me, and to refuse would have been an insult, so I stopped complimenting what people were wearing and the possessions they had. In spite of my learned cautions, I came home with paintings, an air rifle that was one of a kind, and books galore.

Jim Callahan, who was our government's liaison and was in charge of me and my safety, provided a couple of days of R and R at a beautiful house on the water, which belonged to a famous television talk-show host, who had opened it up for us. I never felt that I was in any danger, but besides Jim, there was also a security guy to drive me everywhere.

I returned one more time to the Philippines in 1995, and that time I lectured and taught in cities on all the major islands: Manila on Luzon; Cebu City on Visayas; and the largest city in the country, Davao, which is on Mindanao. I worked with a wide variety of actors, which was a wonderful learning experience. The Philippines had a population of fifty-seven million at the time, and everyone who could read a newspaper or listen to the radio or watch TV knew I was in the country and what I was doing there! One of the newspapers carried a full picture of me on its back page. While I walked down the street with Johnny, many people would point at me and say, "Look, Morris, Morris!"

During that same year, 1987, in Los Angeles, I received a call from a man named Jost Heider, who had a discernable German accent and said that he was here from Germany and wanted to explore an acting career in Hollywood. While walking up Sunset Boulevard, he had run into an actor, and they had struck up a conversation. Jost had shown him his head shots, and the actor had told him that he looked very sad in the pictures and that he should go and take some classes with Eric Morris. The first time Jost had heard my name, however, had been from Heinz Gerhard Luck, his acting teacher at the Prestigious School of Performing Arts in Hamburg, from which he had graduated. Luck had been using *No Acting Please* from the seventies and had mentioned it to Jost. He, however, didn't make the connection until after he came to my class. I invited him to audit a class, and he did. So started what would be a very long and fruitful relationship.

I must describe Jost, so that you can get a mental picture of this man, who would probably qualify for the *Reader's Digest* feature "The Most Unforgettable Character I Ever Knew." Jost could have been the poster boy for the Nazi party. He is over six feet tall, with thick blond hair, a muscular body, and a rosy complexion—a true "Aryan." I don't mean to say that Jost would have been a Nazi if he had been born forty years earlier. He just has the physical qualities that those little rats like Hitler and Himmler didn't have.

Jost studied with me for a while, and I directed him in a couple of scenes and monologues to be put on tape. He was full of energy, and whenever he walked into a room, he would shout, "Halleluiah!" At first, people in my classes didn't know what to make of him, but in time they accepted his idiosyncrasies and embraced him as one of the group. He had been touring Germany with a number of plays for several years, but since he really wanted to be a Hollywood movie star, he had made the move to Los Angeles. He told me that the walls of his bedroom were covered with large posters of Steve McQueen and Marlon Brando. Over the years Jost has become an astrologer, a preacher, and an inspirational speaker! Recently, he informed me that he had returned to acting, with great vigor. When he went back to Germany, he arranged for me to do a weeklong workshop at the school he had graduated from—which I will talk about in the section on the nineties.

That same year, when I announced I was going to do a whole day on the megapproaches, one of my students in New York, who was a sound engineer for a film company in the city, asked me if I would like to record the session and put the tapes out for other people to hear. He assured me that the sound quality would be on the highest professional standards. We recorded that session, and I did publish the set of three tapes covering three of the megapproaches, including subpersonalities.

On February 8, 1988 the D.C. group, which now called itself the Actors Ensemble until it could legally become a branch of ANT, did a standing-room only, two-hour demonstration of the Eric Morris System at the National Theater. It included instrumental and craft exercises and demonstrations of the work by people in the group. They did scenes from *The Dining Room* and *Crimes of the Heart.* I hosted a Q-and-A session at the end, followed by a book signing of *Acting from the Ultimate Consciousness.* More than two hundred actors showed up. The D.C. group was very active. They did another "Monday Night at the National" later that year, but I was doing a film in Argentina at the time and couldn't be there. At the end of March they also did a staged reading of *Hubris,* by John F. Morton, at the Source Theater.

One of my students in L.A., Adriana Fernandez, approached me one night in class and asked me if I would like to meet with an Argentine director who was looking for an American actor to play a part in his film. I of course agreed to meet with him the following day at the Source restaurant, which was one of my haunts. His name was Jorge Coscia. We spoke for two hours, and at the end of that time he told me that he wanted me to play the part in his movie. It was the role of an English colonel, most likely a graduate of Sandhurst—the British version of West Point. The film was a musical with eighteen production numbers.

"I don't sing or dance!" I remarked.

He laughed, and replied, "No, no, your part is straight acting, no singing or dancing."

He then told me the story of the movie, which I liked. It was to take place after the Falklands War between Argentina and England. In the film, the British had ostensibly occupied Buenos Aires—which in reality they never did; that was the fantasy part of the film—and the Argentine youths were rebelling against them by staging tango dances on the streets all over the city. My job as the officer in command of the occupation was to chase down those groups, confiscate their phonographs, break their records, and instead of making arrests, disperse them with stern warnings. I rode around in the sidecar of a motorcycle driven by an army soldier under my command. The Spanish title of the film was *Cipayos* (I don't have a clue what that word means), but the English title was *The Tango War.*

I flew to Buenos Aires. The name of the city means "good air," but nothing could be further from the truth! I was the only non-Argentine in the film, an American playing a career British officer! I have always prided myself on a good ear for accents, but a classical, high-born British accent was tough. I had bought David Allen Stern's accent tapes at Samuel French and worked on the accent feverishly, and I got fairly competent with it. Many of the scenes were shot outdoors on the streets of the city, and for what I think was a low-budget film, the production numbers were great. Thirty or forty dancers' performing to playback on uneven pavement was incredible. My part, however, had no real depth or character structure. The scenes were one-dimensional and very much the same. There wasn't any room for creating or establishing any colors in the character. I created a complete background journal for him, using what I knew about military schools such as West Point, and drew upon my own military experience. I wore the uniform even when I wasn't working, to get a sense of a relationship to it. It was a makeshift outfit created by the wardrobe person, and while it looked good and somewhat authentic, it wasn't real. I invented some things about the ribbons on my jersey and kept up the British accent all the time. I attempted to work with the actors in the scenes I was doing with them, but the language problems got in the way. The only actress I was able to have somewhat of a relationship with was Adriana Fernandez, because she was in one of my classes. I had a couple of very short scenes with her, but they were the best work I did in the film. Not only could she understand English and speak it quite well, but she was also able to respond emotionally to me, so those two short scenes had somewhat of an ensemble quality. My shooting schedule was a month long, so they structured all my scenes to be shot during that month, since I had to get back to my classes in L.A. I had spent too much time on effecting an authentic accent and felt I might have spent more energy on the character instead, even though it was very thin. All in all, I wasn't happy with the results of my work. Jorge Coscia, the director, wasn't much help, and there wasn't anybody else I could speak to or work with, so I was really on my own, and since many of the other actors in the film had language difficulties, that also complicated my process. It was an interesting experience, however, and I learned a lot about working under adverse conditions. Like a Monday morning quarterback, I thought after the fact of a lot of things I might have done.

While working on the film, I was asked by the producer if I would do a three-day workshop for the acting community in Buenos Aires. I agreed to do so, and they agreed to pay me a stipend for my efforts. He also asked me if I would give a free lecture at Carlos Gondolfo's studio. Carlos was one of the two or three most established acting teachers in all of Argentina. I said yes and showed up at his studio, which was filled with young, eager actors, relishing what they were about to hear. I laid out the work, emphasizing the whole concept of being and not doing. I stressed the importance of preparation to get ready to act, demonstrated personal inventory and selfless involvement, and generally outlined the two parts of the work, the instrument and the craft. When I finished the lecture and was about to leave, a very pretty woman approached me. She had long dark hair and seemed quite enthralled with the lecture. She told me she had read all my books and intended to come to the States to study with me. I was polite and told her to contact me when she got to California.

Two thousand people attended the seminar, which was held in the General San Martín Theater, a huge and opulent theater with a lot of historical-period décor. (An interesting aside here: All over Buenos Aires there are statues and plaques of military officers of high rank, and the cemeteries are filled with monuments for generals and high-ranking military men, and yet, I am not sure of it, but I believe Argentina never won a war!) Many of the attendees were directors, acting teachers, or film makers anxious to hear what I was going to talk about. Adriana was my interpreter, since many of the people didn't understand English. I started the seminar with an introduction to my work, making a statement about one-sentence long: "The work is divided into three parts: obligation, choice, and choice approach," at which point I turned to Adriana to interpret what I had just said, and she spoke for ten minutes. I just stood there, thinking that if this was what was going to happen every time I said a single sentence, it would take three days to get through my introduction! I know that Spanish is a different language, but my God, how many more words had to be spoken to communicate what I had just said? This went on for about an hour, and we finally got through my introduction. At the beginning of the second day I got another interpreter, an actor who had spent time working in New York and was much more facile with both languages. It moved somewhat faster, but I must say Argentines like to go on speaking for long periods of time! I did a number of individual instrumental exercises, working with actors in the first few rows of the audience, explaining as best I could what I wanted them to do, and the transformation in their behavior was phenomenal. I asked if anyone had a scene or monologue, and I got a few volunteers, who did their monologue in Spanish. I worked with them on an emotional basis with equal success.

An actor named Jamie Murray was in the film, where he played a subordinate English officer who worked under me. Jamie had an English or Scottish background but lived with his parents in Buenos Aires. He spoke perfect English and was equally fluent in Spanish. He was sitting in the first row in the audience, right next to the woman who had approached me after my lecture at Gondolfo's. Her name, as I learned later, was Susana Tanco, and she was a good friend of Jamie's. She wore a pair of red-rimmed eyeglasses that took up a significant part of her face, and she was equally attentive at the seminar. After I finished the first day, a group of us went out to dinner, among them Jamie and Susana. I was attracted to her and asked her to have dinner with me the following night, and she accepted. I also invited her to an outdoor location where we were filming the next day, and she came. We saw each other several times in the next weeks, and when I left to go home, she said she would write me. We corresponded and spoke on the telephone during the following year. I did see her again a few months after I finished filming. I went back to see the premiere of the film, and we became involved more seriously at that time. About a year after our first meeting, she came to L.A., got an apartment, and we became romantically involved. Some years later, in 1995, we were married.

Sometime in 1989 David Anspaugh asked me to meet him in Baltimore. I was working in New York at the time, so it was a short train ride from the city. David was there to talk to Johnny Depp about some project David was trying to put together, and he wanted me to meet with Johnny and possibly work with him on *Cry Baby,* the film he was there to do. At the time, Johnny had mostly been on TV, on a series called "24 Jump Street," and this was one of his first films. I met with him, and we liked each other. I spent the next four days in a Baltimore hotel room working with him on his role in the film. I immediately recognized his enormous talent. He was very much in touch with his child energy, and I knew that his charisma would ultimately lead him to stardom. We broke the scenes down, and I helped him find an approach to each, using my work and making vocabulary adjustments in our communication. He didn't want the director to know that he was working with a coach, so we kept our meetings on a low profile. I did some emotional demonstrations for him, and he was quite impressed with my impulsive facility. I saw him just one more time a few years later at my house, just before he started to work on *Edward Scissorhands.* The director was adamant about not working with anyone else on the role.

Right at the end of the eighties or at the very beginning of the nineties, Tom Mesereau walked through the door of my theater on Cahuenga. I was immediately struck by his look. He had a shock of white hair and very blue eyes. His smile exposed a complete set of very white teeth, and his ambience was ingratiating. He told me that he was a lawyer and wanted to take my class to improve his expressive skills in the courtroom. Tom is a unique person and has earned my respect for the commitment he has to the justice system. He has on many occasions gone down South, pro bono, to defend poor black men on death row and has successfully gotten them off.

Tom stayed in my class for many years, doing all kinds of large commitment exercises, such as abandonment, primal moans, primitive abandonment, and different types of confrontations, and he was really able to grow and evolve expressively. He displayed a great deal of courage and always did what I asked him to do without hesitation. Being a criminal lawyer is largely dependent on being able to *act* from a real place. Over the years Tom has become quite successful and famous as an attorney, defending Robert Blake in his murder trial and successfully defending Michael Jackson.

We were now in the nineties, a decade still filled with classes and out-of-town workshops. In 1990 I had three classes each week. Wednesday was a full day of classes, morning and evening, and I also had a Thursday evening class, which in '91 was turned into a scene-and-monologue class, where we also worked with craft and imaging exercises.

I was still starting each class with the preliminary relaxation cluster, followed by a craft workout, as I continue to do to this day. I had also introduced self-regulated exercises. An SRE, as it is called, is an exercise that the actor has brought into the class. It is usually an instrumental involvement but can also deal with craft. My purpose in adding this to the work was to get each student to take responsibility for himself and during the week between classes to think about what he needs to address. Quite frequently, after an actor finishes an SRE, I ask him why he did what he did, what the purpose of the exercise was. Only occasionally do I take issue with his choice. At the time, I was also working a lot on imaging, developing the approach and using imaging techniques in each class. The classes were divided, as they always were and still are today, between instrumental-therapy work and the craft. The balance between the two is very important.

That year, I finished the outline for the imaging book and started writing it. I also did thirteen weekend workshops, getting around all over the country. For the most part the focus was instrument and craft, but I varied the content depending on the level the students had reached in their evolution and facility with the work. If, for example, I repeatedly visited a place where the same actors were attending frequently, some sessions would be totally about craft, while others emphasized instrumental work. I was developing the use of subpersonalities and imaging, and I combined them in two-day workshops, working exclusively in those areas. I also did complete workshops on the megapproaches.

In March 1990 I shared a two-day workshop with Sally Kirkland at Yogi John's studio. She took the first day, and I the second, although we both participated in each other's teaching. Sally is a wonderful actress, and as a teacher she is very inspiring. The major difference between us is specificity. She excites the child energy, accesses the imagination, and helps to free the actor's instincts, and while I certainly attempt to do the same, I have created a process that is very pragmatic and specific for addressing the obligations of dramatic material.

I was also busy being the artistic director of the American New Theater, which was in full swing. They were doing work in New York, and I was directing *'night, Mother* in Los Angeles. I had seen the third preview performance of the play in New York, before it opened officially. Kathy Bates was playing the daughter, and Anne Pitoniak was her mother. I had been blown away by their performances and had liked the intensity of the play. Right then, very much as I had decided to direct *The Glass Menagerie* after I had worked crew on it at Northwestern, I made up my mind to direct *'night, Mother,* although this time I did it only a few years later. I cast Cynthia Sanders as the daughter and Rachel Bard as her mother. Both actresses had been working with me for a number of years and had a very good sense of truth. Scarlett Gani was my assistant and attended all the rehearsals. She was quite helpful taking my notes and making excellent suggestions.

In the first five minutes of the play, Jessie, the daughter, informs her mother that at the end of the evening she is going to kill herself, and the next two hours are devoted to her explanations as to why she is doing it and to the mother's attempt at stopping her. Jessie has been handling all the things related to the running of the house, such as the bills and a multitude of other duties, which she has to instruct her mother about before committing suicide. She is resigned to end her life because she is so unhappy and unfulfilled. She is divorced, she has a son who is a criminal, she is an epileptic, subject to grand-mal seizures, and she has nothing to look forward to. She has a line in the play: "Mother, if you have lost your appetite, shouldn't you push yourself away from the table?"

I worked with each actress on identifying the parallels in her own life. I had Cynthia doing a "litany of woes," finding and exploring her dissatisfactions and sadness. Rachel talked about her failed marriage, her responsibility to her own real daughter, and so on. I had both women sit and share their personal lives with each other, and I encouraged Rachel to stay overnight at Cynthia's house, so that they could get up at the same time in the morning and talk over coffee. I asked them to express all their feelings to each other, and I privately instructed Rachel to try to "fix" Cynthia. When I went away on vacation in December, I asked Scarlett to take over the rehearsals while I was gone. When I returned, I was very pleased with what she had contributed to the play. Both actresses had taken her suggestions and added depth to their relationship.

Opening night of the play was the exact day the Gulf War started, and we had five people in the audience! The play was sensational every night though. At the end, when Jessie goes offstage and we hear the gunshot, her mother just sits there for a moment or two, then goes to the telephone and calls her son to tell him what has just happened and to ask him to come over quickly. At that point I had the crew take the lights down slowly. The audience sat silently in the dark for the longest time, with no applause or response, until I started clapping. The play was so impacting and shocking that they had just sat quietly in the darkened theater.

Cynthia was getting very depressed as the play continued. She developed dark circles under her eyes and became much less verbal offstage. I could see that the work was creating a despondency that I thought could be dangerous to her health, so I closed the play two weeks earlier than had been scheduled.

After *'night, Mother* the American New Theater did a couple of other plays, one of which was *Hearts* by Gabe Walsh, whom I knew from the writers' unit at the Actors Studio. I don't remember what the others were, but I know that Michele Martin, the assistant artistic director, directed a couple of them. Around '92 or '93 they worked on one called *Criminal Minds*. I came and saw the final rehearsals and was outraged at the level of the work. It was really terrible! The actors were being presentational and obvious, and there wasn't any reality on that stage. The plan was to have two or three previews and invite the press to review the play. They had even put together elaborate press packages. I spoke to Diana De Mayo, the stage manager, and told her that this play would not preview or open until I could come in and do a week of direction on it to get the actors to a level of reality and authenticity. I thought that my decision would be respected, since I was the artistic director and my name was all over everything. I dropped by the theater the following evening and saw that it was filled with people, most of them from various papers and magazines. I flipped out and resigned the next day as artistic director of the American New Theater. I intended to kick everyone out and just use the place for my classes and an occasional independent play I would do. I had mortgaged my house to build that theater, and it seemed that they wanted to showcase themselves on my nickel. I was angry and disappointed, because the whole purpose of founding the American New Theater had been to promote "the work" and do honest, real productions.

A couple of weeks after my resignation, several members of the group came to me and asked if I would rent them the theater so that they could do productions under a different banner. By that time I was a little less enraged, so I replied that I would think about it, predicated on the fact that my name would not appear at all on their promotional materials or in any way be mentioned anywhere. After a great deal of soul searching and contemplating, I agreed to rent them the space for a small fraction of what any Equity-waiver theater was getting for weekly rentals. They formed a company called the Mojo Ensemble, with Michele Martin as artistic director. In the following two or three years they did a number of plays, one of which was *The Mayor's Limo,* written by one of my New York students, Mark Nassar, who also performed in it. Several of my former and present students were in their plays, and I thought that some of the work was pretty good. When Mojo folded, I rented the theater to a group that called themselves the Candlefish Theater Company, and I charged them the same fractional amount Mojo had been paying. The entire time they were there was a complete nightmare for me, however. Too many things happened to go into in this book.

My classes continued to evolve, and in '91 I started using video in the Thursday class, which was now a scene class. We would do the scene or monologue, record it, and then the class would watch the tape and I would critique the work. This went on for a year or so, but I finally discontinued doing it because the actors were very camera conscious and seemed more interested in seeing themselves on screen than in being involved with the process.

That year I also did twenty-one weekend workshops, adding Chicago, Piedmont College in Georgia, and Hamburg, Germany, to the list. Hamburg was a very interesting experience for a multitude of reasons. I was invited there because Jost Heider had spoken to his school about the work I was doing. It was a very famous performing-arts high school, much like what we have in New York, except that what they call high schools there are really college-level institutions. The school holds yearly auditions and is very selective. Of the hundreds of people who audition each year, only a handful are admitted. They were having a theater convention that went from

September 23 through 27, with a variety of classes, including classical drama, stage combat, voice and movement, and various acting classes.

I walked into a room filled with young aspiring actors, about twenty in all. I was dressed very western, wearing a leather-tooled vest, jeans, and cowboy boots. That was my look in those days. I heard a small voice from the back of the room saying, "Ach, John Wayne!" I started the way I always did, by introducing the work, and then had everybody get up onstage to do the preliminary preparations. I followed that with a being workout, and then I asked the students if they had been successful in accomplishing a relationship with their partners. I might as well have asked them if they wanted to expose their private parts with the response I got. I quickly learned that to claim success in any of their work was *verboten.* It was like praising themselves. The two words most prevalent in the German vocabulary are *verboten* and *controller!* I also learned that everyone was very critical of everyone else. It seemed that the attitude was it could always be better and you shouldn't be proud of what you did. In other words, even when the work was good, it was only O.K.! I might have been a tough teacher and quite demanding in my early days of teaching, but I was always encouraging and supportive of the people I worked with.

After the group work, I did a slew of instrumentals and discovered that almost all of those I worked had a great deal of tension and a lot of social obligations. I had them do a variety of relaxation techniques and selfless-involvement work, and I attempted to get some of the more uptight ones to do some antisocial exercises, but that proved extremely difficult for them. In their monologues they were very presentational, and I realized that I had my work cut out for me. To get them to be more organic I told all of them to use their own words to paraphrase their monologue and in some cases to talk about their own personal experience that somehow mirrored the piece. That also seemed very difficult for them, since they had resistance to exposing personal things about themselves, which in their view were private. In spite of the resistance I encountered that first day, I was able to slowly involve them in reality, and the difference in their work was so obvious that I began to get the cooperation I needed. I had twenty students on my first day and one hundred on the last! Each day there were more people in the class. I guess the word got around that this "crazy cowboy American" was doing something important. That was my first experience in Germany but not my last.

Back in Los Angeles I was still teaching my two classes on Wednesday, the one on Thursday, plus a Tuesday class, which was my advanced class. I was also working occasionally as an actor. In 1992 I had fifteen weekend workshops. I was really covering this country, continually adding cities and countries to my schedule. I didn't advertise in those various places. I would generally get a call from someone who lived there, asking me if I would be interested in doing a workshop. I always wanted to know how they had happened to hear about me and found out that 90 percent of the time it was from one of my books.

One day I received a call from a man by the name of James Burns in North or South Carolina, asking me if I would come to Hawaii and do workshops. I was surprised, since he wasn't calling me from Hawaii, so I asked him where he lived. He told me that he worked as a bodyguard for Doris Duke, the famous billionaire who was the heir to the Duke tobacco empire, and that she had houses all over the place, including Hawaii, which is where they spent most of their time. Doris's adopted daughter, a woman named Chandi Heffner, was with Doris a good deal of the time, even though Doris had bought her a three-hundred-acre ranch on the Big Island.

So I began to teach workshops in Hawaii and was invited to stay at Chandi's ranch, which had thirty or forty horses running freely on the property. In the mornings the horses would congregate near the front of the house, and a couple of them would eat the paint off the front of Chandi's Bronco. I admired a gorgeous white Arabian that seemed to stand out from the rest. He was wild and quite spirited. He had a little brown patch of hair between his ears and wild curious eyes. Chandi saw my fascination with him and said that I could have him if I wanted him. At first I thought she was kidding, but she wasn't! I told her that I thought the horse was very valuable, and she said, "Yes, about three or four hundred thousand dollars." It was a thoroughbred and rare. I never did take it. How would I have gotten it to the mainland? Where would I have boarded it? Who would have broken it for me? It would have been tragic to put a horse like that in a stall at some stable in L.A.! Not long after that call from James, he and Chandi got romantically involved, and Doris disowned her.

I went to various places in Hawaii, met a lot of people there, and was well treated. An acting teacher at one of the colleges, whose name was Ed Gillweit, invited me to teach at his school with a combination of my people and his.

At the end of the year, I received a call from Jost. He was going to do the lead in an Agatha Christie play, *Love from a Stranger,* and he asked me if I would be interested in coming to Germany to direct it. I replied that I would have to think about it and see if I could adjust my teaching schedule. He told me that it would only be for two or three weeks and that they would pay all my expenses and also compensate me for my time. I arrived in Munich and was driven to Shtarnberg, a town about fifteen kilometers from Munich. I was to stay in the house of Ellen Schwier, the producer of the play. She gave me a room up some stairs in the guest house, which was separated from the main house. I was very uncomfortable there and slept with the light on every night. I felt that there was a presence in that room. At first I thought it was my imagination and the fact that I was in a foreign place, but each night I felt more and more energy surrounding my bed. I didn't say anything, because I thought that they would laugh at my fears. Later, however, when we got to Ludenscheid, Ellen told me that her son had died in that room, that he was ever present there, and that his spirit lived in the tree right outside the bedroom window. I'm glad that she told me *after* I had left that house, or I might have died of fright!

Ellen's company was called *Das Ensemble,* and at the time of my arrival she had been doing the directing for a couple of weeks. They had rented a hall in Shtarnberg about a mile from her house, and when I arrived there, I felt that the air was thick with angst, and that fear hung over the room like a dark cloud. I actually had a physical reaction to the atmosphere. I told Ellen that I wanted to watch some of the rehearsal before I took over the reins. It was in German, but I had an English translation of the play, and besides, I understood a lot of the language. Yiddish is a Germanic language, so it has a lot of similarities with German; and since I am fluent in Yiddish, I could understand about 40 percent of what was being said. I sat there watching a scene, which Ellen interrupted several times to rail against one of the actors, Robert Remmler. Robert had the part of the doctor in the play and was obviously having some line problems, directly as a result of the tension and fear created by the heavy hand of Ellen. She had been relating to the actors as if she were a Nazi SS officer in charge of a prison camp, rather than the director of a play. At one point she screamed at Remmler, "If I had the money, I would have hired a better actor than you! If you don't remember the lines, I will play your part myself!" Everyone in the company was uptight and, to say the least, not having any fun. Shortly after that outburst, we broke for lunch, and I put my arm around Robert and walked with him for a while. He had very little English, and I had only some facility with his language, but we communicated quite well. I told him that if I had cast the play I would have hired him, because I thought he was perfect for the part. I continued to compliment him and to build his confidence, which I was able to do honestly, since I really believed everything I said to him. When we returned to the rehearsal after lunch, I had the cast repeat the scene, and Robert was not only letter perfect, but he was actually great in it! Ellen just looked at me with the kind of confused curiosity that people have when they witness something astonishing.

Within twenty-four hours I had everyone in the cast loose, confident, and eager to act. I spent a little time with each actor, discussing what I saw and what I wanted him or her to do. No one except Jost knew the language or my terminology, so I invented various ways of communicating with them. My emphasis in the early rehearsals was to create an atmosphere of permissiveness and acceptance. I had them do some parallel improvising, which seemed alien to most of them. At times I asked them to use their own words and was extremely generous in my direction and critiques. I would take each one of them aside and, when necessary, talk to him or her in private in another room. It was a complete turn around from what I had walked into on the first day. I later found out that Ellen had wanted to replace Jost in the part, largely because he wasn't giving her what she expected. They had worked together before on other productions, but they were having difficulty with this play.

We were to open the play in a town called Ludenscheid, which had a population of about a hundred thousand at that time. The theater sat two thousand people and was an elegant plant. It had incredible equipment and was beautifully decorated. The man who ran it was a short, balding guy with a pointed nose, who always looked like he had to be someplace else and who moved with a gait that indicated he had better get there very soon! His name was Schwerer, and from the moment he laid eyes on me, he was giving me the evil eye. He pulled Ellen aside and berated her for hiring an American director. "Ve haf plenty German directors!" he protested. He would often stick his head into the theater to see what was going on. Usually I was just sitting there, watching the action in the scene, so he complained, "Vat is he doing? He just is sitting there!" When I took actors into another room to talk to them and give them some pickups, he would ask Ellen what I was saying to them. I really think that my presence was traumatic for the poor man!

As director, I not only concentrated on the organic character of the work, but I also structured the action to heighten the suspense and the impact of the play. I rarely block a play when I direct, but in this case I had to do some inventive staging to service the fear and threat in the piece. The play is about a psychopathic man who charms women into marrying him and then kills them and takes all their possessions. At one point the woman attempts to escape from him and runs to a door on the opposite side of the stage. I asked Jost to be behind that door, quickly and from a backstage position, when she opened it. The shocking impact of his presence drew screams from the audience. And in the same scene, while he is trying to get her and kill her, I had him stalk her around a table while she scurried around avoiding him. It was quite exciting and theatrical.

Opening night was a smash. The play was wonderful and the most successful the theater had had up to that point. Jost was great in the role and responded to all of my direction. Ellen's daughter, Katherine Jacob, was playing the female lead, and Ellen was her aunt in the show. A cute girl, Heiki, played a maid, and a couple of other actors filled out the cast. I was invited to take a curtain call with the cast, and we then had a celebration dinner, where Mr. Schwerer went on and on about what a wonderful director I was and how he had underestimated the great talent I had brought to the theater. Before I left to go home to America, Ellen pulled me aside and said, "You are not just a fine director; you are a guru." The play had opened in early January and ran through May. It successfully played in over one hundred cities in Germany, Austria, and Switzerland and was not only artistically rewarding but also financially a hit.

Shortly after I returned to Los Angeles, I started to investigate selective memory as a choice approach and introduced it to all my classes (I will describe all the newer approaches at the end of this book). I also began doing scene parallels, after first giving all my classes a lengthy explanation of what they were and why and how I was adding them to the work. Doing a scene parallel is exactly like doing a written scene. The only difference is that there are no written words. The actor is paralleling a written piece of material and addressing all of the obligations to the piece, using choices and choice approaches in the same way as he would approach a scene. The major difference is that he uses his own words, and the main reason he does that is that it allows him to develop the life of the character without falling into the trap of concept or logic. By the time he gets to say the written words, the relationship, the emotional life, and the time-and-place issues have been established, so that he is able to avoid all the representational and conceptual traps. In later years I began to do *arbitrary* scene parallels, where the actors create a circumstantial structure replete with relationship responsibilities, emotional obligations, and conflict. Those workouts have a different emphasis. While a scene parallel addressing a written scene is supposed ultimately to take the actors to the written words, arbitrary scene parallels are designed to help them use the basic elements of the process—obligations, choices, and choice approaches. I still do them now, and I think they are an important tool in the training of actors. Over the years I would see actors who were waiting to read for an audition going over lines and experimenting with a variety of ways to say them. Not only does that lead to conceptual behavior, but it also creates a situation where the actor is listening to himself—which short-circuits reality and organic life.

In '94 I started the "intensives." They were a yearlong series of workshops, designed to cover the craft from A to Z and at the same time eliminate any instrumental issues the actors might have. The same people met once a month at my house in Lake Arrowhead, which is where I held them for a number of years. We ate and slept there, I hired maids and cooks to prepare the meals, and I bought futons for people to sleep on. It was amazing to see how the students bonded and how close they all got. Because there were no distractions and we were in that space for forty-eight hours, the concentration was awesome. The major difference between the intensives and the regular classes was that we had much more time to explore the instrument. Sometimes I would spend as much as an hour with a single person if he or she needed it. In addition to doing the instrumental work, I was committed to cover the entire craft process in a year—which would be impossible to do in a regular class. We explored one or two choice approaches in each session and spent two or three weekends on the megapproaches. The actors did their monologues and scenes, using each choice approach to create the choice that addressed the author's intention. I do the intensives at my theater in L.A. now. It still works very well, but it has a different quality. Some students have done all, or almost all, of the twelve years of intensives and still learn and grow.

My personal life was much better. The war of the Morrises was over, and Joy was out of my life, even though we remained friends. Susana had started to teach privately. At first, she didn't charge anything for her time. She wanted to be sure she was doing the work and being helpful to the students. I was a little upset by her pro-bono efforts, since she would take a taxi to the theater (she doesn't drive, and we can all be thankful for that!), so that her first few years of teaching were costing us money. However, I understood what she was doing and admired her for it. She also started to help me with the business and encouraged me to get off the road, which I did. I was still doing workshops, but by '95 there were fewer trips out of town. I am not exactly sure when it was, but one morning in New York I woke up and didn't know where I was for a solid minute. I took that as a cue to cut down on my travels and went from twenty-six workshops out of town to three. I did go to Atlanta that year, though, and did a workshop there. All this travel was an incredible education.

We started the second series of intensives in '95. I began to give the students a test around the seventh month to see what they had learned and whether they could articulate the information. At the end of the twelve months we did a review of the whole year, not only talking about what we had learned, but performing craft exercises and material too.

I was also concentrating quite heavily on subpersonalities as an acting tool at that time, adding various approach techniques for accessing the different subparts. What I had learned from Hal Stone was voice dialogue and a couple of other techniques for accessing the other selves. As I worked with those, I began experimenting with other approaches, such as *role playing* and using *choices, movement, music, externals,* and later *imaging*. I found that certain subparts responded better to one technique than another.

All through the nineties we continued doing a major jamboree each year, sometimes in New York and sometimes in Florida, as well as in Los Angeles. Over the years I cut down on the attendance radically, so that we now have only about twenty-five students at each of the jamborees. For a while I had to rent a large house in Lake Arrowhead, stock it with food to feed twenty-five people for a whole week, and hire a staff to cook and serve the meals. It was an overwhelming task, even before the actual teaching would start. We had problems locating the right house, dealing with the staff, getting the food, and transporting it up to the mountains. At the end of the week we were left with the chore of putting the house back together, cleaning it up, and replacing the damaged items. That went on until 1999, when we started doing the mini-jamborees and the major six-day one at the UCLA Conference Center in Lake Arrowhead. That made all the difference in the world. It is an elegant place, the accommodations are first rate, and the food is gourmet. It has allowed Susana and me to walk in, teach the workshops, and leave when we are finished.

I was teaching much more than acting and wasn't really doing much to get acting work. I imagine that I was fulfilling my creative needs by innovating new techniques and choice approaches. A young woman by the name of Zoe Williams had come to my class around the same time as two of her friends. Since they all lived in Malibu and had had somewhat of a privileged life, I affectionately called them the Malibu Brats. Zoe's father, Paul, a film director, would occasionally sit in on my class. He approached me one time and asked if I would like to be in a film he was planning to do in Palm Springs. Of course I was interested. He told me I would play the part of a captain of police in the Palm Springs police department. The stars of the film were Sean Young and Edward James Olmos, and the film was called *Mirage*. Paul Williams also had a big role in it, and Zoe played a waitress in a couple of scenes. Paul used two of my other students for smaller roles.

I had a scene on the inside of a police car, talking to another detective, who was my subordinate. Supposedly, we had known each other for almost twenty years and were quite familiar with our respective work and living styles. The scene, which consisted of about fifteen or twenty lines, was about some conflict over why my subordinate had staked out this house and why it was important. The dialogue contained his justification and my concern over the reasons for his involvement. When I arrived at the location at about nine in the morning, Paul introduced me to the actor I was going to do my scene with. He was one of the leads in the film, and Paul had worked with him before on a couple of other movies. We went to his trailer and talked to each other about everything in our lives—our marriages, divorces, alimony payments, affairs, and so on. We were in that trailer a total of seven hours, getting very familiar with each other. We shot the scene as the sun was dropping low in the sky, around 5:00 P.M. The relationship responsibility was that we knew each other and had had a relationship for a very long time. The seven hours in his trailer had established a mutual knowledge and familiarity that worked in the scene. I don't know that anyone noticed the effects of the history we had created with each other, and I also question how many actors would have felt the need to do what we did; but when I watched the scene, I could see that the relationship seemed to have history. I also used other choices to address the emotional issues between us. Fortunately, we had had all that time to get familiar with each other. I think that if we had shot the scene when I had first arrived at the location, it would not have had the depth it did. It was fun to be acting again, no matter how small a part it was. Whenever I return to class after working as an actor, I bring with me an increased respect for the obligations an actor has in doing film. Some of the work we do following an acting experience includes various kinds of preparations to accommodate the technical demands of that medium.

In March of '96 I started the third series of intensives. We were still doing them at my house in Lake Arrowhead. They were getting deeper, and the work was evolving. The people who repeated them each year developed a deeper understanding of the work, their instrumental obstacles began to disappear, and it carried over into their scenes and monologues. I was also continuing to travel—not quite as much but still hopping on airplanes.

I guess one of the highlights of that year was getting a part in a pretty big film, *Eye for an Eye,* with Sally Field, Keifer Sutherland, Ed Harris, Joe Mantegna, and Beverly D'Angelo. The director was the legendary John Schlesinger, who had directed *Midnight Cowboy; Sunday, Bloody Sunday; Cold Comfort Farm;* and many others in his career.

Mali Finn, an important casting director in town, called me in to read for the part of a magazine journalist who was writing a review of the museum where Sally's character was working. She and her friend, Beverly D'Angelo, oversaw the administration of the place. My scene was with both of them—about a dozen or so lines as we walked from the museum to the street. Schlesinger was at the audition, which surprised me, since it was such a minor role. I gave the character a somewhat officious and effete quality, and I could see that Schlesinger loved what I brought to it. The entire experience was a lot of fun. The director started with a table reading of the whole cast, catered on a soundstage at Paramount. After that, he invited all of us to a screening of *Cold Comfort Farm,* which he had directed in England.

Every day, new colored pages were delivered to my home, each time of a different color, but none of them had anything to do with me! I thought that this was one of the reasons making movies in Hollywood is so expensive: a lot of waste! Schlesinger was a funny little man, full of energy and excitement. Whenever we would start to do my scene, he would run up to me and say, "Eric, say this line here!" So I would replace the original line with his suggestion. By the time we were ready to shoot the scene, none of my original lines remained. He had changed them all, fortunately adding to the original script. We were invited to see the finished film at Paramount a couple of months later, and I was disappointed: at least half of my scene had been cut. I understood why. It didn't promote the action or story and was only there to establish what and where Sally's character had been before her daughter was murdered. About a year later Mali called me in again to read for the part of a waiter in a Madonna film Schlesinger was directing. He remembered me, but I didn't get the part.

Meanwhile, my classes continued as they always have. Recently, I have come up with five new choice approaches, a couple of them invented in the nineties I believe, and the others in the twenty-first century. I now have thirty-one. My last book, which was published in 1998, was on imaging, which is the twenty-sixth. The newer ones are SELECTIVE MEMORY, DÉJÀ VU, MIND'S EYE TRANSLATION, DYNAMICALLY IMPACTING SINGLE WORDS, and SELECTIVE LISTENING.

EPILOGUE

As I am writing this, we are in November of 2006. I will leave for the next book the specifics of what evolves as the decade finishes and am only going to explore here the highlights of the last six years. At the top of the 2000s we moved from the Cahuenga theater, which for me was traumatic. I had had that theater built from scratch and had been there for over fifteen years. It was a functioning Equity-waiver theater, and a lot of work had been done there. However, Alba Morino, who owned the property with her husband, had sold or somehow lost it to other people, one of whom was a horrible man, who made my life very difficult. The neighborhood was declining, and there were a lot of street people out there. To get to the theater in the back we had to drive through a tunnel, where the bums would urinate—which made entering very unappetizing. My classes went until twelve or one at night, and I feared for the safety of the young women in them. Susana and I began to look for a new location—which sounds a lot easier than it is. I wanted a space where I could just have classes and workshops, since I felt burned out on doing theater.

We found a place in a five-story building on Wilshire Boulevard on the Miracle Mile. It had been used as a post-production space and was a long room painted white, with fluorescent lights running along the entire ceiling. It had a sink against one wall, a discolored cement floor with steel spikes sticking up in various places, and an unfinished wall at the back. I am not a person who can look at a room and visualize anything other than what I see. Among my various talents, that one doesn't exist! So I hired Erik White to design and build a theater out of that barren place. He had already helped build the Cahuenga theater and had spent many years as an actor studying with me. Susana helped with the design and the work.

I had enormous separation anxiety leaving Cahuenga. I took all of my lights, seats, and sound equipment with me, so I could use them once we had a theater built. I guess I have always liked things to stay the same and have had great difficulty with change. When I was married to Joy and she would rearrange the furniture, I would freak out. However, when the new place was finished, it was beautiful—clean, elegant, and conducive to creativity. We have about two thousand square feet, which include a generous lobby, two offices off the lobby, and two in the back—one for storing my books. The walls are maroon, which complements the color of the seats, also maroon. The stage area is painted in a flat black color; the entire place is carpeted, including the stage; and there is some wonderful art on the walls of the lobby and in every office.

I only go to New York once a year now, and, except for the mini-jamborees and the major one, I do very little traveling elsewhere. In Los Angeles we conduct all the intensives at the theater, which makes things easier for everyone. Susana is teaching about twenty-five private lessons a week. Besides running the business, she structures the intensives and teaches at least half of each weekend. She also completely organizes and outlines all the jamborees and mini-jamborees, and has made it possible for me to finally be able to walk into the classroom and just teach. She chooses scenes and monologues that fit the actors perfectly and continues to be a source for the people in my classes, who constantly go to her for suggestions on which scene or monologue to bring into class. I will forever be grateful to her for all the wonderful things she has brought into my life.

Besides three new choice approaches, I have added character explorations and character parallel monologues to the work. The whole concept of character obligations was not a new thing; sometime in the 2000s, I just started to put a specific emphasis on what we had already been addressing in trying to fulfill the obligations of character. The way we approached addressing the four elements of character—what is the character like physically? emotionally? intellectually? psychologically?—had always been predicated on finding choices from our own life experiences. I, however, structured two exercises that the actor can do onstage, or wherever, when preparing to work. The *character-exploration workout* is done as a stream-of-consciousness sharing monologue. The actor talks about his personal life, selectively emphasizing the parallels between him and the character. Let us imagine, for example, that the character in the play is depressed and despondent and has failed to find his way in life. He is confused about the choices he has made and cannot find a direction that might change his life for the better. The actor who doesn't feel the kind of depression or confusion that the character does can generally selectively emphasize and creatively manipulate the things that depress him and make him feel confused about his past decisions and the path he has taken. He can emphasize his lack of success and fulfillment in his career and in his personal relationships and express all of that in his sharing monologue. When done in class as an exercise, it is said out loud, but if the actor was doing it in a professional environment, he would approach it as an inner monologue.

The *character-parallel monologue* is done somewhat differently. Again using personal realities, the actor structures a monologue that fits the character's behavior and is something that the character might actually say in a play or film. The entire content of the monologue is organically related to the actor's personal life and experience. By employing those techniques an actor establishes a personal connection to the character. In most cases we all have similarities and parallels to the characters in dramatic material; however, if finding enough similarities becomes difficult, the actor can use believability as a support system.

Usually a new choice approach is a result of something that is happening in my life or a discovery from an exercise onstage. *Déjà vu*, for example, happened quite by accident. I was meeting someone for lunch and had arrived at the location about half an hour early, so I sat in my Bronco, tilted the seat back, and stared up at the visor, on which were several feathers that I had picked up at the beach in Carmel. I wasn't concentrating on the visor or the feathers. I was just aimlessly staring in that direction. For some unknown reason, I began remembering a humiliating experience I had with my older brother in New York. It had been so traumatic that it had really changed the course of my life. I was about seventeen or eighteen at the time and was planning to pursue a career in photography. The day before the incident, we had taken a trip on the Staten Island ferry, and I had taken some pictures with a Brownie camera that belonged to my brother's stepdaughter. I had photographed the Statue of Liberty from a great distance and had taken some other snapshots on the ferry. When we picked up the developed pictures, my brother looked at them and flipped out. On a public street with people passing by, he shouted at the top of his voice, "You call yourself a photographer? These pictures are awful! You have no talent. Give it up, son!" I remember standing there, feeling totally humiliated and embarrassed, not able to speak. I didn't touch a camera again for ten years!

I recalled that event vividly while sitting in my Bronco staring at those feathers. After lunch I returned to the Bronco and casually glanced up at the visor, and the entire event came back instantly. I re-experienced the humiliation and the entire impact of the scene emotionally. At first, I didn't trust that this could be a tool for acting, so I personally experimented with it for a couple of months before trying it in class. It worked amazingly well and quite consistently. It became one of the new choice approaches, which people in class have reported using in the film work they have done.

In 2004 I was approached by a former student, who was directing his own films. Right before the start of one of my evening classes, he appeared with his producer and literally begged me to come in and do a part in his film the following day. It was the role of a psychologist in a therapy session with a male patient who was having marital difficulties. The film was titled *Love, Hollywood Style.* I agreed to do the part and showed up the next day at the director's house, where one of the rooms had been made to look like a psychologist's office. The scene was not a great stretch for me, since much of my work is being involved with the actors I teach and being perceptive about their problems and issues. It was like having a private lesson with one of my students. It went quite well, and we did everything in one or two takes.

Another one of my students, Norman Crawford, has been working with me since the early eighties. He is about seventy years old, is a hydrologist by profession, but has been acting avocationally for about thirty years. I started working with him in San Francisco, although our first contact was at a jamboree in New York. He is still very active in the work. He attends all of the jamborees, and I believe it is his sixth or seventh year in the intensives. Besides acting, he also writes. He has written a play called *Love Always,* a two-person piece structured very much like *Love Letters.* In the latter play, which has been done all over with name actors, a man and a woman sit on opposite sides of the stage, reading love letters that they had sent to each other. Norman's play, on the other hand, is about a father and his daughter who are somewhat estranged. Because the father has been an archeologist for most of his life, he has spent very little time at home and hasn't been privy to his daughter's growing up. The play starts with several back-and-forth voice-mail messages informing him that his wife has died and notifying him when the funeral will be. It is well written and is a good play, even if it is possibly a little too verbose and poetic. Norman approached me, I think sometime in 2005, and asked me if he could take some private lessons to work on it with me. The actress, Courtney Birch, was also a former student, who had spent several years in my class. I worked with them every time Norman came to L.A. for an intensive. He lives in Mountain View, near San Francisco. We would work for two or three hours, with me giving the actors feedback and suggesting choices and approaches. After several months, it became apparent that I was directing the play. Because we all had a common language and approach, I was able to work with the actors without having to find ways of being understood.

We performed the play once at my theater in L.A., and there was also a performance in Utah, which was arranged by another former student who lives there. This year we did the play in New York at Anthony Vincent Bova's new little theater, where it ran for two weekends. Recently, Norman went to Berlin to work with another former German student, Magdalena. He rehearsed and performed the play there. At the present time he is going through a rewrite, adding more scenes where the two characters actually talk directly to each other—which would make the play more dramatic and theatrical. Our intention is to mount it in an Equity-waiver theater in the near future.

The work is always growing and evolving. I keep reaching for new and better approaches in the instrumental and craft areas. I have been asked to do a weeklong workshop next July in Australia, where there are three acting schools that exclusively teach my system, and I just came back from New York, where I was invited to give a lecture in the Bruno Walter Auditorium, which is part of the New York Public Library at the Lincoln Center. Titled "From Stanislavski to Eric Morris," the lecture consisted of an exploration of the system from its origin to where I have taken it in the present. It went very well. The two hundred seats were filled, and about twenty people who had been turned away were able to listen to the presentation over the loudspeakers in the lobby. What had been billed as a two-hour session turned into a three-hour talk, with twenty people participating in the Q and A after the lecture. It was followed by a presentation of a scene from a Clifford Odets' play titled *Nine Ten Eden Street,* which had been written in the thirties but had never before been published or produced. Two of the actors doing the scene were from Anthony Vincent Bova's workshop and had been rehearsed and directed by Anthony, who teaches my work in New York. When they finished the scene, I critiqued it, with an emphasis on what their approach had been as they used my system. Everyone was quite elated by the whole experience, including me! I followed it with a two-day workshop, which also went very well.

The journey I have been on started at birth. Everything I have come up with as part of an acting system has been the result of all my living experiences, all the people who have affected and influenced me, as well as my desperation to find ways to act from a real place. I don't think that my life is unique or so unlike everyone else's, but I believe that I have created this system of acting because so many of the components of my life have impelled me to search for, explore, and experiment with, the techniques I have invented.

MY SYSTEM

I have said earlier in this book and in all my other books that my system is based on the foundation of Stanislavski and also the influence of Lee Strasberg and Martin Landau. I always claim that I went from A to E with what I learned from Marty and Lee and that I have, in the forty-five years I have been teaching, gone from E to T on my own. I believe that my work and my system go light years beyond Stanislavski and Strasberg, but without their incredible contribution I would have no system. I believe that to date I have created a complete system of acting that addresses not only the craft of acting but the incredible importance of liberating the actor's instrument, which has sorely been neglected for over three thousand years. Not only do most acting teachers avoid digging into the problems actors bring with them to their training, but many fear crossing that line into the personal and psychological. My God, isn't acting personal? Isn't there a psychological aspect to almost every character an actor approaches? Among the master master teachers, Lee made the greatest contribution in my opinion. He attempted at least to address the actor's obstacles with some of the exercises he did in his classes. He also modified, updated, and made more specific the work of Stanislavski.

My journey to find answers and to learn how to achieve organic results, and the failure of most of my teachers to answer that question, created a desperation that led me to this unending journey.

Without going into deep specifics about my system, which is covered almost in total in my five other books, I will attempt to give the reader an overview of what it is.

The system is divided into two parts: **the instrument** and **the craft.** The actor's instrument is himself, in the same way as a violinist's instrument is his violin. We all grow up in a society that affects us in many damaging ways, creating inhibitions, fears, insecurities, dependencies, emotional blocks, and social obligations—just to name a few of the problems actors come to the theater with. **There is no separation between living and acting**, and when an actor attempts to act in spite of the blocks that keep him from BEING REAL, he is destined to be presentational and separated from his real feelings, thereby having to impose emotions that do not come from a real place. Truth can only be created from a place of truth, and so, reaching the basic level of here-and-now truth is the creative starting point. I call that state a *being* state. It sounds so simple, and yet, with lifelong issues and obstacles, compounded by the need to succeed, most actors will attempt to fulfill the obligations of material by assuming behavior, while the greatest degree of their talent and their real emotional life are suppressed by the overlay of that assumed behavior. In my approach to training actors, I start with dealing with their instrument, identifying the problems, blocks, and so on, and doing antidotal exercises to address and eliminate them. Throughout my teaching career I have invented over five hundred instrumental exercises and techniques to free the actor from those walls. Most of them are described in my other books. The freedom that evolves as a result of doing them not only liberates the actor to act, but it also dynamically enriches his life.

Instrumental exercises are progressive. When you eliminate one obstacle, you lunge head first into the next, but if an actor is willing to go the distance and divest himself from the issues that keep him from achieving a comfortable and permissive being state, then he can approach material from an honest and organic place. In my classes I work in both areas simultaneously, knowing that while we are eliminating instrumental obstacles the actors can still address material from whatever place they are in at any given juncture in their training. Quite often, when I watch an actor do a monologue or scene, I am able to address an instrumental obstacle and to free him from either a dependency or a block. The concept of becoming a "professional experiencer" is totally predicated on the actor's ability to *organically* create the inner *organic* life of the character and to allow that life to be expressed on a moment-to-moment level with unpredictability and the ability to discover the next moment in the next moment.

As for the craft part of my system, I learned about obligations and choices from Marty and indirectly from Lee, but there was no specificity related to obligations. Marty would ask, "What did you want to accomplish?" or "What was your obligation?" Lee would say after an actor had completed a scene, "What would you like to tell us?" My system codified the obligations. I discovered seven major ones—time and place, relationship, emotional, character, historic, thematic, and subtextual—and I specified their importance and their place in the structure of material. They are all described and explored very specifically in *Irreverent Acting.*

In the choice area (a choice is a person, place, object, event, or thing from the actor's life), I worked to expand the type and number of choices an actor can find and use by doing "choice hunts," eliciting energies through subpersonality work, and exploring unconscious content. In my last book, *Acting, Imaging and the Unconscious,* I describe a process for accessing the unconscious so that it will liberate the memory banks to yield potentially exciting choices. I worked for years on techniques to elevate awareness and consciousness. Many of my exercises are also designed to stimulate curiosity, an important component in establishing a conscious state.

I feel that my greatest contribution to my system, however, is in the area of **choice approaches.** This is how an actor creates his choices. Identifying obligations and selecting the right choice for a scene are essentially intellectual processes, but the pragmatic work of the actor consists in correctly using the right choice approach to create the choice that will address the scene and hopefully produce the desired result. When I started teaching, I had three choice approaches, but they were not called that. The term is mine. They were sense memory, affective memory, and animal characterizations. Sense memory comes from Stanislavski and was made more specific by Lee Strasberg. Affective memory, which Stanislavski called memory of emotion or emotional recall, was renamed by Lee. Alvina Krause first introduced me to animal characterizations at Northwestern, but she had just instructed us to go out and watch animals and try to get a sense of them and had never told us *how!* Marty was a little more specific when he said to watch the animal for its rhythm and limitations, but that was it! After spending the better part of three days each week at the Los Angeles zoo for a year, I created an approach for observing animals and then getting a physical sense of them through one's own body. The approach blueprint, as specifically described in *Irreverent Acting,* contains about ten descriptive steps. I call this choice approach, which is also a megapproach, EXTERNALS. The animal is just one of its four parts, the other three being people, insects, and inanimate objects. The approach technique addresses all four, which are then translated into human behavior, so that many of the seven obligations can be addressed.

Among the thirty-one choice approaches in my system are five megapproaches: sense memory, affective memory, externals, subpersonalities and imaging. A megapproach is a choice approach so powerful and rich that it could possibly comprise an entire system of acting.

The reason I created so many choice approaches over the years is that some work more efficiently with certain choices than others. The actor should use the rehearsal period to explore which is the right one for the choice he has selected and to settle on the one that creates that choice effectively. The question I hear most frequently from actors is, "What am I doing while I'm acting besides saying the lines and being emotional?" My answer is, "Creating the choice that impels you to experience the life of the character in the scene by using a choice approach and allowing the created choice to impel you to the emotional life. Once the choice is working, get out of its way and go with the impulses that are stimulated by it."

In summary, my system concentrates on liberating the actor's instrument so that there aren't any obstacles to achieving a being state, a place where he can be comfortable doing no more or less than he feels and from which he is able to address material by identifying the responsibilities, selecting choices, and creating those choices by using one of the many choice approaches. The goal of the system is to become a PROFESSIONAL EXPERIENCER. The philosophical underpinnings are BEING, IRREVERENCE, and reaching THE ULTIMATE CONSCIOUSNESS.

The Five New Choice Approaches

The following are the new choice approaches I have created since the publication of my last book.

SELECTIVE MEMORY

This approach enables the actor to edit or modify an experience so that the part of it he selects addresses the obligation of a given scene. This can make a choice usable when in its original form it does not affect the actor the way he wants it to. It also multiplies the use of a single choice.

Example: An actress is addressing a scene where the obligations are to be excited in a romantic way and to be very attracted to the other actor. It may be the start of a meaningful romantic relationship. After searching for the right choice and having difficulty finding it, she decides to concentrate on one that might work if she used selective memory. The original experience was a blind date she had. The man appears at her door with an orchid in his hand and is strikingly handsome. He takes her to a very nice upscale restaurant and orders their best wine. In the middle of an intimate conversation, while gesticulating with her right hand, she knocks over a glass of red wine, which spills all over his beautiful and expensive suit. He responds graciously, assuring her that it can be cleaned, but she feels terrible. A short time later, she feels a funny sensation between her legs and realizes that she has started her menstrual period, and of course she is wearing a white dress. She excuses herself, attempts to hide the spot on the backside of her dress, and heads for the ladies' room. A short time later she returns to the table, dragging a long piece of toilet tissue attached to the heel of her shoe. The entire experience up to that point can be classified as a nightmare! The rest of the evening, however, continues without incident. Her date takes her home, kisses her, and promises to call her the next day.

This is not an experience that would in any way address the original obligations of the scene. However, if the actress uses selective memory, she can find in that event all of the ingredients that would excite her and generate romantic feelings. So she creates part of the experience, starting from when her date appeared at her front door, flowers in hand, and editing out all of the bad stuff. She constructs a beautiful evening, without spilling the wine or getting her period. She might approach the choice by using affective memory or just sense memory, evocative words, or evocative images. Selective memory is something we do all the time. We choose to remember things that serve our purposes, even unconsciously at times.

DÉJÀ VU

I have already spoken about how I discovered this choice approach. It is an amazing tool for actors. Besides creating impacting choices, they can "endow" many objects on the stage with meaningful associations, so that every place they look at and any object they relate to can be full of impacting stimuli. If used properly, it can cut down on the number of choices needed.

How to use the choice approach: Looking at an object of little meaning and just staring at it aimlessly, the actor creates an impacting event or experience by using imaging or sense memory or just by visualizing the experience. He might spend ten or fifteen minutes recalling the event, never taking his eyes off the innocuous object. Once he has finished, he might walk away from the object and get involved with some other activity. After some time has elapsed, he should go back to looking at the object, and hopefully the entire event will be re-experienced, replete with the emotional life it stimulated. He might have to repeat the process several times to make sure the object is properly endowed with the experience. In a scene where there are several emotional transitions, he can endow a number of objects on the stage with a variety of impacting events and just go from one object to another. When I do this exercise in class as a group workout, I ask the actors to relate to each other after leaving the object and to get involved with small talk before going back to it. If they succeed in creating a meaningful experience, the object will contain the impetus to being affected.

MIND'S EYE TRANSLATION

For many years I was adamant about how sense memory was approached: Never, never respond intellectually to an object you are trying to create! Always respond with the specific sense which you ask the question of—with the outer eye, with the tactile response, with the auditory response; really hear with your ears the sound the object makes. Sense memory and the creating of an object when it is not really there are totally dependent on seeing, hearing, tasting, smelling, and feeling the object as if it were *really* there, in other words not in the mind or in the imagination. This has been my mantra for forty-five years, and until recently I was unmovable in my relationship to the sense-memory process.

One evening in my class one of my students doing a sense-memory approach to create a choice stopped and said, "Eric, I know that you have to start the process by asking the first question, 'How far away is the object from me?' and responding visually with the sense the question was aimed at, but the moment I suggested the object, I had a response. I saw the object in my mind's eye. It was there! I smelled it, and I even had a tactile response before asking the first question. Should I disregard all of that even if it affects me emotionally?" I must say that for a few moments I was speechless. I didn't know how to respond to the question. It seemed to me that by disregarding the initial response the actor was short-circuiting something valuable, something that could have supported the sensory approach. I said that I would explore it and come back with an answer after doing some research on it. Even though I had been doing sense memory successfully for more than fifty years, I started to work with the initial response I had with an inanimate object, encouraging myself to allow the first reaction to the suggestion of the imaginary object. I found that I did have an immediate response that was a "mind's eye" response, so I used my early inner responses to encourage myself to ask sensory questions, and I discovered that it was supportive to the process. It was like a kick starter to sense memory. I immediately identified the traps and dangers of going too far with the initial responses, so I cautioned everyone to start the conventional question-and-sensory-response process shortly after experiencing the mind's eye response. As a choice approach and technique, it is a helpful way to begin, especially when the mind's eye responses are there and strong.

DYNAMICALLY IMPACTING SINGLE WORDS

I was teaching a private lesson to one of my young students and we were talking about his early life and growing up. He said that he used to watch a TV show called "Airwolf" and that every time he says that word, it immediately takes him back to that time in his life. He continued by telling me that it is not just a memory, but a complete experience. He can smell the environment from that time, he can hear his father's voice, taste the cereal he used to eat for breakfast, and feel the clothes he wore at the time. I was impressed with his story and thought about it for some time after that day. It seemed like the choice approach I was already using, called "evocative words," but it also felt somewhat different, since evocative words is a string of words or short phrases related to an experience or a belief structure, while this was one single word that was pregnant with dimensional impact. When I introduce a new choice approach, exercise, or technique, I always work with it personally before exploring it in a class, so I experimented by saying single words related to my own background and found that many of them produced a meaningful response. Some were more affecting than others, and some brought with them sensory and impacting emotional responses. I saw great potential in this as a choice approach, particularly for making quick emotional transitions as well as creating a total emotional life for a scene. I started exploring it in my classes and found it to be very useful. It can be done audibly or as an inner monologue.

SELECTIVE LISTENING

The last of the new approaches is something we do naturally. How many times have you heard someone say, "You only hear what you want to hear"? Almost everything in my system is natural to life. None of the techniques violates the natural way we function. In a scene or in the preparation for doing the scene, the actor can selectively hear only those things that affect him and promote the emotional life of the character. He can listen only to those lines of the material that have specific meaning and a particular effect on him. It is a process of deliberately blocking out the words that he doesn't want to hear and emphasizing the ones that he does want to hear and that will affect him.

Example: The lines of the scene are, "You know that I love you! And I have supported everything you do; but you are irresponsible, selfish and uncaring for the people around you. You say and do insensitive things that hurt people, and I want things to be different. I will always be there for you, no matter what!"

We can use those lines in two different ways with selective listening. Suppose the actor only wanted to hear the love and support from the other person. He could edit out all the criticism and just listen to the supportive lines; or if he wanted to feel diminished and criticized, he could only listen to the criticism. It is a very simple approach technique, easy to apply to preparation or to the author's words.

You can learn about the other twenty-six choice approaches in my other books. As I continue to teach, I expect there will be many more than the thirty-one I now have. As long as I stay hungry and reach for more, the work will continue to grow and evolve.

INDEX OF NAMES

H

I

J

K

L

O

P

Q

R

S